A LAWMAN'S VOW

Yes, Sagan had courage, dignity and strength—she was a superior woman by anyone's standards. He'd never met anyone like her. That very first handshake at the depot had his body responding. He'd known it then, but was too proud and intent upon his mission to acknowledge the attraction. Life up to this point had been boring. Except for punctuating instances of terror. Wherever he went lately, one sector of space looked like any other. Here, with this Earthling, he'd rekindled a fire that had long ago burned to embers. Keir felt a renewal of passion and hope that too many hours of traveling from one star system to another had dimmed. He was paper, she was the match. She was defiant and he would tame her. All he must do was finish this mission without her discovering his deceit; then he'd find a way for them to be together.

CANDACE SAMS

Electra Galaxy's
MR. INTERSTELLAR FELLER

LOVE SPELL NEW YORK CITY

LOVE SPELL®

July 2008

Published by

Dorchester Publishing Co., Inc.
200 Madison Avenue
New York, NY 10016

ISBN 10: 0-505-52762-6
ISBN 13: 978-0-505-52762-2

Printed in the United States of America.

10 9 8 7 6 5 4 3 2 1

Visit us on the web at www.dorchesterpub.com.

DEDICATION & ACKNOWLEDGMENTS

I want to dedicate this story to my husband, Lee. Without his support, writing wouldn't be possible. I want to gratefully thank my family back home in Texas...all of whom hail from or near the community of Palacios. I send greetings to the rest of my distant relatives throughout the United States. Your collective whimsy and great senses of humor have allowed me to become a better storyteller; especially those of you who've gone on ahead and who I know I'll see again: Mildred, Ed, Chester, Fred, Arlene, Dumps, Littley, Sterling and Lela. Of all of you, only my mom, Winifred, remains. She taught me to love a good book. Warmest regards also go out to my deceased grandparents, Henry and Ruth. You did a very good job.

I'd like to gratefully acknowledge my husband's family in Tennessee. Thank you for your wonderful support and the motivation to keep writing. And thanks for producing Lee.

With *great* appreciation, I also dedicate this book to all the readers and reviewers who've been e-mailing for years, supporting my work. I hope you enjoy this story. Please contact me at any time; I'm almost always at my desk. You can reach me through my website at www.candacesams.com.

Finally, I want to express my gratitude to my personal trainer, Cindy Pierce, and my workout partner, Dana Seale, for their instruction regarding bikini waxes...like I had a clue!

Good reading to you all. *Reach for the moon. If you fall, you may still land among the stars!*

Disclaimer: No pillow mints were harmed while writing this manuscript!

Electra Galaxy's
MR. INTERSTELLAR FELLER

CHAPTER ONE

The Future
Headquarters, Earth Protectorate Force

Captain Sagan Carter crossed her arms over her chest and shook her head. The man whose profile she'd just finished reading would never go for this crazy idea, and that certainty raised concerns about his motives. After watching for another full five minutes, she switched off the recording to take in the real drama unfolding throughout Los Angeles.

The vid screens mounted in every conceivable niche of the office now advertised the Mr. Interstellar Feller Pageant. Everything from mouthwash, male cosmetics, clothing and even prophylactics were being sold as the brand names used by the pageant contestants. Several times she heard a biography about Electra Galaxy. There was a detailed account of how the woman had risen from almost abject poverty to her current status as male pageant diva. Included in all the hype was the fact that Electra owned most of the downtown area of Los Angeles, including the exclusive, ultra chic Stardust Hotel, right in the heart of the city. Since that hotel would house all the contestants, Sagan's interest was in studying

blueprints of the place. Detailed knowledge of its lay-
out would stand her, as an undercover operative, in good
stead. From those same building plans, she'd learned
that the entire top floor, including a huge private ballroom and entertainment suites and offices were all al-
located for Electra Galaxy's private use. All but a few
of the remaining one thousand rooms and suites were
booked.

More publicity on the vid screen followed. In every
area of the city, females of all ages, shapes, colors and
sizes, waving human or alien appendages, were holding
signs welcoming incoming contestants. Banners flew
from every lamppost, noting the pageant dates as Au-
gust 15 through the end of the month. Electronic
kiosks located in shopping centers flashed the pageant
location as the new Los Angeles Colosseum, built as a
domed facsimile of the Roman structure bearing the
same name. Camera crews from local news stations lit-
tered the Stardust Hotel where the contestants would
stay; from Sagan's perspective, they resembled flies
hovering around excrement. Men and women bearing
hair-styling accoutrements and costume trappings were
scurrying from one boutique to another.

She finally turned off the vid screens in disgust. About
to voice her misgivings, she turned to the only other person in the room: her supervisor.

Overchief Lement Snarl held up one hand to stave
off her dismissal. "I know. I know what you're going to
say, and you can keep it to yourself, Sagan. From our
side the deal is done."

She let out a long breath and tried to reason with her
boss just once more. "Sir, I've read a bio on this man
from Oceanus. There's no way that he'd be willing to let
us do this to him." She pointed to the now blank video
screens behind her. "Those men are *not* the kind of people he'd ever associate with, let alone compete against. I

can't envision any creature with half a brain going for this . . . idiocy."

"He'll do it, or he'll turn around and take a very long journey home. Until his planet's Supreme Council backs down on their demands for trade exclusivity, he isn't supposed to set one foot on our turf. Shuttle pilots, mechanics and workers from Oceanus are welcome as always, but this enforcer is here only at our consul's discretion." He shrugged and wearily swiped a hand across his face. "Dammit, I don't like this any better than you do, but his cooperation in this scheme might just make it easier for his world and ours to come to some agreement as to diplomacy and barter. It would go a long way toward showing some willingness to bend. So far, his leaders have been absolutely implacable about their demands. Yet, here they are practically demanding our cooperation in allowing one of their law enforcement people to follow a lead to Earth and investigate it." He sat down and straightened a scattered pile of paperwork on his desk. "No. If he wants his investigation and his planet demands it—and it seems they do—then this officer from Oceanus is going to have to agree to this cover. Otherwise, he can get back on his ship and let us kiss his alien butt good-bye."

Sagan waved at the empty brown leather chair before her supervisor. "May I?"

Snarl nodded readily and leaned forward to hear whatever she might add.

"Sir," she began. Then, sinking into the ultraluxurious leather seat and straightening her shoulders, she saw that her supervisor's expression was less than malleable. "I have to assume this officer doesn't know what's been planned for him. Is that correct?"

Snarl nodded. "It is."

"May I be so bold as to ask . . . who's going to tell him?" She watched as her overchief placed his elbows on his desktop, clasped his hands together and shot her what she could only describe as a wickedly evil grin.

"You're not serious," she blurted.

"Quite. Since you're the officer chosen for this duty, you'll be the one informing our, uh, law enforcement *guest* just what his cover story will be." Snarl stopped speaking, opened a file cabinet with his right hand, extracted a folder and plopped it down on the desk. He shoved it at her. "Your cover is set as well. He knows one of us will be meeting him, by whatever means he chooses to land, but that's about all."

Feeling trapped and reluctant to look at the file, Sagan only did so when Snarl poked the folder at her again. It was now sitting precariously on the edge of the desk. Swallowing hard, she picked up what she assumed were her instructions. When she was done reading, she gently placed the papers down and glared at her boss. "Tell me this is a joke of some kind. Please?"

"Sorry. You're now the official manager of 'Mr. Keir Trask.' It's supposed to be some kind of Earth-sounding version of his real name." Snarl tried to pronounce a name several times but couldn't.

Sagan picked up the file, opened it and said, "The man's real name is Keirstrandst T'raskchrdtniq'. Of course, that would be the Earth pronunciation. How they'd say it on his world is pretty damned incoherent. There's a lot of clicking and wheezing that really gets stuffed between the syllables."

"Whatever," Snarl muttered. "You'd think these people, who love to brag about their advanced intelligence, would buy a few damned vowels. The hen-scratch representing their language doesn't indicate that we're supposed to have the same, star-roaming ancestors. Christ! Other than their coloring, they *could* be us. Our physiologies are amazingly the same, but look at this crap that passes for a language and look at how they so conveniently forget our common ancestry to act so frickin' superior. Where the hell did a people so physically similar come up with this dialect?"

Sagan simply sat and waited for this inept, insecure ranting to pass. The Oceanuns' language had nothing to do with the fact that they shared the same internal organs with humans. But her boss had to get his bias out of his system.

Snarl quickly cleared his throat and continued, "At any rate, this captain will be posing as the newest entrant to the Mr. Interstellar Feller competition, and happens to be representing the planet Oceanus. As we see it, the cover is perfect."

"We?" Sagan choked out. Others had agreed?

"Myself and a discreet handful of Earth representatives. In the interests of law enforcement, we've approved this story. That's the only way any Oceanus cop is going to be allowed to set foot on Earth until some kind of diplomatic trade compromise can be arranged. Oceanus can't have things all their way and expect us to bend over backward when they demand it. Besides, the competition is open to any man from anywhere in the known universe, as long as he qualified under his own world's competitive rules. Even the planet Ussar is sending their pageant representative along with their runners-up. There's been publicity about it for weeks. And if a planet of thieving, no-good, conniving cutthroats can send representatives to the pageant, then—"

"Sir, I realize all this is true. This year there are representatives from planets that most folks have never heard of. But I highly doubt Oceanus ever had a male beauty pageant—"

"I can see where you're coming from," Snarl interrupted. "Such an event would be cause for unbelievable scorn and derision in Trask's neck of the galaxy. His people view such pursuits as unworthy. But don't you see? That's why no one from his home planet is going to care that he's representing them. Protesting his appearance as a contestant would be even more undignified as far as the Oceanus hierarchy is concerned." Snarl thought for a moment before continuing. "I'll have my staff leak it to the tabloids that there were no contests held on Trask's planet and that he's decided to represent his people on his own. As I understand it, there are a number of contestants who've done the same thing. Under the existing rules of the competition, this is allowable. His late entry in the competition is a result of his last-minute decision. He can say that his motives are to break with his world's superior bearing and make nice with the lowly Earthlings. I leave it to you to get the details straight when the press questions him, as they most certainly will."

"Yes, sir, that *could* work. But, with all due respect, Trask would probably be incapable of passing himself off as any one of those conceited asses I watched parading around in the video. It's my guess that he's going to tell us where to get off, even if he was given his orders recently and can't get out of the assignment now."

"If that's the case, you can escort him back to the nearest transport station to catch his ship home. He has no choice."

"Sir, surely we could make an exception and allow him to operate as a law enforcement liaison to Earth. Just this once?"

Snarl shook his head determinedly. "No. If we make an excuse for him to come here hunting one criminal or another, then we'll have to do so for cops from every other half-baked world that hasn't signed diplomatic treaties. We'd have every bounty hunter and armed alien lawman from here to the Crab Nebulae wanting access to our turf, obeying no laws but their own. And possibly putting our citizens in jeopardy." He snorted. "We've already stretched the rules far enough. Though we need his planet's help in fighting off pirates, they need us, too. We're wise enough to realize it; their leaders simply want us to make the greater sacrifices. They think we're as backward as hell and that it's beneath them to be collaborating with primitives," he finished angrily. "In short, they want us to give and give—"

"While they take and take," she finished.

"Precisely." Snarl leaned forward and put one index finger against the top of his brown oak desk. "You're not just acting as this man's manager in a beauty contest, you're serving as an example of the kind of officer and citizen we want the Oceanuns to know. We want Trask to fly his ass back home when this is all over and give a brilliant report on just how in control of our enforcement system we are."

Sagan took a deep breath and let it out slowly. "So, I'm the diplomatic guinea pig, is that it?"

"You're one of our most decorated officers and highly qualified for the assignment on a number of levels. I wouldn't put just anyone on this mission."

"You knew nobody else would do it," she said, and watched him try to suppress a laugh.

"Look at it this way. While you might have to work with this man, who in all likelihood will be a superior, swaggering prick, as all Oceanuns I've ever run across are, you're still in charge. This is our planet, after all. He plays by our rules or he goes home and won't get his man."

Sagan stared at her supervisor for a long moment.

"What?" he curtly asked.

"Maybe we're wrong about him. How do you know this particular Oceanun is a swaggering prick? All you've ever dealt with is their diplomats. Maybe this guy is different."

"I'll tell you how. First, he's an Oceanun. Second, he's an Oceanun," Snarl repeated.

Sagan paused a moment. "Not to sound insubordinate, but why do I get the feeling I'm being hustled?"

Snarl laughed heartily. "You're paranoid. I'm not hiding anything."

She glared at him, picked up the paperwork and scooped it all back into the file. "I'll need to do some more research on Trask."

"Remember: as far as we're concerned, you're away on vacation. Only a handful of people will know what you're really up to. It has to stay that way. If the media gets ahold of our little operation and the special consideration we're giving to Oceanus, all our collective butts will fry—not to mention we'll lose the smugglers and their cargo."

"I understand, Overchief." Sagan got up to leave, then turned at the office door. "This guy is going to be awfully visible as a contestant."

"Since he refused to hide the telltale markings from his planet through the use of temporary cosmetic surgery or makeup, this was the best we could offer," Snarl replied.

Sagan frowned and left her supervisor, paging through the paperwork again. Something wasn't adding up. Why was so much importance being attached to these smugglers? Politics aside, it made no sense. Still, submitting to this farcical cover should boost her career—if she could pull it off. Unfortunately, the mission depended on the cooperation of a man with a reputation for being unyielding. Captain Keir Trask had been *charitably* described as rigid. To make matters worse, she, a reputed loner who'd come from a background where the only three people she'd ever cared for had lied to her, would be forced to trust a total stranger.

The Oceanun enforcer soon to be known as Keir Trask looked over his information again and handed the electronic programmer back to his second-in-command. As he'd ordered everyone to speak English to keep the language familiar, he did the same. "Everything appears in order, Navigator. Lay in a course for Earth's moon. We won't go any farther in this vessel."

His best friend and lieutenant—Da'nequwit, now to be called Datron—regarded him with interest. "Wouldn't it be easier to just land on Earth, Captain?"

"No. We'll shuttle to their surface. I don't want anyone to see this enforcer ship. There's too much at stake."

Datron turned to make arrangements for the new orders, then addressed Keir again. "Request permission to speak freely."

Keir carefully regarded the bridge staff, motioned for Datron to move closer, then nodded to indicate permission was given.

Datron took a deep breath. "Sir, this mission is asinine. We've already been forced to adopt more easily pronounceable names and speak the Earth language just to accommodate the ignorance of their population. That's insult enough. Now we're being inflicted with this infantile cover. It's degrading. I'd like to say we'll have a good laugh over this stupendous adventure in the future, but it's so far beneath us as to be harmful. Even if we pull off the entire mission without a hitch . . ."

Keir shrugged. "It's the best way to find the smugglers. Certainly it'll be much easier than choosing some other Earth occupation as a cover. We'll be right in the thick of things. That should shorten our stay on this backward little rock considerably. That alone is worth the imposition, wouldn't you say?"

"I suppose," Datron said. "But we'll never live it down."

"Think on this," Keir suggested with a smile. "We at least have the satisfaction of knowing it was an Oceanun diplomatic trick that put us in the middle of the assignment. Leading the Earth Protectorate to believe they came up with this entire scheme should be worth a few laughs on the way home."

Datron waved his hand in a conciliatory gesture. "Yes, I'm well aware that Oceanun representatives lured Earth Protectorate envoys into this agreement. But that won't make the acting any easier. Or the revolting stunts in which we'll be forced to engage. Every law enforcer in the Oceanus Protectorate—including those of my home world—will be laughing at our expense. Or they'll find what we've engaged in so distasteful that they'll have nothing to do with us in the future."

Keir turned to look at the video screen, noting the passing planets with only moderate interest. He'd seen so many. "So long as we get those weapon-smuggling vermin, I don't give a Kreskian's green knobbly ass what anyone thinks. When the Earth officer greets me and describes my cover, I'll act the part of the enraged Oceanus enforcer to the hilt. The Earthlings must believe they put one over on us. And that I only learned of my assignment when I was too close to Earth to refuse it. In that way, their agency won't know exactly what we're looking for until it's imperative that we tell them. Earth's Protectorate is too backward to get their hands on that kind of advanced weaponry. I don't care what our comrades think. I *will* find those responsible for taking those Ache blasters."

"I realize the importance of this mission and I'll do my part, Captain. You can rely on me. But I doubt I'll ever be able to wash the foul taste of this experience from my mouth. I'd almost rather be subjected to body worms from Vargus than this travesty."

Keir chuckled at his friend's sour tone. "Just remember your role, and don't ever address me as sir, Captain, or any other title when we meet on the Earth's surface. You'll shuttle in ahead of me. Your cover is set. You're arriving from your home world of Valkyrie. You're a contestant who quarreled with your manager and fired him. We won't know each other until introduced."

Datron sighed heavily. "Aye, sir."

Keir focused on the slow blinking lights of the ship's communication center. The steady flash helped him mentally entrench his new name and that of his second-in-command. Every flash, he silently repeated the pseudonyms *Keir Trask* and *Datron Mann*, while pushing back their real, most honored Oceanun and Valkyrian names. The new names had to become very comfortable. It wouldn't do for someone to call out and get no response because he and his partner didn't recognize their aliases.

At least they were lucky enough to understand common Earth speech, so neither he nor Datron would need a universal translator. While the devices had been in existence for some time, Earthers rarely used them: many among their population suffered serious lesions from the temporary cranial implants. For some strange reason, their brains didn't seem adaptable to the small translation microchips. As a result, aliens landing here often found communication problematic. It was incumbent on every alien landing on Earth to have his or her translator implants attuned to English—or learn the language, as Keir had from a very young age. Conversely, Earthers never seemed to want to learn any others' languages in return. They also never showed any interest in improving translator technology so communicators would be safe for them. Keir found this lack of motivation to be arrogant. Simply because they couldn't use the devices currently available didn't mean they should force everyone else to speak what was now Earth's primary language. How hard could it be to learn a few sentences, in several alien tongues, just to be polite?

To further his annoyance, Keir shared Datron's disgust about the assignment. Even though he had chosen this most recent course of action, the current case demanded the most unusual and denigrating tactics he'd ever suffered. If it hadn't been so important, he would never have agreed. And he hated to rely on his best friend's loyalty. No other enforcer would have ever accepted this duty. It made it worse that he knew his friend would never have refused his request for help, no matter the circumstances, and Keir still couldn't enlighten Datron regarding all the truths of the case.

Yes, it was bad enough that thugs had stolen illegally-built Ache blasters. The weapons were aptly named: by inhibiting the formation of an enzyme known as Acetylcholinesterase—abbreviated in Earth English by the letters AChE, or simply *ache*—they killed their victims after several incapacitating minutes of excruciating agony. Those inflicted with the beam from an Ache blaster died the way pests do when exposed to a short spray of insecticide. There was always a painful, contorting convulsion before breathing halted. Victims always knew horrific suffering during the last few moments of their lives. But those insidious weapons were only part of the matter. Someone had taken something much worse: the Lucent Stones. Objects so powerful that no one could know they'd been taken—not Datron, not his Earther allies, not anyone.

Keir considered the ease with which his foes had been able to smuggle their goods from port to port and planet to planet while under the guises of contestants and while on their way to the competition held on Earth. He, too, had to take on that same identity as a competitor. In such a way, he intended to avoid discovery as an enforcer, just as the smugglers joining the Mr. Interstellar Feller contest had eluded detection. Because each of the contestants had been vetted by the contest sponsors—Ms. Electra Galaxy and her backers from a company producing Pluto Pillow Mints—no law enforcers took the time to thoroughly check them or their luggage. It was assumed that competitors were above such dastardly deeds. To be honest, most enforcers wouldn't credit the kind of men competing with the intelligence it took to smuggle anything. But while Keir usually shared that belief, there were some exceedingly conniving and deceptive entrants this time.

Keir leaned forward. "Put us into hyperdrive, Helmsman. I want to be in the orbit of Earth's moon by this time tomorrow." *And get this farce over with as soon as possible.*

The ship's helmsman nodded. "As you command, Captain."

CHAPTER TWO

Sagan waited at headquarters for three weeks. Finally, word came that her new partner was arriving via a commercial shuttle from the moon's surface. He won points for not landing where his enforcer vessel could be seen, but she awarded them grudgingly. She'd been informed that Trask had told his crew to stand by on the far side of the moon as if they were on patrol. After he landed on Earth, they could proceed to Mars Colony for a well-earned bit of shore leave. Since Trask's vessel was a specially equipped, deep-space police craft and didn't need refueling for a standard year as Earth measured time, the crew hadn't made any ports of call from the time they'd left Oceanus. Their flight so far had consisted of three months. That meant they'd avoided all the lawful disembarkation checkpoints between his world and hers. By intergalactic treaty, law enforcer vessels from other worlds weren't subject to search even if they had made port at some distant world. That meant the Oceanun vessel could be carrying any number of arms that Earth would never allow on the surface. Hence her supervisor's order that her new partner was to land without any weapons. But she couldn't expect him to show up without some kind of arsenal. Especially since she wouldn't if the situation were reversed.

All in all, she wasn't getting the warm fuzzies about either this man or his mission. There were about a hundred unanswered questions filtering through her brain as she stood on the shuttle dock.

Casting a glance around, she saw that there didn't seem to be anyone taking notice of her presence, other than a few passing men giving her bold stares. She was used to that and ignored them as always. Most of those present strained to see the new batch of arriving contestants. Everyone wanted to bathe in the glow of these males whose alien features were considered gorgeous in their respective cultures.

When the right shuttle finally appeared on the horizon and slowly hovered at the dock, something in Sagan's gut told her to be very careful. The hair on the back of her neck was on end, and that never happened unless she was being watched. Surreptitiously glancing over her left shoulder, she saw only a tall, blond giant of a man whose bare torso and angel-like wings designated him as a denizen of the planet Valkyrie. She vaguely remembered that it was a mountainous world somewhere in the Orion sector. He wasn't looking at her at the moment. Rather, he seemed to be studying a local news video displayed on a kiosk screen. Nevertheless, she would bet that he had been watching her.

She wanted to shake off the suspicious feeling, attribute it to one more stare from a lecherous passerby. But something about the bronzed, winged megalith's presence disturbed her. Something just wasn't kosher.

She moved away; he didn't follow. After she turned the corner to enter the shuttle depot and came out on the other side, he was gone altogether.

Sagan frowned, then took up her position again on the platform. The shuttle was just landing, and she heard a voice on the loudspeaker announce a momentary disembarkation. Now her skin began to tingle and she could feel her heartbeat pick up. There would be no mistaking someone from Oceanus, especially since the fool hadn't taken the opportunity to disguise himself. Egos ran to the extra-large size on his home world. Knowledge of that, and knowledge that she'd be demanding a very long explanation for a number of unsolved riddles thus far, was giving her a case of anxiety the likes of which she had never suffered. A man like him wouldn't accept being interrogated.

She lifted her chin, unclenched her hands and licked her dry lips. *Get a frickin' grip. I'm the one in control, and he's gonna know it.*

Keir exited the passenger shuttle with the one large carry-on bag he'd brought. All the rest of his gear had been sent ahead with Datron. They'd both approved the idea of Datron taking charge of their luggage since Keir's physical appearance might draw notice and require a search; Earth now had some ridiculous edict that only subordinate workers from Oceanus be allowed to land, and Keir didn't know how seriously the local constabulary took that order. He needn't have worried. The security guards at Earth's docking stations, as had other guards throughout the galaxy, wrongly assumed this contest's competitors held the status of ambassadors. The guards, therefore, didn't want to incite any incidents by asking too many questions or by going through luggage. Datron had informed him he'd passed the entire inspection without a question being asked or a strap on a piece of luggage being unbound. Keir's disgust over that serious security lapse was doubled since they could have been terrorists or spies bent on killing thousands—as were the smugglers he sought.

He let out a frustrated breath and searched the crowds for the person who would be his contact. He didn't know the party, had only been told that his contact's appearance would most certainly make itself known. He now wondered what the man looked like.

For a full five minutes, Sagan simply stared. While the males on the platform ogled her, the man fifty yards away was being equally scrutinized by every female within sight. He stood there, a little over seven feet tall and mesmerizing.

That he was from Oceanus was readily apparent. His light green skin and bright blue eyes were as striking as his size. Sagan didn't miss the luxurious quality of his long, straight black hair, which blew like a banner in the afternoon wind. There was one bright blue star on his left cheek, absolutely labeling him as a citizen of the ocean world. Oceanus: the name Earthlings had given the planet, and the name by which its own people referred to it when visiting Earth, as they pretentiously assumed no one here could pronounce their native tongue. This assumption was, she guessed, also the reason for the man's new moniker.

Keir Trask. Square-jawed, with shoulders broad as a bridge. Sagan continued to stare at him. She saw him gaze at his new surroundings with an expression of contempt that was plastered unmistakably on his perfect, godlike, crazy-gorgeous face. For a brief moment she was sure she'd seen a statue that looked exactly like him; then she remembered her frequent visits to the Los Angeles Metropolitan Museum and the likenesses of deities on display there. Looking him over, there wasn't a single marble structure in the hall of Greek mythology that could stand the comparison to this unworldly visitor . . . except for one. *Poseidon.* If she had to pick a single deity to represent this man, Poseidon was perfect. Keir Trask even appeared to have the arrogant and thunderous personality of that god.

She couldn't see any of his body, for he wore a black cloak that fell just to the tops of his high black boots. But she could guess from his dimensions that her new partner was carrying enough muscle to take on the entire local football team and then some. The only thing that marred his magnificent presence was the lack of any semblance of joy. Sagan got the impression that he didn't smile much. It was either that, or he wasn't finding his current environment pleasing.

She took a deep breath, exhaled slowly, then walked forward with calm deliberation. If she was scared, this immense creature would sense it in a moment. That would put her on a level of defensiveness that wouldn't help their working relationship. And they had to be close, given their cover. Very close.

Keir didn't like being made to wait; nor was he amused by the pictures being taken of him and the catcalls from dozens of women. There was no mistaking his presence or his home world's markings. If this delay was someone's idea of "putting the alien in his place," he'd go to the hotel and leave his Earth counterpart far behind, wondering what had happened. He'd have done it sooner, but this mission was too important for one-upmanship. He and whoever had been assigned as his partner had to operate as a precise team—even considering the secrets he kept—or all might be lost. Still, his limited patience could only strain so far. The trip had been long and he needed rest. He gazed about the platform one last time, then decided his counterpart would have to come looking for him. That was when he saw *her*.

He'd been about to turn and summon a transporter to the hotel when she came sauntering out of the crowd like a graceful dancer. She had a subtle sway to her hips that would put the lovely silver dancing women of Denudion to shame. Her figure was long and lean, made slenderer because of the black one-piece garment and matching boots she wore. Her long brown hair, a medium color with a touch of golden shimmer, was currently bound up in some kind of tightly woven braid atop her head. For some ridiculous reason, given the day's standards of dress, he found himself hoping it wasn't a hairpiece but real. Then her eyes captured his and he forgot to look at anything else. Three long months aboard his ship had him missing female companionship. Rules dictated that he couldn't touch one of his crew women, and they were far too professional to let him. But the situation being what it was, he found that first sight of her sexually engaging.

Her eyes were a very clear violet. His study of Earthling physiology didn't account for that strange but exquisite color. And he was under no delusion that she was only approaching to make his acquaintance, as many women did: Though he'd thought his counterpart would be a he, his counterpart was a she. As he kept his gaze locked with hers, something in her stare said, "Don't screw with me." She was as determined as she was beautiful.

Keir had to force the reason for his presence on Earth into his mind, while trying to control the urge to begin a torrid seduction. In his whole life, he'd never experienced the sudden loss of his mental faculties so quickly and totally. His new comrade-in-arms was nothing short of stunning. He saw men turn their heads as she undulated by, and felt an irrational, illogical desire to break faces because of the gawking. As she drew nearer, he saw the flawlessness of her skin, the high cheekbones and full lips that would probably drive a lesser man insane with desire. But he was no lesser man. He was an Oceanus enforcer of the highest rank. As such, she was as far beneath him as desert sand to a star. All that considered, why was his body responding this way? Why couldn't he focus?

"Keir Trask? I'm your escort. Just call me Sagan," she smilingly introduced herself. Then she held out her right hand—believing he'd be well versed in Earth languages and customs, no doubt, as were most aliens visiting her world, and believing he'd understand her extended hand was a friendly greeting.

Keir lifted his hand, slid his palm against hers and felt a bolt of energy shoot straight through him. Her palm was soft, but her handshake was firm as he closed his grip. The sensation of her skin against his unnerved him immensely, but he struggled not to show it. She wouldn't have felt the electrifying shock, but he did and knew its meaning. "Keir Trask," he quietly said. "I'm sorry. I missed hearing your surname."

"I won't be using one," she replied. "If we can gather your luggage, we'll be on our way. There's a great deal we need to talk about, and this place is a little too public."

Keir glanced around at the crowds, took in the ultra-modern glass-and-steel depot that echoed sound all too readily, and nodded. "I agree." He picked up his bag. "Shall we go?"

She arched an eyebrow in surprise. "That's all your gear?"

"I wasn't expecting this assignment since my crew and I left Oceanus with a schedule for deep space patrol. Except for uniforms, I ordinarily travel light." It was a lie even a rookie could have detected. Though he'd been told her department would issue whatever defensive weapons would be necessary for this assignment, she probably wouldn't believe for one second that he hadn't brought his own arsenal. No self-respecting Oceanun enforcer would be caught dead without their personal armament.

"Come along, then. I have private transportation ready."

Keir followed, noting that her beguiling gait hadn't changed. It wasn't an affectation just to draw attention; not as far as he could tell. She had a long stride that was probably due to a lot of physical training. There wasn't an ounce of spare flesh on her body, judging by that second-skin suit that hugged her every curve. He allowed himself the extreme luxury of letting his gaze slide up and down her back.

Three damned months in space. Had he been on another planet and off duty, he'd pursue this woman with the intention of thoroughly bedding her. Oceanun and Earthling physiologies were thought to be highly compatible, but it wouldn't have mattered if she were a Bog Hag from the swamp planets at the galaxy's outermost rim; built the way she was, he'd have still desired her, as he did right now. He silently thanked the Creator of all things for his good judgment in wearing his traveling cloak, else his overt pleasure at just having her near would be readily apparent to anyone. He could feel the cloth of his trousers rubbing him as he walked, and the soft abrasion was adding to his titillation. Sagan, whatever her last name was, had rapidly affected him in a debilitating way. He couldn't think straight with the lower part of his body so engorged.

Sagan reached an open, flat, silver piece of floating metal that would serve as their transportation—a *hover disc*, she called it—and turned to him and nodded toward the rear. Keir readily tossed his bag into the back. There was only a large seat in the center and a control panel in front, but the vehicle looked similar to most on his home world. He stored that knowledge away, in case he needed to use one without her aid. With luck, almost everything he and Datron needed to accomplish would be centered in the Stardust Hotel. But he couldn't mention that he knew the name of the place yet. He wasn't supposed to be aware of too many details, considering the lie that he'd just been assigned to this mission. Had she been just a little later in getting to him, she'd have eventually found him registered at the right place. He'd have passed it off as a coincidence and, given Earthlings' lack of perception, he was sure she'd believe it.

He mounted the passenger side and belted himself in as she got behind the wheel of the disc. Curiously, she turned the craft away from the lighted city skyscrapers that towered in the evening light. Keir glanced over his shoulder, then pointedly looked back at her. "Would you mind telling me where we're going? In case you hadn't noticed, the city is behind us . . . and getting farther behind by the moment."

The woman kept her eyes riveted on the desert ahead of them. "We need to get some things straight, Mr. Trask. I don't like people screwing with me. I have a real problem with people who lie."

The anger in her voice immediately put Keir on guard. She'd either found out something or was about to go on what Earthlings referred to as a fishing expedition. Having researched how the police on her world operated, he was prepared for a full interrogation, but vowed to keep his temper until she finally relayed the part about his pageant obligations. At that time, he'd act outraged and put-upon. Knowing that was coming, it was all he could do to keep a smile off his face. And while the competition was contemptible, she'd probably find out he'd known about it far longer than originally believed, and that he'd been playing her. That eventuality would be worth the imposition just to see the surprised look on her gorgeous face. But only just.

Using all the speed she could get out of the little transport disc, Sagan was able to quickly put many miles between them and Los Angeles. She found a quiet landing spot on an overhanging desert rock. They were quite alone. And though she was risking much by bringing this gargantuan man into the middle of nowhere with only a stun laser tucked into her boot, she was aware he'd know the consequences of harming an Earth enforcer while on a mission from his home world. The penalty would be death.

She got off the transport and walked toward the setting sun. It was just about to sink below the horizon and made a beautiful view. However, her reasons for coming into the desert weren't for the spectacular scenery. She abruptly turned to find him standing behind her. Taken aback that a man of his size could move so silently, she backed up a few steps.

"I assume we're here because you've taken exception to part of this assignment?" he asked.

"I've taken an exception to a great many things, Mr. Trask. I want about a hundred questions answered. And if I don't like what I hear, you'll be on the next transport back to your planet, just as soon as I can arrange to have a few local constables haul you to the depot . . . in handcuffs. Is that understood?" She saw his eyes narrow and knew she'd never get to her stunner in time if he really wanted to wring her neck. The anger in his gaze proved he wasn't used to being spoken to in such a manner. But he'd better get it clear from the get-go that he wasn't on his home world anymore. This was Earth, and she was in charge. The lies she'd gleaned so far were already enough to send him packing. But she wanted to hear how far he'd go to cover his real mission, just so she could include his deceit in her report. That way, Earth's diplomats could correctly say he'd been given every chance to reveal his real motives and failed to do so.

Keir pressed his lips together firmly before saying, "Ask your questions. Please be quick about it. Three months on board a confined craft makes a long trip. In deference to your inability to understand, I'll try to be succinct."

She let out a long breath, willing herself not to smack the smug expression off his gorgeous face. He may as well have just called her an ignorant worm. "Why the hell are you really here?"

Keir steeled his features at the directness of the question. Considering their location, he guessed she was interrogating him away from the city because she was the only one who knew about his planet's real agenda. At least, he hoped that was the case. "Officials from my planet forwarded the information. I got the same communiqué that was delivered to the Earth Protectorate. We're to look for smugglers from Lucent."

She stared at him for a very long moment. "We were given a list of goods to search for. Rare silk, even rarer spices and artwork. That's all."

When she didn't continue, he had the strangest feeling she might actually know something she wasn't supposed to. This didn't fit the profile of Earth law enforcement personnel. Perceptiveness was never something with which he would have credited them. "And your question is?"

She stepped closer and tilted her head back to look him in the eyes. "Quit shitting me! What the hell else are you supposed to be looking for? Smugglers paying off customs agents and coconspirators wouldn't make enough on the black market to pay for this shipment they hid all the way from Lucent. That planet is roughly two star systems away from Oceanus. That would make the smuggling time here, if everything went perfect, at least fourteen months using star jumps. Even a half-wit would see it'd be far easier taking minor goods and selling them in smaller ports closer to the theft. Now, I'll ask you one last time: *What else was in that shipment?* What was smuggled from Lucent that caused their government to look two star systems away for law enforcement?"

Stupefied by her perception, Keir actually had to gather his wits before answering. Clearly, the lie was uncovered. To stick to it would most certainly get him ejected from the planet's surface. The loss of face would be untenable—and the possible lives lost if he wasn't present to stop the smugglers would weigh even heavier on his conscience than any loss of position. Releasing a long, slow breath, he decided to relay what truth he safely could. He began with: "All right, you've done your research. Let's see if you can handle the truth."

Sagan swallowed hard. This was something very big. She'd known it would be after weeks of intensive hacking into computer databases that yielded nothing but top-secret codes she couldn't begin to decipher. No one went to that kind of trouble over goods routinely smuggled by pirates. She lifted her chin and prepared to hear the worst. Whatever it was, this huge man had taken a three-month space voyage because he was deadly serious about what he was doing. He hadn't found out about this assignment while on regular patrol and just a few weeks from Earth as local officials had been led to believe. From what she'd learned of his record, Keir Trask was particularly chosen or may have even asked for this assignment. Moreover, the serious look on his face said everything. He was ready to die for his job. Was she?

CHAPTER THREE

Y ou're correct about the misrepresentation of the goods for which we're searching," Keir solemnly said.

His colleague snorted. "Misrepresentation? It's a bald-faced lie. One I'm sure you thought I'd buy, given my 'limited Earthling capacity for the deduction of facts.'"

There was that. But he wasn't going to take the bait for that argument; not at the moment. Since she'd stumbled onto a large part of what he'd tried to keep hidden, she might as well know the gist of the matter— less the part pertaining to the Lucent Stones. "The truth is, the smugglers seem to have broken into a warehouse on Lucent and stolen a sizable cargo of lethal weapons. Ache blasters, to be precise."

For a long moment Sagan simply stared at him, clearly horrified. "There's a universal ban on neurological disruption weapons. Lucent signed the treaty as well as every other known world!"

"Lucent didn't make the weapons. Pirates did."

"Keep going," she urged.

"About a month before the theft of the weapons, Lucent's constabulary got word of a pirate den hiding on one of their moons. Their top law enforcement operatives were able to swiftly plan a raid that yielded twenty cases of Ache blasters. While some of the thieves got away, the man responsible for drawing up the plans and actually constructing the weapons was among the pirates caught. He was a dispossessed scientist from Pegasus Minor, looking to make more money than he could on his home world. This so-called scientist was able to hook up with the looters, and they gave him the ready supply of blaster technology he needed by raiding small transports shuttling to and from Lucent colonies and the surrounding sector. When the pirates were caught, Lucent authorities immediately warehoused the booty until it could be destroyed. Lucent's high commanders were in the process of questioning some of the thieves they'd captured when those pirates who were still free broke into the storage facility and took the entire shipment. Eight of Lucent's law enforcement people were killed in that attack."

Sagan silently considered that bit of news then asked, "What's Oceanus's part in this?"

"Lucent, as you probably know, is a very small colony. They don't have the law enforcement manpower to handle a protracted operation across the universe. Especially not after losing eight of their best. They approached my home world for help. As far as the smugglers know, my world and its law enforcers have nothing to do with searching for the blasters. There's the added benefit that we Oceanuns have the best enforcers in the known universe. Lucent's officials know this. It was perfectly logical of them to come to us, given their limited powers and resources."

Sagan turned away and began to pace. "Now everything is beginning to make some damned sense," she muttered, though she obviously still couldn't countenance the lie behind this subterfuge.

"It should now be obvious to you that I knew about the smuggling all along, and that I came straight from

Oceanus for the express purpose of locating the thieves. More to the point, I was fully prepared to engage the cover of a competitor in the Electra Galaxy competition as your officials demanded. This is necessary to support an excuse for my presence when I wouldn't be allowed to land here for any other reason."

"Go on," she encouraged.

"I concede the lie that I was coincidentally in the area, on scheduled patrol. That story had to hold in case your media actually found out my real occupation and we could no longer put me in the pageant because my enforcer status was revealed. In the event that happened, Oceanus authorities would have admitted to a minor co-operative law enforcement exercise between your planet and mine, but an operation that is of no consequence and only for the sake of diplomacy. Furthermore, though communication from my ship to Earth's surface has always been encrypted, I took no chances that higher intelligences might break my codes. Again, in the event my identity was discovered, my superiors would have stated that your enforcer vessels and ours were engaging in some trumped-up training mission in space. Our procedure is to always have backup plans. Still, I would have told you all this . . . eventually."

She rounded on him. "When frost formed at the outermost regions of hell—is that when you planned on letting me in on these minor details? I shouldn't have to tell you that a backup plan only works if everyone on the mission is apprised of it."

Keir opened his mouth to speak, but the woman's tirade was just beginning. She stalked right up to him and poked a long, red-tipped finger into the middle of his chest. Momentarily flummoxed by a gesture no one had dared make in his entire life, he simply stared at her, speechless.

"If I were a betting woman, I'd lay odds that you've got even more information you're not sharing."

"Please elucidate," he said as he gazed down at her.

Sagan lifted her chin and stared him straight in the eyes. "Okay. Here's what I think. I believe that the only way twenty frickin' cases of Ache blasters eventually got on this world is that the pirates who raided Lucent's warehouses had some very integrated help. They couldn't have just got in and out of spaceports easily if Lucent had enacted the proper all points bulletins. I imagine Lucent didn't do that out of fear their planet would be blamed for not immediately destroying banned weaponry."

She moved even closer to him and asked, "Did you think I wouldn't be able to figure all this out? Did you believe that I'd simply buy the story that you'd come all this way for stolen *carpets?* While I had no idea what you were really looking for, I knew it had to be something very dangerous. And it had to be something smuggled in such a way that no standard security guard, at any spaceport, would notice."

Keir was amazed. This woman's magnificent perception was confounding.

She backed up and sat on the edge of her transport vehicle. "One good way to smuggle something a routine security search wouldn't find would be to make yourself highly noticeable. No one would possibly believe a pirate smuggling weapons would enter and leave a spaceport under the guise of a Mr. Interstellar Feller competitor—would they, Mr. Trask? I mean, everyone on the planet, including me, has been watching competitors arrive. There've been vid screen transmissions of the spaceports every night for weeks. People want to know all about the contestants in this year's contest. It's the hottest topic on the whole damned planet, never mind Los Angeles. And because every disembarkation area is covered by the media, the population can see everything and so can I. And what I see is that the local transport authority lets competitors breeze right through the gated checkpoints without as much as a by-your-leave. Everyone takes the position they're diplomats. Even the local police department has been instructed to give special latitude, as some of the contestants are sons of dignitaries—dignitaries of planets with whom Earth hopes to establish an alliance."

Keir could almost hear what she'd say next. And the little fireball didn't disappoint him. She was exhibiting an almost uncanny astuteness.

Sagan watched him grind his teeth in exasperation, then said, "I listened to the recorded transcripts of your world's ambassadors trying to hammer out a trade and defense alliance with ours. Your people did one hell of a job, using semantics and tricks to get my people to come up with the idea of putting you in the Mr. Interstellar Feller competition. It was all very subtle, how your envoys listed one unsuitable occupation after another for your cover. When Earth's response was always negative, your guy sarcastically remarked that the only thing left was a competition spot in this pageant. And of course the entire Earth council seized on that idea. No, you wouldn't be allowed on the planet *unless* you agreed to be in the contest. Which is exactly where you wanted to be all along."

She shook her head, angered by all the stealthy plotting his people had deployed. "Your diplomats worked mine like modeling clay. Let me paint this picture for you just a little more and see if it all fits."

Keir clamped his jaw shut only to keep from saying anything he'd regret. Sagan simply continued her angry monologue. "The smugglers used the pageant as an easy way onto Earth's surface with their goods. As I've said, your envoys deliberately did everything they could to make it look like adding you to the contestant list was *our* idea. All so you could keep the Earth Protectorate from really knowing what you were searching for, and hide Lucent's neglect in not destroying those weapons sooner. My guess is that you'd have found the damned blasters and got them off the planet without us being any the wiser."

With the swift motion of one hand, Keir threw off his cloak and tossed it into the back of the transport. "Are you going to keep me in this wretched heat, interrogating me for the rest of the night? Since you so cleverly figured out the truth, I see no reason to continue this cross-examination. Unless it *is* your intention to keep stating what you know."

Sagan pushed away from the transport and put her hands on her hips. "We're here until I've had our hotel suite swept for bugs and any kind of recording devices. I've set up the equipment to do so, but that kind of filtering takes a few hours. And I wasn't about to have this damned conversation with you in a hotel room that wasn't, as yet, secure."

"*Our* hotel suite?" Keir blurted.

"That's right, Mr. Trask. We'll be sharing a suite. Most of the contestants will have their interpreters, entourage and whatever paraphernalia they need to help them survive in our atmosphere. My sharing a suite with you, since I'll be posing as your manager, will seem quite normal. And I can keep my eye on you at all times. I'm certain you intended to send me off on what we refer to as a wild-goose chase while you looked among the contestants for the smugglers. And we both know they *are* among the pageant assembly. Weapons with this kind of destructive power had to be transported in such a way that normal security measures could be circumvented. It makes absolute sense that our criminals are among the pageant contestants as we both now agree. But what you don't understand is that every year when this pageant takes place, Earth's defenses are dangerously lowered. Because this contest is so well hyped and women are especially determined to see as many of the competitors as possible, Los Angeles's population almost doubles. The port authorities are overloaded. Our security personnel have to work overtime and they tire easily after fifteen-hour shifts. What's worse, we have to be very tactful about how security risks are handled. Businesses stay open much later and all that adds up to some serious revenue for the city. Local law enforcement agencies like the LAPD have been ordered to use great diplomacy with everyone. Emphasis on the word diplomacy."

"I can imagine that the city's profits probably triple, and money talks," Keir said, rolling his eyes.

"Exactly. At any rate, we must keep what we're doing as quiet as possible. But I demand to be apprised of your every move. Our butts will be on the line if we besmirch Electra Galaxy's competition. Never mind Lucent's government; Ms. Galaxy has so much pull downtown that I don't even want to go into it. Her money runs a lot of politics in Los Angeles. More to the point, if anyone finds out what we're doing, the smugglers could panic and start using those blasters. That means innocent people could get killed."

After pausing for a deep breath she asked, "Are you certain the people we're looking for are still in ignorance that Lucent ever approached your world for help?"

"The pirates were long gone when envoys from Lucent landed on Oceanus," Keir said.

Sagan nodded. "Okay. That brings me to the next part of our little discussion."

Keir spoke up. "So far, the *discussion*, as you call it, has all been on your side. This isn't what I'd call a good start to a working relationship."

"And whose fault is that? Who lied, Trask?"

He lifted his chin and stared down at her. The little ice princess definitely had a Thorian thorn in her panties concerning lying. Yet that aspect of their jobs was almost a given. They were undercover enforcers! Such work, in and of itself, was a lie.

Sagan shook her head and asked, "Why the hell are the weapons being brought *here?* Why didn't the smugglers simply drop them off at one of their ports of call? Security on all the other planets was probably just as lax where contestants are concerned. My research indicates that they seem to have gotten a free ride through every disembarkation area through which they traveled."

Keir swiped at the sweat running off his forehead. The desert heat was as daunting as this little flame of an Earthling. "Unfortunately, Lucent's constabulary was a bit overzealous in their interrogation of the jailed pirates. The criminals . . . *expired* during questioning, so their statements were never corroborated by anyone from Oceanus. But the information gleaned concerned a weapons buyer on Earth. No name was given by the pirates as to who this person was. My superiors assume that, if the story is correct, the thieves would probably have to transport their cargo to the buyer. This would make perfect sense, given what I've seen of the poor security measures and the fact that your local enforcers are spread so thin. If the general slump in security is common knowledge during the pageant dates, then it's a good guess the thieves know about this breach of safety as well. Hence their desire to gain admittance to the competition. They'd want to take advantage of not having their belongings scrutinized. As to what the weapons are for, my guess is as good as yours. They could be turned over to any radical group. There are many in existence, and each would pay a great deal of money for an arsenal of the kind we're talking about. With that kind of weaponry, insurgents could take over a small country."

Sagan nodded then slowly looked him over. "You

know you're going to stick out like a supernova. It's going to be damned hard to convince anyone an Oceanun would enter this competition. People believe Oceanuns are the pretentious pricks of the universe. The only reason we bought it is because officials on Earth believed you'd been suddenly ordered off a routine mission and on to this one. But all that considered, how did you think you'd go poking around hotel rooms and luggage without drawing attention? How were you going to pull this off?"

Her acerbic remark concerning his race being pretentious was inappropriate. He quickly addressed that comment. "The idea was to pretend to have an interest in changing our reputation as 'pretentious pricks,' as you put it. Just as the pirates used the most obvious form of transportation for their loot and thereby evaded detection, we hoped being so obvious an entrant would lend credence to the possibility that I'm not here for any other reason."

She laughed. "Use their own plan against them. Hide in plain sight. Is that it?"

"More or less," he bit out, and stared at the now darkening horizon.

Sagan considered backing off, but she couldn't help herself. This Oceanun had intended to give her the runaround, and his diplomats had deliberately lied to Earth's. As she saw it, he was owed a butt-chewing. And it would come from her, both as an enforcer and a citizen of Earth who was righteously enraged by his deceit. "You don't like this Mr. Interstellar Feller thing one bit, do you? Even considering the entire idea came from your superiors, though it was supposed to look like it came from us." She paused. "Brother, you must want those blasters pretty damned bad. To think you would sink so low as to pose and primp in a male beauty contest. That has to hurt. I'll bet your pride is pretty shredded."

He kept his mouth shut and deliberately slid his gaze away from hers. When he didn't respond, Sagan blurted, "Just so you know, you're going to play the part of competitor to the hilt. If you don't, I'll have you on a transport out of here so fast you won't know what hit you. Is that clear?"

Keir was taking no more from her. He slowly walked toward her, with the effect of making her back away, down the side of her transport and toward the edge of the high precipice where she'd parked.

Upon his approach, Sagan dropped her righteous indignation enough to again look him over. Without his cape to cover his torso, the weight-lifter's, broad-shouldered physique was more than readily apparent. Over seven feet of angry, pissed-off alien was now stalking her in the desert. His color seemed to darken, though that could have been a trick of the fading light. His blue eyes were narrowed and his countenance was, to say the least, bleak. If he didn't kill her now—after discovering his lies and shoving them in his face—they might just be able to hammer out the semblance of a team. But she had to survive.

"While I stand here, as yet unconditioned to your planet's atmosphere, there are men ready, willing and able to hand over dangerous weapons to Creator knows who. And all you can think of is your righteous indignation at having been left out of the informational loop?" Keir put his hands on his hips and continued to back her up, step by slow step. "Did it ever occur to you that we had no idea it wasn't some of your Earth Protectorate who might want the blasters and paid the pirates to get them in the first place? It's a known fact that your world is years behind the rest of the universe concerning certain technology. How did we know Earth officials wouldn't take the damned weapons and use them for research? Even knowing that if they got into the wrong hands it could cost thousands of people their lives, your Earth engineers and scientists are still taking great pains to access technology that even *they've* agreed is too dangerous for common use. During the last general assembly of planets, it was discovered that certain physicians from your world are still attempting to clone sentient beings, which has been outlawed by even the most backward of planets. Your diplomats craftily tell the entire galaxy that they'll sign treaties barring certain technology, then turn around and covertly locate it. I can name at least a dozen times when they've been caught doing this very thing. People in your governments believe they know what's best for everyone else and can control the powers they seek to exploit. There are many in Earth's history who have thought this same thing, to the detriment of millions. And they never seem to learn."

Sagan opened her mouth to vehemently protest, but he held up one hand and moved forward at a more rapid pace. This forced her to momentarily consider her personal safety more than arguing.

Keir continued his monologue as he gave chase. "In the past centuries, your people have shown apathy regarding the preservation of your planet's resources and, indeed, your own lives. First, you almost bombed yourself out of existence on several occasions. Second, you had the almighty damned gall to move yourselves into space and bring your self-centered, thoughtless, trashy ways with you." He gently but deliberately began prodding her in the center of her chest, the way she'd done him. Right between her breasts. "Third, your populace steadfastly refuses to learn anything about your world's history, so you keep making the same infernal mistakes over and over! You don't respect yourselves, but demand it from others. To this damned day, visitors to Earth are forced to speak *your* language and endure *your* English translations of their names and home planets. Yet you won't even make half an effort to learn other traditions. It has always been about you, hasn't it?" he finally finished. He looked like he expected her to babble an apology.

By now, Sagan had retreated to the boundary of the ledge and couldn't move any farther. The sheer drop behind her served as a metaphorical backbone. She wasn't backing down anymore. She rallied and let him have it. To hell with what he decided to do to her.

"You pompous, conceited, arrogant, pretentious son of a bitch! Where do you get off judging the only planet in the entire universe that, last year alone, took in over a million refugees? Where were the Oceanun ships when asteroids struck the third mining colony at Trigus Four? *Our* ships were there taking in survivors, bringing them back to Earth and finding them homes and rendering medical aid. And when every dissident and political prisoner has a choice of leaving their own world and relocating, why the hell do you frickin' think they end up on Earth instead of your planet?"

She stood taller, drawing on the love she had for her home world. "The rest of the sentient universe has managed to chase away everyone who doesn't fit into their little mold of how to live, act, think and even breathe. Those people come here, knowing the free and democratic countries of Earth will give them room to grow and chase their dreams. When we *ask*—and yes, we ask, not demand—that you speak Earth language, it's to keep an irreparable misunderstanding from taking place. The word *frisati* in Kordian means 'friend.' On the second planet in the Bootes system, that same word translates into calling someone a fornicator." She angrily continued, "We have to live in a world where we can get along. There are billions of people on this planet, most originating from elsewhere, whereas your planet can only boast half that population, despite being three times larger. We've made more advancements in the last three hundred years than most worlds have in double that time. Our people live in an environment that rewards motivation and ingenuity. And, yes, we have our problems, but we're the freest crankin' planet in the entire universe, and that's why everyone ends up here or wants to be. So get off our collective cases and shelve the judgmental crap!"

Most of Sagan's defense was made as close to Keir's face as the much shorter woman could get, and she'd yelled the last two sentences at the top of her lungs. Her violet eyes literally flashed with a pride and love that he'd never seen in any creature before.

In that moment, Keir greatly admired her. More, he felt a fierce attraction that bordered on obsession. What would it be like to stroll through a garden on Oceanus arguing politics with this lovely creature? And what would the night bring when they put aside their differences to warm each other in bed? The very thought riveted him in place. All he could do was stare and fight his need of her.

Part of his brain told him he was responding to the stimulus of argument with a beautiful woman. Part of it said he'd never found anyone like her and never would again. For that reason, and that reason only, he backed away. One didn't destroy something so wild and untamed with further negativity. Doing so would counter her tremendous spirit. And Keir simply couldn't do that. Furious, Sagan was a vision to behold; rare and wonderful.

He watched the angry rise and fall of her chest as she

dragged in heated desert air after her passionate outburst. *Passionate*. Yes, that was the word to describe her.
He already knew she was far more intelligent than he'd
bargained for. But add that to her immense emotion
and she was captivating.

Not just for the sake of the mission, but because he
was enthralled with her courage, Keir made a peace offering of a magnitude he'd have never before considered. "I apologize, Sagan. I have no business judging
you or your world. There was no excuse for hiding the
fact that Ache blasters were involved in the smuggling
operation or that I'd intended to take this mission all
along. If someone had come to my home and hidden
pertinent facts, I'd be just as outraged. I can only say I
did so out of ignorance. Your argument is a profound
one. I'm afraid that not seeing things from another's
view is one of my weak points. I shall definitely have to
work on that."

Taken aback, Sagan simply stared. Then, she put a
hand on her chest and took a deep breath. "I-I'm usually
not so out of control," she said.

Keir slightly bowed his head, but his gaze never left
her face. "I provoked you. Again, my apologies."

"Why . . . why don't we get back to the hotel?" Sagan
suggested, looking calmer. "I think we can gather our
tempers and start over."

Keir nodded. He waited for her to mount the hover
disc before doing so himself. And while they said very
little on the way back into the city—a metropolis
that looked very modern and bright by comparison to
almost any of another planet's—Keir began to feel a
deep sense of regret that he couldn't tell her about the
Lucent Stones. But he'd sworn, at all costs, never to reveal their existence to humans. Or even to his partner
Datron.

Glancing at the woman beside him as she concentrated

on operating the craft, something in him realized there would come a time of reckoning. He hoped she never found out there was one more lie he'd told, for whatever small peace was newly formed between them would be forever lost.

CHAPTER FOUR

After checking into the Stardust Hotel, Keir took note of his surroundings. Using one of the bullet-shaped glass elevators that allowed for a view into the building's foyer as well as outside into the city, he and Sagan were on their way up to the sixteenth floor of the most luxurious building he'd ever seen outside the confines of Oceanus. The exterior of the building had been constructed to look very much like a narrow pyramid, the kind he'd once studied as a child and which existed on a number of humanoid planets throughout the stars. Instead of brick and mortar, however, everything was steel, chrome or glass.

The sun was down now, but would surely illuminate the interior of the hotel come sunrise. At the moment, lights from the surrounding buildings glittered around them from enormous heights. From his extensive study of Earth culture, Keir had learned that land on this part of the Earth's surface was at a premium, especially in the downtown Los Angeles area. To make the most of the space available, contractors had decided to build up in spite of warnings of a fault line just beneath the city. Luckily, no major earthquakes had disrupted the community in over a century.

From his research he further gleaned that the pageant diva, known as Electra Galaxy, owned this building and almost everything surrounding him for five city blocks. Since his travels had led him to many exquisite locations, he could appreciate how immaculately dressed her staff was, in their gray uniforms trimmed in silver, and how well trained they were when approaching guests. Everything in this ultramodern facility was polished to perfection, including the white marble stairways and banisters that had bits of shimmering quartz embedded in them for effect. Of course, the elevators kept guests from having to drag luggage to the heights of this enormous facility by use of the stairs, but one could certainly make an entrance by strolling down them.

Right now, he preferred the elevators for no other reason than to get a good view of the hotel and the outside city through all the glass in the structure's facade.

But even the most innocuous details, from elevator buttons to wall computers had been addressed. Even the banners welcoming the guests to the thirtieth annual Electra Galaxy's Mr. Interstellar Feller pageant were hung precisely and made of the finest silken materials. Appropriate for such a contest, they were black and adorned with small golden planets and stars.

Further perusal indicated crystal sparkling from chandeliers, from cut-glass decanters holding beverages, and from elaborate sculptures of stars, planets and moons located in every conceivable nook and cranny.

If he had to sum up his surroundings in one utterance, the word *opulent* covered it. But the design, elaborate as it was, could never equate to the outdoor scene he witnessed from his small oceanside villa on any given night when the stars blanketed the sky and reflected in the sea like diamonds.

Thoughts of home brought warm remembrances of

his family. His brothers, sisters, parents, grandparents, uncles and aunts had all been at the enforcer airfield on the day he'd left Oceanus. It wasn't that they knew of this mission's importance or the danger involved; indeed, most of them didn't. It was more about his loved ones always being there before another space voyage took him away for months on end.

He tried to hold back a smile over his parents' and grandparents' request that he make this his last space mission, take an academy teaching position and find a good woman with whom to settle down and breed children. It wasn't as though they didn't have enough toddlers running around with nine born and another on the way. But he was the only one of his siblings not to have married or to have children. In this day and age one didn't necessitate the other, but his parents were somewhat old-fashioned in the universal way of wanting him married *before* producing heirs. Wherever he went, there were still some that clung to this belief, though many more, on hundreds of worlds, certainly didn't.

By his own desire, he'd never sire a child by a woman he didn't worship with all his heart. And if he loved her that much, then she'd surely be his mate before he'd get her with child. Still, he considered himself a virile warrior with a man's needs. An occasional woman crossed his path that was just too alluring to pass up. For those instances, he did what all his crewmen would on deep-space voyages and inoculated himself with a birth control serum that would last until he was given the reversal serum.

As his thoughts aimlessly wandered from hotel décor, the faces of his beloved family and finally to birth control, he glanced at Sagan's perfect profile and again noted the creamy, flawless complexion, the hard little body the woman displayed with such unaffected grace and her unusually colored violet eyes. May as well enjoy his imaginative wanderings now, while he had the time to do so.

His body hardened yet again, so he took a deep breath and concentrated instead on looking out the glass elevator doors, and studying lush tropical plants that were beautifully displayed on each level. He put his mind on the perfectly balanced earth tones decorating the floors they passed, and off what it would be like to tame this temptress during a long night of torrid lovemaking.

Trying harder to note his surroundings the way any undercover operative would, he'd perused many contestants in the competition registering for rooms at the hotel desk. Sagan had whisked them through the process, already having their accommodations handled. As she'd told him, her belongings were in their suite, so all they'd needed to do was secure a room access code for him.

Continuing his survey as they climbed ever higher—which took longer, given the crowds using the conveyance—he remembered a few more mundane details of his research. Electra Galaxy owned the only green areas left in Los Angeles. Keir began to appreciate the empire of power and wealth this woman had built by showcasing men. He'd also amusingly learned that her real name was Myrtle Crabtree, from someplace called Ipswitch, Oregon. She'd started her competition thirty years ago with a few men from off-world mining colonies and built her influential profile from there. And Sagan was correct in her summation of the woman's power and money being unequalled in this city.

When they finally got to the sixteenth level and stepped out of the elevator, more plants surrounded them. Their relaxing scent wafted through the air-conditioned space. Keir noted that Sagan presented a beautiful smile as she gently touched the leaf on one large specimen. Clearly, she loved plants. They had that in common. But he kept his opinion on the matter to himself as he was sure the little warhead accompanying him wouldn't want to hear his comments on the environment.

When they got to their room, he watched as she efficiently keyed in her access code. After entering, she unnecessarily put a finger to her full lips in a gesture for him to keep quiet. Then, she quickly closed the door, locked it and checked a tiny sweeping device attached: If anyone had entered and placed any equipment for monitoring sound or movement, this white disc on the back of the door would tell her. He appreciated that she'd gone to the trouble. This thoroughness wasn't an attribute common to humans as he saw them, but there was no question the device she was now scanning was state-of-the-art. He'd brought another just like it for the same purpose.

"We're clear. You can speak now," she told him, watching him toss his bag to one side.

"Unless there's some change in the schedule, I understand the main competition doesn't start until Saturday. That leaves us little time to coordinate efforts," he replied.

She tilted her head and studied him.

He arched a brow in response. "Yes?"

"You have an unbelievable command of our language. I don't detect a trace of any accent," she said.

He crossed his arms over his chest. "That's because I've been studying your world since I was a young boy."

"Really? Why? I mean, at the risk of starting another argument, I'd have thought we'd be too boring a race for anyone from Oceanus to bother over."

"It's as you stated," he relented. "Those of us in the outer reaches of space aspire to visit Earth at one point or another. I, uh, had the mistaken belief for some time that I'd actually get to see cowboys riding through the street if I could just get here."

She grinned. "Some stereotypes die hard. And that one is centuries old."

He smiled back. "You can't tell that to a young boy looking for adventure and trying to escape the rigors of a dull yet meticulous higher mathematics instructor."

For a moment, Sagan had to stare. Keir's smile was gorgeous. Yet she still got the impression he allowed himself that luxury very seldom. Even as she admired the brilliance of it, he pasted back on a grim expression and turned to survey the room. Too bad. She'd just been about to question him on his admiration of cowboys. That time period and topic, she adored.

"Which is to be my quarters?"

She was going to have to work on his stiff attitude and demeanor. That would never do for the cover story in which he was about to engage. "The larger room on the right is yours. Mine is there." She gestured to the left.

Keir picked up his bag, but stopped to study the fountain in the center of the room. "My villa on Oceanus has such a water feature on the balcony," he said. "From there I can look out on the ocean and see what you'd refer to as the porpoises playing in the surf."

Porpoises were another happy subject for Sagan. She'd just watched a documentary about them only two weeks earlier. "That must be lovely. I've heard your entire world is balmy and tropical. To have a place right on the beach would be heaven. I love the beach."

He nodded, and reached out his hand to let water spill over his palm. "It's a paradise unlike any other, my world. Of course, you might not recognize the porpoises. They're purple, with fins that glow in the dark."

"God, I wish I could *see* that," she blurted.

He glanced at her. "Perhaps you shall, someday." Then he cleared his throat and continued to his room.

"I'll unpack and grab a quick shower. After, we can discuss this mission further," he called back.

"Would you like something to eat?" she offered.

He turned at the door to his room. "Please. I'm a vegetarian, so anything from that part of the menu will do just fine." Then he disappeared into his room.

From her studies, Sagan already knew some Oceanuns avoided meat, but how surprising that Keir was one of them! This was another common aspect to their lives. She, too, was prone to choosing fruit and vegetables. Feeling hungry, she grabbed up the hotel menu and scanned it for foods she knew Electra Galaxy would have in stock. The cuisine was designed to satisfy thousands of different tastes from around the universe. There was no problem finding something any weary traveler would find sumptuous.

After placing her order on a menu grid, she walked to the wall computer panel, flipped out the keyboard and began to access files pertaining to the Mr. Interstellar Feller competition. Then she quickly went about showering and changing into something less confining, assuming neither she nor Keir would be going out for the night. She returned to the main room just as the buzzer on the door sounded.

First making sure that it was the hotel staff with their food, Sagan opened the door and allowed the staff to set up the dining table. They were leaving when her giant green companion strolled back into the room wearing a black bathrobe with some kind of muted silver designs embroidered on the silky fabric.

She tried not to gawk, and pretended to put more interest on the meal and pouring them each a glass of wine, but it was one of the hardest things she'd ever done. When the man made an entrance, he flat out made an entrance—whether he meant to or not. He'd walked into the room nonchalantly, drying his long black hair and shaking it back over one shoulder. The vee created by his open robe, which was loosely tied around a very trim-looking waist, was stupefying. He seemed unaware of all the chest muscle and gargantuan pectorals showing, but Sagan sure as hell wasn't. It was all she could do to keep her hands from shaking at the glorious glimpse of skin. Here she was, one of the Earth Protectorate's best operatives, shaking at the sight of a huge alien— Check that. A very *virile* and huge alien wandering around her now too-small hotel suite, wearing what she assumed was nothing but a robe. Against the sumptuous white decor of the suite lounge, he stood out like a beacon, and one desire became imperative. Before this case was over, she wanted at least one chance to touch that shimmering blue star on his left cheek.

Keir finished drying his hair and tossed the towel across the back of the sofa. He hadn't been prepared for Sagan to be similarly clothed. The silvery-gray dressing gown she wore perfectly set off the long brown hair now falling over her shoulders and high, pert breasts. The gown clung to her svelte curves the way her one-piece black outfit had, and he realized she availed herself of no artificial devices women sometimes used to give themselves just such a shape. What he saw was all real, and he craved it far too much. Three months in space was still weighing on him.

Shaking the image of her from his mind and focusing on his hunger, he waited until she was seated, then took up the larger of the two luxuriously padded chairs opposite her. He arched his brow and gazed at the lit white candle surrounded by flowers in the center of the table.

Sagan followed his gaze to the candle. "Um, the hotel staff did that. This is an eight-star facility. All the competitors are given the royal treatment." When he lifted his eyes to hers, she cleared her throat and added, "Speaking of competitors, you still have to sign the pageant entry forms. The Protectorate has leaked your entrance into the pageant to the media . . . as a way to explain your presence on our world. So I assumed you hadn't filled out the forms until that cover story was in place. Suffice it to say, since word got out that an Oceanun was coming to Earth and that there was a connection to the Electra Galaxy venues, every tabloid has drawn the conclusion that you're here to compete, no matter what the Protectorate and your dignitaries decided to report on the subject."

"I had assumed all this would be so. But you're quite right. I haven't filled out any forms for the contest. I thought it more prudent to appear before my so-called manager first."

"It would make sense that you'd want to sign with me witnessing," she agreed. "Anyhow, I pulled the forms up on the computer, on the wall over there. You can read through them and sign after we've eaten. If you electronically submit, that'll keep you from having to leave the room tonight. Your cover and mine will be all set. You should get a confirmation back and an entrant's welcome packet."

"You're very efficient. I admire that."

She gazed across the table at him, then quickly removed the silver domed lid from their meal. "I hope you approve of the food. If not, I can order something else. . . ."

He quickly scanned her choices and found the plentiful fresh cheeses, crackers, fruit and salad much to his liking. "No. This looks quite refreshing. I've only had protein packets during the flight. Forgive me if I employ a bit more gusto than manners."

Sagan smiled. "I think anyone could forgive that." Again she was treated to Keir's beguiling, boyish grin, and he dug into the food and genuinely seemed to enjoy himself.

She'd never taken a voyage beyond a two-week trip to the Mars colonies using stellar gate technology. Indeed, she might be ready to crack after such confinement, but her companion seemed none the worse, except for his voracious hunger. And the way he ate: it wasn't devoid of manners as he claimed, but something about it was exceedingly sensual. He took the food into his mouth, closed his eyes and seemed to savor every morsel. It wouldn't take a great stretch of the imagination to see him taking a woman with the same care and delight.

Sagan picked up her wine, sipped it and tried to pry the wicked images from her mind, most of them having to do with him taking her.

Keir tried the beverage and sighed. "This is grand. I don't recall having eaten this well in a long time. And the wine could rival any of those on Oceanus." He glanced up worriedly. "I didn't mean to imply the wine or food on Earth wasn't comparable . . ."

She put up a hand, interrupting his apology. "I understand." Finally, she found herself relaxing and able to share the meal with him. After a few minutes of eating, and as the intensity with which he attacked the food faded, she remembered the other covered platter set to one side. "Don't forget to leave some room for dessert!" It was one of her favorites, and Sagan unaccountably hoped he'd like it as well.

He followed her gaze and briefly put a napkin to his mouth. "Please say that's something chocolate."

Sagan was warmed all over by the look of expectation in his eyes. She reached for the platter while he cleared a small space on the table. "Ready?" she asked.

He nodded, his eyes trained on the dome.

With teasingly slow deliberation, Sagan lifted the lid

to reveal a slice each of chocolate cheesecake and chocolate layer cake. "Which do you want? Or, we could share."

"Share," he blurted, still staring.

After handing him the chocolate layer cake, Sagan hesitated, watching him in delicious lieu of taking a bite of her dessert. Never in her entire life had she seen a man exhibit such an expression of pure lust while tasting a forkful of cake. "You've never had chocolate before. Not in any form," she guessed.

He gazed at her, and slowly shook his head.

"Here, try some of this," she coaxed, and proceeded to load her fork with cheesecake. She leaned over the table and simply stuck the fork out, and he opened his mouth and took the offering. Again, Sagan allowed herself the pleasure of watching this mountainous, striking alien eat. This time, however, she was feeding him, and feeling sensuous effects.

Once the food was gone, she quickly withdrew the fork. "H-how was it?" she stuttered.

"I can only describe it as . . . carnal," he responded. "I'm beginning to see why beings from every corner of the galaxy and beyond wish to come here. There are treasures for the tastebuds, and delights for the eye to behold. I'm honored to have both this night."

He'd been looking at her when he said it. Sagan lowered her gaze and took some more cheesecake on her fork. Then she raised and ate from it—the same utensil he'd just used—and found something very arousing in the action. Indeed, he seemed to think so as well, as he was pointedly watching her with a heated gaze that could melt iron.

Keir continued sampling both desserts. Far from minding, Sagan seemed to enjoy his taking food from her fork when she offered it. But, when the food was gone and she finally stood, he grounded himself back in the reality of their mission. This enchantingly lovely woman was his partner. He had to remember that, though it was becoming more and more difficult. The candlelight reflected in her bright violet gaze was almost hypnotic. He'd have given his soul, right then and there, to toss aside the damned reason he was on Earth and take her to bed for the night. Never in his life had he allowed such thoughts while undercover. He could only attribute his unprofessional mind-set to the long voyage— and to the breathtaking sight she made as she walked across the room, tucking one long strand of hair behind her ear and putting those long graceful fingers to the keypad of a computer.

"I . . . I think you should read over and sign the entrant documents now," she remarked. "After that, we should get some rest. I'll have the staff clear away the dishes when they bring breakfast in the morning."

Back to business it was. But the sensuality of the moment still clung like a nimbus to a goddess. Keir approached the computer and took his time reading every word, knowing Sagan wouldn't leave the room until he was done. Finally, he electronically signed his Earth name to the forms, then sent them. In a moment, a computerized voice loudly heralded acceptance:

"Thank you for entering the Mr. Interstellar Feller competition as sponsored by Electra Galaxy and the makers of Pluto Pillow Mints. We hope you enjoy your stay on Earth and that your experience is simply spectacular. We'd like to remind you that all entrants will be receiving written confirmation of their acceptance as well as extra information regarding schedules. Look for your welcome packet to be delivered to your room within twenty-four hours. Please let the Stardust staff know if there's anything else we can do to make your competition the thrill of a lifetime. Good luck, and

thank you once again for entering the Mr. Interstellar Feller competition."

When Keir turned, he saw Sagan trying to suppress her laughter. After trying to do the same and failing, they both ended up with their heads bowed, shoulders shaking at the absurdity of the assignment. Yet, there they were, still moving forward with it.

When he finally regained his composure, Keir looked Sagan's graceful form over and asked the question he'd wanted to ask since arriving. "I don't suppose I could finally get your last name?"

"Carter. But I won't be using it."

"Why not? I assume no one knows it. You've worked undercover elsewhere, not in this immediate area, or the assignment would have been given to someone else."

"That's true," she readily agreed. "And everyplace I was undercover, I wore an extensive disguise, even using laser surgery to change my facial features. But I was hoping this assignment would be my last as a field agent. I want to command my own operatives. If that happens, I want to still have my name. So . . . I'll just use my first name here. It won't be strange. It'll fit in with all those other Hollywood elitists who use one name."

"Ah, much like some of the old singers, Carbuncle and Flatulentia?"

"Precisely. And as you say, since I've never actually worked the Hollywood scene, I need not worry about anyone recognizing me. No one except perhaps my supervisor." After a moment, she paused and moved closer to him, leaning nonchalantly against the wall. "May I ask a question?"

"Just one?" he joked.

She smiled. "Okay, maybe a couple of questions. But then I'll let you get some rest, I promise."

He nodded, glad she hadn't gone straight to bed. Any

excuse to stay and converse with her was fine by him. He told himself that the more they knew about each other, the better team they'd make. And while that was perfectly true, his real motives ran deeper.

"There are going to be some parts of the contest you won't like," she remarked.

He sighed heavily. "I know. But we *know* the smugglers are part of it. We have no choice. *You* certainly can't compete. And this pretext gives me access to every part of the hotel where simple staff might not be allowed."

She did not speak for a moment.

Keir saw her hesitation, so he wryly prompted, "Go on. I can see you've got issues on your mind. Let's get the air cleared so we can get on with our jobs."

She gulped. "Has it occurred to you that if you don't accrue enough points to final that you will be dismissed from the pageant? If that happens, you'll be forced to leave the planet. My supervisors will want you escorted to the depot. Of course, since I know what we're looking for, I *could* go it alone if that should happen . . ."

He sidled closer, also using the wall for support. They were now very close. "But then we wouldn't be setting the precedent both your world and mine want for future relationships—if you were working alone. And there are other political implications. Your supervisors would have to get the blasters to Lucent and explain why an Oceanus operative, someone they approached and trusted, was forced into revealing their secret and then released from duty by the Earth Protectorate. It might create some ill will toward Earth, both with my world and Lucent. But the point is, I fully intend to do what's necessary to final— whatever it takes to get those weapons."

She chewed on her lower lip and gazed past him.

"What now, Sagan? What else do you need to know?" he asked softly, absently moving a stray strand of hair off her cheek.

She gazed deeply into his eyes. "You said the Lucent government questioned the pirates until they died. Just how did that happen?"

He let out a long breath. "I was told they used mental probes."

She gasped. "That's outrageous! It's illegal on most planets—Lucent included, if I remember the treaties they signed."

"I totally agree. I said as much when I learned of their tactics. But seeing as how a mental probe *was* used, we can trust the information they got as most certainly reliable. The uncaptured pirates were to smuggle the blasters to Earth using the pageant as a way to get by security. And that makes me even surer these pirates are keeping the weapons very close, not in a storage area or outside their immediate control. I believe they will be in this hotel."

"I don't like this. Lucent's playing pretty loose with the rules regarding criminals. What's to say they were ever going to get rid of the blasters? What other treaty specifics are they disobeying?"

"That's exactly why they aren't going to get the Ache blasters back," Keir solemnly supplied.

Clearly shocked, Sagan put one hand in the middle of his chest. "What do you mean?"

Keir moved even closer when she touched him, inviting further intimacy. "Just that the ministers of Oceanus thought long and hard over Lucent's failure to destroy the weapons in a timely fashion, and their use of illegal methods to get a confession from criminals within their care. It was decided that once the blasters were found, they were to be immediately destroyed. Even your Protectorate isn't to get their hands on them."

"I'm not sure I like the implication there, but I can assure you this particular agent of the Earth Protectorate would be happy to help you do the deed. It's not that I think my agency isn't trustworthy, but any time you have weapons like these, some criminal element seems to get ahold of them no matter how protected the technology is. My world would be better off without them, even if I have to take heat for their destruction."

He liked that answer, and he liked Sagan's integrity. Altogether there was more and more to admire about her as the minutes passed. "We'll make a pact. You and any Protectorate members of your choice, and me and a cadre of officers from my ship—which will return to stand ready outside of Earth's radar range when I give them the signal—will quietly form an alliance of third-party witnesses. After the blasters are found, they'll be inventoried by us, taken to the desert of this planet and blown up. Is it agreed?"

She nodded. "And what will you tell Lucent's authorities?"

"We'll send the regrettable message that the weapons were accidentally destroyed while being relieved from the smugglers' possession. There'll be a tactful note from my government stating that it'll no longer be necessary for Lucent to go to the trouble of dismantling them. Lucent authorities can hardly raise an objection, since that's what they said they were going to do with the damnable things to begin with." He saw Sagan smile broadly, and knew he'd finally scored points with the proud beauty.

"I'll have a similar message sent from Earth Protectorate," she confirmed. "You won't have to haul them through space, praying no pirates get word they're on board your ship."

"Exactly," he confirmed.

"Exactly," she echoed, and ran the hand on his chest across the muscles there.

Keir looked down at the hand, then back at her face. She was positively glowing with anticipation. If words could bring that response, what would she be like when a man made love to her, slowly and deliberately, all through the night?

She immediately jerked her hand away. "I've kept you up too long. You've had a hard trip. Get some rest. We can talk more in the morning."

The loss of heat from her palm was almost painful. Keir watched her slowly walk toward the door of her room. She paused and turned after opening it.

"Good night, Keir. Sleep well."

"Rest well, yourself, Sagan."

He watched until long after she'd closed the door. Then Keir went to his room and withdrew the communication device from his luggage and tapped a crystal on the inside. The circular band looked like a simple piece of jewelry worn on his right biceps, but it actually served as his communication with Datron and an eavesdropping detector. His friend would now know he was settled in the hotel and looking to retrieve his equipment. Keir had no intention of searching rooms where smugglers guarded lethal weapons with no armament of his own. The stunners Earth Protectorate operatives like Sagan commonly used, and with which he'd most likely be provided, were meager defense against the arms such as smugglers carried. While he tapped the crystal he had a twinge of guilt: he still hated lying to both his best friend and the woman in the next room. But that was the way things had to be.

Re-dressing himself, Keir waited. At last, deep into the night, he crept to Sagan's door and carefully opened it. Light from the moon filtered through a window and illuminated her slender form as she slept. For several moments, he regarded her steady, deep breathing and saw she slept soundly. He wished he could lie beside her. The warmth that body and spirited personality could provide was alluring. But such a connection wasn't to be.

If she found out what he was up to, her explosive temper would get him hauled off to some spaceport at the hands of the local police, and whatever alliance they'd formed would be gone. Before that happened, he had to find the Ache blasters and Lucent Stones. For that, he needed Datron.

CHAPTER FIVE

Keir carefully shut the door to Sagan's room behind him. He prayed she didn't awaken. Then, he thought of the perfect way to explain his absence if she should. He'd simply leave a note and tell her he was restless and had gone for a drink. That part was true. He and his second-in-command had long since done their research and determined the hours the Stardust Hotel bars kept, and it was there that the pair would meet. It was the *rest* of his liaison he'd leave out of his message. He could only hope the reacquisition of his gear would take place before his absence was noticed. He wouldn't put it past the clever little Earthling to check on him as he slept, and assume he was off on the mission without her.

He made his way to the Cosmos Pub to meet Datron. The get-together was intended to look accidental, as if two competitors struck up a friendship while enjoying a drink.

As Keir entered the bar, he was surprised by the number of men sitting around, amiably sharing a late snack or beverage. There were also quite a few women present . . . very beautiful women dressed in evening attire. Keir shook his head in exasperation. *Groupies.* He was pretty sure that was the Earth term for the bevy of lovelies now hovering around the competitors. And when he saw Datron snuggled up with two women, Keir had to smile. He leisurely chose a spot at the other end of the bar. That was when a sultry brunette with huge breasts approached.

"Looking for some company?" the woman asked.

Keir looked her over and smirked. He took her hand in his, kissed the back of it and shook his head. "Another time, sweetness."

The brunette pouted, raised her hand to touch the blue star on his cheek and leaned in to plant a soft kiss on his left temple. "I'm Francie. Room 1014. Just give me a call when you're ready. I've been with Oceanuns before and know what they like," she whispered.

Surprised but not offended, Keir regretfully watched Francie sway away. Part of his anatomy had responded splendidly to her come-on. Three months in a cabin the size of a closet was hard. If he were on leave, he'd have been more than happy to follow Francie anywhere. But he had to stay focused.

He captured the attention of the barkeep, ordered an Earth whiskey and handed the man some currency. From time to time, he'd been able to sample this beverage, imported to one spaceport or another, and found it greatly to his liking. He favored the woody taste and bold smell, and it had a decidedly relaxing effect he needed at the moment. Despite Francie's wonderful offer, Kier had another woman on his mind, and had to purge the image of them together that he'd been harboring all evening.

What would Sagan look like in a shimmering gown like these local groupies? It would cling to her lithe body like a second skin and accent every perfect curve. He had a notion she wouldn't have to request the attention of any man; they'd be all over her. He frowned at the thought, then shook his head to rid himself of such possessive feelings. Little Miss Intensity wouldn't be caught dead parading her goods to barflies. She'd most likely meet a fellow enforcer on duty and discreetly invite him back to her apartment when her shift ended . . . then leave him lying aflame with desire as she went off on some mission or other. Her lover would be taking cold showers to quell the lust. She probably wouldn't even leave a note. Her love interest would be pacing back and forth, wondering where in the universe she was, worrying himself sick and still needing to massage her firm, pert breasts and slide himself between her slender thighs. The poor bastard would only be able to imagine the cries of satisfaction as he pleasured her. Yes, there he'd be, with all that need, and Miss Protectorate would be—

What was he thinking? He'd suddenly personalized the scenario and it was *himself* cast as the man left behind. He was the one whose insides were torn up, wondering where Sagan was and why she'd left in the middle of the night. Keir suddenly threw his drink down his throat with much more force than intended, then signaled the man behind the bar for another.

Datron noticed his superior's angry countenance and the unusual act of ordering another round. Keir normally never drank so fast, and not while looking as if someone had just kicked a dent in his perfectly polished command ship. "You look like a man who needs a friend," he loudly announced as he moved to stand next to him. "My name is Datron Mann, from the Valkyrian System. Of course, I recognized an Oceanun right away."

Keir accepted his second drink, then turned and offered his hand. The two men shook as if meeting for the first time; then Keir gestured amiably to a nearby seat. "Join me."

"Don't mind if I do." Datron lowered his voice. "But you might want to back off the alcohol, Captain."

Keir glared, then nodded in agreement.

At a loss as to why his commanding officer was in what could only be described in Earth terms as a "crappy mood," Datron silently drank until he finished his own beverage, then made a suggestion: "Why don't we go for a walk? It was a long trip here, and I could use the exercise."

Keir glanced at him, clearly recognized the wisdom in that remark, and stood. He followed Datron out of the bar, through the lobby, and then the two dodged slow-moving hovercraft to cross the street. The cooler night air of the park, the surrounding trees and subdued lighting—all would be a balm to chaotic thoughts. Datron checked his wristband for recording devices, just as protocol required, then lifted a hand to signal safety in speaking freely.

"I saw you at the station with the most striking creature. Don't tell me she's the Protectorate officer assigned to work with you," he said. "I could hardly take my eyes off her."

"One and the same. Her name is Sagan Carter and she knows everything," Keir replied.

Datron stopped walking, which forced his captain to do the same. "About the blasters *and* your pretended ignorance in competing?"

"All of it—with the exception of your presence here as my backup," Keir relayed. "The little comet had it figured out before she picked me up at the depot. She already had a suite reserved for us at the hotel, and is acting out the part of my manager, if you can believe it. She even took me out to the desert to interrogate me about what she perceived as my deceptiveness regarding the smugglers. Can you imagine *me* being interrogated . . . by that little *Earthling?*" He placed his hand on his chest to emphasize the indignity.

Datron just lowered his head and began to laugh.

Keir glowered at him. "I'm glad one of us is amused." Hearing the sarcasm in his friend's voice and not wanting to get on Keir's bad side, Datron reined in his guffaws. "I-I hardly know what to say. I suppose neither of us expected that kind of perceptiveness. She must have had her doubts about this mission all along."

"To say the least. She even had the audacity to put me in my place as to who's in control of the operation. The little Voragen she-cat presented the ultimatum that if I fail to final in all the pageant events, she'll have the local enforcers around to put me in restraints and drag me to the nearest deportation point. Like a common criminal." He breathed out once and lowered his rising voice. "Her reasoning is that I'll have no plausible excuse to remain if I can't final. Earth's ministers have made it clear that this is the only cover they'll accept."

Again, Datron couldn't control his humor at his friend's expense. It was the first time he'd ever heard of his captain being bested, and the first time in his knowledge an Oceanun had ever been upbraided by a human. Being a Valkyrian who signed a contract to work with the Oceanus enforcers, he had seen more than his fair share of the legendary Oceanun self-righteousness. But his commanding officer was an exceedingly fair man whose integrity had never been disputed.

Then again, Keir had now been caught in a lie that could see him deported and on his way back to Oceanus in shame. Many other planetary law enforcement officials would likely have done as much, intending to keep the glory for themselves. Datron had to give the beautiful Earthling points for allowing Keir Trask to stay and work after obtaining enough information to finish the assignment herself.

"Uh, I think we can maneuver around this," he said. "After all, she can't possibly mean to approach these smugglers with only a stunner. Unless something's recently changed, that's normally the only weapon Earth enforcers carry."

"She'd not only take the damned smugglers on, she'd get herself killed doing it," Keir declared. "You have no idea how contrary I've already found her. It's like . . . like talking to a rock."

Something about the way Keir was arguing made Datron think there was more going on than met the eye. "She's gorgeous. At least you'll have her all to yourself in a suite. I'd think you of all people would be able to . . . charm her into submission. Think of the cause. These smugglers are desperate. They've already killed."

"I explained all that, and she's implacable." Keir paused. "Still, there might be something in what you say. We had a very long talk and seem to have come to a compromise, though it's not entirely to my liking. She still insists she wants to run things. But I have noticed a . . . a vague interpersonal connection between us that might be utilized."

Datron watched the expression on his captain's face drift from anger to rapture. He'd never seen such a look on Keir. "If she doesn't know about me, then we have that added edge, sir."

"Yes . . . and don't call me sir."

"Yes, sir . . . uh, Keir."

Blinking and shaking his head, Keir changed subjects. "What about our weapons? Can we get any to my room tonight?"

"Ask and I deliver," Datron replied with a smile. "I've dismantled most of it for easier hiding and put it in a shopping bag. It's in my room, locked within another piece of luggage. All you have to do is take it to your quarters. If your little Earthling sees it—"

"I'll just say I bought some personal items and walk away," Keir finished. "Excellent thinking."

Enraged, Sagan hid in the bushes, listened to the exchange between the two males and tried to keep a firm grip on her temper. God, she hated lies! She'd known when Keir entered her room, sensed his presence looming over her and realized immediately that he wouldn't stay put. Then thinking he was simply scouting the hotel, and only moderately angry at him for doing so without her, she was now beyond furious. She'd had no idea he'd brought a partner. Worse, he still believed her so ignorant that the deception would be easy.

He's gonna wish like hell that he'd never heard of Earth! She quietly backed through the shrubbery, intent on getting back to her room and her computer. She circumvented the walkway where Keir and the winged Valkyrian she'd seen at the depot were now conversing and patting themselves prematurely on the back. Of course, she could pick up her communicator, call Overchief Snarl and have them summarily removed from the planet's surface. But she was sure there were still more lies to come and she wanted to know the rest of the story. Interrogation wouldn't work on them, either; conditioned as the men were, they'd die before revealing anything.

There were two ways to handle this: lose her temper and have them arrested, or let them know they weren't playing with a dense Earth flatfoot. She chose the latter of the two solutions. She'd take the high road and throw their lies back in their faces.

After entering her room, she pulled her small personal computer from its case beneath the desk. Entering an encrypted code, she tapped into Protectorate computers to cover her trail, then hacked directly into the hotel's registration data. It went much quicker than she'd expected. Apparently, Electra Galaxy and her security people didn't think anyone would hack into contestant information that would eventually be made public anyhow. The only thing Ms. Galaxy's personnel had placed in a more secure file was the men's room numbers. Accessing that information took an extra five minutes, but she finally had what she needed.

Sagan tucked her hair behind her ears and steeled herself. "Screw with me? I'll screw right back," she muttered.

After a long walk in the park, Keir felt much better about his situation, though Sagan's mastery of the situation still rankled. She was still on his mind as he agreed to meet Datron outside the hotel gift shop and accept what would look like a bag of sundries.

He waited for nearly thirty minutes by the clock in the lobby, but Datron still made no appearance. He was just about to approach a communication center imbedded in the lobby wall when his best friend appeared from the elevator, wearing a concerned look. Keir sensed a problem.

Datron approached his commanding officer and held out the note he'd found in his room, exactly where he'd stowed all their weapons, communication devices and tools. "You'd better read this."

Keir took a look and swore under his breath. "Why, that little . . ."

"Your Earth Protectorate officer is the craftiest creature I've ever run across or I'll cut my wings off," Datron said. "What do you want to do?"

Keir glanced at the note again, words carefully chosen so as not to alert anyone but Datron and himself to their meaning. It read, *I have your toys.* Sagan's name was at the bottom.

Datron witnessed something he hadn't seen since the slaughter on Cetus 5. On that planet, raiders had attacked in the night and robbed the few colonists who lived there. They'd killed all opposition, leaving children orphaned and every home in flames. At that time, he'd seen his superior display the rare tendency of Oceanuns to change color. Like then, Keir's light coloring was now rapidly darkening to a shade of forest green. Datron began to actually fear for the Earth woman's life.

Keir stared at the elevator, and Datron watched his friend's eyes begin to take on a silvery glow. "Captain, calm down," he said. "We've been caught. Let's just find your woman and speak rationally to her."

"First, don't call me captain," Keir growled. "Second, she's not *my* woman. If she was, I'd request a firing squad at dawn just to be free of her. And third, when I get my hands on her, I'm going to strangle the demoness and skin her alive!" With that, he wadded the note into a ball and stalked away.

"Omicron's balls, he's pissed!" Datron muttered. Then he ran to catch up, as Keir's stride was now twice its normal length.

Sagan waited. She stood in the middle of the suite with her arms across her chest, knowing he'd be there any minute. She heard someone accessing the keypad outside and didn't flinch when the door opened so hard that it crashed into the inside wall.

Keir stormed up, face within inches of hers. "Where's our gear?"

She simply pointed to the large black bags of devices neatly piled on the far side of the room.

"You followed me, didn't you?" he asked.

"Don't you *hate* it when that happens?" she blithely returned.

Keir moved close enough that she could feel his breath on the top of her head, which had the effect of making Sagan tilt her head far back to look up at him. "You could have blown this whole operation," he accused.

"You can blow *me*, you lying son of a—"

"Please!" Keir's companion in deception interjected, entering the room and softly closing the door. "Why don't we all calm down?" He forcibly moved the two adversaries apart by pushing at their shoulders, which was no small task. They were locked in place, ready for mortal combat. He said to Keir, "Sir, you can't blame her. We brought our gear to this planet illegally. In the vernacular of this world, we're 'busted.'"

Sagan turned her head to look at the blond, winged giant. "I saw you at the depot watching me. Who the hell are you?" she asked.

"Datron Mann. I'm Captain Trask's second-in-command—a position I'm proud to hold, by the way. I'm working with an enforcer of the first rank who's known as one of the most decent and selfless persons in existence." He stepped in front of his commanding officer while pushing Keir back with his hands. As he pushed on Keir's chest, experiencing great resistance in return, he turned around and used his feet to better propel them away from Sagan, also managing to grunt out, "He's a veritable paragon of virtue and rationality. Why, a nobler, more patient soul never existed. He's the very epitome of integrity and reliance. You'll be happy to have him on your side, and proud to call him friend!"

Keir was still glaring at her, and met Sagan's flashing, recalcitrant gaze. He wanted to both throttle Sagan and push her to the carpet and engage in feral, mindless sex, both at the same time. Even as his best friend pushed him away, he tried to move forward to get at her. He didn't know what he was going to do when he got his hands on her, but he was quite sure some suitable scenario would present itself.

She crossed her arms over her chest. "Let that big green piece of kelp go. I can deal with him," she taunted.

"That's *it!*" Keir ground out between clenched teeth. "Three months cooped up on a ship, landing on this rock and being inflicted with this deceptive little web spinner is quite enough!" Keir pushed Datron to one side.

Sagan noted her opponent's dark green color and knew what it meant, but she was beyond caring. How dare he assume the position of the wronged party? She was the one who'd been duped from the beginning. It was time someone took this arrogant fool down a peg. "Would you leave us alone, please?" she quietly asked his partner.

"I-I don't think that's a good idea," the Valkyrian countered, and tried to get between her and Keir again. "My captain is a bit upset right now."

Sagan put a firm but gentle hand on Datron's shoulder. "Just go. I'll call you tomorrow and we can figure out your role in all this. Right now, muscleman and I need to sit down and work out the definitions of the words *duplicity*, *liar* and *cooperation*. They seem to be among several terms he didn't grasp when learning our language."

Datron backed away as she asked before addressing his captain. "Sir, she's right. Please consider our position here before you speak. I've never known you to be this angry, but we have a mission to complete. Sagan has it within her power to relieve us of our welcome here."

Being corrected by his subordinate in such a soft tone, and in front of the very woman who frustrated him, had something of a deflating effect. In his gut, Keir knew Datron was right, but his pride simply wouldn't allow him to admit it. He'd already backed down once tonight, and he wasn't used to the taste of defeat: It was bitter and unpleasant.

Why was this woman able to thwart him, a trained professional enforcer of the finest caliber, at every turn? This wasn't supposed to be happening. He could only see sorrow coming from this alliance. Not yet on Earth for twenty-four hours, he'd already had the metaphorical rug pulled out from under him. He'd never lost control this way—not to such an extent that his fellow shipmate had to intervene. His behavior was unworthy, and yet he couldn't help himself. This woman was doing something to him no one ever had. Whenever she was near, he lost his composure.

Datron glanced between the two of them for a long moment. Then he nodded at Sagan and walked toward the door. "As you wish, I'll leave you alone. Please understand that we didn't come here to cause trouble . . . just to stop it."

Once his lieutenant left, closing the door behind him, Keir moved toward Sagan. This time he was able to control himself and get a grip on his anger. "I don't know how to handle you," he blurted. He stood, staring down at her.

Her expression softened very little. "Why do you keep lying about your plans? More to the point, what did I do to deserve all this subterfuge? We're supposed to be working together. Is this what our planets can expect from one another? Is this the best we can do?"

"You don't understand."

"Explain," she demanded.

"I'd been led to believe you couldn't handle this operation, and that innocent people would die if we couldn't get the weapons quickly and be on our way. I was told to do what I must to facilitate that."

"And the pact we had about destroying the weapons in front of witnesses? Was that a lie, too?" Sagan demanded.

"No," he said. "But we need weaponry to match what our opponents have. I had no idea you wouldn't run to Protectorate Headquarters and have the weapons and us seized."

"Wouldn't you have done just that if the situation

were reversed—if I was on your planet and required to obey your laws?"

That was the bottom line: She was right, and he was wrong. "Yes. Yes, I would," he admitted.

She shook her hair back. "Then why are you so damned pissed?"

"Because I've never been in a position where every backup plan I had was destroyed, and that seems to bode ill for us."

She walked slowly toward him. "And what if I have backup plans I'd have shared with you if you hadn't pulled this crap?"

He ignored her question, instead changing the subject. "What if you'd been caught by hotel security while carrying our equipment. It's unlawful. What would you have done?"

"I wasn't caught, and could easily ask the same question of you."

He sighed wearily and ran a hand over his face. "You could have been intercepted by any guard with detection equipment, and you know it. It would have been more prudent to confront Datron and me in the security of this room or some other safe place instead of breaking into his quarters and absconding with our arms."

She shrugged. "Do you want to work this mission or not?"

"I have to, Sagan. It's a matter of interstellar safety. That's the only thing I care about."

She paused, moved very close and stared up at him with steely resolve in her eyes. "If you lie to me one more time about anything . . . if there's even just *one* secret left, you'd better tell me now or I swear to God I'll have you put in jail and charged with so many offenses that you'll never see your world again. I won't just have you deported, Keir. I'll put you away. The punishment for bringing the kind of weapons you have to Earth is life in prison."

She was deadly serious, but so was his mission. The Lucent Stones had to be found before anyone knew they'd been taken at the same time as the blasters. Again, his conscience warred with a need to come clean and win the trust of this woman, but he had his duty above all things. "You know it all," he lied.

"Will you agree to use the weapons available to Earth enforcers and leave yours secured in this room?"

After a moment he said, "Agreed."

"When you leave this planet, you can take the damned things with you. If we can really work together on this mission from here on out, I'll keep my mouth shut in the interest of future diplomacy. But tell your people when you get back that they can't come to our world and disregard our rules. We fought wars and lost millions of lives to earn the freedoms we have, and we won't let any sons of bitches take that away by disregarding us at the drop of a hat."

Again, Keir's anger ebbed and he felt a searing desire swell within him. "Shall we seal the bargain?" he asked.

She slowly held out her hand.

He took it, then gently pulled her forward. "A handshake wasn't what I had in mind." He lowered his head, slanted his mouth over hers and felt passionate, torrid heat rush through his body as they shared a slow, scorching kiss.

CHAPTER SIX

Sagan opened her mouth wide, her tongue touched Keir's and she felt every nerve in her body come alive. The kiss seemed to go on forever, and she found herself sliding her hands into the half-fastened black jacket he wore to touch his massive chest. All that muscle could be hers if she wanted. He had to have biceps that were easily eighteen inches around, according to the old English measuring system she preferred. And if the rest of him was proportionate, her night could be very satisfying indeed.

She felt him slide his hands down her back and caress her butt. It felt so good to finally have a man in close proximity whom she respected, who wasn't afraid to pursue what he wanted, no matter the cost. And that was the impression she got of Keir Trask. They'd been at odds and she'd bested him, but he wasn't afraid to make sacrifices and complete his mission. And he'd lost none of his aggressiveness. She admired that. Perversely, she was sexually charged by it.

The first streaks of light broke the horizon outside, and slowly Sagan broke the kiss and pushed Keir away. She could almost feel the brilliance of the upcoming warm, beautiful day. Sunlight would soon fill the main area of their suite through the crystal clear glass of the floor-to-ceiling windows. That had the effect of putting her back on track, getting her mind again on the matters at hand and off her arousal. She slowly moved backward a few inches while keeping her hands on Keir's chest. Then she gazed up into his face and said, "I-I didn't know Oceanuns kissed in that way. I thought it was a human tradition."

"So it is," he murmured, running his hands through the fall of her thick, shining hair as if its softness enchanted him. "But there are some of us who prefer the lovemaking techniques of other worlds. By old tradition, an Oceanun male only brushes his lips over his woman's, then he trails them across her face, down her neck . . . and farther. Does that interest you, Sagan? We could put our differences behind us, work through them in bed."

Her mouth went dry at the thought of having his huge, muscular body pleasuring her, but she had never let her body rule her mind. She wasn't going to start now; not when so much was at stake. "I-I think we'd better save that for another day."

When Sagan moved out of his embrace and took a deep breath, Keir had to actually focus on her words to make the mission come back into focus. For a split second, he found himself mentally asking: *What mission?* His professional bearing finally took hold, however, and he pulled himself together. How had they progressed to this fiery interlude from wanting to kill each other? How could his emotions run to such extremes in such a short period of time? Nothing like these feelings had ever plagued him. And was *plagued* the right word? Wouldn't it be better to say that he was enraptured, bewitched and beguiled?

"I suggest we get some sleep and try one more time to get our act together," she said.

"I agree," he replied. "I'm on your planet. I'll play by

your rules. I have no more secreted allies, no more weapons or covert devices. You know every detail Datron does." That truth was the most he could give her.

When she found him looking straight into her eyes, she nodded. "All right. The plans for the day include the competition details. I already have my computer set up to list all the competitors, and that will make it easier to begin our search—which will be done together, either by floor or room. We'll decide that later. As it happens, Datron could prove useful. If you vouch for him, we could use another pair of eyes."

"I pledge my life on his loyalty."

"Okay. First get some rest. I'll lock your gear in the hall closet and install an extra coded padlock to keep out the cleaning staff. I'll make excuses to the hotel supervisors, too." She gazed up at him and asked, "No more meetings behind my back?"

"As you wish," he responded. Then he glanced down at his hands and saw the color was back to normal. He was in control again.

Sagan nodded, turned and walked to her room. But she left the door cracked open as she showered and changed.

Keir also left his door open. For him it was a peaceable gesture to show he wasn't going to leave or hide his actions behind any barrier. As he lay back against the mountains of pillows in a soft, layered bed that easily accommodated a man even of his size, relaxation came much easier than he'd have believed. The only thing that could have made his rest better was having Sagan's soft body next to his. After this mission, she might relent. That possibility filled his mind as he drifted into a very deep sleep.

"You're using the encrypted channel?" the disembodied voice asked.

Burl, the leader of the Ussar Warriors, bristled at the assumption he'd be stupid enough to do anything else. The person on the other end of his communicator was, as always, using a voice scrambler. That device made it impossible to tell if his contact was male or female. "Do you think me a fool? I know what's at risk. Though we were disguised so no one will recognize us as the original thieves, we will eventually be discovered and hunted throughout the universe. That's why I'm now demanding twice the sum agreed upon."

There was silence on the other end of the communication device.

"Did you hear?" the Ussarian leader gruffly asked. "We've risked much and have been paid too little for the trouble to move this cargo so far. You'll either pay what we ask, or the goods can be sold elsewhere."

"I'll agree to your demand. In return, you must perform one further service."

Burl growled out, "We've already done what was required."

"This is to our mutual benefit, Ussarian. You're close to being discovered. Enforcers know of the theft and are endeavoring to gain control of the shipment and incarcerate those responsible for its pilfering. They're hard on your trail."

"What?" Burl came to his feet and clenched the hand not holding his communicator. "We traveled this far without detection."

"Perhaps," the voice advised. "But the means of smuggling was known. Enforcers discovered the connection with the pageant. As you say, it was unknown who the thieves were, but some of your compatriots back on Lucent were not fortunate enough to have escaped. It's a matter of time before you're caught."

"Those captured by Lucent were warriors. They'd never give up details that would lead to the discovery of their comrades," Burl proudly declared. "Also, those captured didn't know my name or the names of my men."

"That may be true. But under illegal mental probing, your warriors gave up enough vital information as to reveal that there was a smuggling operation connected with Electra Galaxy's contest," the voice cautioned. "As I say, the enforcers will be upon you shortly."

Burl struck the top of the table with his free hand. "You know who these enforcers are? If they've become aware of our operation, why haven't they made their arrests?"

"As to the first question: Yes, I know who they are. That brings me to the added task you must complete before I meet your demands. You will kill the undercover operatives who seek you out.

"As to the second question: The enforcers didn't stop and search all contestants who made their way to Earth. They feared the goods would be divulged by doing so. They're as anxious to keep the theft a secret as you. It would create a diplomatic nightmare were it publicly known that such lethal cargo exists and was pirated from Lucent's control. The authorities were reluctant to create upheaval by insinuating the pageant was used as a smuggling route. Electra Galaxy is a powerful woman with strong allies. Since there are so many entrants, searching their various routes would have been impossible. All the enforcers needed to do was wait until the cargo made its way to its final destination. They correctly assumed the goods wouldn't be diverted elsewhere. They've followed you to Earth."

"That doesn't explain why they haven't moved in now that we're here," Burl said.

"*Think*, Ussarian. These enforcers intend to go quietly. They desire to recover the stolen goods within the confines of the hotel, arresting those responsible without making their actions public. This will protect the operatives' identities, as well as the pageant and its competitors. They may also fear you'll use the weapons on innocents if forced into a standoff."

Burl considered. "I'll kill these enforcers myself, and will do so with stealth. Will that satisfy the terms for greater payment?"

"Yes. And I'll triple your fee if you expedite this matter."

Burl let out a low rumbling laugh. "I like the way you deal. You have the names of these enforcers?"

"There's an Oceanun in the competition for the first time. This is no coincidence. He's picked up an Earthling manager along the way who's probably his Protectorate contact."

Burl felt his chest tighten. "Triple is not enough. To kill an Oceanun operative is no small task. This will call for more capital up front, too. We'll have to run far and fast to escape their planet's justice."

The voice responded in anger, "Have a care, Ussarian. You've no idea who you're dealing with. There are repercussions for those who don't know the meaning of an agreement and whose greed gets out of hand. We know where you are."

"Yes, but you can't approach without making yourself known," Burl countered. "The media keeps all us contestants under constant observation and will continue to do so until after the pageant. As you've said, there's reluctance among law agencies to interfere in Ms. Galaxy's operation. That's why we chose this method of smuggling the goods. This is also how I know you will *not* seek to harm me. You won't approach while we're watched by the eyes of the universe. Only when the pageant is over will it be safe for you to crawl from your hiding place." Burl sneered. "You'll meet my demands, my anonymous friend. I'll take care of the Oceanun. It'll look like an accident. And the diversion of that will allow us to leave this planet quietly when our transaction is done."

The disembodied voice warned, "I'll make no further contact until the lawmen are dead and the pageant is over. Take care with those blasters and the stones. There are those among us who consider you expendable if you lose the goods or attempt to use them for your own purposes."

Burl cursed in Ussarian, but the communicator was shut off from the other end. "Oceanun or not," he said, "the enforcer and his comrades will be killed quickly."

Sagan rapped on Keir's halfway open bedroom door but heard no response. Padding into the room on bare feet, she gazed at the huge man in bed and couldn't help smiling. He had the most peaceful expression on his face. She could imagine what he must have looked like when he was a little boy . . . if he'd ever been little. But he surely had. That massive bare chest and those loglike arms were the result of years of physical training.

Glancing at the wristband she wore, she noted the time was almost three o'clock. Keir had been exhausted. The events of their meeting had worn her out as well, but they needed to get down to business. Still, she found she didn't want to rouse him. It seemed a little sadistic to even think about it after the lengthy voyage he'd made to Earth.

As she turned to leave, Keir opened his eyes. "Did you want something, Sagan?"

She stopped and turned back to him. "I was going to wake you but decided against it."

He threw back the cover and stood, and grinned broadly when Sagan's eyes grew round with shock. She immediately turned to face the door again. "Don't tell me that an enforcer with your experience has never seen a male body before," he taunted.

"I wasn't aware you were nude." The glimpse she'd gotten of hard-packed muscle almost made her turn around for another look. She wasn't shocked by his nudity so much as surprised he'd expose himself to a new female partner. But all seven feet of him were magnificent. But then: "What do you mean, about *'my experience'*?"

He chuckled. "I didn't mean sexual. I was referring to your professional experience," he explained, pulling on his robe and looping the sash around his waist. "You must have seen a nude body or two in your time. Dead or otherwise."

"Oh. I thought you meant . . . never mind. I've got some breakfast on the way. Electra Galaxy's people sent your welcome packet to the suite. We'd better go over it and start making plans. Saturday night is your first function. I don't know if there'll be a way to search before then, but we could try. And we'll need to get Datron here. Since you were seen in the bar talking with him last night, it shouldn't be suspicious for him to be invited to the room. But you need to do it, not me. If the hotel operator is listening in, she might find it strange that your manager was asking to see him. Just invite him up to eat."

Keir grinned to himself. Sagan was trying to act the part of a prudent, thinking enforcer, but he had just seen an innocent side of her that she was desperately trying to cover. Her instructions were perfectly appropriate and businesslike, but somehow he recognized her words as babbling to cover embarrassment. He both enjoyed her discomfort and was a tiny bit ashamed at having caused it. And when she quickly walked out of his room, he decided to follow her lead. He went to the outer lounge to contact Datron.

"Datron is in 1242, remember?" she said.

Keir took a deep breath and let it out while punching

in his friend's room number. Sagan was just trying to one-up him by reminding him that she'd broken into Datron's room and stolen their gear. He wasn't going to take the bait, especially not after having lost control earlier. Instead he waited while the com buzzer sounded, and finally he heard the device being activated.

"Datron Mann here."

"Come up and have some food," Keir suggested.

"You're speaking my language," Datron replied. "I'll be right there."

Suddenly, Sagan rushed to the intercom and yelled, "Bring all your clothing. I need to go through it."

"Uh, as you wish," Datron replied.

Keir heard the com switch off; then he rounded on Sagan. "Why would you risk that being overheard? You have all our weapons. There's no need to—"

"Calm down," she said. "It's not weapons I'm looking for. As you say, I found those last night. I need to see his clothes. Jeez, who put a burr under your damned saddle?"

She went to the suite door, as the buzzer was now blaring. She checked to make sure it was the staff with food; then she let the waiters in. As they arranged breakfast on the table and took away the remainder of the last night's meal, she remained quiet. When they were gone, she turned to Keir. "I suggest you get your clothes together, too. That's if you had time to unpack after your little escapade last night."

"I thought we were over that . . . and what do you want with our clothing?"

She was about to explain when the door buzzer sounded again. This time, however, it was Keir who impatiently stalked over and let Datron into the room.

The Valkyrian dropped two bags of clothing onto the floor. "Luckily, I didn't unpack much," he said.

Sagan half-smiled. "We'll eat first and I'll explain."

"Suits me." Datron grinned and headed for the nearest plate. "I'm starved."

She'd assumed Datron would eat pretty much whatever his ally would, having ordered fresh croissants, butter, cheese, and plenty of fruit. She sat beside the big winged man while a very annoyed Keir sat opposite. Then she shot Datron the question: "Did you get a welcome packet sent to your room?"

Datron picked up a croissant and broke it apart before answering. "Yes. I turned in my entrant application yesterday."

"It details all the competitions," Sagan told Keir. "You'll both need the proper wardrobe to compete."

Keir sighed in relief, having feared his Earther partner was onto yet another nefarious little plot. "Why didn't you just tell me?" he asked.

"I'm not sure either of you has a real grip on this pageant, or the need to fit in," Sagan shot back; then she grabbed up a packet of papers listing the exact details of the competition. "You'll be wearing formal attire Saturday night for the first function. It'll be a mixer with the Miss Milky Way contestants. Then there's a photogenic competition, a pose-down, a swimsuit contest, a talent contest and an interview. By that time, the finalists will have been chosen."

"We're here to arrest thieves," Keir reiterated.

"And you won't stay if you don't final. That goes for Datron, too."

Keir put his knife and fork down. "Why? Your Protectorate edict was about Oceanuns, not Valkyrians."

"These are the instructions I was given. As Datron is an Oceanun enforcer, the same rules apply," Sagan said. "You'll both final, or that's that."

Datron had been listening quietly. He now spoke out. "Uh, I think Sagan has the right idea. We need to fit in. To fit in, we have to want to win—*try* to win. If we can gain the other competitors' confidences, it'll make it that much easier to enter their rooms. Being invited up for a drink could expedite our search and eliminate suspects. We have to plan to win."

"Exactly!" Sagan declared.

Keir glared at his second-in-command, then at the aggravating woman sitting across from him. Perceiving the wisdom in their strategy didn't make the competition and its peculiarities any more palatable. Further, Datron had started siding with the Earthling—something Keir could barely tolerate, and an issue to be addressed as soon as possible. Even if they were right, it galled him to hear them united against him. "Let's just get this farce over with." He continued to eat in silence while Sagan and Datron chatted like friends.

Sagan smiled at Datron, admiring the muscular, bronzed man whose wings were folded neatly behind him. Of the two enforcers, the Valkyrian was unquestionably the more approachable and easygoing. "Did you have a chance to watch a vid-tape of any of these competitions?" she asked.

Datron shook his head. "Not really. The captain turned off the vid screen when he couldn't stomach any more." Sagan stifled a laugh when she saw Keir glare at him.

After a brief moment, Datron said, "You say there'll be women at this mixer on Saturday?"

Sagan nodded. "Some of the most beautiful women in the galaxy."

Datron slowly smiled, picked up an orange and peeled it. "I'll have to force myself to become—what's the term you'd use? Ah, yes. I'll have to compel myself to become a 'babe magnet.' It's a dirty job, but—"

Sagan burst into laughter and placed a hand on his shoulder. "I'm sure you'll manage. I also think I'd better sign on as your manager, too. Otherwise, it's going to look a little strange if we're together too much."

Keir finally spoke up. "Do you think that's wise? You're supposed to be managing *me*."

Sagan shrugged, amused by the jealousy she thought she heard in his voice. "There are other managers who're coaching several contestants. The entire Andromeda contingent has one manager. If you'd done your research, you'd know that," she goaded, popping a small croissant into her mouth.

Datron sighed. "I, for one, am glad to have someone help me through this. It's unnerving."

"We've got a few days left to get it straight, down to the last detail. Your covers are only good as long as everyone believes you want to win this competition," Sagan reminded them.

Keir ran a hand over the back of his neck and tried to blot out the vision of standing on stage in front of ridiculous men and women who thought they had the right to judge others' appearances, never mind the buffoons who paraded before them of their own free will. "Creator, this is going to be the longest assignment of my life," he quietly complained, and felt himself sink further into a malaise. Neither of the other two at the table seemed to notice his ill mood. They were getting along famously. Something in him began to resent that.

He reached for the paperwork that Sagan had been reading. She didn't even glance over. She and Datron were in the middle of discussing the next week's schedule. It was something Keir himself should be paying attention to, but his concentration was too fixated on the Earth enforcer who plagued his every thought.

Shuffling through the papers, he came across a photo and bio of last year's Mr. Interstellar Feller. Apparently that man was a bodybuilder from Cygnus. His *likes* included baby animals, children, stargazing and gourmet cooking. His fondest desire was for universal peace, and he loved romancing women. The fool's *turnoffs* were war, litter, and grouting tile.

Keir dropped the papers in disgust. That any sentient being could equate litter and grouting tile with war was revolting. Knowing that there was such a being, and that *he* was giving chase along that poor soul's footsteps, made him want to walk off the roof of the Stardust Hotel. As Datron warned, they'd be the laughingstock of his entire planet once the transmission of the contest finally reached Oceanus.

Of course, he could always get lucky. The smugglers might kill him first.

CHAPTER SEVEN

After breakfast, Sagan used the suite's computer to add herself as Datron's manager. While her new-found winged friend patiently waited by the suite's fountain, Keir paced. She knew if she pushed too hard, he'd very likely go ballistic again. It wouldn't take much at this point. The idea that he needed to devote any time to the competition was already giving him hell. For that reason, Sagan reeled in the sarcastic comments she might have made and decided to substitute tact.

Walking toward the men, she clasped her hands in front of her. "Okay, let's see what you both have in the way of evening wear. Uh, I don't think tuxedos will be necessary . . . just something nice will do."

Datron flapped his wings. "Yeah. Not exactly the suit kind of guy, if you know what I mean."

Sagan grinned. "I think a pair of dark pants will do. Just choose something nice. Pull your hair back and tie it behind your neck. Use my bedroom to change."

"Got it," he responded, then picked up his bags and walked in the direction Sagan pointed.

Sagan waited for Keir to say something or move, but he stood there like a big green boulder, glaring at her. She pulled the belt of her robe tighter and moved close to him. "Please? We have to do this. I know you don't like it, but we can eliminate a lot of contestants and their groupies by mingling. The more liquored up they get at parties, the more they'll talk. As Datron says, you might get into a lot of rooms just by being friendly."

Keir let out a frustrated sigh, then stalked to his room.

She waited for the men to return and, not surprisingly, Datron came back first. "That's perfect," she remarked, walking around him and looking over the brown leather pants and high brown boots he wore. He'd also slid into a somehow-very-masculine-looking brown halter top that didn't hamper his wings. His hair was pulled back and flowed between his wings in long golden waves.

"May I?" Sagan asked, and lifted a hand to push back a stray curl from his forehead. Datron shot her a broad smile and nodded.

As Keir walked in, he took one look at his best friend and Sagan, crossed his arms over his chest and glared. The elegant little Earthling was on her toes, reaching up to caress Datron's hair with one hand, while her other hand rested on his shoulder. "How cozy," he growled. He had the satisfaction of seeing Datron's face flush with embarrassment.

"Sagan was helping," the Valkyrian mumbled.

Keir's irrational anger over the proximity of the two was assuaged immediately when Sagan turned her gaze upon him. He saw a feral lust in her eyes, which replaced her expression of rebuke. She walked slowly toward him.

Sagan stopped in front of Keir and let her gaze wander. There was nothing that much different between what the two men were wearing. It was just that Keir, in her opinion, seemed so much more present. He had on black, tight-fitting pants and high, polished black boots. His shirt was black, too, and open in front. There were no sleeves. He'd added silver armbands that made his gargantuan biceps look that much larger.

Unlike Datron's golden tresses, Keir's waist-length black hair was unrestrained. It flowed freely down his back. And there was only a very fine dusting of hair on his chest, which Sagan knew would be for the best. She didn't even want to be in the same universe when he heard that his body hair would have to be removed for the pose-down and swimsuit competitions, but that tidbit could be relayed when she'd had time to get across the room and out of his reach. For now, the picture in front of her was altogether masculine and perfect.

No, a tuxedo would have never worked on these two men. There was something wild about them that a formal suit would inhibit. Their choices of clothing worked very well. And, deep down, Sagan found she was beginning to enjoy this assigned cover. In a scary sort of way, she liked dressing the two and making them primp for her. She'd never realized this facet of her personality existed.

"Okay. That'll b-be good. Um, w-why don't we try something else?" she suggested in a rasping voice.

Keir raised one brow and struggled with his mirth, and Sagan valiantly tried to slough off all that raw desire coursing through her.

"H-how about a talent? How were you two going to deal with that?" she asked, putting one hand to her forehead, picking up the informational packet again and pretending to be immersed in paperwork.

"I play a pretty mean Valkyrian harp," Datron responded.

Sagan nodded eagerly. "God, I love classical music—opera especially. I don't suppose you brought your instrument?"

"He did," Keir responded. "We were picked for this mission because of our abilities. We knew what was in store for us. Just because we don't like it doesn't mean we weren't fully prepared."

Annoyance at his arrogance quickly replaced Sagan's desire. She dropped the paperwork on a nearby tabletop, put her hands on her hips and glared at him. "All right, hotshot. What's *your* talent?"

"The captain sings," Datron supplied. "Rather well, actually." Though he would have continued, Keir shot him a glare that silenced him.

Sagan smirked. "Ohhhh, I've *gotta* hear this."

The skin on the back of Keir's hands was beginning to deepen to a darker shade of green again. "Are you sure you'd want to suffer through it?" he asked.

Sagan took a seat. "I'm all ears."

Had the haughty beauty been less contrary, Keir might have enjoyed sharing his love of classical music from many worlds. While his people generally considered the compositions of Earthlings as far beneath them as fish excrement on the bottom of an ocean, he'd secretly found it amazing that such a bourgeois place—using Earth terminology—could produce works so elaborate and beautiful. He might have admitted all this to Sagan, *if* she'd shown the slightest inclination toward respecting his abilities. Since Milady Disdain was expecting the worst of him, he decided to let her have it. He cleared his throat, took a deep breath and sang horribly, praying his family never learned of the musical sacrilege.

> *There once was a virgin named Ann.*
> *She forever was seeking a man.*
> *Experience she needed,*
> *She begged to be seeded;*
> *She found no great joy with her hand.*

He'd sung the bawdy limerick at the top of his lungs and

as off-key as he possibly could. He could see Datron's head bow, and the man's shoulders were shaking with laughter. He saw Sagan stand up and slowly turn away. Her hands went to her face and Keir heard some kind of strange, choking sound that might represent pain or disbelief. Either way, he was immensely satisfied by her discomfort.

Datron finally lifted his head and wiped the tears from his eyes. "I-I thought you were too inebriated to remember that song from Lyra. What a night that was!"

Keir laughed. "I know. I wonder if that bar is still there—"

"All right!" Sagan interrupted, turning back. "Try another song. For the love of God, try something else. *Anything* else," she begged.

Her irritation just encouraged him. "Anything you say, Your Highness." He gave her a slight bow, squared his shoulders and let out with:

There once was a man named Thor.
The ladies he made quite sore.
When women came near,
Their sighs he'd hear;
His privates hung down to the floor.

Datron stumbled into the nearest wall and leaned there, shaking with laughter.

Sagan looked pale. After a moment she said, "Okay. If that's the best you can do, we'll go on to swimwear." Her voice was very soft. "I want both of you in a swimsuit in five minutes. You'll need two outfits—one for the pose-down and one for the actual swimsuit competition—but I only need to see one each."

Her softly phrased request had an enraged undertone Keir didn't like. He motioned for his still-laughing friend to get a move on. As amusing as this was, they both needed to remember that Sagan had the power to throw them in jail or deport them. The flashing fury in her expression conveyed she was nearing that point.

Keir went to his room and donned one of the swim-suits he'd brought for the contest. They were useless to him on Oceanus, as he preferred to swim in the nude, though the suits for this competition were as close to naked as a male could respectably get on Earth. He'd seen just enough photos of the previous winners to real-ize that.

Sagan paced back and forth to get her temper under control. Why couldn't Keir cooperate? Surely he didn't think he could final with those bawdy renditions so hor-rifyingly vocalized. The man clearly had another talent and was playing with her. No wonder her superior had ordered that he be removed from Earth's surface if he didn't go through with this charade: If other Oceanuns were anything like him, Earth's entire diplomatic core must have wanted to shoot their every emissary!

Datron made it back into the central suite first. As he turned and modeled his small white swimming outfit for Sagan, she tried to ignore a sudden rush of unbri-dled desire. The winged megalith had some serious stuff. Sagan simply blurted a few friendly compliments and hoped she was making sense. Even to her, her voice sounded tight and gruff. Then Keir finally returned.

If Datron had been gorgeous, the Oceanun was godly.

Keir had chosen a very tiny bathing outfit like the one he'd seen worn by the contestant in his video briefing. It was only a few short minutes before he'd shut off the recording. He was amazed how anyone could want to parade around, wanting to be judged by another, no matter their state of dress or undress. For a few mo-ments he modeled, arrogantly keeping his gaze off Sagan and riveting it on the view outside the hotel window.

But when he finally dragged his gaze away from the late afternoon sunset and saw that heated look, his attitude changed. If Sagan looked at him like that on a regular basis, he'd wear anything she asked and do anything while wearing it or taking it off. She was staring at him right now as if he was that Earth fruit called a banana, peeling him one side at a time. She was trying not to show her lust, clearing her throat and pretending to have an interest in the information packet Electra Galaxy's people had sent. But her failure to make some caustic remark was an enormous clue.

"I assume you approve?" he quietly prodded when she lowered her gaze further and refused to look at him.

"Y-You'll both do. I suggest you go get changed into street clothes. I need to make an appointment for you at a salon. I h-hope I can get a booking this late in the day," she mumbled.

Keir tilted his head, confused. "What kind of salon?"

Sagan's eyes stayed glued to her schedule. "Just get changed, please." She didn't seem aware as the two men left the room.

If Burl could have his way, he'd burst through the Oceanun's door when the fool was present, toss in a flail bomb that would shatter everything within one hundred meters and leave. But hotel security cameras would record every move he made, and he had no flail bomb to throw. Still, he could kill his enemy and make it look like an accident. He'd made use of his room computer to find the way.

In seeking out his enemy, he'd stumbled upon their room number and the fact that the hotel maids kept to a specific routine. When one of them entered a storage room for linens on his floor, he quickly crushed a fragment from one Lucent Stone and walked in behind her. He'd been curious since the theft to know if their reputed powers were real. Damn his buyer. If he was going to risk his life, he'd have a demonstration of the stones' abilities. The maid would prove a useful test subject.

He sprinkled an infinitesimal amount of the powder in his gloved left hand, sneaked up behind the maid and wrapped his right hand around her mouth so she couldn't scream. He felt her stiffen and begin to struggle, but her strength wasn't his and he had the dust to control her. He blew the shimmering powder into her face and held his own breath until the residue settled. The girl stared straight ahead as soon as she inhaled the powder.

He worded his command carefully: "You'll say one thing if asked, and you won't deviate from this story. If anyone witnessed me entering this room, you'll say that I walked in to ask directions to the nearest bar. You gave me the information I sought, and I left. Nothing else happened. Do you understand?"

The maid nodded.

Burl quickly let the dazed woman go. Her quiet compliance indicated she wouldn't fight him now, so he ignored her for the moment and reached under his black cloak. It took a few seconds to situate a bag and its squirming contents on the maid's towel cart. Then he gave his last commands.

"You'll continue with your rounds as always. When you get to room 1652, you'll complete your cleaning. Then you'll leave this black bag in that room, where it can't be seen. Pull the long tie off the bag, then back away. You won't be frightened. You'll exit the room and forget about the bag. Is that clear?"

The maid nodded again. She heard only the command, and desired nothing more than to complete the task she'd been given.

Burl slowly smiled. The stones' powers were, indeed, everything reputed. More to the point, while the Oceanun and his cohorts were slowly dying, he'd be elsewhere with plenty of witnesses. Even if the maid was accidentally killed, his alibi would hold. He laughed all the way back to his room.

"Welcome one and all, welcome!" Temple d'Amour gushed as she sighted the bronzed Valkyrian and the huge, muscular Oceanun. "It'll be a pleasure to work on you two. Though you hardly need it, we'll polish any rough edges just the same."

Sagan had been lucky enough to get a booking for both her clients at the exclusive Brawné Salon for Men. She'd been smart enough not to tell Keir or Datron anything about the salon, though Keir had kept asking all the way here. And Sagan was pleased to know that, if this appointment didn't push Keir over the edge, nothing would.

Sagan saw the two enforcers glance at each other, and she held out one hand before either man could say anything Temple might not appreciate. "I'm Sagan."

Temple took her palm and fish-gripped it. "Of course, my dear, of course. You'll be handling these two delectable *entrées* for the Mr. Interstellar Feller pageant?"

Sagan nodded and tried not to show any surprise at the woman's bright orange hair or caked-on turquoise eye shadow. As if those elements weren't enough, the beauty diva was wearing a too-snug bodysuit of lime green. Sagan's anxiety over what the men might say to the salon owner was short-lived. Both seemed entirely nonplused by the lady's garishness.

"Will you make the introductions?" Temple asked, looking both men over once more.

"This is Datron Mann and Keir Trask," Sagan supplied, and tried hard not to grin when Temple grabbed both their hands in hers. She almost felt sorry for the men, since the salon owner wore the terrifying expression of a huntress.

Temple abruptly released her clutch and turned to

some nearby assistants. "Tasha, Missy—take Datron to room seven. Keir will go to room five."

Sagan stood back as the two girls led the men away. There was a murderous expression on Keir's face as he glanced over his shoulder, but Datron was already talking his assistant's ear off. Sagan wished Keir could be more like his friend. It would make the assignment easier.

"Shall we do a complete body job?" Temple absently queried, watching the men escorted by her staff.

Sagan nodded. "Give 'em the works. They'll need a wax and an exfoliation for the swimsuit competition and pose-down. Manicures, pedicures, seaweed wraps, facials and deep tissue massages can follow. Also give them a hair wash, deep condition and trim." She'd ticked off the list of those services she'd read other contestants purchased, hoping she remembered everything.

Temple waved a hand. "I love the way you think. Get them all primped and buffed, I say." She moved closer to Sagan and lowered her voice. "We've already had some contestants filter in, and I must admit these two of yours are by far the pick of the litter, at least of what's come through my door. Very doable, those two. Very doable, indeed." She glanced down the hallway to where the men were entering their respective rooms.

Sagan snickered. Temple seemed quite taken. "Thank you. Um, could I be allowed into the rooms while you and your staff work?"

Temple put a sisterly arm around her shoulder. "Of course, my dear! I'll bring you something to drink and will personally make sure my girls do a thorough job."

"I appreciate that, and for seeing us on such short notice."

"For men like these, I'd have come in at any time. Besides, this is the first time I've ever done an Oceanun. That is, the first time I've ever *groomed* one," she corrected, and flounced away to fill a glass of wine.

Taking a deep breath and deciding to put off seeing Keir, Sagan entered Datron's room. "How's it going?" she gaily asked. True to his easygoing nature, Datron's smiling face rose above a dressing screen.

Tasha, Temple's female assistant, pulled a hover cart forward and glanced over its contents, then at the winged man behind the partition. Sagan noted with amusement the woman's sultry look in the Valkyrian's direction, but gulped when she saw the heavy-duty shearing equipment that would be used on his body. Given his smile, Datron hadn't got a good look at it yet.

"Will you be okay? I can check in on you," she offered. It sounded ridiculous that he'd want her to, given his real occupation, but she didn't know how he was going to respond to being shaved all over and given a bikini wax. What if the man's feathers came loose and he lost control?

Datron came out from behind the screen with a towel around his lower half, took one look at the tools on the cart and balked. "Is she going to do with those scissors and razors what I think she is?"

Sagan was about to talk him into the procedure when Tasha spoke up.

Tasha took his hand and softly coaxed, "I promise I'll be very gentle. We just have to cut some of your hair shorter before we wax."

"*Wax?*" he croaked.

Sagan patiently explained: "All the competitors are doing this. You want a shot at that title and all the goodies that go with it, don't you?"

Datron took a deep breath, then grinned as the blonde Tasha sidled up to him and ran her finger across his cheek. "I suppose if Keir can suffer through it then I can."

"That's the spirit," Tasha said. "Now, you just take off that towel and lie down. You'll be in my hands for the rest of the evening, honey. And I'm very good at what I do."

Sagan didn't doubt the girl was good at *something*. She turned and left before he disrobed completely, glad that Datron was so distracted by the lovely blonde.

She strode across the hall and faced the door to Keir's room. Squaring her shoulders, she mentally repeated the mantra, *I can do this. I've had to do worse*, over and over again. Placing the palm of her right hand against the door, she pushed it and found, to her utter shock, that Keir was already on the table, joking with the auburn-haired Missy, who was shaving his legs. There was nothing but a white square of terry cloth over his privates. And while the cloth might have been sufficient for most men, Keir wasn't most men. The swatch was lying in such a way that it barely covered his genitalia.

Noticing that he was laughing with the girl and didn't seem to be having any problems, Sagan was about to quietly back out of the room. But that wasn't to be. He caught sight of her and motioned her in.

"There you are! I was wondering where you'd got to. Missy and I were just getting to know each other better."

Sagan eyed him suspiciously. According to what she'd seen of the man, his contempt for this contest and everything to do with it, he should have been at her throat for this very personal intrusion on his body.

"Darn it! I'll have to get a much sharper blade," Missy said. "He has hair like wire." She giggled, then left the room through a side door.

"Take a chair," Keir said. "I wouldn't want you to miss a single moment."

That was better. His dry tone was more what she'd expected, though he was still showing a great deal of control. "Uh, are you sure you want me in here? This is gonna get pretty personal."

"Absolutely," he asserted, then sat halfway up and stared at her. "In fact, I insist that you stay through the entire appointment. *All* of it."

"I'm sure Missy knows what she's doing. You hardly need me to—"

"I *insist*," he repeated. His voice was soft but steely. "If I'm to be humiliated on the pretense that all competitors do this, then I'll assume their managers would want to stay and see the job done properly. That seems only reasonable. Ya think?" he finished, using Earth vernacular.

Sagan got up, but his next words stopped her dead in her tracks.

"You stay and watch or I leave."

"You can't leave," she insisted. "It's expected that all the competitors go through this kind of grooming. I've researched and—"

"I mean it, Sagan."

"If you fail to cooperate, my orders are to—"

"The threat of having me arrested won't work here." He leaned on one elbow and glared at her. "You see, you made a critical error. We're in a public place. And having a contestant arrested—the first Oceanun to ever compete, no less—will most certainly be news that will circulate all over the city. The women at this salon won't keep the incident a secret, so our cover will undoubtedly be compromised. When that happens, the media will make a circus out of this mission and there'll be a lot of explaining to do on all sides. The smugglers will be alerted, the weapons will disappear and your Protectorate will never hear the end of it. Or, if our cover is blown, the smugglers may look to get rid of their weapons any way they can. They might even use them to fight their way off the planet. People could get killed," he finished.

Sagan knew that was certainly feasible. And she wouldn't have had him arrested for leaving the salon, anyway. "All right, you've made your point," she muttered. "But we shouldn't be discussing this here. I haven't scanned the room for listening devices. Surely you know that many businesses on Earth have them nowadays. Managers like to hear what their clients say when they think they've been left alone."

"Don't try to change the subject. There's a mini-scanner in my biceps bracelet. I've scanned and we're all clear." He paused and took a deep breath. "Now, are you staying or not? I really *must* insist," he repeated.

Sagan sighed heavily. "All-frickin'-right."

Keir lay back down, pasting what he clearly meant to be a pleasant smile on his face as Missy walked back into the room. She held a very large, whirring shaver in her right hand.

"There now. We'll get all that excess hair trimmed a bit. Then, on to the waxing!" the girl chirped.

He turned his head to glare at Sagan. Missy buzzed closer and closer to his privates with her vibrating piece of equipment.

CHAPTER EIGHT

Sagan didn't remember when exactly Temple had come in with wine, but she remembered gulping quite a lot during the appointment. Still, it wasn't enough to blur the image of the man before her. As Missy kept trimming away body hair, Sagan had to grab a tissue from a nearby table and wipe a fine sheen of sweat from her forehead and cheeks. She tried to keep her glance from returning to Keir's, but the intensity in those steel-blue eyes was magnetic.

She tried to hide her discomfort from Keir. As Missy and he chatted, Sagan joined in only if directly questioned. Finally, the unveiling of his privates was about to take place, and Sagan fought the desire to bolt. She sat on the edge of her seat and gripped her wineglass with enough force that her knuckles went white.

"Okay, all that's left is the bikini wax!" Missy said, then lifted the cloth off his privates. "This won't take a . . . Oh, my! You're a *robust* man, aren't you?"

If it had been any other man, Sagan would have said something cutting to the girl and told her to get on with her job. But after seeing what Missy did, she couldn't find air in her lungs. Keir was the most well-endowed man she'd ever seen. Without any erection at all, his penis had to be at least ten inches long. His testicles were as large as tennis balls, green and perfectly symmetrical. And his manhood lay in all its glory for her and Missy to view.

As the girl seemed to get her professional bearing back and picked up a bottle of talc, Sagan too managed to drag her gaze away. Unfortunately, she let her eyes slide up Keir's awesome, muscular frame and found him staring at her. She wanted to look away, but couldn't. Then, something dormant in her cut free. It was like somebody opened a closed door and let a breeze blow through an attic.

She swallowed her wine, put her glass down and walked to the table. "Um, I'll finish this part. I'm a little fussy about how Keir looks in his swimsuit."

Missy stopped short of placing the talc on Keir's inner thighs, blinked several times in surprise, then handed Sagan the bottle. "Well, it's your call. All that's left to do before the waxing is a good powdering." She grinned. "That'll save me time getting the wax ready. I'll be in the next room. Just sing out when you're ready. I'll bring my waxing tray in. Then we'll be doing a facial, manicure and all the rest." She left quickly, surely to tell the other girls what she'd seen.

Almost but not quite stupefied into silence by Sagan's one-hundred-eighty degree turnaround, Keir could only look up from his reclining position and watch as his partner began to work. She was very careful, very methodical . . . and gentle to the point that his manhood began to respond.

"I apologize for all this salon crap. It's just that all the other competitors are doing it," she said.

He found his voice. "I, uh, I've been through worse. I was angry but I'm over it." He briefly closed his eyes as the back of her soft hands and fingers brushed against the shaft of his sex. The movements of her palms as she spread the powder were whisper-soft against his flesh.

Done with the talc, Sagan reached for the shaver, turned it on and began to make a neater job of trimming up his lower abdomen. "This is rather crazy, isn't it? I mean, all this primping just so the competitors can look more endowed in a swimsuit," she murmured.

Realizing he was going to itch badly unless something was done to alleviate razor burn still didn't keep blood from rushing to his groin. Sagan's touch was exquisite. Keir hadn't responded to Missy because she was a professional technician doing her job. When Sagan touched him, it was like being caressed by a lover.

He was about to tell her to put the shaver down and stroke him when Missy stuck her head through the door.

"Ready?" she asked.

Sagan pulled a towel over Keir's midsection and responded, "Leave the tray with me. I'll finish up. Uh, I've done this before, so you can get the next treatment ready."

Missy simply nodded, put the tray down nearby and disappeared.

Keir smiled. "I don't think that technician liked being replaced. She didn't look too happy."

Sagan said nothing, pulled the towel back off and moved quickly to the tray to peruse the paraphernalia. She chose powder: a very special brand from the Aquila star system. Rubbing a bit of the sparkling powder between her hands, she smoothed it over his inner thighs, apparently not caring if she accidentally came into contact with his privates. Then she began to apply the heated wax. It was another specialty item made on Corona Prime.

Keir briefly flinched as the wax touched his skin, but the sensation of heat was oddly sensual. It wasn't all that bad. Indeed, he thought he could get used to having the stuff applied, especially if Sagan was doing the honors. When the heated wax was fully smoothed over his thighs, he couldn't help pushing his hips up and moaning in satisfaction. What she was doing went beyond good. It was extraordinary. He let his imagination take flight and closed his eyes to better enjoy it.

In his imagination, they were on Oceanus at his seaside villa. He was lying on his round, blue pillow-bed and the sea breeze was wafting over his nude body. She was sitting beside him doing what she was doing now . . . stroking, gently and slowly.

In the middle of his daydream, he suddenly realized all that goo was going to have to come off, and that the peeling wasn't going to be pleasant. But he convinced himself he could handle it so long as Sagan was the one doing it. In fact, a kinky part of him began to believe he might even like the experience.

She placed strips of paper over the smoothed wax, waited for the stuff to set as it should, then warned, "Take a deep breath."

Keir did as she said, but he wasn't as prepared as he believed. Inches of groin hair being literally torn from his body was the worst torture he'd ever endured. He yelled in pain and was sure his eyes were rolling permanently back in his skull—and he had another side left to go.

Sagan moved to the opposite side of the table before Keir could rip her head off. His reprieve from the pain being only temporary, she quickly pulled off the second strip without warning. Keir let out a string of Oceanun insults no mortal should ever hear.

She tried to keep from smiling but wasn't having much success. This had been coming all day, and part of her had been sadistically waiting for it. And her pretend

client needn't ever know the truth: a much more advanced
laser method might have been applied for a more permanent effect. However, it was outrageously expensive.
Since her government was footing the bill, this was the
best strategy.

Besides, a man like Keir would never approve of permanent groin hair removal.

He finally pushed back the remnants of pain and
glared murderously at her. "You Earth feline. I ought
to . . ."

"What? What do you want to do to me?" she responded, tilting her head as if she couldn't imagine why
he was angry. "Careful, you're turning a darker color
again. And I'm sure Missy and everyone in the building
must have heard that scream. I'm not sure Datron put
up such a fuss."

His expression tensed before he reached forward,
grabbed the front of her clothing and pulled her to him.
"Kiss me," he whispered.

For a long moment she stared at him, blinking in surprise. But when he sat halfway up to get closer, she
wrapped her arms around his shoulders. He thrust his
tongue deep into her mouth, and she melded hers to it.
In that moment, he could have asked her to do anything. Her mind kept screaming to act professional, but
it had been three long years since she'd been with a
man. Her body was overriding any common sense.

Keir heard the soft, needy little moans coming from the
back of Sagan's throat and was lost in time and space. As
far as he was concerned, they were on a cloud, riding together through the stars in a fantasy of their making.
She irked and provoked him, but this woman was his.
He vowed no man would have her but him, and she'd
want no one else for the rest of her life. How he was go-

ing to accomplish this monumental feat was a mystery, but he'd had tougher assignments. This, as he considered it, was his personal agenda. Sagan and he were meant to be together. His mind had been trying to tell him. That's why they'd struck sparks off each other, fighting the inevitable. She angered him, pushed him to limits he'd never let anyone else approach, and he fervently desired her despite her obstinacy. Perhaps more because of it.

Yes, Sagan had courage, dignity and strength—she was a superior woman by anyone's standards. He'd never met anyone like her. That very first handshake at the depot had his body responding. He'd known it then, but was too proud and intent upon his mission to acknowledge the attraction. Life up to this point had been boring, except for punctuating instances of terror encountered during certain missions. Wherever he went lately, one sector of space looked like any other. Here, with this Earthling, he'd rekindled a fire that had long ago burned to embers. He felt a renewal of passion and hope that too many hours of traveling from one star system to another had dimmed. He was paper, she was the match. She was defiant and he would tame her. All he must do was finish this mission; then he'd find a way for them to be together.

Voices outside the door presaged Sagan breaking their embrace. She drew back, pulling the towel over Keir's erection as she did. He collapsed back on the narrow bed and dragged air into his lungs. Sagan now had her face lowered, but he kept his gaze on her. He wanted to quell any reluctance she might be feeling, and was about to tell her how much her touch had excited him when Temple and Missy walked into the room. It would have to wait. For now, he'd play the part of the primped and pampered beauty pageant

contestant. But there would come a day when he'd separate the mission from what he and Sagan were experiencing.

Sagan kept her back to the hallway door as Temple and
Missy walked in. She raised her face and silently sent
Keir what she hoped was a very clear message. *I want
you.* He surreptitiously nodded. This interlude would be
continued another time.

    "Well, how are we getting along?" Temple quizzed as
she moved about the room, gathering items for Keir's
next treatment. "We heard you crying out. It's unavoid-
able, really, but this is the best method for clearing your
body of hair."

    "He's all right," Sagan responded in a controlled
voice that surprised even her. Now that she had her
mind made up, her reticence was a thing of the past. After this mission—as soon as she could do it and not ad-
versely affect her career—she'd be bedding him.

On the way back to the hotel, Keir kept his thoughts to
himself. Datron, however, was relaying his account of
how it felt being groomed by a beautiful woman. Without actually saying so, his second-in-command let them
know he'd enjoyed sex with the assistant. Throughout
the reaches of deep space and on many missions, they'd
been together far too long for Keir not to recognize
the outward, energized joy his comrade was displaying.
Datron always acted like a new man after sexual satisfaction. As for Sagan, she seemed amused by Datron's
story, though the Valkyrian was chivalrously leaving out
the juiciest parts. But that was the way Datron was:
good natured to a fault. Someone who went out of his
way to respect everyone, including the technician he'd
probably bedded in the kelp bath.

    When they got to the room and Sagan invited Datron

to join them for dinner, Keir almost made some excuse for his subordinate to be someplace else. He wanted desperately to speak with her alone, but saw she was purposely evading a private encounter. She wasn't a coward; he knew that. But she was holding the inevitable at bay for some reason—probably some sense of stubborn pride regarding the mixture of duty and pleasure. He'd always had that tendency himself, but look where it'd got him. He had a history of torn relationships because his duty came first. Now, he wanted more. And when this damnable assignment was over, he meant to grab this connection with both hands.

Sagan ordered room service for dinner, and it arrived quickly. Before they sat to eat, she again checked her scanner. A discrepancy on the biologic indicator caught her attention. According to her equipment, no one had come into the room but the maid. This was confirmed by not only a quick check of the hotel's cleaning itinerary, but the sparkling state of the suite itself. Still, the unusual yet minimal reading persisted even after Datron's presence was accounted for. Confused but stymied, she shrugged the matter off.

As they discussed the dilemma of how to search so many rooms, she saw Keir's worried expression deepen. He, too, was at an impasse as to how only three people could pull this feat off. But they had to find a way. And they could involve no one else without risking a leak. Three worlds were covertly involved and needed to remain anonymous. A lot was at stake.

They finished eating. Deciding to postpone their discussion until morning, and promising herself she wouldn't put either man through any more grief having to do with the pageant itself, Sagan turned to Keir after hearing Datron bid them good night. Now she found herself alone with Keir and hadn't a clue as to what to say. One part of her wanted him; the other part was afraid to get too close. Everyone she'd cared about was now dead, and all had lied to her. The coincidences with those other scenarios and what was happening between Keir and her were too eerie.

Keir watched her fiddle with the scanning equipment, trying to look busy. "Come here," he finally coaxed, and held out his hand.

She glanced at it, gazed into his blue eyes and swallowed hard. "We really ought to follow Datron's lead and get some sleep."

"Was it sleep you needed, or relaxation? There's a difference."

"Keir, I've apologized for dragging you to the damned salon. What happened there was just a response to the situation. Any two healthy beings would normally feel attracted—"

"Sagan, shut up and come here." Again, he held his hand out. "You wanted it. So did I. This attraction is going to get in the way if we don't get it *out* of the way."

"We have a mission to complete."

"And then?"

"I-I don't know about what happens afterward. We have to focus."

"Do you think we can, after being so intimate? All I can think about is being with you," he said. "I saw the look in your eyes and know you want it, too."

She crossed her arms over her chest, recognized the move as the protective gesture it was, then quickly uncrossed and dropped them to her sides. "Yes . . . dammit, I do want you. But acting on that impulse is the last thing we should do. We've got a lot of hard work ahead of us. We'll have to divide up the list of competitors by three and each take a section of the hotel. I've got the security cameras taken care of, so we can—"

"We'll work all that out tomorrow. For tonight, there's

not a single thing we can do. I'm worried about our search as much as you. Let's just give ourselves a break."

She knew the break he was talking about. He didn't have meditation in front of the fountain in mind. "That's very odd, coming from you. You're supposed to be the ultimate professional."

He slowly smiled. "The granite's cracking. I've never let myself get distracted by anything while on a mission. But then, I've never met anyone like you."

He walked toward her, his eyes so full of determination and passion that Sagan's heart almost overran her head. She put up a hand and placed it against his chest when he came close. "I-I can't do this. Not now. Please understand that I *do* want you. But it was hard enough getting where I am, as who I am, with men and women in my organization insinuating I slept my way up. Even in this day and this supposedly enlightened age, jealous and insecure people still exist. I've worked very hard to be where I am. Whatever feelings I have toward you personally must wait. We can't stand the distraction."

He took a deep, calming breath, then let it slowly out. "All right," he said. "But this isn't an end to the subject. We'll speak of our emotions later. And remember, there might come a time when not addressing them could get in our way."

She opened her mouth to deny that claim, but he held up a hand.

"Oh, I know that sounds ridiculous in some ways, but my instincts on this are right. We need to be together. I recognize this as surely as I recognize my need for air. We won't be a true team until we acknowledge our connection. We've been fighting it from the first moment we met, and you damned well know it."

She could cast his comments off as pure male ego, but something deep inside her sensed the truth in his words. They'd been fighting like lovers already. All he wanted was to end the arguments and begin a new relationship built on something besides mistrust. Still, she wasn't ready. Job aside, she'd lost too many people she cared about.

"Let's just get to bed. Okay?" It was a weak retreat, but it was all she had. The new day might bring a new answer to many problems, the worst of which was how to carry out the monumental task of finding those damned blasters.

Keir backed away. "I want you, Sagan. When you're finally good with whatever this is between us, let me know." He turned and walked toward his room.

She wanted to ignore their mutual need. At the same time, she wanted to hold him close all night. But she was too skilled to take the one option, and too frightened to allow herself the luxury of the other. Memories of what had happened three years ago still hurt. She couldn't let that situation recur.

Sagan walked sadly into her room but didn't close the door. They were past any need for privacy. She walked into the bathroom, turned on the heat lamp that also served as an overhead light and began her nightly shower routine. When she was done, she stepped out of the stone stall, wrapped an oversized towel around herself and felt an eerie iciness creep up her spine. As on that first day at the depot, she knew she was being watched. This time, however, the stare came from very close. And it was something far, far more harmful than a friendly Valkyrian. Sagan felt every nerve in her body go almost numb. She carefully turned . . . and froze.

A desert viper.

Many years ago, when Earth almost destroyed itself through pollution, there had been a genetic alteration in certain species of insects and reptiles. One of those dangerous mutations was now lying on the floor, only a couple of feet away.

As dangerous as the animal was, its milked venom had been recently altered into a life-saving drug for Nebulan Flu victims. A picture of her parents came to mind. In this image, she saw casualties of yet another kind of virus called Vagan Syndrome. It, too, had arrived on Earth, innocently carried by star travelers. And though the animal's beneficial attributes skittered through her shocked brain, she was still so frightened by its presence that she momentarily went numb. Nothing in her training had prepared her for a contact of the reptilian kind. Certainly not in the bathroom of an exclusive, ultra-modern hotel.

Sagan finally forced herself to take action. She backed slowly against the wall, as there was no way past the creature. Even her subtler movements captured its attention, and it reared up, sensing what it clearly perceived as prey.

She shivered. Despite its poison glands bringing salvation to humankind, there was still no known antivenom for the bite of this rare and exceedingly aggressive reptile. She kept absolutely still. Its glowing green eyes—an aftereffect of the genetic change that barely kept it resembling its remote cousin the rattlesnake—were now focused on her. Its body was fully as long as she was tall, and its girth was several inches greater than the upper part of her arm. Its brown body, with Day-Glo yellow diamond marks, was horrific. And more important than its overwhelming size and hostile appearance, was the rattle it now began to summon from the buttons on its long tail.

The viper lay directly between her and the door, and she knew any movement would cause it to strike. Somehow, she didn't get the impression it was any happier where it was than she was to have it there.

There was nothing she could use for defense. Standard-issue Earth enforcer stunners had built-in sensors that, once turned on and aimed, allowed for proper shock to the central nervous system given the intended victim's size and strength. She wasn't sure one of those stuns had ever been used on a viper, or how it might work. But her stunner was hidden in the bedroom beyond, anyway, and she'd have to get to it first—something easier said than done. She didn't dare wipe the droplets of water running from her dripping hair and into her eyes, much less try to get out the door.

"Keir?" she called softly, to the only person who might help. There came no helpful answer. The viper, however, responded. Though she knew it couldn't hear, the reptiles were reputed to have extraordinary eyesight. Where this one was, right in front of her, it could certainly see her mouth moving and might be interpreting that movement as an aggressive act. It drew farther back and rattled even harder. From where Sagan stood, pinned against the wall, it was loud as a thunderclap.

"Keir!" she shouted, and retreated farther against the wall when the snake thrust its eight-inch-wide, triangular head right in her face. Its forked tongue grazed her right cheek.

Keir was about to crawl into bed, still pondering Sagan's attempt to push him away, when he heard her shout. Pulling on his robe and belting it, he ran out of his room. Not immediately seeing her in her bedroom, he heard a sound from the bath that made his blood curdle. And what he saw through the door was ghastly. There were no poisonous reptiles or amphibians on Oceanus, but he'd read about the one facing Sagan. And his sudden appearance caused the animal to rear back, glance at him, then focus its more belligerent attention on Sagan.

"By the Creator's balls!" he softly swore. "Sagan, stay very still."

"Wasn't goin' anywhere," she whispered.

"I need a weapon. Something to kill it. Sagan, I need the locking code to the closet. I need my gear."

"No, don't kill it," she murmured.

"*What?* Are you insane, woman? That reptile is seconds away from striking." He could see the beast opening its massive jaws, presenting fangs as long as his index fingers.

"I-I know . . . but they're very rare. Their venom has recently cured Nebulan flu in humans. You can't kill it," she choked out. The snake rose even higher and opened its jaws wider. "S-stunner . . . in my desk . . . in a box behind the computer," she gasped.

"That'll only piss it off!" he said, but decided not to argue. Hurrying to the compartment she spoke of, he found it locked, and was about to yell for the key code but decided he hadn't time. He balled up the fingers of his right hand, thrust his fist into the small black box and felt the lock break. The locking mechanism wasn't meant to ward off an Oceanun's strength, especially not an Oceanun whose panic was in overdrive.

He grabbed the stunner and rushed back to the bathroom. Sagan was very pale, now standing up on her toes as the snake seemed to taste her breath with its tongue. Seemingly satisfied that it had her where it wanted her, it drew back and hissed very loudly.

There was no choice. Keir had to fire, though she'd be in the direct line of the blast. Not knowing how the stunner would sense both Sagan and the animal, he still had to pull the trigger. Better to suffer through a shock than the certain death of a bite from the viper. As he aimed, the animal began to drool, and the glands behind its head expanded to the size of his fists. He fired. Alarmingly, the viper lurched forward at the same time. Both the woman and the snake dropped to the floor.

Keir toed the immense body to be sure it was out of commission. When it didn't move and he saw the snake's green eyes were glazed, he tossed the stunner into a nearby chair, stepped over the still reptile and knelt beside the unconscious woman on the floor.

"Come on, sweetness," he murmured as he lifted her in his arms and carried her out of the room. He placed her gently on her bed, glanced around and finally saw something that would serve as a temporary cage. He had no idea how long the viper would remain unconscious, if he hadn't killed it outright, and containing it was his first priority.

Rushing to a small sofa in the corner, he tugged off its ornate, glittering green cushion cover. It took only a few more moments to drop the unconscious viper into the makeshift bag and secure the ends tightly in a knot. It was a very tight fit, as the animal's looping body was so large.

Once he was sure the viper couldn't get loose, he rushed back to the bed, sat down and leaned over Sagan. He put his fingers to her throat, felt a strong pulse and realized he'd been holding his breath since he'd fired the stunner. Only now could he drag in air.

He lay next to her and gasped out, "Sagan, can you hear me? Come on, love, wake up if you can hear me." He needed to revive her to alleviate his terror. Then he recalled how the damned snake had attacked. He quickly pulled off the towel draping her body and searched for fang marks. The glare from the blast had kept him from seeing if she'd been struck, and if that was the case she'd be dead in a few hours no matter what he did. But he could find no wound, and there was no blood on the towel to indicate so much as a scratch, and relief poured through him. Keir looped his arms around her soft body and gently pulled her against his chest. "Thank the Creator, it didn't get you."

Every bone in Sagan's body screamed in pain. It seemed that even the marrow hurt. "Ow!" she muttered, and tried to push Keir away.

"Lie still," he commanded.

She could hear his words and felt the warmth of his body as he held her, but barely able to loop her arms around his torso, Sagan dropped her head back and gazed up at him. His color had darkened to a shade of almost forest green and the blue star on his cheek was glowing. "Y-you s-shot me," she stuttered.

He kissed her forehead. "Had to. The viper was between us."

"Jerk!" she muttered, then fell into a world of darkness.

Keir chuckled even as he lowered Sagan back to the mattress. If she could summon an insult, the woman was fine. He grabbed a blanket from the end of the bed, but stopped short to gaze at her lovely body. Now that she was safe he had the time and presence of mind to view what the towel had covered.

Here was the most finely designed creature he'd ever seen. Her breasts were every bit as full and pert as they'd appeared in the sexy one-piece suits she liked to wear. She had a tiny waist, narrow hips and impossibly long, shapely legs. "Orion's balls!" he breathed, and spent a full five minutes simply staring. Her long, wet hair spilled around her shoulders and arms. She reminded him of the sultry sea sirens on Praetor Prime. She could have tempted him into that ocean's depths and he'd have willingly followed.

Shaking his head to clear his thoughts, he pulled the blanket over her and tucked it close. Then he shakily stood and gazed at the bag containing the snake. It was moving.

"How in the name of Celestia did *you* get in this room?" he angrily muttered. Then he began a thorough search for vents, ducts and any passageways that might accidentally allow such a dangerous predator into their suite. His exploration was only to satisfy any possibility of this being coincidence. In his gut, he knew it wasn't. And when he found a black bag, a bag that was tattered and old and not one he'd expect Sagan to use, Keir was certain. The bag had been squarely laid out behind a chair near the bathroom door, and the cord was cut long enough so the reptile's handler could safely back away and release the viper.

His anger grew. Someone wanted Sagan dead, or maybe both him and Sagan. This was the only logical conclusion, and it boded ill for both of them.

He rushed to a wall intercom and punched Datron's room number. When his subordinate answered, he instructed, "Scan your room for biologics larger than a sand mite, then grab your medical bag and get up here."

Shutting off the intercom, he walked back into Sagan's bedroom and sat beside her. She might have been killed! The thought had him turning even greener. Yes, someone knew about them. Someone dastardly. That person had used a poisonous creature of the desert to do his or her dirty work, a creature whose venom had no known antidote and would cause its victims a hideous, agonizing death. As a child, Keir had read all about these creatures now populating the area where his beloved cowboys roamed. Somebody was going to pay for this outrage. He didn't know how the guilty party had gotten into the room without Sagan's equipment alerting her to unauthorized access, but he'd hunt whoever had done it down like the bog slime they were.

The confined viper rattled angrily. Despite his people's creed to honor all forms of life, Keir wanted it dead. Still, Sagan's plea to save it and its venom echoed in his ears. Even knowing she might have been killed and that her flesh would have melted from her bones as she lay dying, she'd still had compassion and the foresight to think of others the creature might help. Truly, she was a woman of quality. This made him want her all the more.

He gently stroked her cheek as he gazed down at her pale face. Sagan was the most enchanting woman he'd ever seen. If anything had happened to her . . .

He let out a low growl of pure rage. Whoever had done this wouldn't get the kind of mercy Sagan showed to the snake. Keir swore it.

CHAPTER NINE

Datron buzzed at the door to Keir's suite and was let in. He entered with his med kit and was shocked yet again to see his supervisor the color of a forest shrub, eyes glowing as electric blue as the star on his face. "What's happened?" he asked.

"Come with me," his friend commanded, and led the way. "I had to use Sagan's own weapon to stun her. Can you give her something for pain?"

"You did *what?*" Datron stopped dead in his tracks and faced Keir in confused anger.

"I had to stun her," his friend repeated, then pointed to a bag rattling and hissing horribly in the corner. "Someone put a desert viper in the room. The animal was between me and her so . . ."

Datron heard the frustration in the Oceanun's voice, looked at the bag and nodded. He turned to survey the prone human female. "Her biology is similar to ours, but I'll have to guess at her weight and the exact dosage. I won't know if I've given her enough meds until she awakens." He checked Sagan's pulse, reached into his kit and readied his injection tube. "Why do you think someone deliberately put a viper in here?"

"I think we've been discovered. I'm not sure who was

meant to be bitten, but it doesn't matter. I'll take the viper out to the desert. You take care of her. Don't leave her alone for an instant."

Datron checked his injection tube twice. Too much medicine and she'd be in orbit; too little and she'd suffer. He carefully lifted her head, put the end of the tube against the back of her neck and pressed the meds into her cervical vertebrae. She moaned slightly, and he lowered her head back to the pillow. "I think that'll do." He glanced at Keir. "I know you don't like hurting animals, but why didn't you just kill the beast? Didn't you want to use our weapons? They're still in the closet, right?"

Keir pointed at the unconscious Sagan. "Would you believe she asked me not to destroy it?" He shook his head in disbelief. "I think I've judged these humans poorly. That damnable snake had her pinned against a wall and she still considered its life and the use its venom has for medical purposes." He pushed his hair back in clear frustration. "It struck, but I fired before it found its mark."

Datron smiled and put a hand on Sagan's forehead. "Now, why does pleading for that viper and thinking how it could save lives sound exactly like her?"

Keir frowned. "I'm going to have a hovercraft brought to the hotel entrance. For Sagan's sake, I'll get that reptile back where it belongs. Take care of her."

Datron nodded. Then he watched his partner of many years carefully pick up the bag containing the viper, scoop up the Protectorate stunner lying nearby, and walk out of the room.

After dressing himself and donning a leather duster to hide both the snake and Sagan's stunner, Keir took an elevator to the ground level. He leisurely waited while the concierge readied his hovercraft. Watching his surroundings carefully, as any enforcer under the circumstances might, he vaguely noticed two cloaked, massive-sized men sitting in the bar near the hotel entrance. But he only suspected trouble when they kept their gazes on him and got up as the concierge opened his hovercraft door.

He politely nodded at the valet, then took control of the craft. The viper was rattling incessantly, which caused everyone within earshot to glance his way. Because of Sagan's request to keep the animal alive, he hadn't stunned it again so soon; the beast might go into some kind of shock from which it couldn't recover. He guessed that it would take half an hour to get to the desert at top speed, and he hoped that was enough of a breather before he blasted it again, and that the viper would survive.

He turned on the craft lights, punched in several coordinates to head due west. As he cast a surreptitious glance over his shoulder, he saw that the two cloaked men had exited the hotel and were procuring a craft of their own.

He picked up speed, but soon he saw the strangers' craft catching up to his. He couldn't do anything too obvious on the busy roadways, but managed to alter his pattern enough to ascertain that he was being followed. He dearly wished he had his more powerful weapon, not Sagan's stunner. Unfortunately, his arsenal was still locked in that damned hotel closet.

Calling Datron for help was out of the question. The Valkyrian needed to watch Sagan, who was surely still unconscious and helpless, and his friend couldn't catch up anyhow, so Keir began to weave through traffic. If those following meant to confront him, he would make sure it was away from the innocent pageant tourists crowding the LA streets.

No matter how he maneuvered, his pursuers followed. Taking another quick glance over his shoulder, he saw one of them produce a sawed-off destructor rifle. The weapon was roughly the length of the man's arm, and Keir could clearly see light glowing from its wrist-thick barrel. Keir picked up the pace.

Though it felt as if the trip was taking forever, the desert horizon finally loomed into view. To see the rocky outcrops better, Keir put his front lights on full beam. That was when the first blasts sizzled over his right shoulder, almost singeing his shirt. His assailants had possessed the sense not to fry him in the middle of downtown Los Angeles, but now it seemed they were ready to take him out. More shots followed, and he dodged.

Keir couldn't return fire and maintain control of his craft. While his hovercraft was more maneuverable with only one occupant, his opponents had the advantage of having both a driver and a gunner.

He had only one chance. As he wound through the rocky canyons, his pursuers firing and weaving carelessly after him, he made several attempts to brush against rock walls to send the crumbling boulders into the following craft. Unfortunately, the ploy only slowed him down. One of the destructor blasts hit the left wing of his vehicle. The engine sputtered momentarily . . . then blessedly came back to life. But one of those blasts would eventually hit the main engine and cause his small craft to explode.

That was when Keir saw an outcrop jutting from the desert floor like a stalagmite in a cave. He pushed his little transport to its engine's limit and aimed its nose straight at the outcrop. His attackers were so intent on firing and following that he prayed they wouldn't see his maneuver. His left wing was smoking and might provide the screen he'd need to pull off this stunt. If it didn't work, both vehicles would end up on the desert floor. One way or the other, the encounter was about to end for all of them.

The rock pillar loomed closer and closer. Keir held his breath, counted to three and waited until he could almost feel the daytime heat from the rock's surface on his skin. Then he directed his vehicle straight up. The bottom scraped rock. He held on to the drive controls. Higher and higher he went, skimming the side of the rock pillar and up over the top. He was trying to get control of his rapid ascent when he heard the other craft crash directly into the jutting outcrop, just as he'd hoped.

The chase was over, but Keir still had to regain control of his vehicle. It took him another few seconds, but he finally managed stability, smoking wing and all. Then he circled back to see if his attackers had survived.

The mass of crunched, flaming metal that had once served as his foes' transportation was at the base of the outcrop. Keir slowed his craft and prepared to land. What he found lying in the sand wasn't pretty, but at least the men had met a quick end. *Ussarians.* In the illuminating flames of their destroyed craft, there was no mistaking the facial tattoos, shaved heads or winding insignias on the leather belts and vests. He hadn't been close enough to see the symbols at the hotel, but he knew their kind well. Prior to coming to Earth, he'd incarcerated a band of Ussarian raiders in the Sepor star system. They were merciless hunters, holding to no code save their own. Ussar was always at war, its people fighting among themselves and raiding everyone else when they weren't. These warriors, like most Ussarians, were as large as Keir and as muscular. He'd have been hard-pressed to hold his own if the fight was fair, and Ussarians weren't known for fighting honorably.

So, Ussarians were responsible for stealing the Ache blasters and the Lucent Stones. Now they somehow knew his mission and wanted him dead. And since these warriors didn't bear marks common to Ussarian leaders, he also assumed their chieftain was back at the hotel.

The frightened hissing of the viper broke into his thoughts. Keir gazed down at the bag now wedged under the seat because of his ninety-degree ascent up the rock face. "First things first," he muttered. Lowering his craft to within inches of the ground, he took his stunner from where he'd tucked it beneath his duster and fired at the bag. The animal within went blessedly silent. He hoped he hadn't killed the beast, for Sagan's sake, but such a stun was his only option to stay safe as he nudged the huge viper back into its sandy domain. His conscience made him wait until the animal showed signs of recovery.

"If I'd been trussed up and taken from home, I'd be furious too," he murmured as the viper finally slithered away. But that wouldn't have stopped him from killing it if the beast had harmed Sagan.

He hopped out of his transport and walked back to the remains of the Ussarians spread on the sand. All in all, the scene looked like what it was: a flying accident. He searched the bodies and found the destructor rifle and one lethal neurological Ache blaster. Here was the evidence tying them to the Lucent theft. But his relief in finally knowing the thieves' identities was tempered by the knowledge that there was a leak that had put the Ussarians on his trail.

Keir turned toward his craft and considered the damage. Part of the inside left wing had been completely melted. His technical knowledge allowed a plausible lie: The fuel tank just beneath the wing frame had leaked. In such a case the fuel would have run down the underside of the wing while he was flying, caught fire when he ignited the thrusters and exploded. Such accidents occasionally happened in those vehicles when not thoroughly inspected. And though he hated to get some poor mechanic unfairly in trouble, the lie had to be told. He couldn't lose his cover.

The little hovercraft made it back to the hotel, though barely. When he arrived, he gave the unwitting valet the story of a lifetime concerning the supposed fuel leak, and all seemed right with the world as far as the damage was concerned. As he'd imagined, it didn't hurt that he was a contestant in the Mr. Interstellar Feller pageant.

He bundled the weapons beneath his duster and, relieved that hotel security was on overload due to the heavy pedestrian traffic and guest baggage, Keir plastered a benign look on his face and walked through the lobby as if he hadn't a care in the world. No weapons scanners were being used, to avoid the hotel looking like an armed compound to which dignitaries might take exception. While this was a further sad commentary on security, it stood Keir in good stead.

He waited his turn for an elevator, though traffic was heavy. There were people standing in every conceivable space, some of whom appeared employed by local media companies. Gowned women sauntered by; he assumed they were trying to attach themselves to contestants for the evening. He was on his way to the sixteenth floor when one such buxom devotee approached him.

The woman entered the elevator on the tenth floor, did a double take in his direction, then smoothed the tiny silver evening dress she was wearing. There was no use trying to ignore the girl—the confined space made that impossible—so he simply smiled and nodded.

"Hi, there. I'm Sharyce," she said, sidling close. "You're Oceanun, aren't you?"

Keir let out a long slow breath and kept staring straight ahead. "That would be correct, madam."

Sharyce tried again. "Sorry, I didn't catch your name."

About to tell her that he hadn't given it, Keir relented. He was here to play the part, which meant acting as if her attention was acceptable. Desirable, even. "Keir Trask. Lovely evening tonight, isn't it?"

She moved closer. Keir had no room to back away, as the elevator was crowded. Sharyce leaned forward and made an obvious attempt to get him to look down her very low-cut gown.

"Need a little company?" she asked.

"Thank you, no. I've had quite a full day," he said, rolling his eyes. That was an understatement.

She ran her hand over his large, leather-covered biceps. "I'll bet you win the pose-down. I haven't seen a man nearly as big as you. Not in all the other years I've been coming to the competition."

Why wasn't the damnable elevator moving faster? He needed to get back to the suite, check on Sagan and tell Datron about the attack. "You enjoy the festivities, then?" he absently remarked.

"I, uh, enjoy a lot of things. I know how to show others a good time."

He glanced down at her pretty face, framed by short brown curls, then let out a sigh of relief when the number sixteen appeared on the elevator control display. "I hope you succeed," he told her. "Good night."

There was a semblance of a pout on her pretty face as he nudged his way off the elevator, but her cloying if brief presence was the last straw in a day gone wholly wrong. The only happy event had been his and Sagan's encounter at the salon, but even that pleasure was beginning to dim as his freshly shaved and waxed skin had begun to itch.

When he entered the hotel suite's access code and walked inside, he saw Datron sitting with Sagan on the couch in the main room. While he was relieved to see the Earth woman conscious, her skin was still very pale. It seemed almost chalk white in the silver dressing gown she wore. His temper gone, he prepared to vent. He'd had all he could take.

"With whom must one fornicate to get out of this?" he growled.

Datron turned and stared. "What happened?" he asked.

Keir glanced at Sagan, taking a moment to speak to her before he exploded. "Are you all right?"

She nodded, gazing up at him from her position on the sofa. "You look like somebody with issues."

He waved his hand in the air, shrugged, then began to pace. "Why would you think that? Since I've been on this planet I've fought with you almost constantly. We haven't been able to get any work done. I've been inflicted with body buffing, prodding and poking. I'm to the point that my skin is on fire from your efforts." He couldn't control the rising volume of his voice, or his words. "As I speak, I have portions of a kelp bath clinging to places I won't begin to mention. I'm sore and swollen from lack of release. I've had to shoot you to keep a deadly animal from killing you, acted as a babysitter for the venomous reptile responsible, and was followed, attacked and almost killed out in the desert. What could *possibly* be my issues?" he angrily asked. "To add to my list of irrational complaints, someone has probably known about us from the time I set foot on this world. Our enemies will now be seeking to get us out of the way by any means possible." He stopped pacing. "Finally, I was just propositioned in the elevator by a complete stranger. As if I was a common . . . ho . . . as you Earth people would say."

Sagan's eyebrows rose.

"In short, my fellow enforcers, I . . . have . . . had . . . enough!" He slashed his hand in the air as a gesture of termination.

Before asking about the attack to which Keir had just referred, Sagan ventured a softly spoken offering that might appease him. "We know who the smugglers are."

He held his hands out, palms up. "Let me guess. Ussarians, correct?"

Sagan exchanged a surprised glance with Datron, but didn't want to say anything that would rile Keir further. The Oceanun was as dark green as she'd ever seen him. His eyes were glowing, and the star on his face was an almost blue-white color.

Datron asked the question Sagan hadn't: "You were attacked?"

Keir nodded. "Two Ussarian warriors followed me into the desert while I was trying to put that damned snake back where it belonged. It took some swift maneuvering, but I managed to evade being blasted into cinders." From beneath his duster he pulled a sawed-off destructor rifle and an Ache blaster. "Here're two weapons we won't have to go looking for . . . and your stunner."

Sagan gasped as all three weapons hit the glass top of the ornate coffee table. "Crap!"

"Indeed," he replied. "And the bodies of the men carrying these will be found by law enforcement shortly. They're out in the desert with your friend, the viper."

"Y-you killed them?" Sagan whispered. She stood and faced Keir.

"The snake is the only thing I saw alive. The Ussarians' hovercraft hit a rock outcropping. I lured them into it while trying to keep myself from being incinerated. It'll look like an accident when they're found. And thanks for asking, but I'm just fine," he finished.

"Holy crud!" Sagan blurted. She sat back down. Though she was much better, the side effects from the stunner were far from gone.

Datron spoke up. "Sagan woke after you left. She used her computer to hack into the hotel's security cameras, and we were able to watch the tapes. Since her room scanner only detected our entrance and the maid's, we used the tapes to trace the cleaning staff's movements. It looks like a Ussarian got a maid to put that viper in your suite. We think he must have bribed her somehow."

Keir stopped and stared at him. "Why would a maid do that, even for a bribe? She'd be the first person questioned if anything went wrong. That makes no sense."

Sagan chimed in. "When I played the security tapes, we were able to see the Ussarian actually meeting with the maid in a linen storeroom. I was able to computer enhance and isolate something sticking out of the Ussarian's cloak just before he went in the room. We couldn't see it perfectly, but it looked like a bundled black bag that later appeared on the maid's cart—I think the same bag we found in my room. There are no cameras in our living space so we obviously don't know for certain, but it's a safe guess that the maid left the snake in my room and she got it from the Ussarian."

Keir shook his head. The situation still made no sense. A hotel maid would know she'd be one of the first people questioned if the snake killed someone. The only way he could imagine her committing such an act was if someone forced her. And at that thought, his gut involuntarily tightened. Were the Ussarians using the Lucent Stones? There weren't that many stones to begin with, so they wouldn't risk utilizing them unless it became a necessity. It had never been fully known if the smugglers understood the powers of the stones, but Keir now suspected they did. With even a fraction of one, the hotel maid could have been induced to do anything and never remember it; she'd tell whatever story the Ussarian wanted her to repeat.

Sagan looped her hair behind her ears, took a deep breath and said, "I located the Ussarian suite and hacked into their room computer. It seems these Ussarians have a morbid interest in desert vipers. Someone in their suite used the machine to research the animal, and found out that the beasts sometimes get into people's homes, hovercrafts and offices out here. That's where they got the idea to kill us. They also checked out a number of other natural ways to die in the area . . . scorpion stings and bites from insects, etcetera."

She lowered her head, looking briefly ashamed. "I've, uh, scanned our suite again, more thoroughly this time, and there's nothing here but us."

Datron snorted, clearly amused. "Even though some home invasions have occurred, can you imagine anyone believing a big snake like that got onto the sixteenth floor of this major hotel?"

Keir shrugged. "Ussarians aren't very deep thinkers. They live in the moment and usually credit themselves with more intelligence than they have. They probably thought they had the perfect plan, and that everything was under control. Their egos are immense in that respect."

Sagan looked like she was going to say something amusing, paused, then offered, "Lucky for us they aren't that sharp. These idiots have done half our job for us." She glanced at the Ache blaster on the table. "Now that we know they're the smugglers, we won't have to search all the other competitors' rooms. I can get into the hotel's video files again, computer-splice previously recorded hallway tapes and hide our actions. Any security guards watching the cameras near the Ussarians' rooms will see tapes of an empty hallway. They won't know we're breaking in. We'll obviously need to get into those rooms to make sure the weapons are in their immediate control before we make any arrests."

Keir ran a hand across his face. "Yes, there's no question that we have a better idea of what we're doing now." He sighed and opted to sleep on the matter; weariness was overcoming his thinking. He was also hungry, but he was more tired. All he truly wanted was to put the past few days and the constant moment-by-moment upheaval behind him. "Let's get some rest and discuss these issues in the morning."

Sagan nodded in agreement and stood up. However, as she did so, she stumbled and fell against Keir, clearly overcome by some residual dizziness. He caught her, picked her up and carried her to her room. He told Datron, "Take my bed. I'll be in Sagan's room for the night, making sure she's okay. I want you nearby in case she needs medical attention."

Datron grinned, but did as he was told.

CHAPTER TEN

Inside her bedroom, Sagan put forth her protest: "I can walk by myself."

"Perhaps you'd have taken ten paces, then fallen to the floor."

"Keir—"

"Weren't you wearing just a blanket when I left?" He sat her on the bed and gazed down at her.

Confused by the change of subject, she stared at him for a moment. "Datron helped me into my bathrobe. What has that got to do with anything?"

He gritted his teeth and spoke with his jaw clenched. "He saw you nude?"

"He says he's a medical technician aboard your vessel, as well as your second-in-command. Besides, something tells me he's seen his share of nude women. What does that have to do with the price of tea in China?"

Keir pushed his hair back with both hands, then sat beside her, and Sagan could tell he was trying to get his temper under control. She decided to change the subject.

"You know, the rest of the Ussarians will surmise you had a hand in their comrades' deaths tonight," she mentioned.

"To the media and the local law enforcement agencies,

it'll look like they went for a desert ride and met with a horrible accident, just as I've said."

She put a hand on his thigh without thinking. "The Ussarians will know that wasn't the case. As it now stands, they've pegged us for enforcers. They've tried to kill us twice in one night, so they're obviously mixed up in this smuggling business—unless, of course, there's any other reason they might want us killed?"

Keir shook his head. "Your summation is correct. Someone blew our cover and warned them. As you've said, we need to get into their suite to see what we can find. And we need to do it quickly; the deaths of their men tonight might change their plans," he advised. "It's possible our smuggler friends will try to move the weapons sooner, even fearing every corridor is under surveillance." He paused. "Is it possible they can hack into the hotel surveillance equipment like you have? If so, they can hide their actions."

Sagan waved a hand in dismissal. "Unlikely. For them to hack Earth code would require different technology than they're used to. Besides, I have a special routine running on the main hotel computer. If anyone's entering the system illegally, I'll know. Also, if they could hack into the computers here, wouldn't they have done it when they gave the damned viper to the maid?"

Keir sighed and hung his head. He was clearly tired. But Sagan couldn't tell if it was exhaustion or self-righteousness when he asked next, "I surmise it's legal for you to have hacked into the hotel's computers?"

"It's in the line of duty," she snapped. "So, yes. And you have bigger issues to worry over. I don't think the chieftain of the Ussarians is going to walk away from his two dead warriors without demanding revenge. Not if what I've read about them is correct. Even at the risk of being caught, he'll want you killed now." She paused. "It both-ers me that he's the type who'd make such a stupid mistake. Having those two warriors follow you after putting the snake in our room was a serious error in judgment."

Keir leaned back on the bed. "Yes, he's desperate. He's threatened by our presence, and wants to conclude his deal. He wants us out of the way. The men who came after me tonight were probably commanded to watch for any sign of life just in case the viper didn't do its job. This guy's thorough. It's what I'd order if I were their leader."

"So, they were watching this room and saw you leave?" Sagan asked.

"Not the room. They saw me from the bar, near the hotel entrance." Keir paused. "As I said, I'm sure they were the backup plan. But when the Ussarian leader learns that his backup plan failed, if he can get in contact with his buyers and let them know what happened, he might sell those weapons soon. We need to get into that suite."

Sagan didn't want to be too hasty. "What if they're in there? We can't just go now."

"No. We'll keep an eye on their hallway, choose our moment. Then, assuming we find the blasters, we'll place a tracking device among them. I don't only want the cargo and the smugglers, I want to know who's buying these weapons and why. But we'll have to make sure our bug can't be detected."

Sagan had the equipment and technical expertise to handle that chore. She nodded. After a moment she said, "We also need to learn who put the Ussarians onto us in the first place. We need to plug that leak."

Keir sighed. "I agree. That's a big priority. But for now, let's get some sleep. I've done all I can for one day." He stretched and grabbed the bottom of his shirt to pull it off.

Sagan sat and stared pointedly at him.

"What?"

"You don't think you've got an ice cube's chance in hell of sleeping in this bed with me, do you?"

"Sagan, whatever Datron gave you to counteract the stunner's effects will wear off. You'll likely need help when that happens. As it is, it's late into the night and we've still got the rest of this farce to play out. If the following days are anything like this one . . . I don't even want to think about it," he grimly finished. "I'm not planning anything."

She heard the outright weariness in his voice and saw it in his expression, and he wasn't nearly as dark green as he had been. His anger, at least, seemed to have abated. "I-I'm sorry I called you a jerk. I know there was no other way for you to save me."

"And I apologize for shooting you. I've been stunned, and I know what it does to a person. Especially a frail little body like yours," he said.

She scooted back against the pillows and passed her hand over the switch to dim the lights. "Have it your way. Just so you stay on your side of the bed. But for the record, I am *not* frail."

His only response was, "Don't worry, Sagan. I'll stay where I fall." Then he lay back, let out a sigh of relief and closed his eyes.

Sagan lay motionless for a long time, trying to fight the deep ache in the marrow of her bones and the soreness in her muscles that were the stunner's effects. At last she began to shiver uncontrollably. Datron's medicine had clearly worn off. She tried to sit up, but only managed to moan in pain. It was all she could do to keep from crying out further when a very large, warm body moved against her and muscular arms enfolded her.

"Where does it hurt most?" Keir whispered. He'd been lying next to her, not speaking, for some time now. His conscience had been berating him for stunning Sagan, even though he'd had no choice.

"My back."

He heard the catch in her voice. It would probably be another two days before she felt normal again. And stunning her had put them in another bind: Since the pageant was beginning, he and Datron wouldn't be near to help her if the Ussarians attacked. "I'm so sorry, Sagan. I can't say it enough."

"Better than being bitten by that snake. I'll get over it," she replied.

"I'll get Datr—"

"No. I don't know what he's given me, but it makes me kind of loopy. I'll deal. Just do me a favor, will you?"

"Anything," he said.

There was a pause, and then she asked, "Hold me for a while? I-I think if I can get warm I can go back to sleep."

Keir quickly shed everything but his pants so that he could get closer to her and share body heat. It worried him that Sagan didn't seem to care as she watched him undress. The small dark circles under her eyes indicated her lack of rest.

He pulled extra blankets up from the end of the bed, cuddled up beside her and tucked them both in as best he could without moving her too much. "There, that better?"

She simply nodded, and snuggled nearer. For a few moments she lay in silence. Then she gazed up at him. "I think I'll be okay now. You can go back to sleep."

He almost laughed. "I'm not sure I ever was asleep. Not really. Tired as I am, I don't think I can do it in this situation."

"You've had a lot to think about," she agreed. "You know, most cases I've been on aren't this bizarre."

If she was trying to defend all the escapades they'd suffered, there simply was no justification. But neither was any of it her fault. "It'll be over in a few weeks," he said. "We'll destroy the blasters, then Datron and I can head back the way we came. I'm sure your Protectorate directors will be glad to see the backs of us."

She took a deep breath, exhaled and seemed to nestle even closer.

"Warmer?" he asked.

"Yeah, it's helping. But you must not be all that comfortable. This bed is so small compared to your—"

"You should see the quarters I had on the *Valiant*. Comparatively speaking, everything in this suite is a luxury."

"The *Valiant* is your ship?"

He nodded. The small gesture brought his face much closer to her hair, its clean smell and indescribable softness. As before, he felt himself responding physically to her proximity. He simply couldn't help it. She was a beautiful woman; he was a lonely man in bed with her.

"I-I wanted to ask you about . . . Never mind. You need to sleep. So do I," she conceded.

He gently stroked her back and heard her sigh. "Go ahead. Ask me anything you want."

"I've read about your world. But what's it like in *your* words? You said you had a villa by the ocean?"

"Yes," he said. "In design, it's very much like one of your Grecian temples. I've seen pictures of them and am amazed at the similarities. But then, we're supposed to have had common ancestors. Maybe the architecture is some kind of ancient homage to them."

She leaned her head back, rested it against one of his muscular biceps. "Tell me more."

He shrugged, not knowing where to begin. "My home is very small, but open to the sea breeze so it seems larger. There are no other residences for miles, and I have the beach all to myself. The sand is an amazing white that almost glows in the moonlight. And there are two moons, one blue and one green. The air is cooler than here. And then there are colorful birds that land on my balcony each morning, waiting to be fed."

"It sounds beautiful," Sagan breathed. "Do you have a family?"

"I have no mate, as you know if you researched my personal history," he said, simultaneously pushing a strand of hair off her cheek.

"But there was nothing about sisters, brothers or even parents."

He pulled her closer. "There wouldn't be. That information isn't on any service record. It's for their protection, just in case an enemy comes looking for me," he added.

"Do they? Come looking, I mean."

He felt himself relaxing. The soft sound of her voice had a soothing effect. "I've only had it happen once. Oceanun authorities stopped some criminals entering my home city of Cetacea. The men had information about where I lived." He heard her gasp in alarm, but snorted in dismissal. "They were the remaining members of a band of slavers who'd escaped capture. They'd been raiding mining colonies and abducting people to work on fuel ships when I arrested their friends."

"What happened?"

He placed his lips next to her temple and breathed in her floral scent. "They never made it to my home. I was notified by a member of the local constabulary that they'd been taken into custody. No problem."

"And your family? Did they find out? I mean . . . you have parents, don't you?"

He grinned, pleased by her interest. "My parents, brothers and sisters, uncles, aunts, grandparents and assorted cousins were all duly concerned. But the matter was over before it ever really began."

Sagan was silent for so long that he thought she'd finally fallen asleep. But then, she began a sad story he later wished he hadn't heard: "I had a family—parents, I mean. We lived in New York City when the Vagan Syndrome struck."

He pulled slightly away, and gazed into her eyes. "Sagan, you were part of that? We read about isolated outbreaks. And then there was a year where no alien vessel was allowed to land, though a dozen planets or more—including Oceanus—sent vaccines."

"I was one of those who were immune. My folks weren't. The medicines you mention came by Mars freighter; they had to be off-loaded in space to prevent contamination. All that took time. And when our scientists finally figured out the small chemical alterations necessary for an Earth cure, my parents had been dead for three weeks."

He sat up and looked down at her, horrified. "I'm sorry, Sagan. I can't imagine how terrible that must have been."

She let her gaze drift down his torso to avoid looking him straight in the eyes. Instead of acknowledging her pain she said, "All that was ten years ago. I was eighteen at the time. A lot of kids were left without family. I took up the government's offer of career training, landed myself a job as an enforcer in New York, then applied for the Protectorate and was accepted." She sighed before continuing. "Anyhow, all that's the main reason I didn't want that viper killed. I know what it's like to lose family to space flu. Vipers are rare. That makes the vaccine made from their venom scarce. I couldn't see killing it when it could save lives someday. Besides, something told me you'd get that snake out of the suite without any harm done. Although I never counted on your running into those Ussarians."

Still considering her motivation and not wanting to

backtrack to the subject of Ussarians, Keir kept to the topic of her parents. "I understand your request to save the viper now. It was predicated on what you saw inflicted on your family."

She finally added, "I never saw my family actually come down with the symptoms of Vagan Syndrome. My folks lied to me."

He tilted his head. "I don't understand. They lied?"

She nodded. "They went away, telling me they'd only be gone for a short time. They knew they were infected but I didn't. I thought I'd see them again, but they knew I wouldn't. That's one reason I hate people lying to me, Keir. Every time somebody does it, I feel like that helpless kid again."

He felt like the tiniest, dirtiest microbe in the universe. Among the secrets he kept from her, there was still the undisclosed existence of the Lucent Stones. "You've no family left at all?" he asked.

Her tone became light, carefree—almost. "Better not to have any attachments in this job. It's too hard to hide what you do. Too easy to lose friends you make." She wore a semiforced smile when she looked up at him. "Still, I bet it's great to have a really big family to come home to. Maybe you could tell me about them sometime."

After a moment, she held her arms open. "Please, lie back down next to me again. The pain was just starting to go away. I think I can sleep now."

Keir did as she asked, lay next to her and pulled her back into his embrace. Perhaps she really wanted to avoid the subject of family. The horrors of Vagan Syndrome had hit every planet years ago, but civilizations more advanced than Earth had discovered their own cures early on. With the horrors of the disease's symptoms . . . He was left thinking of a young Sagan left with no other family.

He felt her shaking again, and looped one of his legs over the lower half of her body. Her breathing did not steady. She had faced away from him, was crying and trying to hide it; being stunned had aggravated all her inner angst, as it did with everyone who'd ever been blasted by that weapon. He was quite certain she wouldn't have shared something so tragic and intimate about her life but for this fact. Later, Sagan would remember what she'd said and probably regret the revelation.

As he held her—and especially when she again turned to him and snuggled against his chest—he considered their situation. He still felt the strange pull he had since they'd first met. She was what he'd been searching for all his life, but neither of them could or would give up their separate dreams or worlds for the other's sake; he knew that. Still, he wanted her. Oh, how he wanted her. What a strong woman she was, to have endured so much and to have maintained her desire for righteousness. She could have so easily blamed others and taken a lower road for her life's journey.

Around dawn, when she finally began to breathe normally, Keir relaxed and fell asleep alongside her. That was when a strange series of dreams invaded his mind. And as with any dream, he knew what he was seeing wasn't real but was unable to escape. He simply had to ride the visions out.

First he was walking through the ornate, golden-and pink-colored doors of the horror house known as the Brawné Salon for Men. Two women wearing far too much makeup grabbed him and hauled him to a room where there were leather and chain restraints. For some reason unable to fight, he had to endure having his entire body shaved and waxed, exfoliated, then bathed in kelp. Next the garish women took him to another room and tied him down, and a manicurist forced him to have his fingernails painted an electric shade of pink while his toenails were lacquered a pale purple. Both colors clashed with his skin.

This was where Sagan entered the dream sequence, and as she saw him trussed and having makeup applied, she simply sipped some wine and smirked. Rather than help, she actually aided his tormentors by directing them to change his lip gloss to a shade of red with a bluer undertone. They ultimately chose a tint called Desert Viper Burgundy.

Suddenly the dream progressed: Keir was sitting in a chair with his hands and feet bound. All his nails sported mismatching polish. He sat, unable to do anything as a mud pack was applied to his face. Cucumber slices were placed over his eyes. Somehow he could both see what was happening to him and experience it at the same time. A hairstylist came in and rolled his long black hair onto gigantic metal cylinders to give him what the women all referred to as *more lift*. He could neither stop them nor protest their actions, simply waited and prayed for the dream to end and for him to be free from the indignities.

At last the dream makeover was complete, and as he left the salon it was with Sagan beside him. She was wearing her sexy one-piece suit, but he was in a green sequined gown with his hair piled atop his head and sprayed to withstand a gale force wind. A shiny black hovercraft arrived to take them to a ball of some kind. Datron was sitting up front wearing evening attire: what humans referred to as a tuxedo. His wings were groomed and dyed to match his pastel blue outfit. He seemed happy enough, but all Keir wanted was to hide before anyone saw him. Then the dream took an even more bizarre twist.

He was suddenly thrust into a spotlight in front of hundreds of people. There he was: nude and receiving a massage while his audience applauded wildly. He kept thinking that the massage was the only treatment from the salon he'd actually liked. But it certainly hadn't been given while lying on a stage, and certainly not by a bullocky Ussarian masseur with an Ache blaster hung at his side. To make matters worse, the blaster came to life and was singing out of its barrel-shaped mouth . . . off-key. It was one of the same bawdy ditties he'd performed for Sagan.

He finally forced himself awake.

Sagan sat on the edge of the bed with her hand on Keir's bare chest. She'd been watching him for a little while, and his handsome features were contorted as if in pain. He awoke with such a start that she jumped. "Are you okay?" she asked. "You must have been having one hell of a nightmare."

He sat up. "I *am* awake, aren't I?"

She nodded and chewed on her lower lip. "You were mumbling something about your green pumps being too tight. And that you had a run in your nylons."

He lowered his head and momentarily closed his eyes. "I'm going crazy. There's no other explanation."

Sagan tried to suppress a smile. Not that she enjoyed his discomfort, but the challenging of his male ego was somewhat amusing. "It's almost noon. Why don't you grab a quick shower and join Datron and me for a late breakfast?"

He looked up and gently wrapped his fingers around her forearm, clearly concerned. "Are you all right? How do you feel?"

She shrugged. "A little rough, but I'll get over it." Then she cleared her throat, leaned toward him and lowered her voice. "Um . . . there's some body cream on the counter in my bathroom. Help yourself."

He stared at her, clearly confused.

"You were scratching an awful lot. That's what woke

me up half an hour ago." She pointed to his crotch. In his sleep, he'd undone his trousers, which were the only garment he wore.

He looked embarrassed. "Er, sorry, I had no idea I'd undone them."

He stood and fastened the trousers up, and Sagan stood too and moved close to him. She was overcome with contrition. "I shouldn't have taken you and Datron to that damned salon. I'm sorry. Really I am."

He clearly saw humor in the situation, for his manner changed. He joked, "As long as I don't have to wear anything with sequins, I'll get over it."

His smile was too boyishly charming to resist, and she laughed. Standing on her toes, she planted a soft kiss on his jaw, just below the blue star. "I'll be in the main room with Datron when you're done. Holler if you need anything."

Keir stood for a full minute after she left the room, both warmed and stunned by her innocent kiss. She was still in her robe, and he remembered how soft and inviting her luscious body had been next to his. But this kind of thinking was only making his lower body itch more.

Shaking off the strangeness of the moment and his idiotic dream, he went in search of his robe, a hot shower and Sagan's body cream. So far, nothing on Earth had gone right. Nothing but meeting her. And he could have so easily lost her the night before. As he showered and at last made his way out into the suite where breakfast was being delivered by the hotel staff, the events replayed in his mind.

Datron and Sagan themselves sat rehashing events of the previous day. Keir's second-in-command seemed no worse for his encounter with the salon attendants. Perhaps, Keir decided, he was making far too much of the incident.

He bit into a crumbly croissant and pretended to take an interest in the conversation his companions were having. But try as he might, he simply couldn't focus on their plans. Instead, he kept thinking of his dream, and the intersection of that and yesterday's reality was becoming increasingly hazy.

What in the bowels of deepest space is wrong with me?

The door buzzer sounded, but Keir was so deep in thought that he barely noticed when Datron got up to answer. His lieutenant checked, then opened the door.

"It's one of the staff," he told them, taking an envelope from the man on the stoop.

Sagan sighed, then leaned over and touched Keir's hand. "You're really not okay with any of this, are you?" she asked. "You're wearing kind of a spacey look."

He drew himself up and tried to hang on to the last of his pride. "I'll be fine."

"Delivery for you," Datron said, handing Keir a white envelope with expensive silver embossing. Sagan moved closer so she could read whatever the note might say.

Keir tore open the flap and withdrew the message. It was written in very neat and precise cursive. "Seems Electra Galaxy wants me to escort her to the Miss Milky Way mixer," he explained.

"What? Why?" Datron asked. "Do you think she suspects our motives for being here?"

Keir shrugged, tossed the invitation aside and finally pulled his brain together. "I don't know, but I'll need to do as she asks. You take Sagan to the party and I'll meet you both there."

"No," Sagan countered. "We should stick together. The Ussarians—"

"Will be distracted," Keir finished. "I have a plan. Listen."

CHAPTER ELEVEN

Burl knew the truth long before the enforcers now standing at his door told him. "I thank you for your kindness in this matter, and hope it can remain private in light of the competition. We came here for the pageant. My younger brother was to be our planet's representative, but now I shall have to do the duty, as was our agreement with my world's pageant directors," he lied. "This would have been their wish. My brother and cousin both had a desire to see Earth's vast desert, as we have none on our home world of Ussar. But I *was* worried over their failure to return." He pasted a tragic expression on his face. "It was my hope that they were ensconced somewhere with some admiring women."

The sergeant shook his head. "This is quite unfortunate, sir. I wish my contact could have been conducted under more pleasant circumstances. You should also know that we contacted Electra Galaxy. She has strongly suggested the need for tactful handling in this situation, and I'm certain she'll agree with you taking your brother's place. After all, it was an accident that could have happened to anyone. My department has orders not to interfere. I don't see why you shouldn't do exactly as you please. I offer my sincere condolences. Please let us know if we can be of further service." The enforcer shook Burl's outstretched hand, turned and left him to his grief.

Burl waited until the officer was gone; then he vented his anger on the nearest victim by punching that hapless member of his gang in the stomach and screaming for the remaining seven men to get out of the suite.

"That . . . damned . . . Oceanun! He'll pay with his life!" Then he withdrew to his room, where his blood dagger was hidden beneath some clothing in a drawer.

His fury was endless. His little brother, Cardis, and his cousin, Peron, were both dead at the hands of that cunning Oceanun. And somehow the bastard had made the entire incident look like nothing more than two foolish youngsters' bad decision to go flying in unknown terrain at night. Burl took out his knife and prepared himself for the ritual cutting that was his punishment: the loss of a body part. He should never have let the two young men go. They'd vehemently argued their manly right to pursue the Oceanun if he escaped the viper, and had talked Burl into it. And out in the desert they'd been outwitted by a man with more experience and guile.

Burl undressed, then took his ritual knife in his right hand. He knelt before a small altar he, like all Ussarians, carried with him. The bulbous female deity represented in gray stone was the goddess Enerba, the patron mother of all warriors. He spread his legs, lifted his genitalia and maneuvered until his left testicle was in his hand.

"For having failed my kin, I offer this sacrifice," he said. "I pray to you, Enerba, goddess of those who hunt and fight, to give me the strength and wisdom to seek vengeance against a man I now swear as my blood enemy. I name this man as the Oceanun enforcer who killed my kinsmen."

Burl then cut deep. The pain was excruciating, and it

took supreme effort not to cry out. When he was done, his gonad lay in his right hand and the bloody knife dropped to the floor. Fighting the agony, he wrapped his extracted testicle in a black silken cloth and laid it between the spread legs of the idol. Then he proceeded to clean the blood from the marble floor and his knife. Moments afterward, he allowed himself the pleasure of passing out.

Sagan had watched Keir leave the hotel suite fifteen minutes earlier. He'd been splendidly but simply dressed in black leather pants, a kind of loose, blousy shirt that perfectly framed his massive green chest, and his black boots. His long hair had been flowing freely down his back. As she stared at herself now in the mirror and prepared to put on her evening gown, his image occupied her more than her own.

Datron would be here to pick her up soon, she reminded herself. She needed to keep her attention on matters at hand, including their plan to get into the Ussarian suite tonight to plant the tracking device she'd programmed. But her mind kept drifting back to Keir. How could a man of that size and strength move with the grace of a jungle cat? And why couldn't she forget that he was now upstairs with Electra Galaxy in the elegant woman's penthouse apartment. What did Electra want with him? And why wasn't she, Sagan, acting in the guise of his manager, allowed to go with him? The invitation had been issued only to Keir. And Sagan was pretty damned sure no other competitor in the contest had been summoned to the great lady's quarters.

She finally finished dressing and checked the time. Her mind was so set on Keir that she jumped when her computer signaled an incoming communication. The only person who could contact her this way was Lement Snarl, her supervisor. But he'd never done so on any other mission, keeping his silence to assure that her cover remained intact. She wondered why he now felt it necessary.

Quickly opening up the small lid of her computer, she typed in her reception code, then watched her boss's image appear on the screen.

"Sagan, is it safe to communicate?"

"Of course, sir."

"Thank God," he replied. "We've just been informed that there may be a leak at our end. Our operatives here have intercepted some anonymous communiqués from headquarters. They're being sent to someone at the hotel, but that's all we know."

She nodded. "You're right about that leak, sir. I don't have time to go into it now, but we had an eventful evening last night."

"Would it have anything to do with the two dead Ussarians found in the desert? It's being reported that one of them was a Mr. Interstellar Feller competitor. The crash site looked like an accident, but I'm not buying it."

She nodded. "You're correct in that assumption, sir. I need to be brief, but the two dead Ussarians chased Captain Trask into the desert. He was able to outfly them, but found a stolen Ache blaster on their bodies. *Those* blasters were their smuggled cargo. If it weren't for the Oceanun's silence, local cops would be in the hotel investigating the crash and might have searched the Ussarians' quarters by now."

Snarl pounded left his fist into his right hand. "I had my suspicions about that contingent, but didn't dare say anything without more proof."

"We're on it, sir. They may know about us, but we also know about them."

Snarl leaned forward, filling the small computer screen. "If there are any further developments, keep me informed. As with all operations, use only this private link. That should keep your messages safe. And don't let the Ussarians out of your sight. It's quite possible they'll panic, attempt to get those weapons to another planet and sell them elsewhere. We want the buyer, too. We have to find out what the weapons will be used for. I doubt the Ussarians have that full picture."

"What about the leak?" Sagan asked. "How did anyone at HQ know about this mission?"

"As I told you before this assignment began, a handful of my private staff had to be apprised of the situation. I needed their technical expertise at this end. But I suspect one of them might have been bribed." He slammed his hand on his desk. "When I find out who it was, I'll have his balls!"

Sagan grimaced. "No disrespect intended, sir, but can you get to it quickly? We may be running out of time. The Ussarians will want to unload those weapons quickly."

"I'll do my level best, Sagan. Without saying why, I'm interviewing everyone in this building about their whereabouts and their communications lately. We'll eventually get to the bottom of it, but I'm afraid that won't do you much good. Watch your back. If you need anything, call me immediately."

"I will, sir. And don't worry. Captain Trask and I can handle this."

"That's why you're on this case. You think on your feet," he said. "Just make sure that Oceanun knows that *we'll* take custody of the weapons when this is over."

"Yes, sir. I'll make sure he understands who's in charge. Over." She shut off the transmission and sat back in her chair. There was no reason to tell Snarl that Keir planned to destroy the blasters. To her way of thinking, that was the prudent way to deal with this particular cargo. That way, no one could claim ownership. No one could ever use them to harm thousands of innocent people.

Ten minutes later, the buzzer on the suite door

sounded. When she checked, Sagan found Datron waiting outside, resplendent in brown leather pants and boots with a leather halter vest. She grinned, waving him in, and noted how his beautiful white wings had been freshly brushed and groomed, along with his long blond hair.

"You look fantastic," she said. "But I gave you the access code to the door. Why didn't you just come in?"

For a long moment, Datron stared without speaking. "You're stunning. Absolutely divine," he murmured. "That violet gown matches your eyes and—"

"I'll do," she interrupted. "But you haven't answered my question. Just come in. You don't need to ring."

"Um, I didn't think it was a good idea to startle you. Thought you might be jumpy and I didn't feel like getting stunned. Which reminds me." He took her hands in his. "How are you feeling?"

"Better. I don't think I'll do much dancing, but I'll be okay."

"Good. Just let me know if you need any more meds."

She lifted a hand in refusal. "I want my head clear. It's a good bet that since I signed up to be your manager, the Ussarians will assume you're an enforcer as well. We'll all need our wits about us."

"For that reason, I don't think it's a good idea that I spend any more nights in this suite. It puts us all in the same place—"

"Which makes it easier for an attack," she acknowledged.

He moved closer. "Keir can always have my room and I can stay here," he said. "Looking like you do, I don't know if I can trust my captain."

She laughed. "I'm the one who'll be the loser. I was getting used to having *two* attractive men hovering around." She grabbed up a shawl from the back of the sofa that shimmered like her gown. "Shall we go?"

He held out his arm, grinning when she looped her hand through it. He seemed altogether pleased with himself. "Good thing Keir is occupied with Ms. Galaxy," he said. "I'll have you to myself, even if we *are* on duty."

The compliment thrilled her. And if her mind hadn't been on his superior and Electra Galaxy, she could most certainly have enjoyed an evening with Datron. But duty came first. She set the controls of her door scanner to report anything, even an object as small as a flea.

Keir was admiring some rare paintings by the cosmic artist, Rylander. Before dying of extreme old age, the master had composed the most beautiful fully dimensional depictions of stellar events the universe had known. To own even one was a statement of excessive wealth. Here he was, standing in front of an entire collection.

When he'd presented himself at Electra Galaxy's door, a uniformed maid had informed him his hostess would join him shortly—fashionably late, as women of his acquaintance sometimes were. He took no offense, and was having a grand time enjoying the vivid colors and expertise of the magnificent paintings hung within the room. As with music, art was an important subject on Oceanus.

He continued surveying the works as he sipped a glass of champagne the maid had brought him. The paintings served as a momentary outlet for his frustrated emotions. The smugglers and Sagan were constantly on his mind, but the masterfully rendered stars and planets soothed him as nothing else had. He also found rejuvenation in the bubbling beverage he drank.

"Extraordinary, are they not?" a soft voice echoed through the cavernous room.

Keir turned to see a lovely woman dressed in a white evening gown with a plunging neckline. Her platinum-blonde hair was piled loosely on her head and glittering, silvery stones dangled from her ears. He guessed they were Earth diamonds and very costly. "I was admiring someone's taste," he agreed. He saw her green eyes light with enthusiasm, and she moved toward him. Her smile was captivating.

"Electra Galaxy." She introduced herself and held out her right hand. "It's a pleasure to meet you."

Instead of shaking, as he was sure she expected, Keir turned her hand over and kissed its back. "Of course. I'd be insane not to know who you are. And I must say the pleasure is all mine."

She held his palm a little longer than necessary, taking time to look him over. "I'm happy to meet a fellow admirer of Rylander's work."

"His use of color in a dynamic field is awesome. I have a reproduction of his *Echoes of Nebulae* hanging over my fireplace, but there are some works here I never knew existed."

She was clearly struck by his comment. "Please, feel free to look at anything you like. There are some sculptures in the living room that are free-form composites of gem material. They're all done by Earth artists, none as yet famous. I like patronizing up-and-coming talent as well as collecting works of the masters."

Keir followed his hostess into the living room, still wondering at the point of their meeting. "These are brilliant," he remarked when the sparkling statues of starlike clusters and planets came into view. But it was time to get down to business. He took another sip of his champagne and squarely faced her. "I was wondering why you asked me to see you, Ms. Galaxy. Something tells me you don't require my insight concerning your art."

She nodded and smiled. "Call me Electra. And you're right. I didn't bring you here to look over my pieces. To get to the point, I wanted to meet an Oceanun and ask some questions that may, at the outset, seem blunt."

He raised an eyebrow. "I've nothing to hide."

The blonde walked to a nearby bar, poured herself some gin, then faced him. "Why are you here?"

The question was direct indeed, but Keir was careful to show no outward response. "For the same reason as all the other contestants," he said. "I'd like a shot at the title."

She snorted. "That's crap! You and I both know it, so don't lie to me, Mr. Trask. Oceanuns would as soon cut their hearts out as participate in a beauty pageant, whether it was for males or females and no matter what the monetary gain." She moved closer, stood within inches of him. "Now, I'll ask again. Why are you here?"

Her questions, while straight to the point, weren't aggressively asked. For that reason, he responded jovially. "It's true, some of my fellow Oceanuns are above such pursuits. But far more are not so judgmental. It was my intention to address some stereotypes about my world, especially since my planet and yours are attempting to enter into trade agreements. The competition seemed a way for me to experience some of your culture, as well as a way to expose myself, as an Oceanun, to the billions who'll witness the pageant. We aren't all the pretentious elitists we're made out to be." He remembered those very words being used by Sagan when he'd first arrived.

Electra sipped her gin. "I see. Your aim is to break your planet's image by trading on ours."

He laughed. "Something like that."

She stared at him. "You'll forgive me if I still don't buy that story, but to each his own." After a pause she smiled. "I have to admit that I'm glad you're here. Your presence lends a dignity to my business efforts you can't imagine. I've already picked up several more sponsors besides Pluto Pillow Mints."

"So . . . has your curiosity about me been satisfied?" he asked.

"Far from it." She put her hand on the bared vee of his chest. "I'd like to spend a lot more time with you personally."

"And will that help or hinder my chances?" he asked.

She trailed one finger down his sternum, right between his pectorals. "I pick the judges . . . but they pick the finalists and ultimately the winner. I am simply the producer, and have purposely taken precautions with the rules so as to have nothing to do with the outcome. That keeps things fair." She tilted her head at him. "Does winning mean that much to you? If your aim is only to break a stereotype, that should happen whether you're crowned or not."

"Like my fellow Oceanuns, I like to win," Keir replied. "That's a characteristic most Earthers don't know about my people. But I'll compete fairly or not at all."

Electra Galaxy stared at him. "Something tells me there's more to you than what I'm seeing and hearing, Mr. Trask."

"Call me Keir," he said, and gazed into her sparkling eyes.

"Well . . . Keir. I can definitely tell you that being seen with me will not influence the judges in any way. I run a contest devoid of favoritism. That means you can stay in my apartments or leave and nothing will change as far as your status goes."

He covered her hand with his own and pressed it further into his flesh. "Then I'd like very much to stay. We'll simply be a woman and a man enjoying each other's company. And I'm honored to take you to the mixer tonight."

She made a coy gesture. "I-I'm almost old enough to be your mother. You needn't be publicly seen with me if—"

"What nonsense," he interrupted. "Beauty knows no age. And I know twice now what I did as a boy."

"What is that supposed to mean?"

He wrapped his arm around her. "That a woman of

maturity knows how to please a man in a thousand ways a younger partner has yet to learn. And I'm not just speaking about the sexual side of a relationship, but the spiritual as well."

"Y-You have quite a way with words," she responded breathlessly.

"A beautiful woman is a beautiful woman. Age makes no difference." And the comment was true because it was the way he felt. His own mother still attracted men of his own age or younger, which left Keir's father continually fighting jealousy. It also made his parents' lovemaking that much more passionate, which was why his family was so large.

Electra smiled up at him. "We'll be late for the party and I have announcements to make. I'll just get my wrap."

As the pageant diva walked away, Keir was once again floored by the people of Earth. Electra Galaxy was a brilliant and wise woman. She knew she was still stunning, and didn't need him to say so; she was testing him. She also knew his excuse for joining the competition was feeble at best. But she'd dismissed her misgivings and was willing to let him be. Again, he found himself questioning his people's previous judgment of Earthlings.

He tried to divide his thoughts between the night's party and the job he had to do. Everything kept mingling in his brain, making his task all the harder. Where did the acting start and the sincerity begin? He was beginning to lose track, and that wasn't like him.

When Electra returned, he offered her his arm and they made their way to the main ballroom on the first floor of the hotel. Hundreds of men and Miss Milky Way contestants crowded into the large space, making it seem very intimate. The room was unusually ornate, but tasteful. The black carpet was a perfect foil for the silver columns and ceiling decor. A magnificent crystal chandelier sparkled overhead, and a full orchestra played classical music Keir recognized.

As if on cue, the lights dimmed when Electra entered the room and artificial candlelight summoned a more romantic atmosphere. Everyone had to have seen them arrive together; all eyes had been trained on the door.

Keir found himself looking for Datron and Sagan so that this charade could begin for real. Instead of finding his friends, he spotted the Ussarian. The man also spotted him. The glares the two openly exchanged were telling: Neither was playing a hiding game any longer. And while the Ussarian limped, his face showed his fixation on vengeance.

When a pageant coordinator waylaid Electra and she excused herself to take care of some minor detail, Keir stood his ground and awaited the Ussarian. In a room full of people, even a man of the smuggler's deviant morality wouldn't be foolish enough to start anything. Or so Keir assumed. That was why he'd have to start something.

"I am Burl of Ussar," the villain growled, barely audible above the hubbub. "We've no need for games, Oceanun." He moved closer. "You killed my younger brother and cousin."

"You sent them to kill *me*," Keir responded. "And you're a thief. You'd also sink so low as to plant a poisonous reptile in a woman's room. But hurting others is what criminals do. That's why I'm here to stop you. I intend to take you and your men back to Lucent in irons, before you harm anyone else."

"You, that Earth woman and the Valkyrian are no match for me and my warriors. We know you all work together, so I will make but one promise and shorten this conversation. Your life is already forfeit. If your comrades get in my way, I promise they will also die. Do not put their blood on your hands, Oceanun. Do not bring innocent lives into our fight."

Those words infuriated Keir. "I suppose that viper was supposed to know who was and wasn't innocent?" He grimaced at the Ussarian as if Burl were some sort of insect or reptile. "You don't care who's blameless. You'll never keep any promise you make. Ussarians can't spell honor, let alone live by it. You'll kill me at all costs, and nothing will stop that."

Burl looked ready to put his hands around Keir's neck. "As you have correctly surmised, I have sworn a blood oath to kill you. You *will* pay for my lost kin. But our struggle will remain between us . . . for now. And we will see who speaks of honor when all is said and done."

Keir had intended to goad Burl, but he had not quite succeeded. He regretted his next words, as maligning the dead was beneath him. "Your brother and cousin chose an ambush instead of a noble, face-to-face fight. By your traditions, they'll never reach the afterlife. They'll be branded cowards and forever shunned."

That did it. He saw the Ussarian's meaty fist come up, and he ducked just in time.

CHAPTER TWELVE

From across the room, Sagan had seen Keir enter with the beaming Electra Galaxy on his arm. Some benevolent source had perfectly timed the diva's exit, and Keir now had his opportunity to start a fight. His plan was evolving perfectly, down to the predictable blow the Ussarian threw.

She'd already ascertained the Ussarian's name and room number from the pageant registration lists. As she moved through the crowds toward the lobby computer, she saw Datron slip out of the ballroom. Everyone's attention was on Keir, who was slowly circling the Ussarian warrior.

The Oceanun attacked, and Sagan saw Burl fly backward, into a nearby table. Contestants and women alike screamed and scrambled out of the way. Having left the ballroom proper, Sagan could still see the fisticuffs through the open doors. Her hand made contact with the nearest wall communication panel, punching in the Ussarian room number even as the fight revved up.

A strong, rather unfriendly voice sounded on the other end, and Sagan began her rehearsed speech. She purposely made herself sound rather clueless but breathlessly excited. "Um, are you one of the Ussarians?" she asked.

"I am. And who is this?" the voice asked.

"I'm Miss Aurora Borealis. I got your room number from one of your friends in the bar a couple of days ago. You might want to get down to the main ballroom fast. One of your people is getting the living crap beat out of him by an Oceanun." There was a momentary silence on the other end of the line. She wasn't sure everyone in Burl's group would come, but then she heard a commotion from the other end of the speaker.

"Down in the main ballroom, you say?" the voice demanded.

"That's right. One of your men did me a huge favor in the bar the other night. I thought I'd return it."

"We'll be right down," the Ussarian replied. The connection went dead and Sagan couldn't hide her smile. It seemed Burl's clan would respond exactly as Keir believed.

Following her part of the plan, she quickly punched in a four-digit code from the same lobby computer, connecting to her laptop. Her suite equipment was loaded with the proper video splicing program and ready to go. That data would gently loop into the security system in the Ussarians' hallway. If all the hotel security guards weren't occupied with stopping the battle now raging, the ones left to monitor the cameras would see nothing but an empty hallway on the Ussarians' floor. But that loop would only last for the next fifteen minutes. That was all the time Datron had to search the Ussarian quarters, but first he had to wait for the coast to be clear.

Sagan paused. Everything was proceeding perfectly, but part of this scheme puzzled her. Keir had wanted Datron to start the fight so *he* could be the one to search Burl's suite, though it had made more sense for Keir to be the fighter, as he was the one who'd disposed of Burl's clansmen. Her Oceanun counterpart had only relented because Sagan refused to go ahead with the plan unless things went down that way, especially after her tall green comrade was sent to answer Electra Galaxy's summons. Still, Keir had been angered by the switch and Datron had looked surprised. This had given Sagan the creepy feeling that Keir was still hiding something.

Regardless, her part in the plan was finished successfully, and all she had to do was send a signal to Datron through his arm cuff: a tiny, almost indistinguishable laser pulsing on the inside of his arm.

She quickly counted the arriving Ussarian warriors. All of the remaining seven had come, if hotel records were correct. If there were any others, Datron would have to take care of them, but she was willing to bet they'd all registered as Earth visitation law required. After smuggling those blasters all the way here, they wouldn't be so foolish as to have local enforcers question them for a minor registration infraction. The security rules might have been bent for contestants traveling to Earth, but they wouldn't be for failure to register as visitors once they were here.

Done with her part, Sagan sauntered back into the ballroom. There was a huge circle around the continued battle. Keir's fight with Burl had moved to the far end of the room, and Sagan could no longer see what was happening clearly so she pushed to the front.

When Keir received a blow he dealt one in return. If he received three, he likewise delivered the same. Burl matched his size and strength, but the man was angry, which put Keir at a disadvantage. Sagan believed Keir could take out the Ussarian at any time, but that wasn't the point; the fight had to last until the other Ussarians could get there and Datron found those weapons.

There was a commotion to Keir's left. Burl's warriors had finally arrived, and were pushing through the crowd of bystanders. "I see your cowardice—calling for your men," Keir taunted. Every word was in English so the crowd could hear and understand. "But that's all right. I'll take you all on. Since you began this fight, I'll finish it."

Sagan surreptitiously checked her wrist bracelet to gauge the time. Directly across from where she now stood, hotel security was appearing with Electra Galaxy. As some of the woman's entourage would surely attempt to stop the fight, Sagan sidled up next to a woman with short, silver-blue curls and audibly commented, "Looks like my guy can take on the entire Ussarian contingent all by himself." As she hoped, the remark was overheard by an Ussarian just in front of her, and he gestured to his fellow warriors. All of them moved forward as one.

Eight Ussarians, including Burl, were now in the fight. And they were all encircling Keir. Sagan chewed on her lower lip. As big and as strong as the Oceanun was, he couldn't possibly be a match for the entire clan. But the superb show had everyone riveted.

Keir noticed Electra and her uniformed security people moving forward. "Cowards, all!" he called out. "A Ussarian never lived who could fight fairly. Pirates, cutthroats, thieves and brigands!" He spat in Burl's face. The fight escalated.

Sagan winced at the pileup. Even Electra's security personnel would be no match for the brawl now taking place. She saw the pageant diva turn swiftly around and head for the outer hallway on the other side of the room, presumably to get more security officers. Curiously, there'd been a broad smile on the woman's face, and not the look of outrage and concern Sagan expected.

A loud, warlike growl sounded from the middle of the fray, and Sagan turned back just in time to see Keir emerging like a titan. He was in the center of the eight enraged warriors, several of whom were now flying in different directions as he tossed them aside with seeming ease. From that point on, she couldn't move or look away. Keir, with a grin on his face she could only describe as boyishly energized, stood facing his opponents, and the show was riveting. Those who had been discarded now aligned themselves with the others. They stood before him in a single line.

When they attacked, Keir threw one well-aimed punch after another. He side-kicked several attackers as they attempted to come at him from different directions, then put his back to a wall. But finally one of the warriors waved back the others, displaying a large battle knife in his right hand. The crowd gasped and moved back as one.

Sagan was about to jump to his defense when strong but gentle hands held her back. She turned, and beside her was a bald, glittering-white being. He had gills on the sides of his neck, which indicated his planet of origin was the watery world of Silka.

"No, milady. The Oceanun would not want you injured on his behalf. You are his manager, are you not?"

Sagan simply nodded.

"I am Gilla," the creature announced. "Please, stay here."

Sagan held her breath as the Silkan pushed forward into the cleared ring the fighters had made. The warriors were again moving forward, though Burl attempted to get his man to put the knife down. Their anger stoked, they'd clearly forgotten their mission and were bent only on killing Keir, whose expression had grown as dark as his skin. Now his eyes began to glow, as did the star on his cheek.

"The fight remained between the Ussarians and the Oceanun until now," Gilla loudly announced. "But these eight warriors were not the Oceanun's match. He has proven that. Drawing a weapon is not only dishonorable, it is cowardly."

"Stay out of this," Keir growled. Sagan was surprised he refused the help.

Gilla slowly shook his head, approaching the combatants. "The Ussarians have raided my home world one too many times. All you've said about them is true. Now, I bring my own motivation to this fight. The count is now eight to two."

"Eight to three," a large man yelled as he pushed his way forward. "I am Clitus of Arborea. If the Oceanun must fight eight cravens, then I will add my strength to his. Pull what weapons you will, Ussarians. I need none."

This was an outcome Sagan couldn't have foreseen. As long as Keir was holding his own—and he had been—no one wanted to get in the way. But there were those among the contestants who were nodding in agreement. The weapon had been the last straw.

Someone called out, "Put the knife down, you fool!"

"Fight without it or leave," another voice echoed through the room.

Datron would now have had enough time for a thorough search, Sagan believed, and Keir seemed to realize this too. Keir drew the line. He stepped in front of Gilla and Clitus and said, "I'll see no blood shed on my behalf. I threw the first insult and will accept the consequences. Put down your knife, Ussarian. If you do so, perhaps I'll be able to talk the pageant coordinators into filing charges for no more serious infractions than disturbing the peace. We can both walk away and conclude our business another day."

Burl grabbed his weapon-bearing comrade. "Put that down, you fool! We'll all be arrested," he growled, and grabbed the knife from the warrior's hand. He swiftly turned to Keir. "Another day, Oceanun!" Then Burl and his men stormed toward the exit of the room in one group.

Even from a distance, Sagan could see the fighters'

cuts and bruises. Keir himself seemed oblivious that he'd been hurt. But Electra Galaxy had returned with more security guards, and now the pageant diva was in the process of stopping Burl, apparently wanting to question him.

Sagan checked her wristband and saw a small red light blinking there. Quickly squeezing a tiny button made to look like a jeweled ornament, she acknowledged the signal Datron sent. Apparently, he'd found the weapons, planted the bug and was leaving the room. On the way back to the ballroom he'd stop by her suite, check to make sure the spliced hallway surveillance video was off and the usual cameras were back on line. Sagan would now be able to speak on Keir's behalf to keep him from being ejected from the competition. Datron would join them shortly.

She took a deep, thankful breath and walked toward Keir. There was already a crowd of well-wishers, and those merrily commenting on his stand against a race known more for piracy and lawlessness than anything else. To add to the surprising mix of smiling and laughing commentators, the sparkling white Gilla and the redheaded, burly Clitus were shaking Keir's hands and introducing themselves. She'd hoped Keir's predictions about their enemy's behavior were correct. They seemed dead-on. He apparently hadn't achieved his rank or reputation for nothing.

Keir nodded to Sagan as she approached. At the same time, Electra and her security staff fought for room on his other side. With a shrug, he turned toward the older woman. "Electra, I offer my profuse apologies for the outrageous behavior." He bowed his head slightly. "I didn't come here to fight with anyone."

Electra gave Keir a sultry smile. "This isn't the first time a fight has broken out in connection with the pageant, although it's the first time it was ever over something besides who was handsomest." She turned to one of her staff. "Dismiss the security guards and announce that the party will continue. Have the orchestra continue playing, offer another round of champagne and make sure the newspeople get some diluted story. Just tell them two contestants were fighting over which of them was most photogenic."

She returned her attention to Keir. "Shall we go somewhere more secluded? You need to have those cuts and bruises looked after quickly or they'll show up for the competition."

Keir smiled, looped an arm around her back and followed.

Practically ignored, Sagan fought back annoyance and clamped her sagging jaw shut. Turning, she found Gilla and the brawny Clitus standing behind her, smiling. "Hello, I'm Sagan." she said. She held out her hand and Keir's two would-be defenders each took it in turn. Sagan gazed at Gilla for a moment. "How did you know I was Mr. Trask's manager?"

Gilla shrugged. "Everyone knows. The Oceanun has been the topic of discussion since his entry was announced. It is unusual that one of his race would join such a competition. In fact, one of the staff even told me that you were the person who had paid his entrance fees. That an Earther would be chosen as his manager is even more extraordinary!"

"Quite," Clitus added. "We were under the impression that Oceanus wanted nothing to do with Earth since their trade agreements broke off."

She'd bargained on gossip, but not this much. "Actually, I applied for the position of Mr. Trask's manager when I learned he was interested in the competition. Managing him will build a reputation for me that I hope to use as a bargaining chip during next season's festivities. I'm also managing the Valkyrian contestant."

Gilla nodded. "We heard this as well."

"Would you care to join us?" Clitus offered, and politely held out his arm for her. "It would seem your contestant has found other pursuits, and a beautiful lady such as you shouldn't be left alone. Such a gesture was ill done by the Oceanun."

His last comment was made with a smile, and Sagan took it as the joke he probably meant. She readily took Clitus's arm—and Gilla's when he, too, offered to escort her to a dimmer corner of the room. Everyone around them was laughing, and the party was getting back to normal. The elegantly gowned women especially seemed exuberant. They were probably making up for lost time with the contestants. As Miss Milky Way competitors, they'd be judged on their poise during this mixer, whereas the men's competition wouldn't start until the next day. Sagan silently hoped Keir would keep those upcoming contests in mind as he kissed up to the lovely and powerful Electra Galaxy. For some odd reason, she found herself horribly jealous.

Datron soon made his appearance in the ballroom and covertly nodded to Sagan. She waved him toward her little group and introduced him to the sparkling white being from Silka and the large forester from Arborea. She didn't lack for handsome company, but worried about Keir's missing presence. It was rumored that Electra occasionally dipped into the contestant pool for recreational purposes, and they still had a job to do. They had to discuss whatever Datron had found in the Ussarian suite. Sagan's concern was amplified when the Valkyrian leaned close during a noisier number the orchestra struck up.

"We seriously need to talk," he murmured, and gazed about the room. "Where's Keir?"

"With Electra. I don't know when he'll show up again. He just walked off with her, and I could hardly say anything with everyone watching. The fight had just ended and it seemed prudent to let him go."

"Not as if you could stop him," Datron consoled her. "Besides, he's probably got something up his sleeve. We'll talk later."

Gilla and Clitus had just returned from the bar and were anxious to make friends, and Sagan and Datron both leaned smilingly forward to accept drinks. Sagan's opinion of some of the men in the competition had changed, due in no small measure to her two new acquaintances and their insistence on helping a stranger. Both Gilla's and Clitus's worlds had been ravaged in the past by Ussarian pirates. That her two new friends were supposed to leave politics behind but had tossed that premise aside to stand up for an unknown Oceanun was seemingly lost on Keir. He should be present now, buying them drinks and not snuggling up with Electra Galaxy. On Keir's behalf, she stopped a passing waitress and ordered several more rounds for her comrades. If Keir couldn't be here to play the part of the grateful contestant making new friends, she'd just have to do so for him. But a slow, simmering anger over his having walked away from the mixer began to burn. And she didn't think it was going to be quenched by any solicitous explanations.

Keir took off his shirt and waited while Electra ordered her maid to fetch a small suture laser and a cool cloth. When the maid returned with those, he was surprised by his hostess's comment.

"You can have the evening off, Diana. I won't need you," the woman said, picking up her medical equipment and standing in front of Keir. She pointed. "Sit down in that chair and let me have a look at you."

Keir nodded and took the seat she offered.

Electra knelt before him and chose the medical equipment she'd use first.

"This isn't necessary," he remarked. "My manager can take care of the cuts. And I'm liable to get blood on your gown."

"Don't you worry about my clothes; I can assure you I won't. And it's my pleasure to see to your needs . . . *whatever* they may be," she softly suggested, and gave him an amazing come-hither look.

Keir suddenly had no doubt that she was going to ask him to stay the night. And since she'd already told him that her attention wouldn't matter as far as the judges were concerned, he couldn't use a fear of gossip as an excuse to leave. "My companions will wonder where I am," he remarked.

"Leave a message for them. You'll be back by morning."

Her touch was genuinely tender as she simultaneously held the cool cloth to parts of his bruised face and cauterized his wounds. Though his attraction to her wasn't as strong as that for Sagan, he certainly wasn't disturbed by the idea of sharing a warm bed with this willing woman. Still, Sagan kept coming to mind. She'd be furious. Or worse, she wouldn't give a damn at all, and the thought of that second development was even less to his liking.

He put his hands over Electra's, stopping her ministrations for a moment. "I can't stay. I wish with all my heart that I could, but my manager is already angry with me for my failure to practice my talent and model for her in a way she finds acceptable. And I can't tell how irate she'll be over the fight. If I'm not back in my room, there'll be what you humans call 'hell to pay.' Besides all that, tomorrow is the photogenic competition. It'll be all I can do to get the bruises covered so I can compete."

Electra studied him for a very long moment. "Why don't I believe a thing you're saying? I hear the words coming out of your mouth, but the idea of you primping and posing just to win some contest prizes, albeit very costly ones, doesn't strike me as real."

Again, Keir was taken aback with these Earth women and their propensity to dig out the truth. "But, this is *your* contest. You sponsored it. Why would you have such a patronizing opinion of the competitors?"

"Some are here for very genuine reasons. They want to better themselves and will admit to desiring their fifteen minutes of fame. Others are honest enough to declare they want the money and the luxury that comes with the winnings. Some, such as you, come to this competition hiding something. You and the Ussarians fit here as much as an asteroid fits in the setting of one of my rings. There's something between you, and was before you ever got here."

He was quick on the defense. "I simply want to rid Earth of any preconceived notions about my planet and—"

"Don't start that crap again. There are a thousand different ways you could discourage any ongoing stereotypes about your world. A man like you doesn't show up on my doorstep without a good reason. I don't care for the Ussarians or their motivations, only yours." She leaned toward him. "Why are you here? I've asked you before, but I want a straight answer now."

"Why do you care?"

She began treating his cuts again. "Suffice it to say you intrigue me. I think I was never more impressed with a man than when I saw you standing there fighting off eight brutish Ussarians by yourself. You looked like you'd done such a thing before, on some other planet in some other circumstance. You handle yourself like a trained fighter. And that manager of yours has never been heard of. We have a lot like her who show up every year, hoping to cash in on their clients' winnings. But she has . . . I don't know. From the brief glimpse I got of her, I got the definite impression she was about to stand right beside you and fight. Beauty pageant managers don't usually show that kind of steel."

Keir remembered the brief, fiery flash he'd seen in Sagan's eyes as she'd rushed toward him after the fight. He'd only had a glimpse of the lovely gown she wore and wished he could be with her right at that moment. He could say no more to Electra. She already had him pegged as acting out a role.

"Stay with me tonight and I won't say another word about it. And I won't ask you back to my apartment. You can have your illusion of a competition, and I'll have my memory of a night in bed with a real man."

He stared into her green eyes. "I won't lie to you. I have needs, but I dislike using a woman simply to slake them." He sighed heavily and momentarily closed his eyes in thought. "When I was on some distant planet where favors were offered in exchange for money, I took that deal readily enough. I now know what those women might have felt despite their assurances to the contrary. Sex should be shared by those who desire it for passion's sake. Not by anyone seeking to pay or simply for the expediency of the moment. The act is too important . . . too precious." He paused. "It's as if you're now offering me the position of being the whore, and I don't like it. Whatever my reasons for being here, I despise being made such an offer only to be tossed aside like refuse afterward." He looked into the distance.

"You sound as if this has already happened," Electra commented. "Perhaps that lovely little manager of yours is asking too much of you as well? Or you want more than *she's* willing to give. Is that it?"

"She has nothing to do with this," he quickly denied.

Electra placed both her hands on either side of his face. "I'm not a woman who likes to beg. I usually get what I ask for. And if you give with wholeheartedness, I'll give with the same unreserved enthusiasm. You won't regret the evening. I can promise you no more questions about your business here. But I damned well know you don't give a rat's butt about this competition. Not really."

It was sleep with her or endure further attempts to find out the truth. A woman of her power and influence could do a lot of damage while digging into his past. The Ussarians knew who he was, but the rest of Earth didn't. He'd sworn to keep the Ache blasters and the existence of the Lucent Stones secret. Lucent, Earth and Oceanus depended upon his acting with tact.

"Keir, you're thinking far too deeply about this. Just stay with me. Tomorrow, and every day afterward, we'll just be friends. That's really all I want."

"You ask friends to sleep with you?"

She mischievously grinned. "Actually, I do from time to time. But they don't balk the way you do." Her smile faded and she dropped her chin. "Am I that old and unappealing?"

He let out a slow, long breath. "You most certainly are not and you well know it. I . . . just don't want anyone hurt by what I do."

"No one will know unless you say something. I don't kiss and tell," she announced, and leaned into him.

Keir opened his mouth for the taste of her tongue against his. His body was already making a mockery of his speech requiring ethical and moral reasons for sex. He was trying to do the right thing. But if that got in the way of his mission, then his credo or his job would have to be compromised. This time, it would be his convictions. He had no right putting his personal beliefs or desires in the way of the mission. Sagan would have to understand. Deep in his heart, he knew she never would.

CHAPTER THIRTEEN

Burl winced in pain as he smoothed on the medicinal balm. The blue paste had numbed his genital area so he could attend the party, but its effects were diminished now; nothing could relieve his agony after rage injected him into that fight. It had been a foolhardy action for which his body was now paying. The Oceanun had known Ussarian traditions and what the blood oath entailed. The bastard had purposely provoked him into that public brawl.

He bit the wooden end of his boot knife to keep from screaming in torment. With each tender stroke of his fingertips, he cursed the enforcer who'd taken the lives of his kin and had forced him into defiling himself in such a way that he might never beget children. On that count, he could only pray to the Goddess that his one remaining testicle held true.

As he would suffer, so would the Oceanun. Trask valued his life, but he also had friends whose lives were more important. If there was a way to harm any of them, Burl would.

He slowly sat up from his bed, yelping in barely controlled agony as he did. A knock sounded on his door.

Rather than stand, he simply cried out, "I told you to leave me alone!"

"Sir, I believe someone has searched our quarters."

Burl forced himself into a standing position, quickly clothed himself but almost blacked out from the effort. He stumbled toward the door and his men standing on the other side. Once in the outer room, he ignored his warriors' efforts to help him walk to where the Ache blasters were stored. He pried open the lid of the closest crate, pushed aside the clothing covering the weapons and could see nothing amiss. "What makes you believe anyone was here, Setus?"

"I carefully placed the bag of stones in that top crate myself," his navigator replied. "The stones are present, but not where I left them. The weapons are also accounted for—save the one your brother and cousin took to kill the Oceanun."

"Then why do you bother me?" Burl demanded.

"Someone has been here. I just have a feeling. The enforcers have access to advanced equipment; they could have come and gone without our being able to detect their presence."

"If that's so, they've only confirmed what they already knew. Until our buyer comes forward to set up a meeting, we can do nothing but guard the cargo and wait."

"Sir, please consider another option," Setus begged.

Hurting and wanting to lie down, Burl rounded on the younger man. "What other option is there? The enforcers will be watching every move we make."

"We could sell the blasters to others. There are those who would pay—"

"Not what we're asking," Burl interrupted. "They'd give us no more than a fraction of what our buyer has offered."

"Sir—"

"Enough, Setus! I'll hear no more," Burl cried out.

"The sale of the goods will take place when our buyer is ready. Until then, you'll all remember the blood oath I've sworn."

Ignoring his men's glances at one another, Burl leaned against the wall and waddled back to his room. Stars were floating in front of his eyes. His remaining testicle was swollen and he needed to urinate. When he made the attempt, however, blood ran down the drain with the small amount of urine he was able to produce. The pain was such that he struck the walls in an attempt to quell it. All he could think about was the reason for the traditional cutting of his body. Keir Trask's name echoed in his brain over and over.

Just before dawn, Keir left the expansive apartment belonging to Electra, made his way off her floor and entered the suite he shared with Sagan. He walked to his room, but a soft voice stopped him as he got to his door.

"Rough night?" Sagan asked.

"You have hearing like a feline," he said, slowly turning to face her.

She looked him over and clearly noted his wild, unkempt look. His shirt was outside his pants and his hair was in complete disarray. She said, "Don't worry. Datron is back in his own room where he belongs. What I have to say will remain between us."

Keir arched one brow and strode purposely toward her. "What's on your mind? We have a busy day ahead."

She put her hands on her hips and glared at him. "Since you weren't here to find out whether Datron succeeded or not, I'd thought you'd at least be curious as to what he found."

There was an accusation in her voice that was all too warranted. Keir had no defense. "Datron always succeeds," was his lame response. "That's why he's my partner and second-in-command. I trust him with my life."

"Is that why you argued against anyone but you entering the Ussarian suite to begin with? If you trust Datron so much, then why did you want to be the one to search those quarters?" She eyed him suspiciously.

"I didn't want anyone being hurt if they should be discovered. It was my risk to take."

"Really? Is that all you were concerned about? Or did you know they were smuggling something else besides Ache blasters?"

Taken aback by her words, Keir could only stare down at her.

"Datron found some kind of gemstones in one of the crates. You never said anything about stolen jewels. Not to either of us."

"It's likely they were taken from some other source and are being used to finance the smuggling operations," he suggested, but she clearly didn't buy it.

"What else are you hiding? You told me there were no more secret aspects of this mission. You *swore* it."

"I said that you knew everything Datron did."

"So, semantics makes a lie all right?" she bit out.

"I'm tired. We'll speak of this later, when I can talk to you and Datron at the same time." He turned to leave, but she gracefully but forcefully positioned herself in front of him.

"Did Electra wear you out?" she asked. "Since when is it okay to go off mission to lay a woman who's old enough to be your mother? Where's all that professionalism you flaunt? Why weren't you here to help Datron and me plan our next course of action?"

He shook his head. "Stow it, Sagan. I'm not in the mood."

She ignored his tone and deepening color. "I hope she was damned good. Because we've got a lot to get through, and if there's one more repeat of last night's antics, I swear to God I'll have you thrown—"

"On the next transport off this planet! I know, I've heard it before," he angrily finished. Gripping her by the shoulders he pulled her toward him. "If you recall, it was my plan that got Datron into that damned room to begin with. I didn't plan the rest. What happened afterward was out of my control."

"Oh, there's a new one. 'I *had* to sleep with that woman. She *made* me do it!'" she mimicked. "Christ, that's the worst excuse I've ever heard in my life."

Once again, as on so many occasions, Keir found himself almost staggered by his sudden and uncontrollable desire for her. Even at her worst, he wanted her. "I don't owe you any explanation for what I did. But try to understand that it was necessary."

"Are you gonna blame me now? Because I wasn't giving you a piece of ass, you fell into bed with Electra?"

"I never wanted what you so sadly refer to as a 'piece of ass.' I wanted *you*. Electra has nothing to do with us."

She spoke her next words slowly and precisely: "There is no *us*, Mister, and there never will be. As soon as we close in on that buyer and put the smugglers on your ship, you're off this planet for the rest of your life. And don't let the star gate hit you in the ass on your way out of the solar system!" She stormed away, slamming her bedroom door behind her.

For one brief instant, Keir wanted to wring her pretty neck. Then, an incredible wave of emotion swept over and through him. He felt a curious mixture of both anticipation and euphoria. Why was she so angry? Her ire had started with his not being present for the debriefing after Datron's mission. Then the rage had been directed at Electra and himself. Sagan's animosity seemed more rooted in what he'd done in Electra's apartment than in the course of the mission, or in the fact that Datron had found what she thankfully believed to be simple gemstones in those blaster crates.

He stood there thinking for a long moment, and then actually smiled. She was jealous! That was the only conclusion he could glean from her behavior. A vain assumption it might be, but the signs were all there. And with that discovery, he sauntered happily to his room for some much needed rest.

By noon the next day, Sagan had squelched her desire to kick Keir in the butt. Mostly. Her size-six foot wouldn't make much of an impact, even if it would make her feel damned better.

She'd just finished eating breakfast with Datron, as he'd described how he'd placed the bug on the blaster crates and that it couldn't be detected by anyone not knowing where to look. Datron's armband, along with Keir's and her own, would now register any movement of the crates from their location. All they had to do was wait for Mr. Big—whoever he or she was—to make an appearance.

Sagan hadn't told either of her comrades that Overchief Snarl had made contact. It was a supreme humiliation that any Earth Protectorate officer would betray his fellows to the Ussarians the way this operation had been betrayed. Remembering how Keir had kept secrets himself, Sagan decided to protect that bit of news until such time as it was warranted. After all, Snarl might be wrong. There might be some other excuse for the Ussarians having broken their cover. Thinking through these and other issues while listening to Datron, Sagan was in the process of pouring him some herbal tea when the man she was silently naming "the big green hemorrhoid" made an appearance.

"Good morning." He addressed them both, smiling as he took a seat beside Datron and helped himself to some fruit and cheese. "Ready for the photogenic competition? That's today, isn't it?"

"Speaking of which," Datron said, "we're both on the

competition schedule for this afternoon. We're among the last group to be called in front of the cameras. There's been no sign of Burl and the other Ussarians, but Sagan tells me they'll either have to compete or explain why."

Without looking at her nemesis, Sagan explained: "Burl was supposed to have been downstairs this morning. No one has seen him. Electra's staff left messages for all contestants, giving any of those who partied too hard last night one last chance at the photo competition this afternoon—the same time as you're scheduled. If Burl doesn't show, he'll be eliminated from the competition. Something tells me that isn't going to happen. I'll bet money I don't have that he's going to make an appearance when you do." She glared at Keir as she made the last comment, slammed a filled teacup down on the table in front of him.

Keir glanced at Datron, who was clearly trying to keep from laughing. He seemed to get a little smirk himself. "You'll be there for the photo shoot, won't you, Sagan?" he asked. She couldn't tell if he was baiting her.

She bit back a suggestion that Electra should score today's competition, regarding how photogenic he was, since she had seen him up close and personal all night, but pride kept her from going that far. Instead she said, "Will you take the rest of this competition more seriously? You and Datron have to final," she reminded them.

Keir donned a more appropriate expression. "I intend to compete with my full interest in the project. But I'll need you present."

Suspicion overwhelmed her. "Why? You can stand in front of a camera by yourself. Both of you can."

"Leave me out of this," Datron interjected. "I'm fine either way." He leaned back in his chair, amused by all the tension in the air.

Keir sipped his tea before answering; then he winked at Datron while he thought Sagan had her attention on the competition schedule in her lap. "The rules say that at any time during the pageant I can use any props I need, just so long as I provide the main entertainment or focus of each competition. Isn't that so?"

Sagan put down the schedule and stared at him. "Your point is?"

Her question was asked with such foreboding that both Datron and Keir burst into laughter.

Keir finally stifled his mirth, and took on a more stoic air. "I just need you to be there, Sagan. What if I suddenly need a prop? And . . . it'll look better if you're present when both of us go downstairs. You're supposed to be our manager," he reminded her.

She almost snorted in disbelief. "A prop? And who'll be watching the Ussarians?" she asked, glaring between both men. "Even with the bug in place, I think their suite should be monitored."

"As you suggested," Keir replied, "it's likely Burl will want to start something with me again. He won't stop until he sees his blood oath to an end. For that reason, more than any, I think it highly unlikely he or his clan will move those blasters. I just imagine he now has another fixation."

"That's likely," Datron spoke up. "They're single-minded beings when it comes to their oaths. Burl will see Keir dead or he'll never be able to go back to his home world with any honor. Such honor as he ever had."

"That makes him unpredictable," she immediately countered. "We aren't here to play games with that Ussarian idiot. All we want is to place the smugglers and the buyer under arrest at the same time. Who knows what Burl will do during the competition to avenge his dead clansmen? Some innocent bystander might get hurt. This puts us in a whole new bind!" she realized. "I was hoping we could just avoid him until he was ready to make the sale."

Keir put his hand over hers. "Don't worry. I know his type. Burl wants to fight *me*; no one else. And after last night, he won't risk being placed under arrest. No matter how obsessed he becomes, he'll pick a more private spot for our next confrontation. Until then, he'll try to embarrass me as much as he can. That's why I'm sure he'll show up at the competition with his men. Now, will you accompany us to the photo contest or not?"

Datron's voice became coaxing. "It'll look more convincing, Sagan—our cover, I mean. All you have to do is just stand in the background while we do whatever we're instructed. However odious those instructions might be."

She glanced from one man to the other. The Valkyrian seemed open and genuine about his request, but Keir was up to something that she was sure to regret. Exhaling slowly she said, "Oh, all right. But no screwing around. Act like you're totally serious about what you're doing," she warned, and menacingly held up one finger. "Whatever you do will be recorded for the judges, and they'll know if you aren't earnest. After last night, we're probably not the favorites to win."

Keir shot her an innocent expression. "Whatever we have to do to honor our deal with the Protectorate."

Sagan sat chewing her bottom lip while the men went their separate ways to dress for the contest.

"The pain isn't so bad now. At least I can walk, where I couldn't this morning," Burl muttered to Setus. He gently massaged his genitalia, hoping to make the swelling diminish. "I can't miss any further appointments or we'll be asked to leave the competition. If that happens, our buyer will be angered by the change of plans. Being ejected from the pageant will make us conspicuous. The authorities may check our baggage more thoroughly than when we arrived."

"Then, you'll continue the competition on behalf of your sibling, sir?"

Burl nodded "I will. And if I must proceed, I'll best the Oceanun in every way. He'll know public humiliation before I kill him." He paced the length of the room, though it was painful for him to do so.

"In his culture, this competition is already a shameful affair," Setus suggested.

"Yes. But his is a race of competitors. Trask may hold this pageant in contempt, but he'll want to win. It's in his blood." Burl placed both hands against his crotch in an unconscious gesture of protection. "By beating him in this absurd pageant, I'll humble him before the entire universe. Imagine, an Oceanun enforcer being bested by a race they abhor!"

"It'll be a day to remember, sir."

Burl lifted the corner of his lip in contempt. "This, I think, is a better plan than killing him right away. To humble him first is better. But, there's one other thing I'll do before he dies."

"Sir?"

"I'll ravage the woman with him and rip the wings from the Valkyrian's back. All this will the Oceanun see as he takes his last breath," Burl promised.

Setus nodded in agreement. "I think Keir Trask will beg to die after that."

Burl tilted his head and considered that image. "Yes . . . in front of me begging. That's where I want him." For the first time since his kinsmen died and he'd cut off his testicle, Burl actually smiled. "Come, Setus . . . make sure that I can hold off the pain during the competition. I have an Oceanun worm to disgrace."

Keir watched in amusement as Datron primped for the camera and followed the director's commands. The camera crew and judges seemed immensely pleased with the Valkyrian's performance. And, as the winged man stepped off the stage and approached, a muttered oath from him caused Keir even greater personal delight.

"Blood of the gods!" his friend softly swore. "Those Pluto Mints are by far the nastiest things I've ever had in my mouth. I was told they were produced for customers in the Pillowarian star system, but that the manufacturer is toying with new flavors. Foods from that part of space always had a lingering, moldy tang that reminds me of rotting vegetation." He pulled a sour expression at that memory. "Still, there are those in the pageant who seem to find the damned things refreshing. *Unfortunately*, I'm not one of them." He shook his head as if the action could rid him of the foul taste lingering in his mouth. "Orion's balls . . . I need some water! I feel like something old and sick crawled down my throat and laid eggs there."

Keir had to drop his head to keep everyone in the room from seeing the tears of glee in his eyes. "Datron, you need to get off the fence and tell me what you *really* think." He snickered again. "Your disgust aside, you certainly convinced everyone you enjoyed the mints."

Datron frowned. "Yeah, well, after this I'm asking for a damned raise! I at least deserve some kind of award for that acting performance I just put on." He watched Keir laugh harder. "Ohhh, laugh while you can. You'll see what I mean when you take your turn. In our time, we've had to eat some damned nasty things for the sake of diplomacy, but screw me sideways if I ever *think* about putting one of those mints in my mouth again." He stopped and nodded to something behind Keir's back.

Keir turned to see Clitus and Gilla walking toward them. "Good day to you both. Have you competed yet?" he asked, still recovering from his mirth.

"I have," Clitus responded. "Those mints were enough to make me gag. Gilla was kind enough to help me to my room, and to buy me some alcohol to wash out my mouth."

Keir tried not to laugh harder. "Surely they aren't *that* bad."

Gilla lifted a webbed hand. "Have you ever been forced to eat wallow slugs from Armenius? They're small, grayish things with orange eyes and smell rather like festering wounds."

Keir blanched. "That bad?"

"Decidedly." Gilla slowly nodded. "If I had the choice between the two, I'd rather consume the slugs. I simply cannot understand how the Saturnians and the Mystonian contestants raved about them so. But then, they live on planets where sewer vapors are considered cologne." He thought for a moment. "Perhaps it has something to do with our differing biology. Though both those species consume matter through facial orifices, I'm told their tastebuds are located in their butts. I've often wondered how they sit and eat at the same time. Would it be too indelicate to ask?"

Keir shook his head, trying to rid himself of various mental images they were painting. And though they were trying to be gregarious, none of what they relayed was encouraging. Still, there was nothing for it; Pluto Pillow Mints was sponsoring the pageant and wanted their share of exposure.

He was still reeling from their descriptions when Sagan approached. Lovely as she was in her violet, one-piece outfit—with plenty of cleavage showing—he couldn't rid himself of the trepidation the men had put in his mind. His best friend's next reaction didn't help.

"E-Excuse me. I-I have to find a lavatory," Datron stammered, and he ran from the backstage area with his hand over his mouth.

Sagan stared at the retreating Valkyrian's back, then shrugged. She smilingly acknowledged Gilla and Clitus, then held up her schedule to check it again. "You're up after the Sprellian contestant," she told Keir. She was about to say something else, but the lavender, yellow-haired contestant currently on stage ran past, gagging just as Datron had.

Keir had faced many dangers in his life. But if a Sprel-lian warrior—a being fully two feet taller than himself, who could swing a battle-axe such that it could split open the hull of a space vessel—couldn't take the mints, then he was sure he'd make a fool of himself. He turned to Sagan for support and saw a demonic gleam of light in her eyes.

"What's wrong?" she asked innocently. "You don't look so well. In fact, I'd say you were turning green, but . . . seen that, done that," she joked.

Keir was about to tell her he had no intention of filming this commercial to test his photogenic ability if actually eating Pluto Pillow Mints was involved, but then the gazes of both Clitus and Gilla fell on someone behind him, and the teasing expressions on their faces disappeared.

"It's the Ussarian," Gilla announced, moving closer to Keir and keeping his voice low. "Be careful of him, Trask. It's rumored he has taken a blood oath against you. If that's true, he'll do whatever it takes to finish it."

Clitus agreed. "Whatever your fight was about last evening, the Ussarian means to best you at everything. I don't care what brought you to this world or this pageant, but take heed, my friend. This spectacle is now danger-ous for you."

Keir was gratified by their friendly warnings. Gilla and Clitus didn't know that he was already aware of the damned oath, and they were under no obligation to say anything at all. Perhaps the men in this competition were not as shallow as he'd once thought.

He glanced over his shoulder to see Burl glaring at him, his full complement of warriors straggling in behind. There was what could only be described as pure hatred in their expressions. And Keir's two new friends had been astute enough to realize that.

He turned back to them and said, "Wish me luck. I'll venture that swallowing those damned sweets will be much worse than anything that Ussarian can mete out."

"Do not jest concerning a blood oath," Clitus advised.

Sagan stopped Keir, put her hand on his arm and slowly shook her head in warning. "No more fighting. Promise me." The urgent and quiet request was clearly about keeping him from being ejected from the competition. Electra Galaxy might forgive one such transgression, but not another.

He covered her hand. "Don't worry, *shala*. I won't start anything first." A second after he'd said it, he recognized his use of the Oceanun endearment. Roughly translated, it meant *darling*, and was a slip of the tongue probably originating from his deep feelings for her. But she seemed not to notice; her beautiful gaze lit on the Ussarian now approaching.

To his chagrin and amazement, both Clitus and Gilla placed themselves in front of Keir, as if offering protection. It was at that moment Datron reappeared, and he also took up a position between Keir and the Ussarian.

Burl grinned wickedly. "I see you have your protectors well at hand," he sneered. "In the end, they will do you no good."

One of the film crew called the Ussarian's name and began to berate him for being late. Burl walked forward, taking no notice of the man's censure. He smiled benignly at the judges in the audience, then took his place onstage. It only took a moment for him to remove his shirt and pose for their inspection. Every camera angle and light reflected the great mass of musculature that was his to command. Women in the background began to call out his name, and he spoke, expounding on the luscious taste of Pluto Pillow Mints and their ability to make a man even more masculine. He nodded in satisfaction as the performance brought a round of applause from the judges, as well as from many of the Miss Milky Way contestants standing nearby.

Keir watched Burl swallow more mints without even flinching. The Ussarian leader had turned in the exact commercial that the Pluto Pillow Mint company seemed to desire, and from his place in the background Keir could see some business-suited men in the audience nodding and grinning. It seemed that those must be the representatives of the company.

Keir summoned the stamina to outdo his opponent. He hated losing, and would hate it even more so to this enemy.

Burl left the dais, wiping away sweat caused by the hot cameras. He glared at Keir as he passed, looking him in the eyes. "Beat that if you can, Oceanun. Try not to sprain your ego in the process." He walked by with his head up, though he seemed to have an odd gait. The cheers from the audience trailed him into the wings.

"He *is* challenging you," Clitus confirmed. "You must now win this competition, Trask. It is imperative. He must be taken down a few pegs . . . in front of his comrades and the billions who will eventually see this competition when it is aired tonight."

Gilla placed one hand on Keir's shoulder and likewise encouraged him. "There is no one but you who can beat that performance. We wish you luck."

Some inner brick of challenge formed in Keir's core. He felt a magnificent crescendo of nerve enter his body. Demeaning as this would be, he'd do his best.

"It's your turn," Sagan quietly informed him. She stood on her toes and planted a soft kiss right on his facial star. His cheek tingled where her lips had touched. "Good luck."

Keir summoned every bit of acting ability he'd ever laid claim to, and he approached the stage. He knew there were others gathering, including the Ussarians, to watch what the rest of the universe thought would be the humbling of one of its most pretentious snobs. Everyone wanted to know what he, an elitist Oceanun, would do in the way of promoting these disgusting mints. Everyone was full of preconceived notions, and tension was rife.

It was a chance to change some attitudes, and he meant to do it.

CHAPTER FOURTEEN

Keir held his head high and walked onto the dais. The light was so intense that he could no longer see anyone sitting in the auditorium, but a hushed silence followed his entrance. It was as if he was expected to come up with something even more dramatic than what Burl had just presented.

The director approached. "You'll be expected to read the words on the teleprompter, and will have a chance to go over the lines before we begin. Also, if you have any preferences or props you'd like to use, now is the time to let me know."

Keir took a deep breath and turned to view the sky-like background depicted on stage behind him. "Would it be possible to dim the lights and put up some kind of celestial backdrop?" he asked.

"Absolutely," the director said. "I'll find one in my program and display it on the screen behind you. Anything else?"

"No, that will do. Oh . . . and I'd like to include my manager, if possible."

The director nodded. "That's perfectly acceptable. Go ahead and familiarize yourself with the lines. Each script is different, so you won't be using the same one as your competitors. That means there's no point in rehearsing the lines you just heard, if you were. You'll have only a couple of minutes before we film. You'll have only one shot, so make it count. You can go ahead and remove your shirt now."

Keir tried to keep composed as he stripped off his shirt, the same as all the other competitors had. He heard some soft murmurs coming from the Miss Milky Way section, and tried to ignore the women's admiring comments. The thought began to weigh on his mind that his parents didn't know what he was doing; only that he'd been assigned a distant and important mission. After a few months, when this transmission had time to make its way to his home, everyone in his family would see this. He could just imagine his father's embarrassed outburst and his older brothers' refusal to speak to him. But he pushed all that to the back of his brain and kept himself in the present. He had a job to do.

Sagan appeared on the dais. "The stage director said you wanted me?"

"I need you to respond."

"Huh?" she squeaked, and raised her brows in confusion.

"Follow my lead," he murmured. "I need you, Sagan. Please, just do this."

She placed a hand on his chest, and surely could feel how hard his heart was beating. When she did, she smiled up at him and nodded. "Whatever it takes."

Keir turned to the teleprompter, read the lines that were posted there and gulped. Then he steeled himself. The lights went low. A sparkling image of a quarter moon and stars appeared on the backdrop. Keir looked into Sagan's eyes, and took the box of mints the prop man gave him. Making sure the box faced the audience, he opened it and tapped one of the yellowish-green sweets into his hand. Then he paused.

"You can begin anytime," the director advised. "Roll film . . . and action."

Keir gently pulled Sagan toward him. Someone had activated a stage fan to offset the tremendous heat of the overhead lighting, and the breeze gently lifted her long hair off her shoulders. He pretended he was on that beach he'd so wanted to get her to: the one on Oceanus where they were alone under the starlight. He gazed deeply into her eyes, keeping the box prominently displayed toward the camera, and popped the mint in his mouth. It was *disgusting*. But fighting the taste, he slowly dipped Sagan over his left arm. She kept her gaze riveted to his and made her body more pliable.

Keir spoke the line he'd been given. "Pluto Pillow Mints . . . the mints that melt in your mouth and provide an orgasmic moment for your taste buds." He held the box higher with his right hand. Leaning Sagan farther back over his forearm, he stared at her. Then, in one swift move, he swooped in for a kiss. She responded magnificently, long and deep. The kiss went on and on. He almost forgot to stop. But then he remembered where he was and what he was doing, and he finally broke the sweet encounter to look straight into the camera while pulling Sagan deeper into his embrace. The hand with the mint box was still facing forward. "Enjoy the moment," he recited.

Applause broke out across the audience. He could neither see nor hear what was being said, but he didn't care; he turned and kissed Sagan yet again. He could feel her hands running through his long hair. There wasn't a distraction in the galaxy that could rival her touch—or the sensuous look she was now sending him.

"Keep the camera rolling!" someone shouted from the audience.

Keir kept nuzzling Sagan's cheek. She finally tucked her head against his chest and looked into the camera.

"Stupendous!" a loud voice cried out. *"That's* what I want! That's it! That's exactly the mood I want for my product!"

Keir heard the applause continue, and he reluctantly let Sagan go. The lights came back up and a small, rotund gentleman approached from stage left. Keir smiled in acknowledgment. Apparently the sensual, romantic mood he'd created was more appealing than the coarse posing offered by the Ussarian. In his gut, Keir knew he'd won this competition.

Someone tossed his shirt back to him and he slipped the garment on without buttoning it. Some inner voice told him not to worry over what his family and friends back on Oceanus would think. A jubilant Datron, Clitus and Gilla were quickly walking forward to congratulate him. But Keir turned to Sagan and kissed her once more, to the gasps of the women standing nearby.

"I wish I was her," one girl blurted.

"I can't wait to see that footage," said a stagehand. "That kiss was hot as hell. It almost warped the damn camera lens."

The portly gentleman Keir noticed moments earlier finally pushed his way through the crowd. "Sir . . . Mr. Trask . . . I'm Pierpont Horizon, the owner of the Pluto Pillow Mint Company." When the grinning bald man held out his hand, Keir took it and smiled.

"I've been waiting all day to find someone who could illustrate a special moment using my new flavor for Pluto Pillow Mints," Pierpont continued. "It's called Cosmic Catastrophe and will likely be a big hit back home in the Pillowarian Sector. I so very much want to thank you for your interpretation. I'd like to ask you to dine at my table tonight with Electra Galaxy. There'll be an impromptu party for everyone in her private ballroom at eight sharp, but you'll be the special guest of the evening. Everyone else will have to be contacted;

rehearsals will have to be cancelled. But I wanted to extend my personal invitation. We need to make sure you're present. I think we might just have a contract you'd like to look over."

That assured Keir that he'd won. When Pierpont walked away to make his party arrangements, Keir turned to see Sagan smiling up at him. And it suddenly only mattered what she thought; no one else.

She stood on her toes and whispered in his left ear. "That kiss would have rocked my universe more if not for the taste of that damned, revolting mint in your mouth."

He grinned down at her. "Next time, there won't be any." There was a glee in her eyes he found all too engaging, but their private little reverie was soon interrupted.

"We've got a replay," a stagehand yelled.

Keir and the rest of those present turned to the large screen at the back of the stage. The starry, celestial facade faded, and it played the footage he and Sagan had just recorded. As it played, several of the women gasped—including Sagan. Keir felt another thrill of desire.

"Tonight at seven," Pierpont gaily told him. "Electra and I will be expecting you in her suite."

Keir led Sagan offstage and his comrades followed. The joy of the moment was slightly abated when he saw Burl wearing a snarl. The Ussarian leader and his men spoke together in low tones and huffily left the area.

"I cannot tell you how much care to take," Gilla repeated softly. "Please, watch yourself with that one."

Keir took a moment more to speak to his new friends and accept their congratulations. They sauntered off eventually, leaving Sagan, Datron and him alone.

Datron announced an intention of being elsewhere for the evening. "I think it'd be a good idea if I took in the gossip at the bar. Gilla and Clitus will be there, as well as many of the other contestants. If the Ussarians show up, it'll be a surprise. Everyone seems to think they'll hole up in their room and regroup after that beating you just handed them."

A director's assistant walked up and handed Sagan a list. As the smiling woman walked away, offering her congratulations, Sagan began to laugh. "Seems you placed second, Datron. Burl was third. That won't make our little band of Ussarians any happier. You *both* took this round," she crowed.

Immensely pleased, Keir burst out laughing at the surprised, shocked look on his friend's face. "According to the rules, you'll be approached about a contract as well. It might be a good idea if you were in the bar—just to make yourself accessible." He winked.

Datron rolled his eyes and shrugged. "Seems I was forgotten in the rush to sign you up, Keir. Be that as it may, I'll be available." A lovely blonde girl walked by, ran her hands suggestively over his wings. "Um, excuse me. I'm off to shower and get downstairs."

Sagan smiled at the Valkyrian's rapidly retreating figure. She wanted to insist that both men be in the suite watching the Ussarian quarters, but the sponsor would call Datron and Keir to meet him whether she liked it or not. That commercial had been riveting. She herself had been mesmerized. She'd never seen herself on film before, but that wasn't what captured her interest as much as the man she was hanging on. The look in her eyes as she gazed at him had been, in a word, enchanted. His startling blue eyes were hypnotic, especially when he'd looked into the camera and said his lines. The heat of their kiss lingered even now. And she'd been cuddling next to him as if he were the only important thing in life. It had been a little embarrassing for her, but no one seemed surprised that she clung to Keir like a vine

clings to a stone column. And when the camera closed
in on Keir's face, women in the room had gasped. In
truth, she'd only noticed the lingering taste of the foul
candy when the entire scenario had been acted out. All
her attention had been on the man and the moment,
nothing else.

"Guess I'll be the one watching the hall monitors tonight," she said to cover her discomposure.

"We have a date upstairs, in Electra's private ballroom
and—"

She placed her fingers over his lips. "The invitation
was for you. Not me. Besides . . . *someone* has got to
watch the Ussarians, just in case they try something stupid." She stood on her toes and kissed him. "Well done.
If there was any doubt about why you're here, you just
dispersed it."

He sighed heavily and followed her back to the room
in silence. Sagan knew the invitation to dinner was
meant for her as well as him; Pierpont's gaze had included her when the invitation was made, but she was
choosing to ignore it. She didn't think it'd be wise for
them both to go.

When they reached their room, she turned on her
computer and pulled up surveillance of the Ussarian
hallway. Keir seemed about to say something that might
be too personal, so she jokingly turned the comment
aside and asked, "I only got an aftertaste of that mint.
How on God's green earth did you not gag?"

"Curious enough, I don't remember eating it. There
was something else on my mind." His gaze slid over her.
Then he stood and slowly approached. There was a look
on his face that compelled Sagan to stay where she was.

"I want to try that kiss again," he whispered. "Maybe
we could do it better." He lowered his head and gently
pressed his lips to hers.

Despite her reluctance to get too personal earlier, she

now gave in to her desire. She opened her mouth to let her tongue entwine with his. Excitement welled within her, and all thoughts of the mission and contest flew from her consciousness. Keir ran his hands down her back and caressed her bottom, which prompted her to moan and move closer. She looped her hands around his neck and let the kiss deepen, linger and grow more intense. When he finally broke the embrace, it was to walk her back toward her room, still keeping his hands around her waist.

"We have a few hours before we have to be upstairs," he softly said.

"I'm not going with you."

"We'll discuss that later. Right now, we have time for ourselves. Let's make good use of it."

Sagan stopped him, put her hands against his chest and shook her head adamantly. "We're on duty. That comes first."

He ran his hands through her hair, looking deeply into her eyes. "The Ussarians aren't going anywhere. Burl has made it clear that he's fixated on getting even with me. He's not just a smuggler now. He's a man bent on revenge. As long as he keeps that uppermost in his mind, he won't budge. That's the way his people are."

Sagan wasn't convinced. "What if his buyer shows?"

"I have a feeling Burl won't sell to him until this blood oath of his is satisfied. That's the great thing about having him after me. Any race that has a ritual of removing a testicle to—"

She tilted her head in confusion. "You think it's great that he cut off a testicle to swear an oath?"

"Ussarians get crazy that way. In fact, to leave now would probably cost him the loyalty of his crew and his place on his home world. And since I beat him tonight, that's even more reason for him to hate me. He's a man with a mission, and that mission is to destroy me in every way possible. For the last time, I'll stake my life on his not selling those weapons until he's done with me. That being the case, you and I have some unfinished business." He nuzzled her neck and began to plant soft kisses down her throat to her cleavage. Slowly unzipping the one-piece suit she wore, he revealed the lovely, black lace camisole underneath. "Mmmm, you smell like fresh flowers."

Sagan tried to ignore the passion stirring in her abdomen and the way he was taking her every rational thought and destroying it. She did want him, but not until the mission was over and she could leave on her terms. She slipped her hand between his lips and the places he kissed. "I can't. Not until our arrests are made."

He dropped his hands and backed away, clearly frustrated. "I don't believe you. This isn't about the Ussarians or the damned blasters. In fact, I don't think any of your reticence when we get close has anything to do with the mission or your purported desire to remain professional."

She licked her dry lips and tried not to look at him. But his gaze was so compelling that she simply couldn't cast her eyes elsewhere. "It . . . it was something that happened a long time ago."

Keir looked concerned. "What was his name?"

"What makes you think . . . ?" She stopped speaking, unable to deny that there had been anyone else. "Mark," she whispered. "His name was Mark Gallant."

Keir took her hands in his. "Tell me."

"It was a long time ago. I shouldn't have said anything." She tried to pull away, but he kept her hands clasped firmly in his. The warmth of them steadied her.

"Apparently, not long enough."

She tossed her hair over one shoulder and tried to make light of it, but the catch in her voice made her

words sound pitiable, even to her. "He . . . Mark was
with the Protectorate, too. He was sent on a mission to
Mars, where there was a colony setting up on the far
side of the planet. A rebellion was started by some mal-
contents that didn't believe the recent elections there
were democratic. They kept claiming the results of the
Mars council elections were due to voter fraud . . .
mostly because their candidate lost by such a landslide."

Sagan took a deep, shuddering breath, but Keir didn't
interrupt as she'd half hoped, so she finally continued.
"The dissenters kept attacking the oxygen replenish-
ment stations. The main Martian cities were in imminent threat of losing their life support. Mark took the
mission to infiltrate the rebels and find out who was
funding them. Somehow, his cover was blown. The an-
archists killed him. But they didn't do it quickly. They
took him into the wilderness, tied him up and took his
oxygen supply. Mars constables found his body a few
weeks after he lost contact. That was about three years
ago. The worst part was . . . he lied to me, the same way
my folks had. As another Protectorate enforcer, he
could have told me what he was doing, but didn't. And
he swore he'd come back to me, just like my parents did.
The truth was, that mission had a high probability of
failure. Mark kept the danger to himself. The bastard."

Keir briefly closed his eyes, hearing Sagan's pain and beginning to understand her outrage over all deception.
So far, three loved ones had misled and hurt her. And
his lies concerning the smugglers weren't done yet.
That tore him apart.

He quietly said, "You loved this man very much. And
you don't want to get close to another enforcer." For
him, everything made sense now except her stated desire about possibly being with him at the end of their

mission. Then it hit him. After she slept with him, she'd walk away. He'd go back to Oceanus and they'd likely never see each other again. She could make love to him and then leave him? The thought engendered bitterness in his heart he hadn't imagined possible. He let her hands go.

"I-I'm sorry," she said. "But I don't get involved on a long-term basis with enforcers. There's too much to lose."

"Yet you already have feelings for me, Sagan. You can't deny it. Nor will I."

She dropped her head and muttered, "You won't be here much longer."

"So . . . all we could have is a one-night stand? Isn't that what you Earthers call the situation you'd see between us?" he angrily asked.

She finally looked into his face. "As you say, I'm already getting too close to you. I don't want to go any further."

He fought down his rage. "Too late, little Earther. Another of your sayings would apply: You've already crossed that bridge." He pulled her against him again and kissed her with much more intensity than ever before. She resisted, so he bitterly let her go. But when he did, she surprisingly wrapped her long fingers around the nape of his neck and pulled him back down. The second kiss wasn't so harshly delivered, but exquisitely tender. Keir heard himself moan in need. His entire body was on fire for want of her. No other woman had ever elicited such a wild, abandoned response.

"I won't let this drop," he murmured against her hair as she took his earlobe between her lips and gently sucked. "I told you once that'd we'd eventually be a real team. I meant that we'd be able to work together once this passion between us was addressed. We need to give

in to it. You know this. Fight your fears, not the passion," he breathlessly admonished.

Against her better judgment and reason, against all logic
and fear of future pain, Sagan shed her suit and moved
against Keir's chest. As he slipped out of the shirt that was
draped around his frame, her fingers skimmed over all
the muscle, the giant pectorals and smooth body made
smoother with the removal of its hair. Even the fact that
he'd spent the previous night with Electra Galaxy didn't
hold Sagan back. All she wanted was one night with him.
Just one night in his arms and she could try to forget him.
She could try to get back to her work without wondering
what making love to him would be like.

"Keir, I want to know that you're safe to be with. Do
you understand me? I want no regrets or fears afterward," she blurted out in a rasping voice.

He seemed to understand and approve of her question.
"*Shala*, as enforcers we're inoculated against any sexually transmitted diseases, and I'm on birth control meds.
I'm not crazy; neither are you. We're adults. We know
what can go wrong on any mission." He cupped her face
in his hands. "Tell me you trust me. I want to hear you
say it. I would never, ever, do anything that would hurt
you. Never."

She simply nodded and let him kiss her harder,
deeper and longer.

Finally, he maneuvered her toward her room, alter-
nately kissing her and removing an article of clothing at
a time. His boots and hers were kicked off and tossed
aside by the time they made it to the edge of the bed.
She momentarily pushed him away to pull off the black
camisole, but otherwise she never let go of him. He
gasped as her perfectly round, pert breasts came into
view.

Sagan moved back against him, rubbing her chest

against his bare skin. She reveled in the feel of his flesh next to hers. If she would regret what they did, it was best to do all she could. She wanted to be taken in every conceivable way, and on and on until neither of them could walk or move.

Keir moaned in appreciation of Sagan's softness, then lowered his head. As he had during the photo shoot, he bent her over one arm and kissed her. Then he brought his free hand up to caress her breasts. She was his everything. In the short time they'd known each other, they'd shared more than a great many couples did in a lifetime. There had to be some way to keep her with him forever, some way to convince her they were meant to be as one.

He quickly unbuckled his pants and began to shed the rest of his clothing even as she did. He got a quick glimpse of Sagan's perfect little, black-pantied behind as she pulled off the rest of her outfit. When she turned to him and he saw the black lace on the panty front, and how it barely covered anything, he wanted to tear the little garment from her and take her while standing. He was so erect that he couldn't move closer without his shaft getting in the way. But that didn't stop Sagan from surprisingly solving the problem: She knelt in front of him and took him in her mouth.

Keir shuddered hard through the first moments of a sensual pleasure the likes of which he'd never known. Sure that he'd embarrass himself like a young boy and ejaculate too quickly, he took one more moment to savor the wonderful sensation of her tongue, then pulled her up his body and went with his first inclination. He slipped his thumb into the side of the panties and simply ripped them off.

The suddenness of Keir's movement set Sagan off as nothing before. She lifted one long leg up to his hip and wrapped it around his hard waist. The shaft of his erection pressed partly into her, and she cried out at the electricity of the sensation.

"I want you. God, I want you," she gasped.

He placed his hands and arms around her body, lifted her up and laid her across the bed. "This is only a beginning, *shala*. Never doubt that."

From then on, Sagan simply kissed him and stroked his body. Keir was moving like a man possessed and she didn't try to stop him. More to the point, she didn't want to; she wanted to do as he desired. Of course, the heat inside her seared to such a degree that if he didn't end her need soon, she'd find fulfillment on her own.

His hands soothed her body, his tongue laved the center of her pleasure and his voice was low and encouraging. She spread her legs several times, waiting for him to penetrate her, but he would only stroke her or kiss the sensitive skin, readying her for something else. She was about to beg when nothing else worked. That was when he finally moved between her thighs and thrust forward with one, well-aimed jerk. His body was deep inside hers in an instant, and they cried out in unison. The pressure was so perfect. He moved in exactly the right way, circling his hips while still speaking softly.

"Come with me, Sagan. Feel me deep inside you and forget everything but what you want. Listen to the sound of my voice." He gasped, looking overwhelmed. "You're so damned soft. Every inch of you is so perfect and silken. And you're tight . . . so tight that I don't know if I can stand much more."

She kept her gaze on his. He'd turned a dark shade of green; his star was glowing, as were his eyes. "Keep moving in me . . . keep doing just what you're doing," she pleaded.

"There's more, *shala*. Much more," he rasped out. And then, Sagan felt the tip of his manhood begin to turn. It was an exquisite sensation, and her quick intake of breath and startled expression made him stop. "Did that hurt? Do you want me to stop?" he asked in a whisper.

"No. I . . . I had no idea you could do such a thing!"

"You should have researched certain aspects of Ocea-nun sexuality a little more. But never mind. I'll give you a firsthand lesson, if you're willing."

"Yes, keep going," she responded, trying to sound as airy as she could, and closed her eyes as the tip of his penis began to circle inside her once again. She gripped his shoulder, cried out his name and felt a deep orgasm begin from the back of her body. It rolled forward, quick, tight, and with extreme intensity.

Keir felt the motion begin and timed his release to match Sagan's. He had that ability, and wanted to experience this first moment of bliss with her. His release came harder than normal. She was so tight, and squeezing him like a clamp. But the sensation wasn't painful; it was exotic and hot. Her sheath was milking every drop from him, along with the ability to do aught but call out her name even as she cried out his. Within a few seconds, he collapsed his weight on his thighs and elbows. Sagan's fingers were still clawing at his back as the last of her orgasm ebbed away. They were both covered in a fine sheen of sweat, and still deeply connected. He lowered his head to her shoulder and planted small kisses there and on her neck.

"You enchant me, Sagan. I'm bewitched and can never forget you. Not ever."

She smiled, closed her eyes and ran the insides of her thighs up and down the outsides of his hips. "I can still feel how hard you are. Don't let me go. Please, don't let me go."

He growled possessively, wrapped his arms around her slender body and silently swore he'd die before ever leaving her behind. Stroking her body and feeling her whispery soft breath against his shoulders was how he wanted to end his days and awaken each morning. He loved this woman with all his heart. She was in his blood and his mind. And with that realization, there came a sudden idea.

If he won the damned contest, the Protectorate would be hard-pressed to ever have him evicted from the planet, no matter the politics of their individual worlds. Even after the smugglers and villains were arrested, Electra Galaxy wouldn't take kindly to having her champion whisked away. It was standard process that the new Mr. Interstellar Feller would spend one year on Earth, living in a penthouse apartment of the hotel. It was a wild idea, Keir acknowledged, but he was well on his way to accomplishing that very feat. Tomorrow, he had the pose-down and the swimsuit competitions. After that, all there was to endure were the talent competition and interview, then several mixers with the judges.

He pulled Sagan closer and felt her relax in his arms. Sleep seemed to find her easily. Finally moving away enough to see her face, Keir let his gaze wander over her sensuous body and caress each and every curve. He whispered, "You are the life and warmth my heart has craved. Once this mission is over, we'll be together. Never doubt that, little Earther."

She'd be so surprised when he went after the pageant title with a new gusto. But now, there was a reason to win. Even if his planet shunned him for his efforts, he'd have Sagan.

He stretched out next to her, pulled the covers over them both and kissed her. "You don't know it yet, but you're waking up with the next Mr. Interstellar Feller," he murmured, smiling broadly, then snuggling closer to her. They had little time before dinner, but he'd soon put his plot into action. Nothing was keeping him from winning this title.

CHAPTER FIFTEEN

"Shala, *mena dallos encha poorna igns, shala,*" Keir murmured, and turned toward Sagan. She was smoothing cream across the waxed area of his groin in order to stop the itching. He could only assume he'd been scratching in his sleep again. His words, spoken in Oceanun, had been more subconscious than anything else. Basically, he'd just said that she was the most sensual, beautiful woman alive, and that he loved her with all his heart. But she needn't know that. She would run for the hills if she interpreted his sentiment.

"Good evening," she sweetly breathed. "It's almost time to get ready for that dinner party. I'm sure Pierpont Horizon will want everyone to try his mints. That being said, you might want to hold off eating."

He chuckled at the thought of losing his dinner over those vile sweets. "Don't we have anything better to talk about? After all, I just had the best sex of my life. And what you're doing isn't going to get us to Electra's party any sooner."

Sagan stopped creaming his inner thighs, put aside the tube of lotion and wiped her hands on a cloth. She asked, "Did you know you talk in your sleep?"

He sat up. "What did I say?"

His obvious concern made her laugh. "You were speaking in Oceanun."

He let out a tremendous sigh of relief. "Oh. I suppose I must dream in my native language."

"And what were you dreaming?" she asked, leaning into him and planting a small kiss on his lips.

"That's not up for discussion right now, and we still have time to improve our technique. Now, I'll ask again. Don't we have anything better to talk about than that damned party? Aren't you going to ask me about my alien capabilities?" He waggled his brows in a mischievous fashion.

"I think we'll shelve that conversation for another time." She patted his thigh playfully. "Get up, or you'll be late."

With his renewed interest in the competition, he did as she requested, but only because he needed to impress those judges. It occurred to him that his family would never understand his actions, even after explaining he'd started out on a mission that was top secret. How could he explain the complete turnaround in his own mind except for wanting Sagan?

He quickly hopped out of bed, stretching until he noticed Sagan turning away with a look of pure lust on her lovely face. The little she-cat wanted him, but was too afraid of committing to anyone to admit it. Once they got through the next few competitions, he'd sit down with her and have a serious talk in reference to their futures. It simply wasn't possible that she'd ever refuse him.

He left her room so she could dress; otherwise, they'd never make it to the party. His desire for her grew with each moment, and was currently at an almost uncontrollable point. In fact, this was the first time in his life that he'd ever put his concerns and his future before a mission. It felt good to do so. He was tired of being alone, tired of walking into an empty home, and sick of realizing that his life meant no more than the next criminals to chase down. In such a short time, Sagan had completely realigned his motivations. Now, his personal life, including family and friends, would come first.

In her room, Sagan dressed to kill. For her, the party was on after all. She kept telling herself that it shouldn't matter what she wore or who she impressed, but the woman in her—and she had been a woman long before she'd ever been an enforcer—wanted to look special. Keir had ideas in mind that couldn't include her. She could see the homey look in his eyes and didn't want to leave him, but that time would come, sooner or later. His planet would call him home. Hers would eject him. Since the trade talks between their worlds had broken down, it could be years before anyone more important than an Oceanun shuttle crew was allowed to land. She shook off all morbid thoughts and decided to enjoy the moment and to just live in it. There was no changing the future.

Burl limped as he paced yet again. His warriors, now watching as he moved about in agony, wanted to leave the suite and go to the bar. But months of having been cooped up inside their vessel had made them surly as well as restless, and he couldn't risk a single argument between them and any competitor in the pageant.

"Sir . . . may I ask how long we must endure the enforcers' presence? It is dangerous for us to remain here any longer. I say we sell the weapons and stones and leave," Setus insisted once more.

"You've broached the subject too often. If you speak of it once more, I'll assume your tongue is uncontrollable and will remove it from your mouth," Burl growled. He grabbed the younger man by his vest front and swore, "I will see them denigrated, then dead, before we leave. And the payment we were promised from our original buyer will be enough to live on for the next three solar years. It will supply our ship with fuel and our entire clan with the ability to raid planets farther from home."

"The Oceanun makes fools of us—especially you!" Setus snarled. "After the competition today, we will be the punch line of every joke in the known universe. Trask has beaten you. He is too cunning. We must leave now, while there's still time. We should not trust a buyer who has never shown us his face. I smell a trap."

Burl drew back his right arm and struck with all the force he had. The power of the blow knocked Setus— his navigator and the only medical technician he had— off his chair. The others in the group might have wanted to help Setus, but they were too frightened to do so. Burl had to keep them fearful or he'd have no power to command.

"Once and for all, it was your comrades as well as my kin who were killed out there in the desert. They will never see their home world again, and I will have to explain how those two young ones died." He drew himself up to his full height and wiped a drop of sweat from his brow. "If they'd been successful and Trask buried in the desert as planned, other options would be open. As it is, the enforcers know who we are. We can't leave this world without ridding ourselves of all witnesses."

"We could use the stones against them," Setus bravely suggested, wiping blood from his mouth and leaning against a far wall.

Burl glared at him, but went back to pacing. He'd have honored his threat to cut out the youngster's tongue except that Setus was the son of his own little sister. "If we crush the stones, we'll receive little compensation from our buyer. Too little to justify the deaths of our men. Only fourteen have ever been found. I already used part of one on the maid. Had I known about the Oceanun and his people sooner, I could have eliminated these enemies in space. But our informer chose not to make the information available until we landed."

Setus spoke boldly, clearly having had enough. He pulled a long knife from his boot. "I can follow you no longer. You're obsessed with revenge. It was *you* who publicly provoked a fight in the ballroom, and *you* who lost. You lost again today," he snarled. "We have been unmanned in front of billions of sentient beings. Had your younger brother and cousin not wanted to impress you, they would still be alive. You should have gone after Trask yourself and not sent younger warriors to do your job."

He approached Burl, and was aware of how the others made space for him to do so. "We're now trapped in this place, in a situation of your making. We have the blasters and the stones and greatly outnumber the enforcers. I say we attack, kill them and not concern ourselves about witnesses. By attacking when they do not expect it, we can gain ourselves an advantage. Then we could be off the planet in less than an hour." He moved steadily forward. "We cannot trust some unknown buyer who says he'll take our goods at a high price but won't share the risk by showing himself. This entire scenario should have been handled differently. I will not stand by and wait to be captured, incarcerated or killed just to satisfy your twisted need to play both the virile leader and avenger. You have proven you are neither."

Burl stared at Setus with fury. Setus turned to his comrades. "Come with me," the man told them. "We can be on our way home tonight. The enforcers can be dead, and Trask's part in killing our kin will have been avenged. We'll still have the blasters and stones to sell another day, on another planet."

Burl took his opportunity while Setus's back was

turned. Despite his relation to the boy, this betrayal was all he could take. He pulled his own knife from his boot and planted it deeply in the middle of the betrayer's back. A strangled, gurgling sound crept from the younger man's throat, and he fell to the floor in a heap as Burl removed the blade.

"Cover his wounds and use his cloak so he will look drunk. Take him to the desert and bury him. Then, spit on his grave as I spit on his remains." Burl finished his directive by doing just that.

All the warriors slowly stood and gazed down at Setus's body. They clearly realized that he'd been the only other soul besides Burl who could order their onboard computers to plot a course and start their ship's engines. Burl had just ensured his own safety as well as silencing an enemy. They watched Burl as leaned his head at an angle and gazed into the distance.

"Any more questions?" the Ussarian leader asked. "I'll be in my quarters, planning our revenge." Then he left the room, certain that his orders would be followed.

Once he was in private and his door was closed, he quickly shed his trousers and walked to the mirror. Both his cock and his one remaining testicle had turned a curious shade of green and were oozing a substance that both smelled and looked grisly. He'd have to lance the wound and let the infection spill out. To do so, he would use the knife he'd just bloodied. For some reason, that seemed appropriate.

Burl pulled three chairs forward. One of them he positioned in front of the mirror; the other two were set on either side, close enough where he could prop his feet so he could get a good look at what he was doing. Then with Setus's gore still dripping from the weapon, he plunged the tip into his infected wound.

Intense agony overwhelmed him and darkened his world.

Keir was watching Sagan's computer screen when she made her entrance. His attention was immediately pulled from the Ussarian doorway, which was only visible because of his partner's expertise, and he had eyes only for the brilliant, lovely possessor of such technical skill. Tonight, however, she wasn't an enforcer of superior skill or the human who'd totally changed his view concerning her species, but an enticing young beauty he wanted to love. He stood and offered his hand as she glided toward him, elated that she'd finally agreed to accompany him to the party.

"You're exquisite. *Shala, d'methor facdrostan.*" He'd repeated the same phrase in his own language, hoping she'd show both an interest in what he said and in learning more of his ancestry, but she didn't take the bait. He saw her simply smile.

"You, uh . . . are looking very nice yourself," she replied.

He grinned at her attempt to avoid the intense attraction they shared. In the long black halter dress that swept over her figure, she was classically beautiful. It was the first time he'd seen her hair arranged in loose flowing curls down her neck. Part of it was fastened with a sparkling, star-shaped clasp that reminded him how much he wanted to get her beneath the sky of his home world. She was a superb creature in any light, but Oceanun starlight would make her a goddess.

"Shall we go before I decide to keep you all to myself?" he asked.

She nodded, and kept her gaze straight ahead as they headed to the gala.

They arrived fashionably late, and easily located Datron,

Clitus and Gilla. Keir took one look at the way Datron inspected Sagan's appearance, saw that it was hot and wanted to tell his subordinate to keep his attention elsewhere. But such petty jealousy wasn't warranted. He couldn't justify it to himself, except that he'd now advanced his amorous attentions in a more permanent direction. Sagan was his and always would be. He felt he knew her heart, even if she wouldn't admit her feelings for him.

"You look spectacular," Datron remarked, taking Sagan's hand and kissing the back of it.

When Clitus and Gilla made the same gallant gesture, Keir couldn't have cared less. But he kept his attention on the brawny Valkyrian, and on Sagan—just as a matter of course.

"I see you got your invitation and won't be in the bar tonight," Keir remarked as he gazed at Datron, and then tried to appear more interested in the silver and blue streamers and glittering, planetary ornaments hanging from the ceiling. "Looks like someone went to a lot of trouble for an unannounced party."

Datron shrugged with a smile. "As Electra Galaxy and Pierpont Horizon have asked that everyone attend, I could hardly refuse. Besides, there's food here and I'm hungry."

"I do hope the buffet is generous," Gilla announced.

"As do I," Clitus agreed.

Datron surreptitiously nodded to Keir, then stepped close. He kept his voice quiet. "My arm bracelet is picking up so much surveillance equipment in this room that I can't keep up," he remarked. "We were all invited to an unplanned party, in a room that's heavily bugged. Am I the only one who thinks this is odd?"

Keir grinned, as if Datron had just told him something funny but personal, and nodded in agreement. His own armband, hidden beneath his shirt, was tingling. The others in the group had their eyes on the buffet, with the exception of Sagan. She, as always, was watching everyone very closely. Keir put his finger to his lips, and she lowered her eyes in acknowledgment. He needn't have worried over her talking indiscriminately, he realized; she was a pro and should be treated as such. Were it not for his promise concerning the stones, he'd have told her everything that very night.

Sagan saw the way Keir was looking at her and felt a little shiver of delight. Still, she knew they needed to focus on work. "Shall we mingle?" she suggested, taking a glass of champagne from a passing waiter's tray. She was about to suggest a direction when several young beauties approached the men in her group. The women seemed to capture the gentlemen's attention, and Sagan shrugged, smirked at how quickly her companions forgot her appearance in favor of some new prey, and strolled off to find her own amusement.

She was standing in another room, gazing at a beautiful landscape of the American Southwest when a low voice made her skin crawl. She recognized it immediately.

"I will kill your man eventually. But perhaps I have something more pleasurable in mind for you."

Slowly turning, she saw Burl standing behind her, several of his warriors also present and sneering, looking her over as if she were a fresh pastry. "Why don't you go find a cave and evolve, Ussarian? And take your trash with you," she growled at his minions. She made no pretense of being pleasant, but neither did she say anything incriminating or specific about their mission.

She would have sauntered away, but Burl stepped in her way. He looked her over yet again. This time, Sagan became concerned, because there was something very sick about the way his eyes moved: They didn't track right, as if his finer motor skills weren't working. Beads of sweat pooled on his forehead, and his skin had a pallor that didn't look healthy.

"You need to get out more," she said. "And get better-smelling friends while you're at it."

Burl stepped closer, ignoring her comments. "I think the last thing the Oceanun sees before he dies will be me having you." He licked his lips in lustful appreciation.

"Get out of my way." Sagan refused to back down, and moving around him and his men again would constitute that. She knew she was safe, in that this group wasn't so foolhardy as to allow their leader to do something in a room full of people. But she almost began to wish Burl would try something, just so she could get in a few punches.

"You think you're too good for the likes of me, don't you, princess."

"I think an amoeba is too good for the likes of you."

He lowered his voice and leaned close. "Guard that tongue when you speak to me, woman. I've beaten females better than you."

"Which proves Keir's point. You're nothing but a coward. And, speaking of beating, didn't my guy do that to you today, in front of everyone? But that's all right. You'll get used to it, because he's going to beat you again tomorrow. Now, if you'll excuse me, something around here doesn't smell very healthy and I'm leaving." The last part was both truth and insult. Something on or near the Ussarian was definitely putrefying.

Burl grabbed her by the arm. His warriors closed ranks and tried to make him let her go, as others were now watching, but he shrugged them off. "I will have you, and the Oceanun will watch. Just before I put out his eyes and cut out his heart."

"You're insane," she blurted, and realized the truth of that statement. Burl wasn't even acting half rational.

And his men recognized that as they attempted to pry his grip from her left arm.

"Let her go!" a low, enraged voice rang out as clearly as any bell ever had. Each word was enunciated with such clarity that everyone turned to look. Keir strode purposefully forward, with Datron, Gilla and Clitus glowering as darkly as he.

"It is poorly done to manhandle another," Gilla proclaimed. "Especially when the person in question obviously doesn't want such attention."

"Leave her be," Clitus added. "Don't be a fool. This is neither the time nor the place to air your grievances, Burl."

Keir spoke no more; he simply grabbed Burl by his leather vest and physically moved him back several feet. At the same time, Datron pulled Sagan clear of the Ussarian's bruising grasp.

"Exacting revenge against you will be sweet," Burl growled, and knocked away Keir's hand.

Keir glanced between the group of Ussarian warriors and their leader. That Burl would dare such a confrontation a second time, in such a short period of time and in front of so many witnesses, went beyond irrational. It bordered on psychosis. "What's wrong with him?" he softly asked the other Ussarians. Then he looked Burl over and recognized the signs of some kind of shock. He'd seen it before, on other planets where battles had laid waste to the population. "Your leader is ill and should be looked after. Have you no better regard for one of your clansman than to let him walk about when he's obviously ill?"

"We will look after our leader," one of the men said, and pulled the feverish Burl back a few paces. He did not add more, simply hauled Burl off as the Ussarian began to mutter incoherently.

Keir saw everyone nearby breathe a collective sigh of relief as the Ussarians left the vicinity. The confrontation had, for the moment, been forestalled. He quickly turned to Sagan. "Are you all right?" he asked, gently taking her arm to look it over. He scowled at the telltale bluish marks that had already appeared. "That bastard!"

Sagan smiled and waved off the whole event. When those strangers standing nearby went back to their conversations, no doubt adding the scene to the list of most-gossiped-about subjects, she lowered her voice so only her companions could hear. "I-I think there's something really wrong with Burl. I'm no doctor, but it's like you said. He looks sick."

"Indeed," Clitus announced. "Septic shock, unless I miss my guess. I've seen it before. Paleness of skin, sweating, what appears to be an altered state of awareness—these are all symptoms. And he seemed to have a hard time breathing as well. I'd say the Ussarian has received some kind of injury that had become badly infected. And rather quickly."

Arching a brow at the level of knowledge his newfound friend had just displayed, Keir felt a sense of shame. Again he was reminded how he'd wrongly assumed the men in this competition were mindless fools. And he'd learned a further, and very noteworthy, bit of information: Clitus had either seen battle or been medically trained. Staring at the Arborean for a moment, he caught the big redhead's expression of acknowledgment.

"He's done himself an injury associated with his blood oath. I've heard of such, but . . . I wasn't aware Burl would go so far," Clitus admitted. He gazed around and made sure no one was listening.

Datron was staring at Keir, but Keir refused to say more. They were being scanned. He, Datron and Sagan knew it, even if the other men in the group didn't.

Sagan pretended not to know what they were speaking

about, feigning all kinds of ignorance and speaking in rather an absentminded fashion, surely to get Clitus's and Gilla's curious looks off Keir and Datron. "Really, does every party or competition in this pageant have to become a battle? After all, if this is just because Keir beat that oaf in the photo competition, isn't he overreacting?"

"I believe the battle began long before that," Clitus observed, and he began to study Keir closely.

"I think there's a longstanding feud of some kind between Oceanuns and Ussarians, isn't there?" Sagan asked, then added, "I mean, it's certainly clear that my men have a great deal more class than Burl. Indeed, Keir's race is derided by the Ussarians for their peaceable and 'soft' lifestyle. Why, just look at what the brute did to me!" she wailed.

Keir knew Sagan didn't give a damn about the injury; she was doing whatever it took to get Clitus and Gilla to forget Burl's illness and its cause. Clearly she was trying to avert their interest to her and away from the Ussarian leader altogether. Their two new friends were already gleaning that matters were far too intense between Keir and Burl. But Keir knew, from Clitus's knowing stare, that Sagan's efforts weren't paying off.

Clitus glanced down at her injury, then focused his intense gaze right back on Keir. That kind of attention elicited Keir's own curiosity as to the Arborean's reasons for competing, as well as Gilla's. But it would no doubt be rude to ask and, knowing they might be overheard at any time, Keir simply blew off the entire scenario.

"It could just be that Burl's had too much to drink," he suggested.

"Something leads me to believe that you know this is not the case," Gilla commented. "Perhaps there is some distinct history between you that would have caused the Ussarian leader to declare a blood oath?"

Datron stepped forward. "Gentlemen, please. Why

don't I find us some drinks, introduce you to some of the Miss Milky Way contestants, and suggest a more pleasurable topic to discuss than what Ussarians choose to do with their testicles. I'm actually curious to hear how you came about your medical knowledge, Clitus. You sounded positively professorial."

Keir almost laughed out loud, for his second-in-command had finally managed to divert Clitus's attention. The Arborean grew a little flustered and turned red, clearly attempting to hide something of his own past.

"I-I see what you mean," the redhead mumbled. "There are surely more interesting subject matters."

Sagan halted a waiter and put her empty glass back on his full tray of assorted drinks, taking another. When everyone else followed suit, looking to quench their respective thirsts with different offerings, she offered a toast. "Here's to good friends and good times."

"Hear, hear." Gilla smiled and readily lifted his glass to clink it against hers.

It was as Gilla clinked glasses with her that Sagan saw another, less dangerous nemesis appear in the room, crossing it. Electra Galaxy stopped to converse with several groups of individuals along her route, but she was definitely coming their way. And the famous woman's green gaze lit on none other than Sagan herself. A shard of jealousy shot through her, and she remembered that Electra, too, had slept with Keir. Her pride took a dive.

She tried to pry her eyes off the way the pageant producer gracefully moved through her throng of well-wishers, like a queen through her court. And it was with a pang of regret that Sagan saw Keir happily welcome the older woman into their midst. Keir was kind enough to make the introductions, though everyone obviously knew who the woman was.

To Sagan's bewilderment, Electra looped an arm

through hers, smiled and said, "Will you all excuse us? I'd like to have a nice, girl-to-girl talk with this lovely manager."

Wondering why Electra would deem it necessary to speak to her alone, Sagan steeled herself for what was sure to be another in a long series of crazy circumstances. This was turning out to be the weirdest mission she'd ever been on. The case was getting more outlandish by the moment. And Electra's next words confirmed her thoughts. The men had already moved away.

"Let's speak in my private study, down the hallway," Electra offered. "You'll want to hear what I have to say."

CHAPTER SIXTEEN

Sagan followed the svelte diva down a hallway decorated on either side with paintings by many masters, and then into what could only be referred to as her lair. Like the hall outside, stunning artwork covered the sparkling silver walls of her large office, and an immense ebony desk sat at one end. On specially lighted tables, there were pieces of crystal, semiprecious jewels and shards of geodes. The entire room looked like a cave filled with treasure.

"Please, sit," Electra offered. "Since the introductions were made already, we'll dispense with the formalities. You may call me Electra and I'll call you Sagan . . . a woman using no last name."

Sagan took the ultraexpensive brandy Electra offered and swirled the liquid in her snifter before taking a slight whiff. "I'm honored by your request to see me alone. I'd have thought you'd had enough of my entourage after entertaining Keir last night."

Electra smiled benignly and sipped her own brandy. "I made him an offer he couldn't refuse."

Sagan leaned forward slightly. "And what was that?"

"Come, my dear. Let's not play games. You're from Earth and know my pageant. You know full well that sleeping with me wouldn't gain or lose your contestant any points in the competition. I'm a figurehead. I simply rake in the revenue from our sponsors."

"Rather lucrative position," Sagan noted, gazing again at the tasteful art and decor around her. "Aside from what I think of the situation, or your part in it, what was the offer Keir couldn't, as you put it, refuse?"

"I simply told him that I get what I want, and that if I didn't, I'd use every bit of power and influence at my disposal to find out who he is and why he's here."

Sagan kept a placid look pasted onto her face. "I'd have thought that was obvious. He wants to win this competition. This year's prizes are the most luxurious in the history of the pageant. Were he to win the crown, he'd get a year rent free in a seven-room penthouse apartment complete with all the amenities. He'd have transport to any place on the planet, exposure to movie and television moguls, commercial contracts, women fawning over him, custom-tailored clothing, twenty-four-hour access to the Brawné Salon for Men along with body work by Temple d'Amour herself, prize money in the millions of Earth currency, staff to wait on him at all hours and, obviously, access to you as your protégé. None of the previous winners has ever wanted for a single thing for the rest of their lives."

"As his manager, a win would also make *you* exceedingly wealthy," Electra suggested. "So, we'd all win. Except for the small fact that I don't believe an Oceanun could be persuaded to have a thing to do with this pageant."

"There are many species competing this year from worlds that've never sent a contestant before," Sagan said. "Why must Keir Trask be any different?"

"As I said, he's an Oceanun. He wouldn't be caught dead even watching one of my programs, let alone vying for the title."

"You think there's something sinister about his presence just because he's different from others on his world?" Sagan blandly sipped her drink. "You're considering his race before his personality. In every species and creed there are those who are different. Having been exposed to so many cultures, I'd have thought you'd realize that. Keir is an example. He just wants to better himself, and is seizing the opportunity to do so. And as you've guessed, I'm along for the ride. I know a winner when I see one."

"Curious," Electra pondered. "I haven't ever heard of you on any of the pageant circuits. Yet you, the Oceanun and a Valkyrian appear out of nowhere and stun the judges completely. They're quite overwhelmed with both your clients. And everyone is completely intrigued by Keir's relationship with the Ussarian."

"I should take the opportunity, since you've brought up the subject, of apologizing for the small disagreement my competitor had with the Ussarian. I believe there's bad blood between their worlds. However, I can assure you there'll be no repeat of such testosterone-driven behavior."

Electra lifted a hand in dismissal. "Apologize? To the contrary, that fight made galactic news and is being commented on by beat writers everywhere. Interest in the competition has never been so keen, and a larger audience than ever before is tuning in to watch the outcome. As you say, there are many entrants from different worlds who've never previously taken advantage of the opportunity. And with the bad blood, as you call it, between Ussarians and Oceanuns, this is also a matter of political concern. Billions across the galaxy will be watching the pageant. My marketing people tell me we're going to triple the revenue we'd expected."

"All that being said, why would you consider Keir's presence so odd that you'd threaten to expose him in

some way if he didn't sleep with you?" Sagan asked.
"Not that he has anything to hide."

"It's the man himself who interests me. He's simply
not the type to join some of the empty-headed, vain lot
who typically show up on my doorstep every year. Neither is the Valkyrian . . . or you, for that matter."

Sagan grinned and lifted her glass. "Does this mean
you'll be asking Datron and me to sleep with you, too?
And will you expose our deep, dark little secrets if we
decline that offer?"

Electra tilted her head back and laughed. "I like you.
There's an underlying streak of contrariness that reminds me of myself—years and years ago, of course."
She moved in front of the desk, sat on the edge and
looked down at Sagan. "Mind you, if you *wanted* to avail
yourself of the opportunity to better our acquaintance,
I wouldn't toss you out of bed."

Sagan had been propositioned many times in her life,
by both men and women. As yet, she'd stuck to men.
"Thanks, but I've got two contestants who need my attention. And it's a full-time job just keeping them and
the Ussarians separated." She paused. "You keep changing the subject rather adroitly, though. What did you
want to know about Keir that had you threatening him
with exposure? And let's not mince words. You *did*
threaten my client or he wouldn't have slept with you."

Electra paused. "Had I not been more bluntly spoken
to in my life, I'd be insulted."

"No offense was meant, I assure you," Sagan hurried
to say. "Under other circumstances, I'm sure Keir or
Datron would have readily accepted your offer, without
the use of any coerciveness. You are, if you don't mind
my boldness, a very attractive woman, and you know it.
I only meant that I know my men well enough to can-
didly state that neither would have put themselves in the
position of inviting adverse media attention, not unless

they were pressured. They're both gentlemen. As such, neither would ever speak of their liaisons, so I never ask. But I believe Keir felt compelled to do what he did."

"And you're jealous," Electra said.

Sagan glanced down at her snifter. "I won't deny it."

Electra leaned forward. "What would you say if I told you that Keir never had sex with me?"

Sagan tilted her head to the side, confused, but she kept her surprise to herself. Something in Electra's voice conveyed sincerity.

"All he did was sleep. Literally. And he held me. I-I don't think I've ever known a more gentle man. As you've so elegantly put it, I'm sure he'd never mention a single moment of our night together to anyone. And yet, when I see him with that Ussarian, he's a warrior through and through. All this is why I know damned well he isn't on this planet, competing in this pageant, for the glory, fame or money," Electra firmly asserted. Then, she walked back behind her desk, placed her crystal snifter on top and pulled a file from a drawer. "You didn't exist before this pageant began. I'll ask you what I asked Keir. Who the hell are you, and what are you doing in my competition?"

That forcefully spoken last sentence led Sagan to believe the woman was seriously determined, but a humorous reply came all too readily: "So, will we be in your bed tonight or mine?" She had no intention of caving where Keir had not. If Electra hadn't found out anything through the Oceanun, she wouldn't through Sagan. They still had time to finish this mission.

Electra laughed again. "I like you more and more, Sagan with no last name."

"It isn't my intention to be obstructive with you, Electra," Sagan admitted. "And despite your claims that you have no pull with the judges, your opinion would still matter to them even if on a subconscious level. I don't want to compromise my clients' competition chances. Neither they, nor I, will be making any trips to your boudoir anytime soon. At least, not until after this competition is over and they can do so without bringing unwanted attention to themselves."

"My dear, attention is *all* Keir Trask has brought upon himself these days. Haven't you been viewing the media reports?"

"No, I haven't had the time. My only concern is what the judges think."

Electra was silent a moment before speaking. "You know, there are those tabloid types who are linking the deaths of the Ussarian's family members and his public altercation with Trask. However remote that actual link might be, some are saying Keir had something to do with the unfortunate accident. The entire incident *looked* like an accident, of course."

"What are you implying?"

Electra held up her hands. "Not a thing. But a Ussarian has sworn a blood oath against your client. You and I both know the cause wasn't any pervasive politics between their worlds, or the outcome of a photo competition. Don't we?"

The woman was showing perceptiveness that amazed Sagan, who carefully chose her next words. "None of us knows the Ussarian leader's motives. He appears to be physically ill and certainly not in his right mind. He accosted me only a few minutes ago. I can only attribute this oath to his obvious degenerating state of mind and health."

"Oh my. Rational thoughts pour from you one right after the other. I do admire you, Sagan. But take care with your safety and the well-being of those in your immediate group. That the Ussarian isn't himself won't keep his oath from being executed. His clansmen will see to it, if he's incapable. And I don't want any more casualties associated with this pageant. Despite the media blitz and the growing income from sponsors who love the lurid rumors, no amount of monetary gain in this world or any other is worth someone's life. I'll do whatever it takes to make sure there are no more pageant contestants harmed . . . by anyone for any reason."

That statement, so assertively made, boosted Electra Galaxy to a higher level in Sagan's opinion. She began to regret some caustic remarks she might have made in the past. "I'll do my best to keep Keir and Datron separated from them."

"Good. The same warning is being sent to the Ussarians. I want whatever is between you all kept to the competition venues, in front of the cameras only," Electra declared. "And, I *will* find out eventually what you're all about. Make no mistake."

Sensing she'd been dismissed, almost the same way a servant might be dismissed by a monarch, Sagan stood. She quietly thanked Electra for the drink then left the room.

When she returned to the ballroom down the hall, she could hear glasses tinkling and saw that people had availed themselves of the sumptuous buffet. She helped herself to some salad and fruit, trying to get a glimpse of either Datron or Keir. Several Ussarians still present were keeping to themselves in a corner, and were avoided by most of their fellow competitors. It was no wonder, since their attitude was as poor as their manners. Sagan tried not to watch their piggish behavior with the food, and helped herself to another drink. A deep voice sounded from behind her.

"I saw you and Electra leaving together. I take it she had a few questions?" Keir asked.

Sagan turned and simply nodded. She couldn't speak without being overheard by the security equipment and staff, especially now in the quieter atmosphere created while everyone ate. But it was obvious that Keir knew the pageant producer had quizzed her the same way he'd been interrogated.

Of course, he'd spent the night with the woman.

"I owe you an apology," she said after a moment.

He smirked. "Perhaps you found out her relationship with me wasn't what you thought."

Sagan studied the top of her glass, mildly embarrassed, and ran her finger around the rim. "You might have said something."

"I wouldn't—"

"I know, I know." She held up a hand to stop his protests. "You'd never be so ungallant as to speak of your trysts."

"And that rule applies to us as well," he said, moving closer. "Tonight. In fact, I'm looking forward to the first really restful night I'll have had since coming to this world."

What he meant was, he expected to be in her bed. She was about to comment on that assumption when an amplified voice sounded from the far corner of the large room:

"Ladies and gentlemen, may I have your attention?" Pierpont Horizon hailed everyone from the dais where the small orchestra was situated. "In past years, the winners of the individual contests in the Mr. Interstellar Feller pageant were always announced at the very end of the competition. This year, however, I simply can't contain my excitement." He rubbed his hands together in anticipation, and there was a small hubbub amongst the audience. "As CEO of Pluto Pillow Mints, it's my great pleasure to break with an old tradition and give you the name of the man who has won a commercial contract with my company for the next year!" He waited for another round of whispering to build anticipation. "Will Mr. Keir Trask come forward, please?"

A round of applause and stares in their direction had
Sagan motioning her companion forward. He had to act
as if he wanted this award, even if he could never fulfill
the obligation: Her government would eject him as soon
as the competition was over and his duty was done. To
her surprise, however, Keir didn't need any coaxing or
prodding. He smiled brightly, walked forward and accepted various rounds of congratulations with humility
and grace, then took his place on the stage with Pierpont. She watched in confusion as he actually seemed to
be enjoying the situation. There might have even been a
glimmer of victory in his eyes.

"For the benefit of those who didn't see Mr. Trask's
performance in the mock commercial made today, I've
brought along a tape. Shall we?" Pierpont invited the
audience to applaud for a chance to see the winning
performance.

Standing far back in the room, Sagan hadn't realized
Datron, Clitus and Gilla had joined her. All her attention was on a vid screen that now rolled a countdown
toward the commercial. It occurred to her she'd be
hard-pressed to ever walk around in public without a
disguise from now on; this clip would probably be aired
galaxy-wide.

It had been edited and improved with the latest technology in color enhancement and special effects, and
Sagan was as mesmerized as everyone else in the room
when the video finally began to play. Again, she was
transfixed by the way her eyes never left Keir's face, and
how she accepted his bold, deep kiss so easily. She was
gazing up at him in adoration. Of course, the way the
clip was cut it was as if the mints themselves made Keir
more attractive. Nothing could have been further from
the truth. The mints were vile. Keir was virile.

As the lights came back up to thunderous applause,
women rushed forward to secure an autograph from

Keir. Sagan could see they held out napkins, contest programs, various bits of paper and even bared pieces of anatomy for him to sign. Debonair and smiling brilliantly, Keir shook hands, kissed ladies and acted the happy pageant contestant to the nth degree. She felt a warm hand on her shoulder and turned to find Datron standing to her right. There was a curious look on his face.

"What's going on? He's acting as though he actually *enjoys* this," the Valkyrian commented in a very low voice. "If it was for real, he'd have to eat Pluto Pillow Mints for the next year."

Sagan simply shrugged. She was equally befuddled over Keir's strange turnaround in attitude.

She should be glad. This was the way she'd wanted him to act to begin with. Now that he was so accommodating, she wasn't sure she liked it. And Keir's behavior seemed just as confusing to his best friend. All they could do was stand and watch until Pierpont presented Keir with a contract, which he quickly read and signed on the spot. Another round of applause echoed through the room.

"That's the best acting I've ever seen," Datron quietly murmured in her ear.

She leaned close to him. "I'll find out what he's up to tonight. I *did* tell you both that you'd have to final to stay on the planet."

"That must be what's on his mind." Datron absently nodded, but she could tell he wasn't totally convinced regarding his friend's motives.

"I'd better fish him out of this," Sagan murmured cautiously. "We have another competition tomorrow and have to keep our eyes on the Ussarians."

Clitus and Gilla had returned after yelling out congratulations to their newfound friend. Sagan saw that both the Silkan and the Arborean were grinning from ear to ear, and she couldn't help smiling back at them. Truly, there were some men in this competition who didn't seem to be hiding their true affection for a new comrade. Of all the people she'd met in connection with the pageant, Clitus and Gilla were the most genuine.

"After I get Keir out of this mob, we can all go back to my suite for a cocktail," she offered. "I'm sure no one will mind. It's getting late and the pose-down and swimsuit competitions start early."

"Too true," Gilla agreed. "I'd be most happy to accept your invitation for a drink, however. I think this crowd will get bawdier as the night goes on."

Sagan moved through the crowd with the others, all four attempting to regain their missing companion. As Gilla spoke, the orchestra had started up again, and the music was a loud dance number instead of something more classical. In her fight through the crowds, she avoided champagne-carrying waiters and women who'd kicked off their shoes to dance.

When she finally found Keir, his massive shoulders hovering above others around him, Sagan was just in time to see a young blonde girl fling herself into his arms and kiss him soundly. She stopped short, almost causing her three companions to barrel into her. Crossing her arms over her chest, she pasted a vapid look on her face. "If you're ready, we need to get back to the suite. We have things to do before tomorrow. I think these ladies will understand that you need your rest, Mr. Trask." She looped her arm through Keir's and tried to smile politely to the groupies who had planted themselves around him like a row of gilded sunflowers.

Keir turned to his adoring audience. "Sorry, ladies, I'll see you all tomorrow at the pose-down." One brunette burst from the crowd, directly in his path of retreat. "Hello, Sharyce," he said with a smile. "Nice to see you again."

Sharyce moved in close to boldly rub her chest against his. "May I oil you up for the competition tomorrow?" she begged.

Sagan felt her mouth fall open, but quickly shut it as Datron snorted in amusement.

"I, uh, have a manager who'll be taking care of me," Keir replied. Then he took Sharyce's hand in his, kissed the back and winked. "But thank you all the same."

Sagan was almost left behind as he bolted toward the nearest elevator. The other men were right in step with him. She glanced back at the woman called Sharyce and wondered from where Keir knew her. Something of her curiosity must have shown on her face.

"I met him when he first got here . . . on the elevator," Sharyce supplied. "I was hoping he and I could, um, get to know each other better, if you know what I mean."

The biblical definition was the one to which the girl was referring; of that Sagan was sure. Confused at how any woman could so easily throw herself at a man and how men so often fell for it, Sagan rolled her eyes and attempted to catch up with the others. She saw them waiting for her at a hall elevator, and kept her gaze on anything *but* Mr. Photogenic, as Keir had now been labeled.

It seemed, in the uncertain ways of karma, that their positions had changed; Keir now wanted to be the perfect pageant contestant. He stood there laughingly joking about his win with his friends, and excitedly spoke of the next competition and what they could do to make themselves more presentable to the judges. Sagan stewed and pondered how the hell his attitude had changed so quickly, and if he even remembered they were on a mission. As they got on the elevator, not one of them seemed to notice her silence. At the moment she did not care.

When they got to the sixteenth floor and exited, all joking stopped. Either the Ussarians had collectively gone mad, or Sagan was hallucinating. Burl and his minions stood in the hallway, bold as brass and not caring if the security cameras were trained on them. She could see, from her position in the middle of her male friends, that the big Ussarian leader was quite ill. Sweat poured off him and there was a kind of tick in his left eye. When he sauntered toward them, he limped.

"I will not be bested," he growled.

To Sagan's horror, he pulled a boot knife and each of his clansmen did the same. She saw Keir's shoulders stiffen, as he stood slightly to the right and in front of her.

He took a step forward and addressed Burl personally. "This is between you and me. Leave the others out of it."

"You started this battle. I will finish it by whatever means I must," Burl snarled in return.

"Put the knives down," Keir commanded. "I won't give you a second chance."

The Ussarian limped forward, unfazed. "I'll kill you and everyone who stands with you, enforcer. I have finally had all I can take."

Burl's behavior got worse every time they met, but Sagan was momentarily taken aback as to who *really* was most insane when Keir refused to back down. He walked forward, instead, jeopardizing the mission. They still needed Burl's contact for the arms sale!

But Keir looked outraged. He growled, "You savage! I'll take you and your men right here, right now. Let these people go," he barked. "For once in your miserable Ussarian life, fight like a warrior."

Sagan heard Keir's goading insult, but she was still surprised when Burl attacked.

CHAPTER SEVENTEEN

She was surprised but not stunned. Sagan went into action automatically; she hauled up the skirt of her dress and withdrew the stunner strapped to her inner right thigh. One shot was all it took. The blast hit Burl square in the chest and he fell midstride, his raised knife clattering noisily to the floor. His men, shocked into acquiescence, picked him up and backed into the nearest elevator. They glared at her and the rest of her group in fury as they did so, but attempted no further aggression.

The recent warning from Electra Galaxy echoing through Sagan's brain, she rushed to their suite, heedless of who followed or what they'd think. There was a chance, if only a slight one, that she could get to her computer and splice in some empty security film for their floor. If no one had been paying too much attention, perhaps she could replace the surveillance camera recordings and the mission might be salvaged.

Keir followed, along with Datron, Clitus and Gilla. Gilla was last into the suite, and he carefully closed the door behind them all and stared knowingly at his Arborean counterpart.

Sagan rapidly accomplished her mission; it took only moments. Luckily, her computer had been set up for just such emergencies. She now had the task of turning around, facing Gilla and Clitus and explaining what the hell had just happened. It had to be done in such a way that Burl's blurted account of Keir being an enforcer was covered. How she'd do it, she didn't know.

Keir was already attempting an excuse. "That fool is out of his mind. I've never seen anyone so irrational in my life. He'd have us in the role of every enemy he's ever accosted." He'd glibly made his best bid, but by Gilla's and Clitus's serious expressions they weren't going to believe him. He ran his hands through his hair, glanced at Datron and shook his head in utter frustration.

Sensing he was defeated, Sagan spoke up. She ignored Clitus and Gilla's presence for the moment and summed up her actions and the repercussions thereof. "Looking into the security system, there's only a momentary glitch in their recording to indicate I've deleted the fight from their tapes. I'm banking on the fact that most of the staff was still at the party, and only a backup officer or two might have been watching all the camera screens in their office. There's nothing in my computer saying the local authorities have been called, and there's nothing as yet indicating that Electra or her people have been notified. We *might* still have a mission here. I'll keep the system closely monitored for another couple of hours and see what happens."

"And if the local law enforcement agents have been called?" Keir asked.

She grimaced. "If I see any sign that they're on their way, I suggest we move in on the Ussarian suite, place them all under arrest and seize their cargo. At that point, Protectorate jurisdiction will take precedence over any local arrests. And we'll have to let my boss handle the flak from Electra and her people. Right now, we have two other problems on our hands."

Turning, Sagan glanced hopefully at Gilla and Clitus,

got up from her desk chair and approached them, hands held out in supplication. "Gentlemen, as that fool blurted out in the hallway, you've accidentally stumbled into a rather secure case involving Earth's Protectorate. I can only go by what I know so far. You both appear to be open-minded men who could maintain your silence. But I won't ask in this instance. I'll beg. The case we're on is of utmost importance. It involves the safety of an entire planet. If I've been successful in covering the confrontation in the hallway, we could still finish our work, but we need your sworn oaths of silence to carry on. Please, can you help us?" she finished.

Keir glanced at Datron, and awaited the other two contestants' response.

Gilla glanced at his companion and nodded. "I think Clitus and I are in agreement."

Clitus nodded. "Go ahead, my friend. It seems we are all on the same mission, coming from different angles."

At that strange comment, Keir faced the men squarely. "Explain," he commanded.

Gilla motioned to the lounge area of the suite. "This will take some time. Shall we make ourselves comfortable? We will need to see if Sagan's technical skill with the hotel security system pays off. In that time, I think much can be accomplished between us."

Sagan followed the rest of the men out of the small room where her computer still monitored security activity, but not before handling a few last things. If any alarm was raised by the hotel staff in reference to the fight, her computer would signal. They'd probably just have time to converge on the Ussarian suite. A quick check of the Ussarian hallway, made after splicing in the empty hall tape, had shown her that Burl and his men had not reappeared after entering their rooms. Her best guess was that they were waiting for their leader to recover before making any decisions. If Burl was still their leader when he woke, she'd bet he'd order his clansmen to stay put . . . if for no other reason than to see Keir dead.

As she took a seat by Keir, it seemed natural to lean against him and wait for whatever Clitus and Gilla might reveal. It was comforting that he placed one arm over her shoulders. The next hours would tell if they could rescue any remnant of their mission.

Once seated, Gilla turned to Clitus. "Shall I begin?"

"Please do," Clitus said.

Gilla cleared his throat, and Sagan watched the gills on the side of his neck move in and out with a sharper speed. If she read that physiological response correctly, the Silkan was as anxious as she, Keir and Datron.

Gilla began: "I and my friend Clitus are both working for the Mars Colony Constabulary."

Sagan gasped in shock even as Keir and Datron did the same. But they all kept silent so as not to impede Gilla's speech. Though what he said next would have silenced them at any rate.

Gilla continued with his explanation: "We were sent here after an arrest was made on Mars and an interrogation of a suspect revealed a plot to overtake Mars's government. The suspect in question cut a deal with our prosecuting attorneys in exchange for information."

"It would seem we are all on the same side in this mess," Clitus added, "but are coming from completely different directions. You see, we know about the blasters and the stones. What we did not know was that Earth Protectorate Force was aware of the case, or that Oceanus sent enforcers. I assume that *is* who you and Datron represent?"

Keir nodded but said no more to either of the purported Mars Constabulary. He wouldn't deny the obvious, but neither would he admit to anything else as yet. The knowledge that anyone knew of the stones as well as the Ache blasters was terrible. He ignored the looks of concern coming from both Sagan and Datron. Neither had known about the true nature of the stones. Now would be revealed their real significance, other than being gemstones stolen by the Ussarians. He'd have some heavy explaining to do. How much he could actually say was governed, however, by his promise to keep quiet. And Gilla and Clitus could still be the enemy. There was only one way to tell: by their actions. For now, he'd let them continue.

Gilla picked up the explanation. "Some years ago, one of Earth's Protectorate enforcers was killed while on an undercover mission on Mars. At that time, he'd been sent to help Clitus and myself in an ongoing operation to seek out and arrest insurgents who'd use violence to overthrow the newly elected Mars council."

Keir knew where their explanation was headed, and that it had coincidentally been Sagan's beloved that had been the very man killed. He could feel her trembling, and sensed that she was stoically withholding her shocked response so that the rest of Gilla and Clitus's mission could be aired.

Gilla took a deep breath, then continued. "Since that agent from Earth's Protectorate was killed, Clitus and I made it our personal mission to track down his murderers. For some odd reason, the very organization that sent the enforcer to Mars in the first place made no investigation of their agent's death. We found this troubling, especially since that man became our friend. When it seemed the insurrectionists had finally come to terms with the Martian election system and faded into the political background, we'd hoped the Protectorate would seek those responsible for their enforcer's demise . . . but they did not."

"As Gilla states, this is a situation we both find reprehensible," Clitus added. "We obtained permission to hunt for the Earth enforcer's murderers. But another arrest led to a *new* conspiracy, and the search for our friend's killer became more urgent. The situation is complicated: Our compatriot's killers are the same Ussarians you are seeking."

Sagan could hold her silence no longer. "H-his name was Mark Gallant, wasn't it?" she said.

Gilla tilted his head in surprise. "You knew him? You knew our friend, Mark?"

"He and I worked together and we . . ." She let her voice trail away.

"Oh, my dear," Gilla offered in the way of apology, "I had no idea. None at all. Mark was a professional who kept his personal life separate from our mission." He briefly reached out and patted her arm.

"He was a good man," Clitus continued. "He did not deserve such an end. Gilla and I are determined that his spirit be laid to rest. That can only be accomplished by finishing this mission. His death is directly related to the Ussarians smuggling both the Ache blasters and the Lucent Stones."

"What the hell are Lucent Stones?" Datron blurted. Keir saw his friend glare at him.

Sagan also took up the question and glared. "You lied *again*."

Keir stood up, walked away and took a moment to consider his words. He slowly turned to his comrades and said, "I was under a solemn oath not to reveal their existence. I'm still under that oath. As for lying . . ." He looked straight into Sagan's accusing gaze. "I told you that you knew everything Datron did. I couldn't even tell *him* the entire range of this mission, and still can't."

Datron stood and approached him. "How many years have we worked together? You know you could have trusted me!"

"Gentlemen, Sagan . . . please." Gilla attempted to calm the growing anger in the room. "Take your seats and let us work out the rest of these issues calmly."

"To whom did you make such a promise of silence?" Datron demanded.

Sagan added, "Your semantics amount to betrayal. You've hidden vital information from both Datron and me . . . likely Protectorate supervisors as well!"

Clitus stood and gently positioned himself between the angry Valkyrian, the Earthwoman and Keir. "As Gilla has suggested, please take your seats. Time is not on our side. Arguing at this point will do us no good."

"I'll have an answer from my esteemed commanding officer first," Datron insisted. "Who gave you the order to keep vital information secret? And what in blazes are Lucent Stones?"

"The order came from the highest source. That's all I can tell you," Keir returned.

"Dammit, what source?" Datron yelled.

"The *highest*," Keir responded.

The expression in his second-in-command's eyes instantly changed from rage to shock. Then Datron backed away as an unspoken understanding filtered between them. The Valkyrian finally understood, and he nodded in acceptance, though he was still upset.

"You didn't tell me for what you deemed a good reason," he openly suggested. "If the mission was to fail and I had no knowledge of that part of it, *you'd* be the only one responsible. And you meant to take the full consequences in that event."

Keir said nothing, but returned to his seat beside Sagan. She was staring accusingly, but her expression had shifted from one of anger to anxiety. He believed she was now beginning to think through his admission, and willing to consider the rest of Gilla and Clitus's story.

"I want to hear the rest of this. *All* of it," she asserted.

When everyone was settled again, Gilla continued. "At the start, I told you that an arrest had been made on Mars and that the suspect made a deal to exchange information for a lighter sentence. This man was one of the instigators in the original Mars rebellion, but had recent news that indicated there would soon be a more dangerous coup attempt. This newer revolution against the Martian government is to take place sometime soon. Those responsible had somehow made a deal for the delivery of neurological Ache blasters and Lucent Stones. This same source eventually led us to the Ussarian smuggling operation, to end here on Earth with the Mr. Interstellar Feller pageant. I surmise you, too, were waiting for the arms buyer to make an appearance so the entire ring of thieves and murderers could be broken. To that end, Clitus and I assumed a cover story that we, like you, are competitors in the competition. Since there were no other entries to the pageant from our home worlds, the cover was set. It seemed this was the easiest way to arrest all those criminals concerned without unnecessary bloodshed. I *am* correct in my assumption that you both"—he directed his glance to Keir and Datron—"were doing the very same thing? And that Sagan was operating as your Earth contact?"

"How do we know any of what you say is true?" Keir asked. "How, for that matter, can I confirm who you are?"

"You cannot," Gilla agreed. "Not any more than we can confirm that you are working for the same outcome."

"That doesn't explain what the hell Lucent Stones are," Sagan interrupted.

Datron stared at Keir, but directed his comment to Gilla. "Yes, please explain that bit of information that was deliberately withheld from Sagan and me."

Keir sighed heavily, but kept his thoughts to himself. It'd be a long time before Datron would ever let him forget this. And, for the moment, he didn't want to think about what Sagan might do.

Gilla looked at Clitus for confirmation to go ahead. Clitus slowly nodded and said, "We must trust them. It is clear to me that Lucent authorities contacted Oceanus for help when the stones and the blasters were taken. It makes sense that they would do so, given their constabulary is hardly adequate and Oceanus has a force many times more powerful. And our source has confirmed that sector of space was the supposed origin of the smuggled goods, and that their destination was Earth . . . then Mars. So far, all of the information has been confirmed. If nothing else, we have the Ussarian's reaction to the Oceanun as evidence. I believe these people are who they say they are. If we combine our efforts, our tasks will be easier. And we have to consider that there are millions of innocent lives at stake. We must take this chance, Gilla. I believe the Oceanun was sent to do the very same job we were."

Keir saw the acknowledging look the men exchanged, and he shook his head. Sagan and Datron didn't need to know this. There was the added problem that someone had already blown their cover and would probably be the same person wanting the stones as well as the blasters. He could only plead his case to destroy the entire cargo or find a way to do so without their knowledge or compliance. No world had any business with either the weapons or the stones. That had been his promise: to make sure both were blown to pieces, and that nothing was left to confirm they'd existed.

Gilla sighed before going on. "The Lucent Stones, as the name implies, originated on Lucent. They are . . ." He stopped, looking unsure of himself.

Clitus took up the explanation. "They're an unspeakable source of power. At first glance they appear as precious gems, but their true purpose is insidious."

"Those are the gems I saw in that case of blasters!" Datron blurted.

"Then, you have seen them and know they *are* with the blasters?" Gilla asked.

"They're there, all right. At least, they were just a short time ago." Datron stared angrily at Keir. "I was led to believe they were simply booty the pirates might use to finance their shipping and smuggling efforts. As contestants in the pageant, security concerning the Ussarians was as lackadaisical as it seems to have been with all the other competitors."

"We, too, found the lack of safety measures shocking," Gilla agreed. "In this instance, however, that apathy concerning secure search efforts might be for the greater good. You see, if the stones had been seized with the blasters, the planet confiscating all the smuggled goods would want to research the stones' origins, possibly their chemical properties. Upon doing so, they'd have discovered the Lucent Stones are not what they appear. And they are far too dangerous for any one world, or person, to own."

Keir finally spoke up. "My orders are to destroy them all: the stones and the blasters. To that end, I'll stop anyone who gets in my way. Anyone."

Her colleague's statement was made with such finality and force that Sagan was taken aback. She believed he'd actually kill any of them who tried to turn the smuggled goods over to their individual governments. She needed to know more about the stones to ascertain why he'd want the universe rid of them. She'd already agreed to obliterate the blasters. But why were the stones so critical?

Neither Clitus nor Gilla seemed to have her doubts. They nodded in unison.

Clitus leaned forward and spoke softly. "As you

might have guessed, Mars wants the blasters and the stones quietly brought to their governing officials. We were supposed to covertly accomplish this on Mars's behalf. Our officials and politicians will publicly want the glory of having captured the Ussarians and their cargo. They'll say their efforts to study the making of the blasters and the stones' properties are all within the realm of their scientific rights, and that they'll use the utmost care. Of course, they'll claim they won't misuse the power they'll discover." He sat back and shook his head. "But we are realists. Most enforcers are. And we know that men's actions and their intentions rarely coincide. This being the case, it's my belief Lucent will want their property back. Perhaps the Earth political sources will claim them as well, and those on Oceanus, and on any world through which the smuggled cargo traveled. Gilla and I both agree with you on the solution. The entire cargo, including those damnable stones, must be destroyed as soon as possible so that no innocent people are hurt.

"We've been lucky so far in that Burl is insanely obsessed with you, Keir," Clitus continued. "Otherwise, he'd have fled into deep space when he first became aware that you were after him. If that had happened, none of us may have ever seen him or his cargo again. Creator knows where the blasters and stones might have been shipped, or into whose hands . . . and that, I think, is your worst fear, isn't it? You know who, or shall we say what, is behind this entire plot, don't you?"

Keir stiffened. He stared straight ahead and said nothing.

Sagan chimed in. "My orders are to confiscate the cargo, while allowing Keir and Datron to take the Ussarians into custody. I'd already agreed with him to destroy the blasters. Any world having that kind of neurotechnology bothers me. However, I still don't understand how a pile of gemstones could be so deadly. What about them would make you all so concerned?"

"Shall you tell your comrades the rest?" Gilla asked Keir.

After a moment, realizing Keir wasn't going to budge any more on the topic, Sagan had to offer a warning. "Before you tell us the dire nature of those stones, you'd better know that someone blew our cover from the very beginning. That's why Burl and his men have had it in for Keir, Datron and me. They know who we are, even if they believed themselves safe because we wouldn't make a move until we could lock up their buyer at the same time."

"It all falls into place." Gilla nodded in understanding. "As cruel as this may sound, Burl's madness has been a blessing for the rest of us. So long as he stays in charge of his men, he will stubbornly resist any change from what we all believe to be his original plan. Of course, his illness also makes him irrational and dangerous. Tonight his behavior put all our missions at risk. If Earth police acquire the blasters while arresting the Ussarians for a lesser infraction—such as disorderly conduct or assault and battery—the result could be awful. The very person who set you up in the first place, some deceitful higher-up in the Protectorate, could get their hands on the blasters and stones. Who knows if that wasn't his or her plan to begin with?"

"Yes. All that considered, *tell us about the stones*," Sagan interjected, tired of being lied to and asking for information no one shared.

Gilla sighed, then finally provided it. "In their common form, the stones have no power. They superficially resemble colorful precious gems, though scrutinized by any reputable jeweler they would appear to have no monetary value at all."

"It was accidentally discovered by miners on Lucent," Clitus added, "that the stones are soft and can be crushed. The resulting powdery residue had a strange, adverse effect on those in the mines. Once the laborers breathed in the dust, whoever commanded them next had complete control over their actions.

"The dust seems to cause some chemical reaction within the brain that renders one incapable of independent thought," the Arborean continued. "To make matters worse, those receiving the commands and acting on them never remember doing so. They simply follow their last orders as if they were part of their normal routine. Unlike hypnotism, where a command would be ignored if it might violate a normal standard of behavior, a victim under the influence of Lucent Stone dust would still complete any order, no matter what that command is, and never recall their actions. And to anyone watching, it would appear they were acting of their own free will. Having completed that command, they go about their lives until the next order is given by the same person. It's that first voice the victims hear that matters. It's that person who holds control over them for eternity."

Sagan began to extrapolate on the possibilities. "Someone could put the stone dust where any authority figure could breathe it, then suggest anything. An entire country could be at the mercy of whoever's ordering its government. And if there were a room of representatives from different worlds negotiating, they could all be exposed to the stones' power at once. The results could be catastrophic! One person could gain control over many envoys from all over the known universe."

"Precisely," Gilla announced. "And that one commanding voice could come from anywhere—a long-distance recording through space, any communication device at all."

Datron snapped his fingers. "The maid! She put that desert viper in your room, Sagan. We couldn't figure out her motives for doing such a thing. Burl was seen with her before she cleaned your quarters. I'll bet my feathered back that he knows about the stones' power."

Sagan turned to Keir and glared at him. "*You* knew. You made all kinds of excuses and plausible reasons for the maid's actions, but you knew all along."

Clitus held up a hand in surprise. "A viper was placed in your room? And Burl had a hand in it?"

Sagan simply nodded. The specifics of that incident weren't as important as the fact that Keir had known how the deed was done. Her next question was, "But . . . why didn't he just put some of that dust where we could breathe it, then tell us to go blow our heads off? He'd have made his life much easier."

"As far as I know, there aren't that many stones in existence, and Burl has them all," Keir admitted, finally breaking his silence. "He may have used part of one on the maid but he couldn't afford to use much. He has a buyer who's probably offering an exorbitant amount for their delivery, and who's probably threatened his life to keep the stones intact. As far as we're concerned, Burl wants a fight to the death. He'd get no satisfaction if we, as his extended blood oath victims, weren't aware of our impending destruction."

Whatever Burl's reasoning, Sagan no longer cared; she couldn't get over Keir's betrayal. He'd deliberately lied about the most crucial part of this mission. Where did that leave any of them? Finding it difficult to digest all the information, especially its correlation to Mark's death and the consequences of that, Sagan stood and walked to the fountain in the center of the suite. The soothing sound seemed at odds with all this intrigue, but the trickling water calmed her in a way nothing else could. This was the worst mission she'd ever encountered. And it was probably her last for Earth Protectorate.

Regardless of what the other three men thought, Keir left the lounge area and followed Sagan. There was still more he couldn't tell her, but he wanted to comfort her and at least explain his actions. The distance between them and the others afforded a little privacy for that purpose.

"Sagan, you have to trust me," he said. "The stones' existence and their powers couldn't be discussed. I was under orders . . ."

She held up one hand to forestall any further explanation. "I know. We're on a mission. This is exactly why I should never have let our relationship go where it did. That's my fault. I could have stopped it and didn't, but this is where it ends."

Disheartened by those words, Keir put his hands on her shoulders. "One day you'll understand everything. The less you know, the better."

"And the more professional we keep this from now on, the easier it'll be to do our jobs," she quietly told him. "I agree with all the others that the stones and blasters should be destroyed. Once this mission is over and we see that task done, I go my way, you go yours. We make whatever excuses we need to for the benefit of our respective governments, and take the heat for not turning over the Ussarian cargo to any one of them."

"And I simply place the Ussarians and their contacts under arrest and head back to Oceanus. I know the drill." He stepped closer. "I never start something without finishing it. Thus . . . while this situation, as bizarre as it has become, may have placed a temporary barrier in our relationship, I won't give up on us. I refuse." He lifted his chin. "Like it or not, we're in too deep."

"Don't make this harder—"

"Oceanuns believe there's symmetry to the universe that can't be denied," he continued stubbornly. "Every event has a reason, though that reason isn't always clear." He put one hand on her cheek. "You and I have been put together for a purpose. That intention won't be stopped." Keir dropped his hand and walked away.

Sagan watched him go, walking away to ostensibly continue his discussion with the others. She'd never in her life wanted to run from any challenge. Right now, however, every instinct screamed to get away as fast as she could. Everything had gone wrong with this case from the beginning. It was only getting worse now. Before she saw one more person she loved die, or heard one more lie from anyone else she cared about, it would be better to shut down emotionally.

She returned to the small group with her own plan in mind. Not truly knowing who to trust but herself, she'd act the part they expected. The first thing she'd learned as an enforcer was to always have several backup plans. She gazed at each of the men and tried to gauge their honesty. The only one whose opinion had really mattered was the same one whose truthfulness was now most impugned. Keir had even more information that he still wasn't sharing; she was sure of it. And knowing what she now did about the leak in her agency, she couldn't go to the Protectorate for help or advice.

Ultimately, she realized, her life was in the hands of these four men from other worlds. And the responsibility for their actions here fell on her shoulders. Hers would be the name never forgiven if this mission wasn't successful. For that reason, she made a terrible decision: it had to look like self-defense, but a certain man had to die.

CHAPTER EIGHTEEN

Late into the night, they plotted.

Keir watched Sagan carefully, and it seemed she'd gone numb. The fact that Gilla and Clitus's role in this case was related to her beloved's death must have come as an eerie shock, but she professionally kept her angst to herself. He wished she wouldn't.

When the others finally left for the night and he closed the door behind them, she silently turned and made her way to her room. It came as no surprise that he wasn't invited to go with her. Too much had happened. Still, he couldn't leave things as they were. Regardless of his need of her, she could use some support. There were too many coincidences. And he could only imagine what she was experiencing.

She was so preoccupied that she didn't hear him enter her room.

"Sagan, are you all right?" he asked, walking up behind her.

"I-I'm not sure," she admitted. She sat on the edge of her bed and looked up at him. "Why didn't you tell us the truth? And what are you still hiding?"

He knelt before her. "*Shala*, I'm not at liberty to say

more. It's better this way, believe me. If something goes wrong, none of you will be accused of anything."

"And what makes you so righteous that you'd go it alone?" she asked.

He slowly shook his head and took both her hands. "Once this assignment is done, I'll ask permission to give you the facts you didn't know. But I can't even contact my superiors now. Aside from the transmission taking too long to reach the source, I can't take a chance that it might be monitored."

"Monitored by whom? Do you know how many transmissions are made from and to Earth every single day? Why would yours, made through an encrypted line from my Protectorate computer make any . . ." She trailed off, clearly thinking. "I'm really tired. We haven't been getting a lot of sleep and our meals have been irregular. All that kind of adds up. If you don't mind, I'm going to bed."

That was his dismissal. But he had to make sure she understood his view of their relationship, such as it was. "Someday very soon, you and I are going to have a long talk and get some problems between us resolved."

"Keir, please . . ."

"Soon," he repeated; then he kissed her forehead and quietly left the room.

Burl cried out in agony while his men held him down and attempted to purge his body of the sour-smelling, putrid mess beneath his botched incision. He'd been tied to his bed while the man with the best medical skills among them lanced the infection. Yet again. As his knife-wielding clansman did his job, Burl could hear the nauseated coughs and gagging of those holding him down.

One thing filtered through his fevered, chaotic thoughts: His men didn't know the code to access their ship's engine, and that was saving him. Without it, they could eventually have the ship's lock reset, but it would seriously delay their fleeing the authorities. Fear drove them to comply with his commands where loyalty would not. Along with his physical condition, a barely avoided mutiny was a bitter circumstance for which he blamed the Oceanun.

Because of Keir Trask, his younger brother was dead. He'd promised his family he'd keep the youngster safe. In his half-conscious state he imagined he was back home on Ussar, instructing his young sibling on the fine art of tracking a man and silently killing him. He remembered how he'd spent hours teaching the basics of flying a ship in such a way as to avoid detection after raiding a planet. He also recalled how he'd captured a woman for the lad's first rape. The girl he'd chosen had been a beauty they'd later killed.

Now, he couldn't even take his little brother's body home. He'd been told there wasn't much left and that the authorities were keeping it for an autopsy. That alone was a violation upon his kin's flesh that would not have been allowed on his home world. His brother's remains would have been taken to the barren, red rocks of Ussar and planted beside his father and mother, both of whom had died raiding a mining colony on Lucent. It had been that reason he'd taken this job in the first place. It had always been his desire to return to the planet where his parents had met their deaths and deliver a decisive, murderous victory.

Of course, all this meant nothing to those men now holding him down and cutting into his burning flesh. They had begged him—with much less spine than Setus, of course—to take the blasters and the stones and run while they could. For that, they'd die. As soon as he was in space again and could set his controls to autopilot, he'd march them into the cargo bay, close the airtight doors and flush them into space like excrement. Their families would be told of their shameful temerity. Their memories would be reviled.

As one of his men applied clean gauze to his wound, he screeched in sheer anguish. Then fell into a limp heap as they walked out and left him to his torment.

Everything he suffered, he reminded himself, was because of the enforcers. He'd stay long enough to make sure they experienced what he had. His buyer would have to wait for the shipment stored within his suite; Burl no longer cared about the money or a timely delivery. The only thing that mattered was destroying Trask.

He dragged in agonized breaths as his groin again began to ache. It seemed like hours later before the pain actually stopped. He sighed in relief as it ebbed away, but the following sleep turned to nightmares where his dead sibling beckoned.

Sagan awakened to find Datron, Keir, Clitus and Gilla eating breakfast together. They'd saved some for her and she tried to act thankful. There wasn't a lot of talk except to confirm their plan to make the final arrest. Everything really depended upon Burl and what crazy stunt he'd pull next.

She considered them all fortunate that whatever manipulating she'd done the night before with the computer had evidently paid off. There were no knocks on the door by Electra's staff; there were no messages on the computers in any of their respective rooms, except to remind them of the pose-down and bathing suit competitions that day.

Since Gilla, Clitus and Datron were scheduled to compete before Keir, Sagan pretended to offer what little encouragement she could regarding their competition. But Keir and Datron still had to final, because she was sure her government didn't know Clitus and Gilla were Mars operatives, and no one from the Protectorate could be told due to the leak.

As the time neared for their competition, Datron, Gilla and Clitus departed the suite to get ready. That left Sagan and Keir alone. She was sitting there, still grimly thinking over the previous night's disclosure, when Keir interrupted her thoughts.

"That was damned fine work covering that fight in the hall. Only you have the skill to pull something like that off," he said. "It was also very clever to have your stunner available."

She managed a smile, but only just. "Thanks. I don't suppose you'd ever consider *backing down* when a man pulls a knife and you're unarmed."

He ignored the censure in her voice and replied, "Ussarians don't respect anyone retreating from a fight. Sad to say, Burl wasn't in any physical condition to take me on. Of course, while beating him in front of his men wouldn't have been fair, fighting fairly with Ussarians is impossible. They don't know the meaning of the word."

"So you'd have taken him on, hosing down the hall with testosterone if I hadn't stunned him. Wouldn't you?"

"Taking Burl out was the only course of action. Embarrassing him in front of his men sent them all back to their suite. We couldn't have walked away unless he was confronted and stopped."

She knew he was making sense; her knowledge of the Ussarian mind told her so. But a few more minutes of fighting in the hall and she was sure she couldn't have gotten back to the room and altered the hallway tapes before security saw the disturbance.

She got up, pulled her robe around her and sauntered toward her room. "You'd better get ready. The others will be waiting on us. We need to be downstairs early so you can get oiled up and figure out a pose or two for the judges. They want to see flesh bulge. So do all those ridiculous women." She sighed.

He laughed. "Oh, don't worry. Remember the judges last night? I spoke to a few, and it's my humble opinion that I've made a good impression."

She stopped and turned around, again surprised. "You sound as if winning this silly competition actually means something to you."

He shrugged, finished drinking his juice and arched a brow. "I *have* to final, remember?"

She nodded absently, then continued to her room. Surprising though it may be, it was better that he wanted to win the competition. She shook off her distrust as nonsensical, and sank into her own dark thoughts again.

An hour later, she stood beside Keir in the exhibition center where the pose-down and swimsuit competitions were being held. Her other three companions had already competed, to the screams and cheers of hundreds of women. Datron, Clitus and Gilla were now waiting for Keir to take his turn.

He was wearing a dark green, silken bathrobe so that Sagan couldn't see his body; nor could the other women who'd been hired to ogle the men onstage as they posed. The sheer foolishness of the entire event was beginning to weigh on her. Sagan's attitude had taken a nosedive since the previous evening. Still, she attempted to smile and coach Keir as she had Datron. The next series of events, however, served as a distraction she hadn't foreseen.

A Pleidian citizen stepped onstage next. Like his entire ilk, the purple man bearing white spots was almost six feet tall and considered at the height of fashion to be pencil thin. When the optional posing music he'd chosen began to play, Sagan's lips trembled and her sense of humor couldn't be contained. To the strains of a very old Earth song entitled, "You're So Vain," the man showed his stuff. And as the slightly built gentleman struck poses only an advanced weightlifter of Keir's stature should attempt, his teeny white posing thong began to slip lower and lower. Apparently, he hadn't accounted for the size of the garment and the lack of anything substantial to hold it in place.

Sagan dropped her head into her hands when, at the end of his routine, the wiry being's thong dropped to his ankles and he had to run for the wings where she and her friends stood. Unfortunately, he tripped in the process and had to half crawl off the stage. What was visible before he disappeared wasn't worth mentioning; the Pleidian's package was nothing to write home about.

"Well . . . that was . . . *special*," Keir remarked with all the tact he could muster. The comment caused his companions, including Sagan, to choke on barely contained laughter. They attempted to maintain their composure so as not to appear unsportsmanlike.

One more contestant had to compete before Keir took the stage. Sagan actually began to relax when a potato-shaped Kaprayan, wearing a black posing suit, took center stage. The denizens of that planet, appearing very much like chubby pink baby-dolls with square-shaped, bald heads, were reputed to be among the galaxy's most amiable creatures. Sadly, that pleasant quality didn't help him in this instance.

Apparently, this poor contestant's suit wasn't any better tailored than the previous competitor's. It couldn't stand the rigors of his bulbous figure, as he posed so attentively. The black thong began to ride up. Sagan put her hands to her face as the Kaprayan's electric-blue eyes began to bulge larger and larger. By the time he finished his routine and bowed offstage, the gentleman looked like one of those eye-popper toys one could squeeze to relieve stress.

Keir simply shook his head at the indignities suffered by these other, normally sentient, creatures. In their attempts to gain fame, they'd made fools of themselves. His comrades' eyes were watering from trying to contain their laughter. Clearly, they didn't want to be seen mocking the competition, but it could hardly be helped.

He found himself thinking that there was no way to maintain pride under these conditions. The only thing that bolstered his resolve was seeing Sagan's bright smile and the way her face lit with glorious joy when she was happy. For her sake, he'd do whatever it took to win this damned thing, even if he had to lose his suit or suffer irreparable eye damage in the process. Luckily, his garment fit a bit better than the previous competitors', even if it *barely* covered him. Luckily, he'd researched enough to know that the body glue he'd affixed to the underside of his posing garment would probably hold it in place, if only just.

He shook his head as the entire audience coughed and snickered, while also trying to keep from laughing outright. Perhaps he'd be the next joke onstage, but he was going to make the attempt to show his stuff anyhow. There was no other choice. He had to win.

When his name was called, he quickly shed his robe and hung it on a nearby rack. Enough Miss Milky Way contestants were present backstage to send up a rowdy cheer on his behalf. Gathering his courage and what was left of his dignity, Keir gallantly waved at them while picking up a container of oil and handing it to Sagan. "You do the honors," he requested.

Sagan had seen Keir nude, but his body never ceased to thrill her. But as she slowly poured oil into both hands and smoothed it over his flesh, and as Datron,

Gilla and Clitus cast jokes Keir's way—just as Keir had before they'd competed—she shook off her desire. She wished the fun was for real. Datron, Gilla and Clitus seemed to have forgotten the serious nature of their discussion last night, and the possible outcome if they didn't complete this mission successfully.

After he was properly oiled, Keir turned to her. He put one finger under her chin and tilted it up so she was forced to look at him. "This will be over soon, *shala*. And any bad memories connected with this mission will fade, I promise."

She tried to smile as he kissed her, but the attempt fell short. Clitus, Datron and Gilla closed in around her and each offered quietly phrased encouragement. It was hard to paste on a grin, and to pretend to give a damn about the competition. Her humor at seeing the previous contestants had fled.

"You're on, Mr. Trask," the stagehand announced.

Keir nodded and turned quickly back to Sagan. "I'll win this for you." He kissed the tip of her nose, accepted an Earth-custom high five from his comrades and walked onto the stage.

Under any other circumstances, Sagan would have wantonly stared at his magnificent figure, his brilliant smile and the bright lights glittering off seven feet of muscular, masculine frame. But all she saw when she watched him stand before the judges in his dark green, barely legal swimsuit was another source of pain. He'd lied like everyone else she'd ever cared for, and he was in just as dangerous a position as Mark.

She blinked away a sudden wash of tears and tried to take comfort in Clitus, Datron and Gilla surrounding her. But watching Keir compete and pose with biceps bulging, pectorals twitching and tight butt bunching, the sadness engulfing her was crushingly abnormal. She could never have him.

She watched Keir twist his perfect body in different stances and heard the women scream until the very rafters shook with their obsessive lust. Even the men were somehow enjoying Keir's performance. And when he was done, waving to the judges and blowing kisses to the women in the audience to win points, she almost wished she were in the audience and an anonymous carefree spectator crying out for more flesh. But those women didn't know what she did. They wouldn't have to do what she would.

Keir laughingly approached the group, grabbed his robe and shrugged into it. But his smile vanished when he saw the tears flowing down Sagan's face. "*Shala*, what in the name of the Creator is wrong?" He gazed at his companions, who were at a loss to explain her sorrow but simultaneously attempting to get her to smile and enjoy herself as before. He moved very close to her and turned to the others. "Could you give us a moment, please?"

Datron, Gilla and Clitus backed away in haste, each clearly hoping Keir could get past Sagan's unhappiness and help her regain her spirit.

Keir led her to a small alcove, away from the milling backstage crowds. "Sagan, talk to me. You've been depressed all morning and it's worrying us to no end. Please, tell me what I can do?" He pulled her into an embrace and held her.

Fight as she did, she couldn't help an increase in tears. She wanted to break something over someone's head. If he had secrets, so did she. But hers were just as bad—or worse—than anything he'd lied about so far.

Someone called for the competitors to change into their secondary outfits for the swimsuit competition. To make Sagan laugh, Keir purposely reached into his robe pocket and pulled out the minuscule piece of black fabric. "Why don't I just tie on a napkin? It'd cover more," he groused.

Sagan actually grinned. "You're showing too much already. Just . . . just go get ready. Make sure the others stay together. I haven't seen any sign of Burl, but I don't want any trouble."

Keir nodded. He gently kissed her and led her toward the bustle where no Ussarian would confront her even if they did show up. Then, he quickly motioned for the other three men to come with him to get changed. They shouldn't be separated long. Who knew what one of the Ussarians might do with Lucent Stone dust? They dared not take any chances.

Sagan used her fingertips to blot away her tears. Feeling like a moron for having cried in the first place, she shook her hair back and waited for the men to reappear in their swimsuits. This part of the competition wasn't about posing, so much as catwalking in front of the many judges and throngs of women in the huge auditorium. The entire scenario began to take on a dreamlike quality. She attributed that sensation, along with her behavior, to too little sleep and too much input.

Mentally shaking herself into awareness and out of her funk, she grabbed at what was left of her frazzled nerves and focused. When the men made an appearance again, she attempted to act more like a manager and less like a lost, helpless little girl.

She watched as Datron, Gilla and Clitus took their turns boldly strolling in front of the judges; then Keir did the same. It came as no surprise when, thirty minutes after he was done, an assistant to the judges told him and Datron to go back on stage with several other contestants.

"That means he's a finalist in both events," Gilla announced excitedly.

Clitus said, "I knew they would. Why, the women love them! What I wouldn't do to have them go with me to any bar on Arborea. We could have our pick of the young lovelies and spend the night st— Oh, sorry, Sagan," he apologized.

She actually felt her good humor return with that mumbled apology. It was clear from his brief carelessness that he now thought of her as one of the guys. That was about as nice a compliment as she could have desired, especially after having acted so childishly.

Looking pleased, Gilla spoke up. "Let's move closer and see what the judges make them do. We can—I believe the Earth term is 'screw with them'?"

Sagan nodded and, with a hearty laugh, did as Gilla suggested. Clitus accompanied them, and they found a spot just offstage where they let out a series of bawdy comments. She cupped her hands around her mouth and called, "Hey Trask, if you want me to be your mattress monkey you'll have to do better than that! Datron . . . take that damned sock outta your swimsuit!"

Hearing, Keir glanced at Datron and they both started laughing. As they were already on stage and being perused by the judges, he began to pose again, to the supreme delight of the crowd. Not to be outdone, Datron spread his wings and moved next to Keir. Whatever his commander did, he repeated. The result was that all attention vanished from the rest of the competitors and landed squarely on them. The judges noticed these boyish antics, and the mock, mini pose-down, and began to laugh.

Seeing the judging panel grinning and marking their score sheets, Sagan felt a wash of pride. Evidently, spontaneity gained points. Forgetting all her earlier sorrow, she yelled out more comments to get the two to behave with even more audacity, and Gilla and Clitus did too.

"Show some *more* skin!" Sagan cried.

Datron threw his head back, laughed and turned his back on the crowd. With his wings lifted, he twisted his swimsuit and bared one of the few remaining expanses of flesh covered by fabric. A large red heart with an arrow through it had been tattooed there.

The cameras zoomed in. The audience rose to its feet and applauded, and Sagan couldn't control her glee. Datron Mann was a huge version of Cupid. That impish heart on his butt was too much!

Keir was not to be outdone. He sidled up next to his friend, knelt on one knee and kissed the tattooed heart. Then he gently rubbed it with one hand and winked bawdily at the audience. The crowd went wild.

Sagan covered her eyes and wept again. But this time her tears were from laughing so hard. She hardly noticed Gilla and Clitus were also in fits of mirth, wrapping their arms around their chests while trying to gasp in air.

Datron quickly turned as Keir rose from his butt-kissing position, shook a finger at his green friend and began to pose again.

Keir bunched his massive muscles and strutted for all he was worth. Women actually threw undergarments onstage, and the rest of the competitors were so overwhelmed by the commotion that they stopped all efforts to get the judges to look at them.

The stage lights suddenly went up, and Electra Galaxy approached the competitors from the audience. She mounted the middle stairs leading to the dais where the men preened; then she held up one hand. It took a full five minutes for the audience to quiet down so she could be heard on her portable microphone.

Sagan looked the elegant woman over. Electra was wearing a long white gown that shimmered under the powerful lights. The men all noticed her perfect figure, but Electra's attention went straight to Datron and Keir. She sashayed over to them, held up an envelope and proceeded to make a great show of tearing it open. She began to read the contents, and everyone went totally silent.

"The judges have tabulated all the points," Electra

informed everyone, "and I'm pleased to announce the winners of both the pose-down and swimwear competitions."

Sagan actually found herself holding her breath.

A drumroll sounded, and Electra used all her dramatic ability to make the moment more suspenseful. "Our pose-down champion is Keir Trask from Oceanus."

Keir smiled winningly and accepted a trophy, the first chest sash to be awarded during the competition, and a kiss from Miss Orion's Belt.

When the applause for Keir died down, another drumroll sounded and Electra made her second announcement. "Our swimwear champion is Datron Mann from Valkyrie."

Datron did as Keir had. He shot the audience a brilliant grin and accepted his trophy, sash and a kiss from Miss Big Dipper. Keir playfully punched his friend in the arm, which had Datron punching him back. Sagan's lungs actually hurt from laughing when the two of them began to girl-swat each other in a limp-wristed fashion.

Again, the audience responded to both of their ridiculous antics by rising to their feet and bestowing upon them a rousing ovation.

"Lord, there'll be no living with either of them," she joked, and was surprised she could do so after feeling so emotionally drained all morning. If anyone had told her the stiff, elitist Oceanun would ever behave in such an outrageous way, especially in front of billions of viewers, she'd have called them a liar. But here Keir was, making her and the whole world smile right along with Datron. And there seemed to be no ire or pettiness coming from the other competitors; they appeared equally as taken aback and entertained as the audience. Clitus and Gilla were laughing so hard they could barely stand.

Sagan swallowed down a sudden lump in her throat. It took very secure men to do what Keir and Datron had, in front of so many. And it took a very special soul to bring joy to others when, privately, they knew catastrophe could be so imminent. In that moment of ridiculous behavior and audaciousness, Sagan realized that she was deeply and irrevocably in love with Keir Trask. Whatever he was hiding, he wasn't doing so out of mistrust. It was as Datron had said: Keir was trying to protect them, even at his own expense. And, at his own expense, he and his friend were bringing happiness to others. She'd be surprised if his boyishness tonight didn't go a long way to opening diplomatic doors between his people and hers.

She shook off a returning feeling of malaise, wanting to keep Keir with her forever and unable to, and applauded right alongside everyone else. She'd gotten to see a side of Keir that was endearing, and she could keep that memory for the rest of her life.

From his bed, Burl watched his vid screen and threw the remote control at the wall. Unable to walk for the time being, he was out of the competition. Since he could not humiliate Trask in front of the billions watching the pageant, the Oceanun would now lose the only thing that really counted.

Trask wanted the smuggled cargo taken into custody and his men in chains. His crew was expendable now. Their simpering, cowardly pleas to leave Earth had him nauseated. As far as Burl was concerned, the enforcer could have them and good riddance. As to the cargo, that too no longer mattered as it once had. The only thought governing his actions now was how to kill the man he considered his greatest enemy. As a fraction of one Lucent Stone had already been crushed to control the maid, there was no sense in not using the remains of that stone.

With his new plan developing, Burl felt invincible. All he had to do was get well enough to close in on the one thing Trask seemed to care for above all else. He would have his revenge.

CHAPTER NINETEEN

After the excitement of the competition, Sagan had no time to speak to Keir or her other friends. A backstage party began where muscular aliens in swimsuits vied for the attention of the finalists of the Miss Milky Way pageant, and Sagan made sure she was seen laughing and talking to as many people as possible. Keir and Datron had been summoned into the circle of the almighty Electra Galaxy and Pierpont Horizon, and they stood a short distance away. The Oceanun enforcer and his comrade were preoccupied with playing elated winners, and Keir's occasional glances in her direction stopped altogether when too many people crowded around seeking his autograph and a chance for an interview or picture.

As the evening wore on, Sagan continually sought a chance to make her escape, and finally found it when the stage doors were opened to important business moguls. They'd been attending the pageant as potential sponsors and now wanted their chance at signing either Keir or Datron to lucrative contracts.

She slipped out a backstage door and quickly made her way back to her room. Once there, she checked her scanner and computer. Everything was well. The Ussarians seemed to still be in their rooms; a playback of their hallway tape indicated none of them had left. Gossip had been rampant at the party about their absence, and that had worried her. Even if he was very ill, Burl would have surely sent word as to why he or some of his people weren't in attendance. Not doing so brought undue attention to them. But then, his physical condition was definitely affecting his mental processes, and his warriors wouldn't counter his wishes if he chose to remain silent.

As she was checking other hotel surveillance footage for any sign that the Ussarians might be loose within the facility, a light flashed on her computer. Taking a deep breath, she viewed it with a growing sense of trepidation, and finally opened communication from her end. She already knew who it was.

"Carter here."

"Sagan, what the hell is going on? I watched the competition and the Ussarians were nowhere to be seen. The announcers said there was a rumor that their leader is ill. Have you been keeping an eye on him?" Snarl asked.

"I have. And I hate to be the bearer of bad news, sir, but it's a safe bet that they're going to cut and run," she lied. Then she added, "As it happens, I was just going to contact you. It looks like the Ussarian warriors are on the move now. They've got the blasters with them."

A look of deep concern crossed her superior's features. "That can't happen," he commanded. "Under no circumstances are the Ussarians to leave Earth. They could use those blasters to ravage entire worlds."

"I know, but there's a problem on my end. Since our officials insisted that Trask had to final in the pageant or face deportment, he's done just that. Unfortunately, he now has the entire universe in his face. He can't do anything without being watched, especially not tonight. In fact, he couldn't even leave the stage without everyone noticing. I'm in my quarters alone. The Ussarians are only making their move now because everyone's downstairs celebrating."

"You have to stop them!" he shouted, pounding on his desk.

She gave him a pointed reminder. "You know that I only have a stunner with me. The Oceanun didn't bring any kind of weapon that will match the Ussarians' blasters. The best I can do is incapacitate as many Ussarians as possible. I'll have no backup until the Oceanun can get himself free of all the attention, however. I don't see there being an ice cube's chance in hell of that happening. Not without alerting the competition officials or even the hotel security. And that's the last thing we need."

Snarl held up a hand. "I'm coming to you, Sagan. I'll have a complement of six enforcers from the Protectorate with me."

"What about the buyer, sir? Whoever that person is, they haven't shown up."

Snarl emphatically told her, "If we can keep tonight's operation secret using pageant activities as a diversion, we *might* still be able to catch that buyer. The Ache blasters are more important than anything right now. Just stay where you are until we signal."

"I suggest we meet on the roof, sir. That's where the hotel cameras show the Ussarians heading. I can loop in previously taped video so the security people here won't see what we're doing, but that'll only work for a short time. Their nightshift officers will walk their rounds soon, and that includes the rooftop."

"We're on our way, right now. Hang tight, Sagan!"

Sagan's computer signaled the transmission was over. She closed her laptop and muttered, "I'll bet you're on your way, you son of a bitch."

She quickly changed into black pants, high boots and a black jacket. It was clothing that lent itself to the stealth she'd need to complete her task. Then, she went to the secured closet where Keir's weapons were hidden. Within his efficiently packed duffel, she found everything she'd need. Grinning like a kid who'd just won a candy store lotto, and wishing like hell she'd had Keir's paraphernalia on other cases, she scooped up equipment. She took Keir's stunner—one a great deal more powerful and with a broader range than hers—a light grenade, and the holo-projector.

Two other pieces of weaponry that interested her were far more lethal. One was the handheld Ache blaster; the other was the sawed-off destructor rifle. Both of these Keir had taken off the dead Ussarians. Sagan hesitated, then grabbed the Ache blaster.

That night Keir had gone to the desert seemed so long ago, though only a few evenings had passed. Sagan gazed at the shining black Ache blaster in her hand and knew it would be put to one last deadly use. Tonight, she'd stop an insidious plot once and for all. And after she completed her chores on the roof, her connection with Earth Protectorate Force was finished.

Keir glanced through the crowd, searching for Sagan for the tenth time. "I still don't see her. Do any of you?"

Clitus, Gilla and Datron shook their heads in unison. The noise would keep any scanning device from easily picking up individual conversations, but they spoke carefully anyhow.

Keir ran one hand through his hair and belted his robe around his body more tightly. "I don't like this. Sagan wouldn't leave alone. Especially not after that stunt the Ussarians pulled last night."

"Why don't you make some excuse to leave," Clitus suggested. "Since you and Datron are the winners of

tonight's events, you can say that you'd like to go upstairs and put clothing on for the party. Gilla and I will
cover for you, then follow shortly. We'll meet you in
your suite."

Keir nodded. "Give us twenty minutes. If you don't
get a message from us through the concierge, assume
the worst."

The two made their mumbled excuses and left the
room. They promised to be back, but that clearly depended on whether they could find Sagan.

Sagan stood behind an oversized air duct on the roof, and
saw two hovercraft approach. The first was a marked
Protectorate craft, which probably bore her supervisor,
Lement Snarl. She didn't recognize the second craft but
had to assume the occupants were in on everything. The
good could later be sorted from the bad. Right now,
everyone was a suspect. She knelt down and waited for
the shuttles to land.

The second part of her plan depended upon Burl's
hatred of Keir. She counted on the Ussarian showing
up, for she'd left a voice message on his room computer.
She'd simply said that Keir wanted to confront him and
his band of cowards on the roof, and that the Oceanun
wanted to finish the fight started the night before. She'd
also added some insults that the Ussarian leader
wouldn't, even in his right mind, tolerate. Most of her
provocative comments had to do with Burl's mother and
who or what she'd slept with to beget him.

After landing on the roof, Snarl exited his hovercraft
and called out Sagan's name. She saw the uniforms he
and the other Protectorate officers wore, and knew
they'd done so to differentiate themselves from any portion of the criminal element about to be confronted:
They wouldn't want to be shot by one of their own accidentally. Snarl was following raiding procedure, as she'd

predicted. This was handy: she could distinguish agency personnel from Burl's minions, even at a distance.

Rather than respond to Snarl's call, she stayed exactly where she was, hoping Burl had taken the bait and would show up soon. If so, she could wrap everything up, all in one nice, neat package.

Exactly as she hoped, and with perfect timing, the enraged Ussarian leader and his warriors burst through the narrow roof door one at a time, all bearing Ache blasters. Those in front took one look at the uniformed Protectorate enforcers and yelled out a warning to their comrades behind.

All the Ussarians were soon on the roof, and weapons were discharged. Everyone scattered, heading for what safety they could. Sagan knew the Protectorate officers only had stunners. To keep them from being killed, she quickly pulled the pin on her light grenade and threw it into the middle of the battle. The resulting explosion blinded everyone on the roof who wasn't shielding their vision as she was. It gave her about sixty seconds before they could recover.

She quickly aimed a holo-projected image of herself toward a different part of the roof, just to the left of all the men now careening blindly into each other. After that, it was only a matter of waiting. She had to be sure who among the enforcers was righteous. The holographic image would give her that chance.

Keir's stunner in one hand and the deadly Ache blaster in the other, she moved forward just enough to witness the men recover. The Ussarians had to be handled first; there was no question where they stood.

She aimed Keir's wide-range stunner at the group of Ussarian warriors and pulled the trigger. Every one of them, including Burl, went down.

"I *gotta* get one of these," she whispered in awe, and then withdrew behind her shelter.

Snarl saw Sagan's image standing some feet away. He grinned, glanced back at the Ussarians and picked up one of the Ache blasters they'd dropped. His voice was sarcastic as he said, "Sorry, sweetheart, but it seems you were killed in the line of duty. It's unfortunate, but that's the way the damn cookie crumbles."

He aimed the blaster at her holographic image, and the other enforcers did the same. Sagan whispered a curse and stood up. Their attention was on the image, so they didn't see her. She aimed her stunner and had to fire twice to hit them all. They, like the Ussarians, fell in a heap. She and Snarl were the only ones left standing.

Snarl froze, shocked. Sagan used that mistake against him. She ran forward and kicked the blaster from his right hand. He was now unarmed, and she still had her stunner. That, however, was for men who would stand trial. The Ache blaster in her right hand had his name on it. She'd made herself and Mark a promise, and she was going to keep it.

"You bastard!" she shrieked. "You blew our cover on this mission and had Mark killed on Mars!"

Nursing his injured hand, Snarl knelt before her. He swallowed hard when he saw her raise the blaster. "Y-you can't use that weapon on me. I'll die. You have to take me in. I'm unarmed."

"You'd have sure as hell shot *me*, you frickin' asshole. And what about Mark? You had him taken to the Martian wilderness, where he died slowly. Why should I show you any mercy?" She saw the look of alarm on Snarl's face. "Did you think I'd never find out what you did?"

"How *d-did* you?"

She glared at him. "I wasn't sure. You just told me." She raised the neurological Ache blaster and put the barrel between his eyes.

"Put it down, *shala*."

That low, soft voice was very near. She stiffened, but didn't turn around to see where Keir was. "Why should I? He was the buyer Burl was waiting for."

Keir kept talking, his voice obviously meant to be soothing. "Sagan, who is this man?"

"Oh, you haven't met Overchief Lement Snarl, have you? He's my boss," she spat. "Soon to be deceased."

Keir could take the blaster from Sagan, but his intention was to get her to put it down by herself. Behind him, Datron, Gilla and Clitus were keeping all the unconscious men guarded and removing their weapons at the same time. He couldn't explain how she'd taken all these Ussarians and Protectorate enforcers out, but she'd had one plan and that was clear. She wanted the cowering man before her dead.

"At what point did you realize your supervisor was the buyer?" he asked.

"Snarl was the only person who could have known enough about this mission to blow our cover. He contacted me at one point and told me it was probably someone else within the organization, but that was too convenient. He wanted me to believe, up until the last moment, that he was on our side. But his real aim was to have us dead by now. Isn't that right, jackass?" She directed her comment toward Snarl, prodding his forehead with the barrel of her blaster.

The vitriolic tone of her voice and absolute stiff posture of her body led Keir to believe she was at her breaking point. Sagan had found the man responsible for a great deal of heartache in her life, and a man who'd betrayed her agency as well as this mission. He could understand her anger, but it wouldn't justify killing in cold blood.

"Sagan, killing him now would be a kindness. Let him stand trial. He and these other enforcers might even

end up serving jail time at the same incarceration unit—
right along with Burl and his men. It would behoove us
to find out what he knows and who else within the Protectorate might be involved. If you kill him, we can't do
that."

His final bit of logic made Sagan falter. She took a full
minute to think over Keir's words, then cursed loudly
and crashed her booted foot into the middle of Snarl's
chest. He fell backward even as she turned and stalked
away.

Keir grabbed Snarl by his uniform collar. "If you don't
start talking, I might just let her do what she planned."

"Not here. We need to get this trash arrested and
take Snarl where we can interrogate him without the
hotel security guards watching." Even as Sagan spoke,
guards rushed up the same stairs the Ussarians had used.
They filtered onto the roof and surrounded everyone.
The security staff had stunners, though a much less
powerful kind, aimed all around.

"Don't shoot!" Sagan called out, holstering her
weapons and putting up her hands. "I'm Captain Sagan
Carter, Earth Protectorate Force. This is Captain Keir
Trask. He's an Oceanun enforcer of the first rank."

Keir still held Snarl. He said, "This man and these
uniformed enforcers were helping the Ussarians smuggle Ache blasters onto your world."

Sagan watched the security guards glance at each
other. "What about *them?* Who are they supposed to
be?" one asked, and pointed toward Clitus, Gilla and
Datron.

"They're enforcers, too," Sagan informed them.
"Don't call Earth Protectorate. We don't know who
among them can be trusted right now." Her gaze shot to
the roof door as a woman in dazzling white appeared.
"Electra?" she squeaked.

The woman took one look at the scene and said, "I heard what Captain Carter said. Do as she commands. Have every one of these idiots taken away by local enforcers. Tell them they destroyed some hotel property and that I'll be pressing charges later, but that they aren't to be questioned. The Ussarian leader and Lement Snarl, on the other hand, will be escorted to my suite. Their presence in my penthouse will remain a secret until I say otherwise."

"You can't do that!" Sagan said. "*We're* the law here."

"And I'm the only supervisor representing Earth Protectorate Force right now who can be trusted," Electra explained, walking toward Sagan. "We've been watching Snarl for some time. We need to get some information before this entire event hits the news. Once the Ussarians and the betrayers from the Protectorate lawyer up, we may never find out what we need to know."

Sagan gasped in confusion, glanced at her male companions and saw the stupefied looks on their faces. "Y-You're with Earth Protectorate?" she blurted.

Without further explanation, Electra spat out orders to her men. "Confiscate all the blasters and stunners and put them into the basement vault. I want five armed guards stationed at the vault at all times, until I say otherwise. And one more thing: When you go to the Ussarian quarters to pick up the rest of the blasters, you'll find a bag of gemstones within one of the crates. Those are to be brought straight to me. Purge all the hallway and roof security tapes. Loop in normal activity . . . the same way Captain Carter has so professionally done on numerous occasions. I don't want any record of this fight to exist."

The guards did exactly as their employer requested. Electra's team proceeded with calm efficiency. Sagan now began to understand why her arm bracelet had so often alerted her to recording devices in several of the pageant venues, and why the impromptu party had been planned after the Pluto Pillow Mints competition; Electra Galaxy had been on this case from the beginning. The interrogation in Electra's office had been planned.

"Don't worry, my people can be trusted," Electra guaranteed. "They were handpicked and are loyal beyond measure. Now, do we finish this business on the roof, or can we retire to the privacy and comfort of my apartment? Snarl and Burl will talk there. If they don't, I'll let you have them both, Sagan."

Sagan shrugged, handed her weapons over to the security guards and took a chance. Electra had to be telling the truth. Her story was just too crazy not to be real. Besides, Electra's armed allies outnumbered hers. There wasn't much else she could do unless she wanted a possibly lethal confrontation.

Thus, in a confused state of silence, she followed Electra, Gilla, Clitus, Datron and Keir. They dragged the unconscious Burl with them, as well as a protesting Lement Snarl.

CHAPTER TWENTY

Once Electra had everyone within her apartment, she ordered the still unconscious Burl to be laid out on a sofa. Snarl was forced to sit opposite the Ussarian while Sagan and her friends pulled up seats nearby.

"Now," Electra began, "start talking, Snarl."

Apparently believing his life was only protected as long as he had information they needed, Lement turned his head and remained silent.

Her patience gone, Sagan got up and slapped him. "I swear to God, I don't give a damn why you did anything. I just want you dead."

Keir grabbed her by the shoulders and gently sat her back down. "I suggest you tell us everything you know. I'm not sure how Electra got involved in all this, but I can tell you there's a very serious mind probe waiting for you on Lucent," he advised. "Unfortunately, Oceanus law can't protect you once you're taken there."

"I-I'm an Earthling. You can't arrest me and take me to Lucent. I broke the law *here*," Snarl argued.

Keir continued: "I'm already authorized to take the Ussarians into custody. Once the local enforcers are finished charging them with minor vandalism infractions—as a means of keeping them behind bars until Electra is done with them—that's exactly what I intend to do. Something tells me no one will object too strenuously if you're among the prisoners I put on my ship." He grabbed Snarl by the front of his black uniform. "Now, talk!"

The overchief cleared his throat. "If I tell you what you want to know, what guarantee do I have that you won't kill me anyway?"

"Just blast him," Sagan demanded, standing again and trying to get at Snarl. It was Datron who held her back this time.

"Let us put it to you this way," Gilla chimed in. "Your cooperation might go a long way toward altering our collective attitudes. My people are a gentle, soft-spoken race for the most part. However . . ." He left the sentence unfinished, and the slightly built, aquatic-like man opened his mouth and revealed fangs that were every bit of six inches long. Sagan cringed as his once pale, friendly face transformed into a hideous open chasm of razor-sharp teeth and gristle.

Snarl seemed convinced he could be eaten alive if he didn't start talking. His hands were visibly shaking by the time Gilla's face returned to normal. "Okay. I'll t-tell you whatever you w-want to know," he offered.

Electra smirked and addressed Datron, Gilla and Clitus. "Before we hear his sordid little tale, I already know about all of you and why you're here. I've had that information for some time." She turned her attention to Keir and Sagan. "As to my getting the both of *you* in private and trying to force you to talk, that's all it was . . . an attempt to see what you'd do if I put the screws to you. Just call it my way of making sure I knew who I was dealing with." She crossed her legs, then glared at Snarl. "I couldn't be too careful knowing some of the Protectorate agents were traitors, and that Sagan was sent by you, Snarl. She, however, has proven herself guiltless—as have Keir and the others. So spill your guts, Overchief. And don't leave anything out."

Snarl gulped as Gilla kept gazing at him in a vicious manner. "It was never about the blasters." He glanced at the still unconscious Ussarian leader lying several feet away. "I knew I couldn't trust Burl and his fools. In fact, I was rather hoping they'd screw things up."

"How so?" Keir asked.

"Ussarians are brutish," Snarl explained. "They think one-dimensionally. I was counting on Burl's greed and his race's fixation on getting even with enemies. Sooner or later, I knew he'd use the blasters and deviate from the plans we made. Fighting and making himself and his men the object of gossip and attention was exactly what I hoped for. While the blasters were a secondary gain in the grand scheme of things, they didn't matter nearly as much as the Lucent Stones. We were prepared to lose the one part of the smuggled cargo through Burl's foolishness so long as we got the other."

"Then, the stones were the point?" Keir prompted.

Snarl nodded. "Knowing Burl and his intemperate goons would get into trouble and that the blasters' existence would be publicized was part of the plan. When Burl eventually got himself arrested on Earth, as I hoped he would, I was going to demand to take custody of his smuggled cargo. If I could get the blasters, fine. If not, I'd make sure the stones disappeared. After all, a bag of what looks like looted gemstones might be interesting, but hardly as important as neurologically destructive weapons. A man with ingenuity could take over a world by using those stones. And no one would ever catch on."

Keir nodded. "To anyone not knowing their power, the Lucent Stones would seem insignificant. And you would certainly use your power to get to them."

Snarl lowered his head. "The blasters can kill, but who wants to rule the dead? The stones conquer without any fighting at all. All I'd have to do is put them in circulation at the Interplanetary Council Meeting on Mars next year. I could make any suggestion to the delegates attending from a thousand different worlds. They'd do whatever I say. Their gradual alteration of law under my guidance would put me in control."

"And the Mars rebellion?" Clitus broke in. "What had that to do with your plans?"

"There are those of us who see that the use of the democratic process on worlds such as Mars, Earth and others is absurd. Real power should be in the hands of a few who have the mental capacity to rule. Most mob mentality is like that of the Ussarians, and you've seen what they've done to their planet. Their warring with each other has destroyed the surface of their world, and they keep widening their raids to other systems."

Sagan pinched the bridge of her nose between her thumb and forefinger. "Great. You wanted to rule the universe. Where have I heard that before?" She shook her head in disgust. "Mark stumbled onto some portion of your scheme and that's why he died. You knew, sooner or later, that one of us might discover the plan on *this* mission, especially if Burl was arrested and later revealed what he knew about the Lucent Stones and their Martian connection. So you pitted that damned Ussarian, half crazy as he is, against Keir and me and hoped we'd all kill each other."

Snarl tilted his head forward in admission. "I and my men would have moved in, mopped up the mess and taken control of the stones—and possibly the blasters, too. Stupidly, I had no idea you'd suspect me and set up a trap. I hadn't figured you'd even be alive this long."

The overchief sighed heavily. "I should have picked allies more intelligent than the Ussarians, but spies we have on Lucent recommended them for the smuggling part of this venture. A self-serving lot who care more about drinking, raping and pirating than ruling worlds . . . we thought that Burl and his cronies would be perfect for the job. After his men tortured one of our Lucent mining associates into talking about the stones and their possible uses, Burl simply wanted more money. He couldn't see what he had. Then again, that's the reason we used him."

Snarl snorted in disdain. "Can you imagine?" He pointed to Burl's unconscious form. "That idiot over there, drooling on himself, couldn't conceive of the power in his grasp because he thought there were too few stones to be of use. He had no long-term vision! He and his ilk are among the reasons why democracy won't work. *Look* at him."

Sagan glanced at Burl in disgust and rolled her eyes. Truly, both men were fools. Worse, they were killers.

"Eventually we could have stopped his people's pirating altogether," Snarl continued. "With the right minds under our control, crime might have been almost eliminated."

"At what price?" Keir broke in. "Who are you to tell the rest of the universe how to live our lives? What, to you, would have constituted criminal activity? The right to govern themselves belongs to the citizens of every world . . . even if they *are* complete morons like Burl. I can't imagine how you thought this scheme would work, Snarl. Or that the sentient people of the universe would stand idly by and let you rule omnipotently. But that's typical of despots." He shook his head in disgust. "Like you, the rest of your conspirators will be rounded up. There won't be any more stones coming your way, and the ones we have will be destroyed along with the blasters. There's no governing body in the universe that should have such power as the Lucent Stones. The ability to so utterly control *any* being is reprehensible."

Electra grinned. "Good. I'm glad we agree. If they

don't exist any longer, no one can argue over who gets them."

Sagan glowered at Snarl. "There was just one little problem with your entire plot."

"The plot was perfect," Snarl began. "Burl—"

"He didn't screw you up any worse than you've screwed yourself," Sagan snapped. "You see, you keep referring to the *others* in your group, and how you think alike. But when you spoke of putting the Lucent Stone dust into the circulation system at the Interplanetary Council Meeting, you said *you'd* be ruling."

Keir nodded, clearly understanding her point. "Eventually, you and your cohorts would be fighting amongst each other. Every time I've met fanatics like you, that's what happens. Remove freethinking and then destroy all stability. You and your power-grubbing friends would have plunged the universe into a darkness from which we might never recover."

Snarl lifted his chin, gazed at the Oceanun in contempt and stared out a nearby window. He was through talking.

Two hours later, the men were still trying to get more information out of him. Sagan stood leaning against the bar, sipping a strong whiskey Electra had poured her.

"I don't know if now's the time to ask," Sagan began, "but if you knew all this was going on and that Snarl was dirty, why didn't you act sooner?"

Electra sipped her own drink and shrugged. "I didn't and still don't know about all Snarl's associates, on Mars or on other planets. It's likely even *he* doesn't know all the conspirators. It's believed they operated in small sleeper groups known only to themselves, and that they only contacted their cohorts on other planets using code names. If one group was caught, they couldn't be forced to inform on the others, not even if we used the

Lucent Stone dust on them. Of those individuals on various planets that we do know about, it seemed prudent for law enforcement agencies to coordinate their efforts on different worlds and act as one. That is, I hope, happening as we speak. Besides all that, I've got a good thing going with this Mr. Interstellar Feller gig." She waved a hand at the priceless objects around her. "Why screw that up along with my cover?"

Sagan shook her head. "But the men we arrested tonight heard you. Your cover is blown."

Electra shook her head. "It's my intention to put them so far away that no one will hear what they have to say on the subject. And believe me, with the power I have in these matters, my name will be kept out of Snarl's or the Ussarians' statements. Besides, our prisoners are proven liars. It isn't likely anyone of importance would listen to what they have to say. We'll only need to prove that Snarl intended to kill you, Sagan, and that he intended to overthrow various governmental bodies. Finally, he aided and abetted the murder of Mark Gallant. The weapons he would have used to do so aren't as important as the insurrectionist acts themselves. Since Burl is Snarl's cohort, he'll be universally charged—as law enforcement treaties require—with any number of crimes as a conspirator in those acts. We won't need the stones or the Ache blasters to prove these charges. The crimes they'll go to jail for, whether here or on Lucent, began years ago. Back with the Mars Colony uprising. In short, the blasters and the stones won't strictly be necessary as evidence. As Keir has suggested, it's better to destroy them so no one ever gets the bright idea to take over the universe again. Suffice it to say, Snarl and the Ussarians will be in custody, on one of several worlds, for the duration of their lives. As a former law enforcer, Snarl will have a hard time surviving in prison. Inmates take a dim view of being housed with former undercover Protectorate operatives. As for

Burl . . . he's insane and will likely face solitary confinement for the rest of his days."

"But there still may be more of these traitorous bastards within the Protectorate," Sagan countered.

"I'm afraid that's true," Electra confirmed, "but since it's likely that Snarl doesn't know all of their identities, we'll have to root them out as we find them."

"I don't like this job anymore." Sagan sipped her whiskey and gazed into the distance. "I'd thought of my coworkers as reliable assets to society, not anarchist pricks wanting to rule the universe."

"We *will* find them, Sagan. I promise you. How many actually know about your work on this particular case is unclear. Anyone in the agency who sided with Snarl won't act suspicious; they won't want to be arrested. To be on the safe side, however, you might be wary about who backs you up from now on." After a pause she added, "Sagan . . . I'd have revealed my cover to you all sooner, but I had to catch Snarl in the act. I had to make very sure I caught him dirty and he could have no defense against the insurrectionist charges. Everything we had on him up to this point was circumstantial. We had enough to watch him, certainly, but not more. I now have video of him trying to do you in on the roof. That alone should be enough."

Sagan drank some more whiskey. Electra was trying to be tactful about why she hadn't come forward sooner. It was far more likely she hadn't trusted Keir, her, Datron or the others until the very last instant, when it was clear where they stood regarding the end of the Lucent Stones. This didn't help her attitude. She settled back into her dark mood from earlier that day.

From his position on the sofa, Burl feigned unconsciousness. The stunner's effects had completely worn off, and he now knew who his buyer was. He also knew the overchief of Earth's Protectorate Force would fare far better than he himself would when taken into custody by local enforcers. There was one last chance to be free of them forever. More importantly, there was one last chance to get even with Trask. His groin still hurt immensely, but not so much that he couldn't respond quickly. The fools thought they'd disarmed him. But he had one weapon left.

"We won't get any more out of him," Keir said angrily, walking away from Snarl.

Sagan put down her whiskey glass. "Can you and your people clean up the rest of the garbage?" she asked Electra.

The older woman nodded. "Yeah, I'll have an extraction team here to take Snarl and the sleeping dinosaur over there to an appropriate facility. I think you can consider this case over."

Without reply, Sagan slowly turned and headed for the door. As she passed the sofa, she stopped long enough to stare at Snarl. "There has to be a very special place in hell for you," she said. Then, as she was about to walk away, Burl struck.

Rising from a prone position behind her, he drew her into a steely-hard embrace. Burl clenched his jaw as he spoke. "I promised I'd make you pay, Trask. Now I'll see your face as I take what you most care for."

Sagan was shocked—as was everyone else. Burl wrapped his huge arms around her neck and body. The Ussarian could crush her throat in a split second, before any of her friends could react. Their stunners had been taken away by Electra's people.

"Let her go," Keir quietly demanded.

Sagan attempted to struggle free, but the man crushing

her to his foul-smelling body had the strength of a madman. When she felt the air being forced from her throat, she stared at Keir and prayed his image would follow her into the afterlife.

"You can't get out of here. Release Sagan," Datron commanded. Gilla and Clitus moved in as well, Gilla's face making the same expression he'd used on Snarl.

Clitus growled menacingly. "You truly *are* a coward. We should have killed you *and* Snarl."

"Take him out!" Electra shouted. "I have Snarl covered." She grabbed a paring knife used to cut fruit at the bar and put it to the throat of Snarl, who had backed into a corner, clearly not wanting to be involved. "Move and I swear to God I'll slit your gullet like a lemon, Lement," she warned.

But Burl kept one hand around Sagan's throat and began to squeeze harder. He slipped his other into a pocket and brought out a packet—likely Lucent Stone dust, Sagan realized. "Remember the maid? She did exactly what I wanted her to. Now, so will this little beauty." He licked the side of Sagan's face.

Keir leaped forward.

"One more step and I'll break her neck," Burl warned. Then he thumbed open the packet containing the dust and put it next to Sagan's face. "I'll let her do my work for me." He blew the powder right into her face.

Frightened more than he'd ever been in his entire life, Keir watched Sagan close her eyes against the sparkling specks now filtering over her flawless skin. But closing her eyes wouldn't help if she breathed in the substance.

Burl put his lips right next to Sagan's ear and said, "You will have no one but me. In my absence, you'll grow so despondent that taking your life will be the only option. If you're restrained from doing so, you'll go mad for love of me." He brutally kissed her temple then pushed her toward the Oceanun.

Sagan lunged toward Keir.

As if the next few seconds were all in slow motion, Keir watched the men in the room rush Burl. The Ussarian seemed to rage out of control. Burl's eyes took on a glassy, piercing glaze and he somehow managed to push Datron, Clitus and Gilla aside and run straight for a plate glass window leading to a balcony on the other side of the room. His huge figure crashed through the glass and leaped.

Datron was the first to get to the rail of the balcony. "I can't even see that far down," he yelled over his shoulder as Clitus and Gilla joined him.

Keir whirled Sagan around to face him. "Are you all right?" he begged.

She finally opened her eyes but pushed him away, and ran for the small sink in the bar. There she splashed cold water over her face. At last, when she was done, she inhaled loudly.

"Sagan, tell us you're intact," Electra demanded.

"I-I'm o-okay," she gasped. "I took a chance it wouldn't work if I h-held my breath."

Keir almost sank to the floor in relief. She'd been trying to rid herself of any remaining dust by washing it off. And if she had the wherewithal to do that and remember the command Burl had given, then she was okay.

Datron, Clitus and Gilla rushed back into the room. They stared at Sagan and sighed in one heartfelt release of air when she told them she hadn't been affected.

"We need to get downstairs and clean up whatever's left of Burl," Datron quickly announced.

Electra pushed Snarl at the Valkyrian. "Keep an eye on this former overchief of the Protectorate. I'll take care of everything."

Keir reached for Sagan, but she pushed his arms

aside. "I-I think I just need to go to my room. I'll wait for you all there." She left without further comment.

"Go with her," Electra mouthed to Keir.

He had every intention of doing just that. He caught up with her at the elevator. "Are you sure you're okay?" he asked.

She simply nodded and kept her silence until they were back in their suite.

Entering the main room and seeing her computer sitting out on the coffee table, Sagan turned to Keir and pointed to the device at the same time. "Who's been using my laptop?"

"When you went missing at the party, Datron and I changed clothes to come looking for you. We were afraid something was wrong."

She was only now noticing that he was back in his black pants, boots and open shirt. His swimsuit and robe were the last garments she remembered him wearing. It seemed her brain was somehow taking a detour down a very slow road, or she'd have asked him about how he'd found her on the roof.

Keir continued speaking. "When we couldn't find you, Datron hacked into your computer, bypassed the looping system you'd set up to trick the security guards and finally found you on the roof. We saw the fight and the light grenade go off and couldn't get to you fast enough. Oddly enough, Electra's people had an even more advanced system tracking your computer hacking. Datron accidentally stumbled across her bug in your system, and none of us ever knew. That was how she discovered what we were up to . . ." His voice trailed off, and he looked drained.

Sagan wrapped her arms around her body and slumped into a chair.

Keir rushed forward, knelt before her and took her

hands in his. "*Shala*, it's over. The mission is done," he softly said.

"I-I don't feel as if it'll ever be over. No case has ever been this hard."

"That's because of all the emotion involved. I feel it, too. But we can relax now."

She gently pushed him away and shrugged out of her jacket. "I need a shower. I can still smell that animal on me. God, I know this is gonna sound sick, but I'm glad Burl's dead."

"Come on, don't think about it anymore." He stood, pulling her with him.

She ignored his advice, kept talking about the mission. "We finally did it, though, Keir. We got all the smugglers and the buyer at the same time."

"*We* didn't do anything. *You* did it, *shala*. You're the gutsiest woman I've ever known," he murmured. And he put his arms around her and carefully propelled her toward her bedroom. "There were men lying everywhere on that roof. You have the most intuitive mind, to have figured out what to do. I still don't know how Snarl was there, but you can tell me all that later."

"He called and was asking about the Ussarians being missing from the pageant tonight. I suddenly got this idea to lure him here by telling him Burl was going to run—"

He kissed her into silence. "We have plenty of time for you to explain details. And I'll certainly want to hear them. Right now, let's just get some rest," he suggested.

Sagan stood in her room as he undressed her. Somehow—she never remembered the sequence of events later—they were soon standing in the shower together and he was holding her tight. It was at that point she began to shake, then cry.

"*Dsrws alla forlas dato cu signia, shala. Fromen drost m' quoestow.*"

Somehow, the gently spoken Oceanun words were

her undoing. She leaned against Keir and let him take control.

Keir knew he had one shot before her government threw him and Datron off the planet. He was pretty sure Electra would stand on his behalf, but he had to stay. Sagan wouldn't leave her world, nor should she be asked to; not after so much upheaval. That meant he had to leave his agency. He held her and stroked her back for a very long time. The hot water sluiced over them and its relaxing flow seemed to help his brain catch up with the moment.

What his family would think was uncertain. In the short time he'd known Sagan, he'd found everything he wanted. His parents, grandparents and siblings would simply have to accept his choice and his next actions as necessary. If they didn't . . . that subject was best confronted later. He began to rock Sagan back and forth in a slow soothing motion, murmuring endearments to her as he did. The case was over, but not the pageant. He had to finish.

CHAPTER TWENTY-ONE

Keir awoke to an empty room. The lights had been dimmed; the covers were over him and carefully tucked in. He called out Sagan's name and had an eerie feeling that she was gone for good. A few of her belongings had been hastily taken from the room, as evidenced by the open drawers and scattered contents. Someone so organized and efficient would never treat her clothing in such a way were she not in a hurry.

He rushed to the wall computer, as Sagan's laptop was missing. There was no message from her, though his comrades had left communications asking to be contacted whenever he was able. They were simply inquiring after his and Sagan's welfare. With no further duties or a woman to comfort, he finally stumbled to a chair and sat for a long time.

He should have known she'd run. He'd been so tired last night and needed rest so badly that he hadn't perceived her leaving. In fact, he couldn't even be sure he hadn't slept through one night and into the next.

There had to be a way to find her. But someone of her training and intelligence could hide and never be located if that's what they truly wished.

One part of him kept trying to be optimistic: She'd

be back and would explain her sudden disappearance. All she needed was some space. The other, more practical side of his nature told him she'd never be seen again. She was running from a job where her once-trusted employer had betrayed her and tried to have her killed. She was running from any commitment with *him*, because she believed there was no way they could politically or logistically work out a relationship. Finally, she was running away from the memory of Mark Gallant's death and its connection to this entire, insane case.

He walked back to the wall computer, contacted Datron and told him she was gone. As his friend began both to commiserate and simultaneously contact the others to help begin a search, a small plan began to form in Keir's brain. It was as ridiculous an idea as he'd ever contrived, but it might work. As far as the pageant was concerned, his cover as a competitor was still intact. Instead of hunting Sagan down—she'd go deeper into hiding if they did—he'd lure her to him . . . just as she'd lured Snarl and the Ussarians to the roof.

The worst that could happen was that she didn't show. He had nothing to lose.

Electra Galaxy stood backstage and listened to the most heavenly harp music ever heard by human ears. The sound caused the audience to weep. "Datron Mann looks and sounds like an angel," she whispered to Keir. "That Shakespearian soliloquy Clitus quoted and the Beethoven sonata Gilla played on the piano hit home in the hearts of all Earthlings. I can predict that all of your points will be high."

Clitus, Gilla and Keir smiled at each other.

Datron finished his harp piece to a standing ovation, bowed and walked offstage. He found the others and asked, "No sign of her yet?"

"I'm afraid not, Datron," Electra answered. "We've all been hoping she'd make contact when she heard what Keir was doing. But so far, there's been nothing. I've never seen a soul so completely disappear. None of my operatives has one clue as to where she's gone. I know it's only been a couple of days, but it feels like weeks. She's out there on her own somewhere."

Keir nodded. Electra had done everything she could to find the missing member of their undercover squad. They'd assumed that Sagan would get her head together and come back. But there was no stalling the inevitable. He had to go onstage, hoping she'd be somewhere where she could hear his voice.

Because the pageant had been so widely televised and had so many sponsors this year, the result was the largest audience in recorded history. Ratings for the program were reputedly through the roof. Billions upon billions of sentient creatures from all over the universe would see this last night of the pageant live, or at least a recorded broadcast later. Keir had no way of knowing where he stood in the scoring since none of the rankings in the private interviews with the judges had been publicized. Those interviews had taken place after the swimsuit and pose-down events, and after Sagan had disappeared. All he *did* know was that he and his friends were finalists. But he had to win. And he had to trust in Sagan's caring nature that she'd come to his side tonight.

Keir patiently waited his turn. His new musical choice had been given to the maestro and passed out to the orchestra. He'd originally planned to perform an aria from his own planet. In Earth language, his choice would have been referred to as the song "Novatron," from the *Music of the Celestial Spheres* opera. But he'd swapped in favor of a very familiar Earth piece that, as he'd practiced it alone in his room, he'd come to appreciate. There was an almost ethereal beauty imbued in each note. His family would be shocked, supporters of the Oceanun arts that they were. But he remembered Sagan saying that she adored opera. That being the case, she'd recognize the song he'd chosen and its meaning. He'd be singing for her; no one else.

As the rules allowed, he'd asked for and been given an Earth orchestra as backup. They'd certainly know the piece he'd be performing. The being now exhibiting a talent was a fluorescent orange octopus-man from Shindar-Degus and his part of the competition was almost over. Keir was up next. There was still time for Sagan to show up. He prayed to the Creator that she would.

Electra stood next to Keir, Datron, Gilla and Clitus. She tilted her head while watching the large, be-tentacled man onstage show his talent. He was blowing a very loud, bluesy tune out of one of his appendages. The music produced from that tentacle sounded exactly like a trumpet and was quiet engaging—in a New Orleans kind of way. Electra turned to the four men with her and found them all smirking quite broadly.

"He's quite good," she remarked. "We've never had a competitor from Shindar-Degus, so I know very little about his people. How is it that he can play tunes through his nose?" When Keir, Clitus, Gilla and Datron all bowed their heads and shook with laughter, Electra addressed Datron, who was standing nearest to her. "What's so amusing?"

"Uh, that's *not* his nose," Datron informed her, then pasted on a wicked grin as he surreptitiously glanced down at his crotch.

Electra rapidly glanced back and forth between the four enforcers and the orange man on the stage. "I'm sure my judges don't know. Should we say something?"

Keir spoke next and gazed at his companions. "I'm not tellin'. Anyone here tellin'?"

The three men with Kier trembled with barely controlled laughter again and Electra finally had to let loose with a hearty snicker. "I've heard of blowing it out your ass, but this takes the cake!"

At that comment, her male companions openly guffawed. The laughter took the sting out of Sagan's missing presence.

"Five minutes, Mr. Trask," the stage manager advised.

"Good luck," Electra smilingly told him.

Keir accepted encouragement from Datron, Gilla and Clitus. If he didn't win now, he was pretty sure Earth's government would call his ship and have him and Datron picked up. Electra's influence had stretched as far as it could. And if he was ejected from the planet, his chances of finding Sagan would be lost forever. She would never come to him. She loved her world. And while he'd give up his for her, she had no way of knowing that.

Later tonight, no matter what happened, he and his allies would destroy the blasters and the Lucent Stones. Using Datron's tracking device, which was still hidden in the crates, he'd determined that the booty—or at least the bug Datron had attached to it—was still within Electra's vaults. She probably knew about the device; a woman with her intelligence and access to advanced technology would have found it. Still, he trusted that she had not done anything untoward with the weapons. And right now, he had another mission to accomplish: He had to walk onstage and sing.

The stage manager lifted a hand and gestured. "You're on, Mr. Trask."

Keir lifted his chin and walked to the marked spot behind the stage curtains. He glanced back, toward his friends in the wings. He saw Electra almost weeping, and he knew she saw his sadness. "If I ever get my hands on that girl, I'll *throttle* her," he saw her say.

The orchestra warmed up. The maestro lifted his baton and the curtains opened to a round of applause.

Keir prepared himself, remembering the meaning of the song and each word he'd sing. As the announcer introduced him, the audience stood and applauded louder. He smiled and motioned for them to be seated and silent. Still they continued. So he simply smiled and humbly accepted their accolades.

At the same instant, there was a scuffling commotion in the backstage area. Electra and the three men with her turned to see a stagehand attempting to keep Sagan from rushing forward.

"Let me through!" Sagan demanded. "I know I don't have a pass, but I'm his manager."

Clearly surprised, Electra rushed forward, waved off the stagehand and put her arms around Sagan. "Thank God you came back!"

"We've been so worried," Datron said, and similar words of concern and thankfulness echoed from Clitus and Gilla.

After Electra was through embracing her, Sagan quickly accepted a hug from each of the men. Then she moved toward the stage. "I have to stop Keir. What in hell does he think he's doing?" she muttered.

Datron put his hands on her shoulders to forestall her forward motion. "While Keir will be elated to see you back, the orchestra is ready and the chorus is in place. Keir must finish."

"Why?" she hastily asked. "Why is he putting himself through this? The mission is over."

"He wants to finish," Electra insisted. "He's doing it for you—so he can stay here and be with you. I wouldn't allow my winner to be deported from the planet, and he knows it."

"He *can't* win," Sagan maintained. "Not if he sings. Have you heard him? He'll make a laughingstock of himself in front of billions." She put her hands to her face, then gripped Datron by the front of his vest. "Do something! You *know* he can't sing a note. We've both heard him!"

Datron was clearly trying not to laugh. "It's too late," he said. "Besides, I think you've got quite a surprise coming."

As the orchestra began to play, Sagan's fear almost strangled her. Keir's strong spirit would be broken and he'd be shunned on his world for taking this pageant any further than necessary. "Oh God, why is he . . . Somebody please tell me what he's singing. At *least* tell me that much," she muttered.

"It's from an Earth opera," Datron announced. "It's called 'Nessun Dorma.'"

Sagan stared at the Valkyrian in shock. "From *Turandot*? H-He's singing Puccini?" she squealed. "*Oh . . . my . . . God.*"

It was at that time she finally perceived the entire chorus from the Los Angeles opera company was on-stage, directly behind Keir. She'd seen them perform previously on her vid-screen. But even their heavenly voices wouldn't drown out Keir's horrifying, off-key caterwauling. "Keir," she whispered, but said no more. There was nothing she could do now. Pulling him off-stage would be as embarrassing as letting him sing. His pride would be shattered. And though he stood there in all his godlike glory, dressed in tall boots, pants and an open vest in a very dark green that perfectly matched his skin, he'd still be laughed at from one end of the universe to the other. She could only pray that looks counted for something.

It was then that she remembered the basic story behind *Turandot*. It was about an icy princess who had her suitors killed when they couldn't answer questions the woman posed to them. It struck her that, in some ways, he'd refused to answer her questions and that she could roughly be described as frosty . . . on some points. But Keir wasn't trying to malign her personally; he was trying to tell her something very important. She was sure he'd have never chosen this piece otherwise.

Keir gathered himself for the first notes and carefully guarded his breathing. At that exact instant, something told him Sagan was near. She was listening. He put every emotion he had into the notes pouring from the depths of his soul.

Sagan's concern filtered away. The voice coming from Keir was not what she'd heard when he'd blown out those bawdy little limericks in their suite. It was magnificent, rich, pure and perfect. She was transfixed by the sound and couldn't have moved if her life depended on it.

Electra nudged the others, pointing at her. They smiled at each other.

Sagan half glowered. Keir had lied to her yet again! She'd have a piece of his butt—*later*; just as she meant to give him a lecture about all the other secrets he'd kept. But she now intended to be in his life. She felt tears course down her cheeks as the wonderful sound kept going and the chorus, equally stunned by his performance, joined in. Their expressions seemed to range from beguiled to rapturous. They sang with their hearts in their voices and reached the crescendo at the exact time he did. The notes all intertwined and filled the building with beauty to the very last row.

When the song ended and the orchestra played its last notes, Sagan held her breath. There was a deafening silence in the auditorium, then a sudden burst of earsplitting applause that had the chandeliers shaking from their rafters. The maestro bowed to Keir and applauded as well. Humbly accepting the adulation, Keir briefly lowered his head and acknowledged the maestro first, then the orchestra. He turned then and acknowledged the chorus, who applauded back.

He finally left the stage and the announcer tried to quiet the crowd for the next competitor. That was when he saw Sagan, who'd dressed in a sparkling silver gown. Her hair was elegantly arranged on her head. Slowly walking forward, his friends parted on either side of them and grinned.

"I-I'm sorry I'm late," Sagan brokenly uttered. "You were . . . I've never heard anything so . . ."

"I was singing for you, *shala*."

She threw her arms around his neck, kissed him and let him hold her tight.

Much later that night, Keir stood with Sagan, Electra, Gilla, Datron and Clitus. Sagan backed away from the pile of weapons that had been carefully stacked in the middle of the desert. Nearby, hovercraft were ready to take them all back to the hotel, and to the results of the Mr. Interstellar Feller pageant. Millions of viewers were partying, awaiting the midnight announcement of the winner. For now, the most important task was to destroy every blaster in that pile.

"Everyone ready?" Keir asked, and gazed around him. He awaited the go-ahead nods from the others in the group. Each had checked the cargo and verified that all the blasters were present.

Word had come to him that enforcers in the Protectorate were being arrested. Since Electra was keeping the statements of these corrupt elements secret, he hoped this entire mission could be kept under wraps as well, and that the scientific knowledge used to create these blasters would never fall into the wrong hands.

He gazed up at the weapons pile to where a small sack of gems sat. The Lucent Stones, as the blasters, had been counted by each of them. Fourteen had been known to ever exist. Discounting the one Burl used, the rest were there. Keir was aware that Electra had contrived a story that Burl committed suicide, having been extremely depressed. It hadn't been difficult to convince people, given his recent behavior.

Now it just remained to be seen when Keir could take the Ussarians into custody. Lucent and Oceanun authorities wanted to question Snarl. The former overchief, like the Ussarians, would be transported back to Lucent. Snarl would later be returned to Earth, though Keir secretly believed it might be better to let the authorities on Lucent dispose of the man.

At any rate, the exact details of the prisoner transfer would have to wait until Keir found out if he won the damned pageant. If he didn't, he and Datron would return to Lucent with their prisoners. He'd have to leave Sagan on Earth until such time as better relations existed between his home world and hers. If he won, however, Datron and the rest of his crew would take the prisoners. Keir would give up his position. This second outcome was the only option, since leaving Sagan was unthinkable.

He took a deep breath, backed away to what he deemed a safe distance. As stars began to shoot across the desert sky, he depressed the plunger on a small, black box he held in his right hand. The entire pile of blasters and the stones vaporized; the explosion rose hundreds of feet into the air. The blast shook the ground, and he guessed a seismologist somewhere was recording it.

Keir turned to Sagan, took her hand and led her back to his hovercraft. The others followed.

At the stroke of midnight, they were all in Electra's suite. And when the word was announced, Keir was indeed the new Mr. Interstellar Feller. He pulled Sagan close and accepted the congratulations of those present.

Sagan saw the smile on Keir's face, but there was a light missing from his eyes. As champagne poured like the messages through Electra's wall computer, she led Keir to a dark corner of the penthouse and kissed him. "You can stay now!" she said.

He nodded. "We'll be together, *shala*. I'll need my manager by my side."

"But you won't be yourself. You'll be playing a game for billions of onlookers. That won't make you happy, Keir."

"Sagan, this is all I want. For us to be—"

She placed her fingertips over his full, beautiful lips. "Once you've done your year here, you have to go home and get your position back. Your world needs you. I won't be the reason you aren't there for them. I'd rather have you safe, out of harm's way. But this is what you do and you're too good at it."

"He won't lose his position. Neither will Datron," Electra informed them, sauntering into their seclusion. "Sorry to eavesdrop on your conversation, but I've got some news that was a bit delayed." She sipped champagne before continuing. "Datron has taken first runner-up. Gilla and Clitus were in the top ten. That means they'll all be receiving endorsement contracts of various kinds."

Stunned by the news, Keir and Sagan gazed at each other in surprise.

Sagan gathered her thoughts. "How can Keir or Datron be enforcers for their agency while maintaining their pageant positions here?"

Electra grinned. "I can swing some weight, young lady. Just leave everything to me." She continued to explain her plans. "Right now, Keir's ship and its crew are on Mars for shore leave . . . or so Keir tells me. They'll be free to go home as soon as he gives the order. But they'll be back for their captain and their second-in-command in one year. When that ship returns, Keir and Datron will both go home with their ranks intact. And they'll be taking the entire damned lot of prisoners back with them at that time. Earth will need that long to question them, anyhow. Of course, that means that you'll have to make a decision, Sagan. After the year is up, Keir and Datron will want to see their families. Keir will be forced to relinquish his crown as the reigning Mr. Interstellar Feller and there won't be a reason for Earth's officials to let him remain, even if I insist. You'll either have to go with him, make arrangements to be with him on some other planet, or stay on Earth alone. What's it to be?"

Surprised but unfazed, Sagan stared at Keir. "I don't care where we go. So long as we're together. I love you."

"Shala, muy dist quot fremon ky shorleu vashno sre . . ."

Electra smiled and sauntered away. She knew she wasn't needed any longer.

To shut him up, Sagan kissed Keir hard again. Then she gazed into his blue eyes and said, *"Shala, m'grue dist en tor myf sli criw, disd anow f'lot secre."*

Stupefied, Keir could only stare down at her. When she finally grinned, he spoke. "You've understood Oceanun all along? You speak it fluently, don't you!"

She tried not to laugh and nodded, "Snarl *had* to put me on this mission for that reason. I was to communicate with you in your language if you couldn't speak English as well as you do. In fact, I speak several Earth *and* alien dialects."

"You lied to me, Sagan!"

"Do tell," she responded. "As I recall, you've told a few tall tales yourself. Besides, you never actually asked me if I could speak Oceanun. You simply assumed I couldn't. So I knew you were telling me how much you loved me and how beautiful you thought I was. You said you couldn't live without me and that your heart would break if we couldn't stay together . . . which is more or less what I just said . . . *shala*."

"And, at the end of the year?" he softly questioned.

"If you've got room for a slightly used, disenchanted former enforcer, I'll go with you to Oceanus."

He pulled her close. "No misgivings?"

"No. The reason I left in the middle of the night wasn't because I didn't love you, Keir. It was because I do. I just felt I couldn't ever have you. There are several reasons for that."

"Go on," he encouraged, kissing her forehead.

"First, I was afraid of caring for you when I knew you could die . . . like Mark. Second, I was pissed because everyone I ever gave a damn about didn't trust me enough to tell me what was going on in their lives. Finally, I was afraid to leave Earth when I knew that was best. But I had a few days to think about it."

He grinned widely, obviously thrilled. "And your conclusions to all these concerns?"

"I want to have you as long as I can. I fell in love with you just as you are and I'm certain you didn't lie to hurt me . . . just like no one else in my life ever did. And vaguely hearing about some bad mission you're involved with wouldn't make me any happier. Worse, I'd have come to regret the time we could have had together." She paused to run her hands over his broad chest. "As to leaving Earth, I can't be an enforcer here. I don't trust anyone in the Protectorate. I think that if they really want revenge for what I did to Snarl, they'll get it if I'm on the planet. That notwithstanding, I want to be with you. I don't care where."

"And what if nothing ever happens to me or you, *shala*? What if we live to be very old and quite happy?"

"Now, that would be something, Mr. Interstellar Feller. That would really be something." She laughed out loud and looped her arms around his neck. The kiss they shared was coincidentally timed with fireworks going off outside the hotel.

Datron stood at Electra's bar and smirked. "One year. Well, contracts aside, I can't leave my captain and his woman behind. They need someone to watch their backs."

Gilla tilted his head in concern. "What might happen now?"

"You never know," Clitus told him. "There could be a few more smugglers hiding in the shadows."

"I suggest you all stay for the year," Electra advised. "There'll be plenty of room in Keir's new living quarters. As the reigning pageant winner, he has to have a *court*, as it were."

The men began to laugh; then they clinked their glasses together in celebration.

They hadn't yet learned their year of living high would also include regular bikini waxing at the Brawné Salon for Men. After all, appearances had to be maintained. Everything came with a price.

EPILOGUE

One year later

Keir looked over his ship and was pleased to see the crew so energized. Datron was back in his old position as second-in-command. Their families had sent messages that they anxiously awaited the ship's return, which only left one small problem: He'd meant to tell Sagan his last, final secret but feared doing so. Now the task couldn't be put off any longer.

As Earth tradition dictated, he'd proven his devotion to her: he'd placed a gold band on the ring finger of her left hand to seal their union, and she'd done the same. The ceremony had been performed the day after handing over his crown to a large affable warrior from Asgardia. Surprisingly, it'd been a rather poignant moment for him, but he was okay with it. He couldn't be Mr. Interstellar Feller forever, though Sagan swore he'd always be that to her . . . and much more.

Once they were on Oceanus, Keir would make sure their union would be publicly announced again, but in *his* tradition. In addition to the rings they now wore, each of them would have their navels pierced and a small silver shield would be hung from the piercing.

That small shield, encrusted with precious stones, would most certainly give his true rank away, and the final secret with which he was concerned.

He cleared his throat and walked toward her. For a long moment, he watched her work. His governing officials, recognizing his importance in Oceanun hierarchy, had bestowed upon her the rank of enforcer of the second class. It was quite an honor, one at which she dutifully strived toward being worthy.

In his eyes, she already was. There simply wouldn't be a better ground enforcer in the entire galaxy. To have a home life he now craved, he was taking a teaching position at the Royal Enforcer Academy. That meant they'd have schedules that were compatible. It was with the greatest excitement that he began this trip home with her. To top it off, she looked exceptionally striking in the black enforcer uniform she now wore, slender, tall and graceful. He yearned to take her to some quiet corner and ravish her until time stood still.

Shaking off thoughts of a carnal nature, he tried to keep his mind on duty. Hiding a grin, he straightened and barked out a command.

"Enforcer T'raskchrdtniq', front and center!" He loved the Earth tradition of her taking his real last name. It was difficult to act professionally around his other crew members when all he wanted to do was kiss her soundly.

Enforcer T'raskchrdtniq' . . . Sagan tried not to smile at Keir's officious tone. It wasn't helping that she could see a glimmer of mischief in his gaze. "Yessir?" she asked, running the words together and standing at attention. She focused on keeping her gaze straight ahead, and tried not to look over that broad expanse of chest with the silver epaulet on one shoulder. Even as she should be considering duty, an image of the night before gushed into her consciousness. He'd made love to her like a wild man. Parts of her body were deliciously sore. Then there was the amusing problem of her hair and his becoming so entangled that it took them an hour to straighten the mess. Then, they'd tangled it all over again.

Keir's facial muscles twitched as he fought to maintain composure. "As you're aware, a Ussarian delegation will be landing in an hour. Though they're suspected of raiding every star system they traversed getting here, and are also accused of stealing parts from no less than eight space stations used by various planets to monitor weather and communications, we have our orders to stand down on making any arrests. Earth wants them on the surface no longer than is absolutely necessary. To that end, we're to release Burl's ship to them as soon as they arrive." He noted her stoic, distant stare while being addressed by a supervisor. That patient, professional posture only made him want her more. "As you know, the former crew of that vessel will soon be incarcerated on our ship, to be taken to Lucent. Did you receive my communication concerning these matters?"

"Yessir. Since the new Ussarian crew is only being allowed access to that vessel, and won't be allowed to purchase provisions on Earth or mingle with the population, I've put crates of foodstuffs and water in their cargo bay so they can depart immediately . . . just as your communication instructed."

Datron heard the exchange and could no longer contain his glee. He gestured to the other new crew members: Clitus and Gilla. As a group they moved forward and also stood at attention before their captain.

Datron handed Keir an electronic clipboard with information on it. "Here's the cargo manifest, sir. However, there seems to be a problem with our own provisions. The count is off."

Keir glanced at Gilla then Clitus and Datron. The three men were desperately trying not to laugh. "What, precisely, is wrong with our supplies?" He glanced down at the manifest Datron had given him.

Datron clarified. "Well, sir, as a parting gesture of goodwill, Pierpont Horizon sent over five hundred crates of Pluto Pillow Mints. I've been unable to account for them."

Keir lowered his head, clearly trying to ignore the stifled mirth coming from Clitus and Gilla. "Please don't tell me . . ." He let the sentence go unfinished, took a deep breath and let it out slowly. Then he cleared his throat and addressed his beloved, innocent-looking wife. "Enforcer T'raskchrdtniq', would you happen to know what happened to the missing mints?"

Sagan lifted her chin and spoke clearly. "Sir, your computer memo didn't stipulate what provisions I was to put on board the Ussarian ship."

He made a choking noise. "You put those vile things on their vessel? Five hundred crates?"

"Aye, sir."

Still standing at attention, if barely, Datron, Clitus and Gilla burst out laughing. The Ussarians would have no way of knowing about the swap until their first meal, and that might not occur until they were far away from Earth's orbit. They'd have to go through many ports to refuel, take on new supplies and pass inspection, and that was if anyone let them land. Until then, they'd be eating Pluto Pillow Mints the whole damned time.

Keir pressed his lips together, turned around and walked the other way. Datron was sure his captain was smiling.

Much later that night, after the good-byes had been said to Electra and the many friends they'd made on Earth, Keir ordered the bridge crew to take off, break

Earth's orbit and head for deep space. He then retired to the quarters that he and Sagan shared. It was going to be a tight squeeze for three months, but she'd brought precious little with her: a few photos, some small mementoes.

When they got to Oceanus, though she'd fight him at every turn, he wanted to make sure she had a lovely new wardrobe. The solid black enforcer garb, brightened only by bits of silver here and there, wouldn't be good enough for the many places he planned to take her and the social events he knew his family would want them to attend.

To his great relief, his family's communications indicated they understood why he'd competed in the pageant and were glad he'd done his best. More important, he was coming home with a mate. His previous bachelor status had been a curse to his mother . . . so much so that any breathing woman was just fine. So long as there would be children at some point in the future, his parents would be elated. And that, too, was something he looked forward to. Making babies with Sagan would be fantastic.

He pulled the side epaulet off his shoulder and let the front of his uniform fall open. He was tired and ready to rest with his lover. It had been a long day filled with the breaking of ties.

As he walked into the room, he saw Sagan sat at the large viewport with her arms wrapped around her knees. She was wearing a robe and taking in a last view of Earth. He could tell she'd been crying, but the smile she presented was brilliant. He lowered the lights and sat beside her.

"I know this is hard, but I'll help you through it."

She scooted into his open arms. "We'll be back someday. But I'll miss Electra."

"She can come to Oceanus any time. Officials will certainly allow her access."

Sagan gazed up at him. "Tell me again about your family. Tell me again how much they're going to love me," she begged. It was the hundredth time.

"They'll adore you as much as I do, if such a thing is remotely possible." He hugged her tightly. She was wearing his robe because, as she so often told him, it smelled of him and she liked having it on.

He summoned his courage. "There's one thing I haven't told you, *shala*. I should have done so sooner, but . . ."

She pushed herself away from him. "Not another secret!"

"Just this one last thing, Sagan, then you'll know everything."

She swallowed hard and nodded for him to continue.

"I know you were angry about the Lucent Stones and why I didn't reveal their existence sooner," he declared.

"We argued all that out. It's over."

"Yes, but what you don't know is why I'd never discussed them. You see . . ." He hesitated.

"*Keir?*" she coaxed.

He let out a slow breath. "The high authority to which I'd promised secrecy was the same authority who wanted me to destroy the stones and the blasters to begin with. That was the ruler of Oceanus—the supreme majesty of our elected council."

"The king? You're on speaking terms with the king of Oceanus?"

He nodded. "You might go so far as to say we speak quite often."

Sagan stared pointedly at him. "*How* often?" she asked.

Keir shrugged and picked at an invisible thread on his uniform. "He's a frequent visitor to my villa."

"And your relationship to him is?"

"He's my grandfather."

She stood up and glared at him. *"Why the hell didn't you ever tell me this?"*

"I was afraid you'd have nothing further to do with me if I did."

She ignored that excuse. "You have the blood of Kryllian Zatoe Doran in your veins. That puts you in line for the throne. Keir, you weren't supposed to marry a commoner like me. I can't ascend to the throne. I'm not queen material!"

He pulled her back down beside him. "See? That's exactly what I'm talking about . . . that attitude."

"I know your traditions and I'm right, aren't I?" she demanded.

"I'm not in line for the throne. Kryllian Zatoe Doran *is* my grandfather, but my father will ascend to the throne, then three older brothers follow him. I have four sisters who can also accept the position as ruler. But that garbage about being a commoner is wrong. We can marry whomever we please. You've seen the communication from my home. None of the messages ever cast any disparagement on you."

"But your family doesn't like the human race all that much. *You* didn't when you first came to Earth."

"I didn't understand them, *shala*. Ignorance clouded my judgment. Despite my having studied your people and planet for many years, there's a huge difference between reading about them and actually *knowing* them. I changed my mind and so did my family. They know of your actions during the mission and are greatly impressed. You'd have never been offered an enforcer position otherwise. And I believe you'll be made a full officer of the first rank after we land. I haven't the power to bestow that, but my grandfather does." He paused for a long moment. "Since I've checked with the physicians and know there's no reason why it can't happen, promise my grandfather some grandchildren and he'll probably give you anything you want. He and the rest of my family have long wanted to see me settled with babies."

She slowly smiled. "Kids? You and I . . . Hey, wait a minute. You're doing that thing where you take my mind off the real issue again," she accused. "I'll have your babies, mister. But you have to promise me I won't have to wear a crown or rule anyone . . . okay? No scepters . . . none of that."

He laughed. "You have my word on that, *shala*. Besides, one former Mr. Interstellar Feller in the family is enough royalty for a lifetime, don't you think?"

"Decidedly."

As they flew through space and into a new life, Sagan made love to Keir as she always did: with passion, spirit and slow deliberation. She took him deep inside her and held him tightly. They were one and always would be. And as Keir released his seed in her, it was with the hope it would grow a new generation to love. He'd walk beside Sagan in the moonlight and bathe with her nude in the sea. His parents, grandparents and siblings would come to visit them and hold the new babies.

Who knew? One day, maybe one of his sons would go to Earth under more peaceable circumstances, and find adventure with an intelligent, strikingly beautiful woman . . . all while being inflicted with bikini waxing and cucumber facials.

He held Sagan as she slept and watched Earth diminish until it was just a small spot in the vastness of space. He knew they would indeed be back one day. His children should know their heritage. They should visit the places their parents had, and if nothing else, they should hear the stories about the time their father was the most unusual entrant and winner in Electra Galaxy's Mr. Interstellar Feller pageant.

☐ **YES!**

Sign me up for the Love Spell Book Club and send my FREE BOOKS! If I choose to stay in the club, I will pay only $8.50* each month, a savings of $6.48!

NAME: _____

ADDRESS: _____

TELEPHONE: _____

EMAIL: _____

☐ I want to pay by credit card.

☐ VISA   ☐ MasterCard.   ☐ DISCOVER

ACCOUNT #: _____

EXPIRATION DATE: _____

SIGNATURE: _____

Mail this page along with $2.00 shipping and handling to:
Love Spell Book Club
PO Box 6640
Wayne, PA 19087
Or fax (must include credit card information) to:
610-995-9274

You can also sign up online at **www.dorchesterpub.com**.
*Plus $2.00 for shipping. Offer open to residents of the U.S. and Canada only. Canadian residents please call 1-800-481-9191 for pricing information.

If under 18, a parent or guardian must sign. Terms, prices and conditions subject to change. Subscription subject to acceptance. Dorchester Publishing reserves the right to reject any order or cancel any subscription.